Praise for Tessa

A powerful story of love, loss, truth, and deep care, this extraordinary saga touches truths that all need to meet and understand.
　—Roshi Joan Jiko Halifax, Abbot, Upaya Zen Center

Let yourself be swept away on this incomparable journey of the noble heart, an intimate, powerful, cherished revelation that is an homage to our humanness. Prater opens a unique window into a raw, deeply personal, and beautifully complex world, filled with remarkable insights and gifts for the soul.
　—Sedena Cappannelli, award-winning author, actress, and theater and television producer

---

Tessa: Eyes on the World is a great gift to readers, filled with tragedy, beauty, transformation, and prose. Surprising and inspiring, this book is a must read.
　—Anna Darrah, producer, Film Nest Studios

This journey takes us around the world and into the hearts of two astonishing women—a mother and daughter who will forever remain seated in your soul.
　—Eb Lottimer, writer, director, and actor

This book is a gift. But open it only if you want your heart touched and if you want to feel the mystery of life and death and the courage it takes on the part of an extraordinary family to face both. In prose, poetry, intimate letters, and above all the deep wisdom of the feminine, you'll be pushed and pulled—and, if you allow it, transformed.

—George Cappannelli, award-winning author, sculptor, and film and television producer/director

TESSA

Eyes on the World

©2024 K. Prater and Salodius Byrd

All rights reserved. No part of this publication may be reproduced or transmitted in any form or by any means, electronic or mechanical, including photocopying, recording, or any other information storage and retrieval system, without the written permission of the author or publisher.

This novel was inspired by a real person named Tessa. This story contains a mixture of actual characters and events. Many names, particulars, as well as details have been changed or fictionalized to allow the author creative license.

The poetry pages art was designed by Tessa Marie Horan with her brothers in 2005.

The cover art was by Jesse Abrams Baca.

Printed in the United States of America

Published in Hellertown, PA

ISBN 978-1-958711-70-5 hardcover

978-1-958711-78-1 paperback

Library of Congress Control Number 20239115917

For more information or to place bulk orders, contact the author or the publisher at Jennifer@BrightCommunications.net.

*To Peggy Day, Xavier, and Maeve
and for the future of
Zomazecawyzawe*

Ships in ancient times were dedicated to goddesses, then eventually to mortal women. These vessels were compared to the care of a baby inside a womb, with men providing steam for propulsion.

Topography

This is a dramatic story of women and their men, who passed down constellations of secrets, loyalties, and subterfuge through several generations.

Peter Hirsch, a Jewish expatriate whose family migrated from Poland in the late 1930s escaping Hitler's genocide, relocated for the rest of his life in Kansas City, Missouri. His parents became wealthy owners of a chain of bookstores, and he met Ruth, the daughter of a prominent Kansas City doctor. They became enamored with one another because of their intellect, social status, and admiration of artistic, bohemian people. They also shared a privileged lifestyle. They mingled with artists and intellectuals. Ruth was stunningly beautiful. They married in 1943, when **WWII** had not yet ended.

A son named Doyle was born in their first year of marriage. They lived on the second floor of Ruth's parent's mansion on Morningstar Drive. Peter enlisted in the army and was quickly promoted to lieutenant, serving overseas.

While Peter was away, Ruth had freedom and the ease of childcare from her mother, cook, and housekeeper. This gave her license to gad about town. She met KW (K-Dub), who was the manager of the prestigious Kansas City Club. KW was also married. His wife was the wealthy niece of the bishop of Kansas City. Ruth and KW soon found themselves deep in a torrid love affair that catapulted them into a future of deceit.

Eventually Peter and KW's wife heard gossip of the affair. Peter was fearful about losing his wife to another man and decided to take Ruth to Europe with him while he worked on the Nuremberg trials, prosecuting Nazi war criminals. He believed if she traveled with him, he could keep her from straying. He arranged for Ruth to stay outside of Paris with their longtime friends, artist Thomas Hart Benton and his wife, Rita. The blend of art, culture, and fashion surrounded the Bentons and their artistic friends in and around Paris.

While in Europe with the Bentons, Ruth often thought of KW and tried to get letters off to him regularly. Although she yearned for her lover, she was distracted and fascinated by the eclectic group of people who streamed in and out of the Bentons' social life in France. Ruth met Alfonzo (Zo) and Avna, two revolutionaries fighting against the Franco regime in Spain, who were also guests staying in the house.

Ruth spent more than a month with this group of radicals, artists, intellectuals, and musicians—a captivating experience for her. She hurled herself into this circle of people, soaking up information and the thrills of such a vibrant group. She became torn between her new friends in Europe, her marriage, her child, and her lover. The yearnings were immense.

Ruth was eight years older than Avna, yet they instantly bonded as contemporaries inside a curious world unfamilar and foreign to Ruth. The complex nature of Avna's accent, attitude, creativity, and political views intrigued Ruth. The two became unlikely best friends as Ruth was drawn to Avna's life experience, and Avna was drawn to Ruth's impulsiveness and curious innocence.

One evening after food, drink, laughter, political conversation, and artistic critiques of paintings, Zo took Ruth into his confidence. He developed a kinship with Ruth, and he opened up to her emotionally and intellectually.

"Everything is about making choices," Zo said. "I'm not a natural revolutionary, Ruth. My true craft is art; this is how Benton and I met. We had a mutual friend who specialized in forging, and

Benton became a mentor. My insurgent persona as part of the resistance was in the name of my loyalty to Avna's family. Our fathers and grandfathers were best friends. My father tried to convince Avna's relatives to leave Spain when Franco came into power and go with us to Chile. My parents were fearful of Franco's extremes. Our families were in support of laborers and spoke out about fairness and equality for them, for us. Franco did not want a middle class to thrive because the voices were strong and determined. When he came into power, his regime incarcerated anyone who spoke against the new government.

"Our families were in business together, manufacturing machine parts," Zo continued. "We were just kids when this was happening. My father was able to get Avna out of the camps if one of my brothers or I would marry her. She was only thirteen, and I was fifteen. We were still kids. This was arranged as part of an agreement between Spain and Chile after Avna's parents, siblings, and extended family were put into camps as sympathizers toward the laborers of the Basque country of Spain.

"Avna was subjected to unspeakable things in that camp. Her father and uncle were tortured and died there," Zo said. "I have promised to help avenge the family. Avna's main purpose now is revenge."

While this story disturbed Ruth, she found herself drawn closer to Zo with the intimate, sensitive honesty. After their time together, Zo, Avna, and Ruth vowed to see one another as often as possible. Zo and Avna were on the run, making plans to disrupt the lives of Franco and his people who had stripped Avna's family and others of decency. The time Zo and Avna had with the Bentons was their only genuine reprieve from the resistance.

Ruth and Peter returned to Kansas City with the intention of staying together. Six months later, Ruth became pregnant with KW's child. She left her marriage to Peter for KW. The scandal of adultery caused them both to lose custody of their children, and their families disinherited them. They were forced out of all they knew—with no money, friends, or family. They too were running from their own resistance.

Ruth and KW moved to Santa Fe, New Mexico, where Ruth

gave birth to a girl. KW and Ruth began to rebuild their lives and eventually bought a candy store in New Mexico.

Ruth wrote regularly to the Bentons, asking about Avna and Zo's safety and situation. In 1953, the Bentons invited Ruth to join them in France—at their expense, hoping Ruth might be able to help Avna, who was pregnant.

More than eighteen months had passed since Ruth had seen her friends. She left KW and their baby in Santa Fe to go to France, where she reunited with Avna and Zo.

Ruth wrote to KW to let him know that she missed him and their baby. Four days into their reunion, Avna's water broke, and within twelve hours she gave birth to a boy. Ruth and Zo did their best to help with the birth before the midwife arrived. Avna was in extreme pain, and minutes later, a girl was born, and twins were before them.

As the days passed, Avna had to choose between being a revolutionary and a mother. Ruth helped Avna care for her twins, with great ease because she was still lactating from breastfeeding her own child and could help breastfeed the babies. Avna and Zo named their son Byrd Ruth Salodius and their daughter Salodius Avna Byrd—for Avna's and Zo's grandfathers.

Days later, Avna asked Ruth to take her daughter back to the United States and raise her as her own. The son remained in France.

Salodius went to the United States with forged papers carrying KW's last name, Powers, and the first name Vivian. No one at the airport asked for anything except Ruth's passport because the baby was sucking on Ruth's breast.

Vivian became the middle child of nine in a blended family. She gave birth to a daughter, Tessa, at home twenty-five years later.

Prologue

When the rain begins in the tropical islands of the South Pacific, there's no preliminary drizzle. No gentle spatters tell you what's coming. It just happens. A big faucet in the sky opens up full blast and then, just as abruptly, shuts off.

Look at a map of that part of the world, and you'll see hundreds of islands: tiny black dots sprinkled across thousands of miles of blue. The vast ocean brings everything from soft breezes to cyclones, depending on its mood. The ocean's moods are nature's moods, which means you don't always get a warning when they're about to change.

The first of February 2006 was a sultry day on the island of Vava'u in the Kingdom of Tonga. A fun, noisy, informal soccer game by the village youth was under way in the tiny village of Tu'anuku. There'd been a late afternoon down-from-the-heavens rain, and they'd gone right on playing. Everyone was soaked, sweaty, muddy, and happy. The rain had stopped, and the sun shone brightly.

The players were brown-skinned with gleaming black hair, except for one. She was a strawberry-blonde girl, petite, fast, and assertive. Like everyone else playing, she wore more than the tropical climate called for: long baggy shorts and a Hawaiian shirt.

Watching from a ridge above the players, dressed in his business clothes and mopping his face in the heat, stood the town magistrate, Heamasi.

"Tessa!" shouted Tatafu, a handsome young Tongan, as he ran to position himself near the goalposts, his eyes following her every maneuver.

At the sound of her name, Tessa flashed him a look and a grin, then expertly kicked the ball in his direction. He took the ball easily and drove it through the goalposts. Their team erupted in joyous shouts. Tatafu rushed Tessa, lifting her off the ground as he hugged her. Tessa's eyes flicked upward, toward the magistrate on the hill, who looked directly at Tessa and Tatafu, his head shaking slowly from side to side. Tessa wriggled playfully out of Tatafu's arms.

"Halftime!" she yelled and dashed down the long concrete jetty with Tatafu, two other young men, and another girl running behind her. From where Heamasi stood, Tessa's effect was plain to see: She was a magnet—the others unable to resist her powerful draw. If she had run in the other direction, they would have joyously followed. If she had flopped down on the ground and turned somersaults, or climbed a tree, or stood on her head, they would have also. She'd been here barely three weeks, and Heamasi had watched as everyone in the village basked in her radiance.

Who is this girl? he wondered, mopping his brow again.

The island of Vava'u has many long, meandering, branching ocean inlets like canals. From the air, the land looks like a cluster of graceful, verdant, curvaceous parts of a jigsaw puzzle that have drifted apart. Each piece is outlined by a ribbon of turquoise where the water is shallow, while the deeper water is indigo-midnight blue.

Tu'anuku is situated just inside the wide mouth of the main waterway that leads to the much larger town of Neiafu. So placid and sheltered is this inlet that mother humpback whales bring their newborns there so the babies can rest, feed, fatten up, and prepare for the 1,200-mile migration to New Zealand. January and February bring the whale sightings in Tu'anuku. Seeing the first whales of the season is a joyous, festive moment for the islanders.

A ferryboat motored past on its way to Tongatapu, the main island to the south. People waved. Tessa, Tatafu, and the others leapt off the jetty, Tessa splashing down first into the turquoise water.

Heamasi first felt a rush of disapproval for Tessa's actions. The water was for work and fishing, not playing. He soon grew envious of her as hearty laughter and splashing filled his ears. *How good that must feel!* he thought. And how beautiful the world must have looked from where they swam: the sun and blue sky breaking through the puffy clouds, the cool water transparent all the way to the bottom, the refracted image of their legs visible down to their toes, the white-sugar sand beach, and the gentle swaying palm trees fringing the shore. Youthful bodies in their prime, not at all tired from the soccer game, still had some energy to burn! Heamasi smiled a little. *Listen to yourself! This girl is getting to you, too, isn't she?*

The friends swam out, Tessa in the lead, leaving the turquoise shallows and heading to where the land shelf drops abruptly and the water turns dark and deep. They went a long way without stopping, swimming steadily until they were far enough from the jetty that people standing there seemed small and distant. One of those people was a boy named Atiata. On the beach near the jetty, Atiata's father, Apolosi, made repairs to his net as he prepared to take his canoe out for some fishing. It was a peaceful scene of late-afternoon, soon-to-be-evening, unhurried island life.

Tessa, treading water and farther out than any of the others, stopped to catch her breath. She yelled a playful challenge to Tatafu in Tongan, "Fakavavevave!" Hurry up!

Tatafu doubled his efforts, moving toward Tessa's shiny blonde head and laughing face.

But suddenly her smile vanished, and she screamed.

"HELP!"

PART I
Cracked Vessel

Narrated by
Tessa

Pieces

Careful elusive vibrant
tiptoeing at midnight
Dewdrops on the grass
rolling with wet hair
Moonlight sits upon me
shadows, secrets gleeful
Unfolding in my arms
embracing words
Senses spring alive
somersaults against the wind
And vines wrap around my little toe.
I squeal,
and the pig in my lap twirls his tail in response.
I fall into mud
as I declare never to eat bacon.
And then I waltz over to the lush vegetation,
remembering the fun of flinging ripe tomatoes
While munching on fresh papaya
smooshing through my teeth.
Want to smear my face with the fruit?
Squished bright orange
becomes my lipstick from eating fantasies!

Chapter One
PEACE BY PIECES

After my going-away party in Santa Fe, one of my fathers (the one I share DNA with) and I drove to visit my brothers who share a house in Venice, California. They were making their way in the film business. Xavier went to video symphony school to become a sound mixer for music and film. Indigo was directing and starring in commercials. Those few days with them were symbolic, sensitive, and satisfying, and they saturated me with tenderness.

My Irish twin brother, Xavier, is wheelchair-bound, and my younger brother, Indigo, lives in a world of imagination and tender sensitivity. I am more porous than usual because my feelings are wide open, like a fresh wound. Indigo and I designed a heart Zia with a wave, and my brothers and I promised to get the symbol tattooed on us when I returned from my two-year assignment in the Peace Corps. Our little sister, Jazie, would wear the symbol on her skin too, eventually.

My mother, Vivian (Viva for short), along with me and my three siblings, got a tattoo of the Japanese "chiari" symbol on our bodies as an amulet of hope for Xavier after his injury. Viva loved this idea because in her mind this was a tribal branding and we all belonged to her. I'm unprotected as separation anxiety creeps into my heart now that I am actually about to leave the U.S., and I know I am going to miss my siblings.

I rendezvoused with my Peace Corps group colleagues on November 1 at a hotel near the airport. A group of Peace Corps administrators counseled and prepared us for our journey, and my new acquaintances got to meet my brothers and father. November 2, 2005, the Day of the Dead. Oddly enough the synchronicities amaze me. I have been reading *The Tibetan Book of the Living and Dying*, and then a week before departing Santa Fe I went to see a Tibetan Book of the Dead documentary narrated by none other than Leonard Cohen. My grandmother and mother had previously introduced me to Cohen as a poet and songwriter and a Buddhist.

I went to the Cinema Café to see the documentary with my father and fell asleep, then tried again the following night with my mother and my friend and godmother's daughter, Kaitlyn, and fell asleep again. I think the symbolism is about old patterns dying and new beginnings arising as I meet the twelve new people who are to be my colleagues, plus me, who makes thirteen—my lucky number. We will be a family training for our new lives in the Kingdom of Tonga.

The first stop on our journey was in a small Polynesian country, Samoa, with several hours' layover. We arrived in the capital city of Tongatapu after twenty hours traveling, exhausted yet filled with anticipation, curiosity, and uncertainty. We were met by the Peace Corp country director, Betty Crowley, and another PC staff member.

A few hours after our orientation, we met our various host families. Komoto, my host father, arrived. He was tall and lean, unusual for Tongan men, with large piercing eyes and a subtle smile. He had a regal stature. Most of the Tongan men I'd seen were shorter and wider, not Komoto. His was a commanding presence, one of the strongest protective father/grandfather figures I had seen.

I lived for two months with Komoto and his family. He is the talking chief for the king. His wife is named Sia; they have six daughters. Komoto's parents live in a little bungalow on the side of the property. I felt as if I had been dropped by a spaceship into a family compound similar to my home in New Mexico—but without luxuries.

The household was busy and productive, and I was immediately immersed in the Tongan way of life. I didn't have a moment to think about missing anyone. I know that living with the talking chief to the king sounds as if I were thrown into an upscale household. No, life was primitive and simple, just what I hoped for when I imagined life in this new home so far away from what I had known.

All the family spoke English, except the grandparents and Sia. When I spent time with Sia and her parents practicing my Tongan language lessons, I couldn't cheat and slip into English with them. During training, we had to learn the language and the dynamics of the country customs, which varied from island to island and village to village.

Komoto's daughters were excited for me to live with them, especially his twin girls, Ema and Voni. After weeks of training and living with my host family, we were assigned to our different island posts. Leaving Komoto and his family was emotional because I had grown very attached to them. I wish I could have stayed in the village of Ahua with them for the next two years.

Several of my colleagues and I were eventually sent to the island of Vava'u for more training. Six of us had our assignments on either the main island or one of the outer islands. Although I was originally going to be placed in the populated town of Neiafu, I insisted on going to a smaller village where no volunteer had previously been assigned. I think the staff was a bit miffed at my strong will and insistence to be stationed in Tu'anuku. I knew I had to go to a village where I could make an impact.

A young man from the village named Tatafu picked me up in Neiafu with an escort from the Peace Corps and drove us to the village of Tu'anuku. Tatafu struck me as having the spirit of a South Seas Bob Marley. His careful openness reminded me of my brothers. I could tell he was curious about me, but he acted reserved. Although he spoke some English, and I spoke some Tongan, we mainly communicated on that subterranean level that has nothing to do with speech.

As we drove and I drank in these new views of jungle and the smells of the South Pacific, Tatafu slipped a cassette into the player. My siblings and I listened to classical, rock, and reggae while we were in the womb and growing up. Bob Marley was our hero. His music inspired me to think about love, community, and humanity, and his message was a big part of what led me to the Peace Corps. Tatafu and I sang along with Bob to "One Love," my face pulling into smiles that I could no more control than the weather.

I savored the odd, alien mix of fragrances as we sang and whizzed along in the open-air car—burning plants, sweet flowers, salty air, and diesel fuel. I quickly fell into the idea of "I'll feel at home here."

I enjoyed Tatafu asking questions, trying to interpret the answers while our Peace Corps escort chimed in with necessary explanations. After passing the tenth ruined car reclaimed by roadside weeds and grass, I had to ask, "What's with all the dead cars?"

Tatafu made a funny pantomime of a proud, virile driver who became weaker and weaker until finally he petered out and stopped, dead in his tracks. "No mechanics in Tonga."

As we approached the village, I realized I was facing another adjustment. Tonight, they killed baby pigs for a village feast. I was a guest—in fact, the guest of honor—so I was polite, yet upset. There was a lot of joking, laughter, and singing while they did the killing, everyone indifferent to the squealing, struggling piglets.

I love the joyousness of the people. They are so eager to be friends with me, flinging open their arms and the doors to their homes. I cried afterward for the baby pigs, and for all suffering creatures. Buddhism stresses that suffering is part of the human experience. Still, I try to escape suffering.

I have not only come far in miles, I've come far into another culture. Finding myself to be the reason animals are slaughtered is too ironic. To regard all life as sacred doesn't square with life being taken in my honor. How many thousands of years have people been doing this? The hamburgers my dad fixes for the Fourth of July are no different from the pigs that were roasted last night. Or are they?

The difference is that everyone at the pig roast knew the pigs were somehow a part of their family. They run free like dogs at home. They had lived their whole lives with everyone knowing (except the pigs, of course) they were to be eaten. Now they were a feast, a part of the recognition that my arrival was an important event for everyone in the village. The pigs allowed the villagers to express their honor.

Dad's hamburgers are given much less respect. Sure, I was used to those hamburgers being part of celebratory events in our culture, but I didn't watch the slaughter of the cow, nor did I know the cow personally. I was raised on macrobiotic food, and organic meat was only acceptable on holidays or with friends. Animals were never slaughtered in my honor, which brought me a whole new perspective on celebration and honor.

Tonga was not my first choice. When you apply to the Peace Corps, you are allowed to indicate three preferences. Jamaica was an obvious choice for me because of the history, poverty, and of course, Bob Marley. I was originally drawn to Central and South America because I speak fluent Spanish.

I had two offers before Tonga, one in Bolivia and one in Vanuatu, both cancelled due to political upheaval. If I hadn't agreed to go to Tonga, I would have had to start the application process all over again. I made the commitment because of my desires to serve others, be part of change in the world, and exercise my independence. I aimed to test myself.

Tu'anuku, with its government restrictions and strong religious customs, acts as a family dynamic. Only 360 people live in the village. An air of innocence surrounds the people due to the lack of consumerism and technology. When I began integrating and observing exchanges, I recognized the villagers as a large family, and now the nuances are notable and familiar. Tonga is a genuine monarchy of three castes: royalty, noblemen, and commoners. This particular village seems to be all commoners, and I'm not sure if there is clan demarcation here in Tu'anuku.

Religious dogma has been around since the missionaries came to Tonga in the early 1800s. According to history, Tongans were so impressed by the luxurious ships and guns that they quickly accepted the Christian belief systems that had seemingly produced such wealth. I would like to know more about their cultural practices before the Westerners came and changed their traditions. I get the impression Tongans see tradition as important, especially when making crafts and utilizing their natural resources for art.

I'm a guest here and I want to be polite. I go to church. Religious dogma irritates me, though I am careful to keep that to myself. Still, the Tongans' singing is remarkable, drenching me with compassion, empathy, and joy. I am also thankful now for my spiritual upbringing. Viva ordained us with the mantles of meditating in nature and finding our individual ideas and attractions. I close my eyes and imagine lying in a meadow with the aspens above me. I hear the wind and remember the mountains.

I understand vastness clearly when I think of the ocean. I feel the miles between my family and me. I have a conversation over and over again with myself about why I chose to take this assignment so far away. I think about the people, patterns, and experiences that I felt I wanted to leave behind in America. I had no forewarning of the impact leaving my family would have on my senses and mental well-being. Viva was that tough pounding in my center that is still necessary. I feel like a compass that has lost direction. Now I have created a fury of emptiness around me, and I am surrounded by yet another cultural myth.

My family didn't want me to come here. Oh, the look in my mother's eyes when I told her I was going to Tonga—I might as well have told her I was going up in the space shuttle. Her firstborn, going so far away! I had mixed feelings about being separated from my family. If my mother had begged me not to go, I don't know what I would have done. But she didn't. She knew better. Despite my stormy adolescence and our mother-daughter battles, we've learned how to manage each other.

My mother, Viva, has a tendency to make decisions for others, whatever she thinks best. She developed this habit from being a mother and a force of nature, I think. Once she arranged a modeling gig for me with *Seventeen* magazine without consulting me first. I was thirteen years old, a soccer player, painter, and a want-to-be musician. Viva, an enthusiast, envisioned me wearing beautiful clothes while I burned with hot resentment every time she insisted on seeing me as a model. My thick, strawberry-blonde hair seemed to carry valuable energy and significant advantage to becoming a model.

In Tonga, I just learned about a custom that when the king dies, all the women of the king's brother's family have their long black hair cut short to honor his passing. Here, women with short hair are deeply admired for demonstrating their respect for the dead.

This reminds me of an incident I shared with my mother, a pivotal point in our relationship. Viva left me home with my little sister, Jazie, one spring afternoon while she drove my brothers to soccer practice. I had done catalog shoots with my brother and mother, and it was not something I enjoyed doing anymore. I sat with a hardened stare looking at my reflection in a three-way mirror in front of my dressing table. I knew my mother valued my thick, reddish-blonde hair. I ran my fingers through the thickness and let it fall where my shirt met my pants. Then I came up with a diabolical idea. I grabbed a pair of scissors and began cutting. *I'm an athlete, an artist!* Snip, snip, snip!

Suddenly, my hair was dropping to the floor, powerless to define me. What was left on my head stuck out in jagged spikes, and I didn't stop there. I took a box of red dye that I planned to use to streak my friend Cate's hair and instead gave myself a quick color job. When I was finished, I looked like a girl-band punk rocker. I was pleased. All I needed was a ring in my nose. My little sister had been lurking in the shadows, witnessing this act of defiance. When she moved behind the scene, she let out a gasp and then we both had a good laugh. I'm sure this episode helped to fuel her future independence.

When I took a final close look at myself, I could feel my defiant righteousness jumping ship. I cleaned up the mess on the floor, vacuumed up every last bit of my hair from the floor, and then Jazie and I sat on the floor drawing in our sketch books as if nothing had happened. Then we heard the door slam with the clack-clack of my mother's clogs, her voice calling out my name, "Tessa!"

I waited. And waited, as if maybe my hair would grow back if I waited long enough. "Tessa and Jaz!" she yelled again. "Come help me put away the groceries!"

Jazie shot me a coy smile as she turned the knob of my bedroom door. "She's going to eat *you* for dinner," she said as she walked out.

My body trembled as I crept around the corner to the kitchen. Viva's back was to me while she put fruit in a basket. "Here I am," I said in the smallest whisper.

"Please bring me the—" she said, turning toward me. Whatever she was about to say froze in her mouth. I will never forget her lips at that moment, forming an "O" with her full glossed lips frozen and stiff. She let me have loud, scolding, angry words. I can't even remember what she said exactly. I do remember scurrying around the island in the kitchen, avoiding her grasp, as she screamed and lunged for me, her eyes welling with tears of anger. She kicked the kitchen cabinets. I knew those cupboards endured her rage, and some of the marks are still visible.

I ran to my room. She continued her fit for a long time. Eventually, the yelling quieted. I pressed my ear to the door and heard her telling Marme what I had done.

My grandmother Ruth, whom we call Marme, came to my room. I felt immediate relief at the sound of her soft, soothing voice. She was always my sanctuary and confidant. She shut the door and looked at me with an unreactive, loving gaze. She said I should have consulted her before committing such a drastic act. She then tilted her head appraisingly. "You look beautiful," she said as she smoothed my spiky hair.

Marme helped me put together an outfit: a pleated skirt, blouse, sweater, and knee socks. "There," she said. "You look like a darling pixie. When Viva sees you, she'll melt."

Well, she didn't exactly melt. When I eventually came out of the bedroom, she sighed a disappointed sigh. Of course, *Seventeen* cancelled when they heard about my hair. My mother wasn't going to get to relive being on a photo shoot with her daughter. She didn't enjoy modeling anyway; the consuming authority of money gave her a sense of security. I felt powerful, and that event changed our relationship forever. Viva continued to let her will be known, and I learned to do the same.

I am making Viva sound pretty assertive, and she is to an extent. But Marme will tell a different story that defends or explains her.

My mother's confidence was greatly altered when the love of her life, her first boyfriend, died in Colorado in a mountain-climbing accident. The trauma arrested her. I can only imagine what the loss of her first love must have felt like. Marme knew Viva had lost too much too soon, and she could tell that the pain was filed away, not measured or processed.

Marme is patient with the entire family. Her softness never falters. Now that I'm older and seeing my mother from this distance, and as a woman, she makes sense to me. She protected herself by having four kids she could love and possess in the way she needed. She constructed her own kingdom, and she sat on a throne at the entrance, guarding her life.

Night Sweat

Rose rain mist beneath a white moon
Stillness
The gorgeous petal's gift
Shadows of light.
Some frantic moment
urges the presence of death,
screaming an approaching storm
of sweet gripping language.
Visions of less love,
growing in my sore head,
powering a thousand beauties.
Deep
inside the sky,
I cry out,
"Tell me I am dreaming!"

Chapter Two
NIGHT SWEAT

When I arrived in Tonga three months ago, it took a couple of days and lots of sleep for the roaring of airplane engines to get out of my head. I breathed in the exotic, unfamiliar air and absorbed the colors, sounds, and smells. The beauty of this place is overwhelming. Nature here is extravagant. My fathers—my biological father, Declan, and Jazie's biological father, Francis—were constantly taking us kids skiing, hiking, and swimming, instilling a need for fresh air and athleticism. Our parents helped to inspire importance of the great outdoors.

I was learning about the caste system—the royals, nobles, and commoners. On the flight to Vava'u, I looked down on the stunning clarity of the sea surrounding the islands as the plane approached. On the ground below, the dense lushness of the islands was covered by crazy tropical flowers, fruit, and luscious white sand beaches. I was on my way to a new village—where I would be living for the remainder of my assignment. The mixture of smells varied from lovely to foul.

There were also some harsh details. On the ride from the airport, I saw plastic bags snagged on bushes and blowing around on the ground. There were cans, bottles, Styrofoam cups, and boxes lying where they were tossed. Old broken plastic chairs were left on the side of the road. In the villages, ugly heaps of trash were piled near the houses. When my siblings and I were small, Viva said that some people in New Mexico think that the state flower is trash. She would be repulsed by the trash here.

This was deeply unsettling. All my life I was taught by my fathers and mother to care for and love the environment. I was travel-dazed, and the sight of this detritus was jarring. How could these people live in such a beautiful place and desecrate the land with trash? Did they not know how beautiful and sacred their surroundings were?

These cheerful, happy, slender, and well-fed people with colorful personalities are anything but hopeless or alienated. You can't call them poor—despite some dirt floors and bare feet—because this place is a cornucopia of fresh, nutritious fruit, fish, and vegetables. I didn't understand at all the contrast between the beauty and the trash.

I remembered my fathers, mother, grandparents, siblings, and godmother asking me again and again before I left home, "Are you sure you're okay with doing this? Things are going to be very, very different." Then I reminded myself that this was exactly what I said I wanted. As much as I came here to teach, I also came here to learn. That's why people go into the Peace Corps, isn't it? Not just to change lives, but to change their own lives. That's what I wanted, and that's what I'm getting. Here was my first riddle. I told myself: *Pay attention!*

I'd been certified through the National Outdoor Leadership School to be an Outward Bound instructor. They're the ones who take youngsters and grown-ups into the wilderness for major life-changing adventures, character-building vision quests. This was what my mother had been lobbying for, along with the rest of the family. I almost signed on. I would have done well, and my family would have been happy. The fit was obvious, and that was the problem—a little too obvious. Outward Bound's own mission statement helped me nail my decision to choose the Peace Corps. The Outward Bound adventures, more than extreme camping trips or wild hairy river rides, were meant to bring "real and powerful experience to gain self-esteem, the discovery of innate abilities, and a sense of responsibility toward others." I remember looking up from the page when I read those words. There was everything I'd been trying to articulate! And I knew I wanted my own "Outward Bound" experience. I wanted to be uprooted from everything I knew, while serving others to the very best of my abilities.

So I chose the distant place, the strange place, the utterly unfamiliar place. And I did that totally on purpose. I wanted to be as much like the explorers of the old world as I could—the adventurers who set out on flimsy, wooden sailing ships into the vast unknown, looking for the Northwest Passage or the city of El Dorado. Supposedly, they took those voyages because they wanted to find gold or a shortcut between oceans. I think the real reason was they wanted to leave their familiar lives behind completely and leap into the risk of exploration.

I have an incredibly complicated family with a tangled history full of calamity, spectacle, secrets, and exhilaration. My twenty-four years of life have introduced me to sadness and disappointment, also to deep love, happiness, and adventure. I am intentionally opening my heart to the possibility and richness of knowing more and revealing my stamina and perseverance.

I hope to discover a way to break through the myth of my family with diplomacy. Doratea, my godmother and Viva's longtime friend, has been a grounding source and inspiration throughout my life. She was with us when I was born and continues to be one of my guides. My send-off party was at her house, and before I could ask everyone to write to me, Doratea handed me a colorful, woven bag and said, "This is the best farewell offering for you." Inside I found letters from my closest and dearest.

She had suggested everyone write about their perception of themselves regarding our consanguinity. I immediately asked her what that word meant, and she replied, "Kinship, my darling Teca."

Teca is my nickname. Those letters are my treasures, my amulets. I've been too homesick to dive my mind and heart into the missives for fear they might make my homesickness even worse. I am beyond curious, though, of what had been shared.

Doratea has always been a calm cradle for me. She has the heart and tenacity of a lion. I must admit I feel frail tonight. I'll read

Doratea's letter because she gives me comfort and a pick-me-up with her philosophies.

Growing up was visual chaos, and we got to use everything we had in our house. Things were constantly shuffled around, rearranged, and reconfigured into an idea of beauty. People would come and go all day long, and often someone would stay for dinner. My parents lacked discipline, emotional competency, and consistency. They didn't have a unified front; we thrived on enthusiasm.

I love them all madly. The family lore has a powerful gravitational pull. Sometimes I feel as if our fates and futures—my siblings' and mine especially, and those of our own future children—have already been decided. I'm busting out, escaping that lure, hoping I can see with fresh eyes, find my own truths, and transform the future for me and my whole beloved family, present and as yet unborn.

My mind is racing like a galloping, wild horse. Why did I come here? Why was I so determined to do things *my* way? All I have to do is look at my family history to answer that question. Here I am in my little third-world house with no hot water or refrigeration, though I do have a bed, a stove, and a sturdy roof.

This night, I lie in the snug but rudimentary bed I've made for myself with windows open to fragrant breezes, and when I drift down into my dreams, they merge with the rich, dense, exotic, untamed worlds of plants and creatures of this tropical place. I feel part human and part of a mystical kingdom; brilliant colors swirl, and bits and pieces of my family lore float like small paintings, forming mosaics of my life.

I awaken before dawn and notice a red, luscious tropical flower opening outside my window, the color of the tailbone chakra, the first of the seven chakras, symbolizing our tribal connection to our family. I begin thinking that I'd made a huge mistake, that my willfulness and defiance had taken me to the wrong side of the world, to a barbaric place where trash is everywhere and they kill animals without a thought. Tears are coming from my eyes. The morning light streams through my window, and minutes later I hear a quiet knocking on my door.

I dry my face and wipe my nose, not wanting anyone to see me crying. I open the door. There stands Lina. I'd made friends with her right away. She is close to my age, outgoing, and full of jokes. She is holding a baby pig, with some of the village boys—Tatafu, Atiata, Hakalo, and Lio—behind her, all smiling.

As Lina hands me the piglet, the boy named Atiata says, "This one will never be eaten, never be killed. He's a boy. He's for you. He's not yet weaned from his mother though."

The piglet feels like a human baby in my arms—warm and wriggly with bright eyes and long lashes. Designs had been painted on his sides and a little bunch of flowers attached to his head. He is calm, as if a special fate had been bestowed, and he knows he doesn't need to worry about ending up crisp and roasted.

The five of them watch me with expectant smiles. They remind me of my brothers, sister, and childhood friends. The natural curve of the piglet's mouth looks like a smile—a grin under his little hat of flowers. I start to laugh and so do they, unable to help ourselves, no translation necessary. Just like that, I am transported up and out of my yearning for my home and relatives.

Shared Revolving Lives

*Time together
filled filtered moods.
Memories of our former selves
crammed into corners of conversations.
Tarnished data
reviewed like flashcards.
Glimmers similarity.
Radiant eye to eye.
Emerging quickly from a trap.
Narrowing winding road soothes
hurt from before.
Threads of sanity repairing the bridge before the collapse.*

Chapter Three
DORATEA

I had dinner next door over at Atiata's family's house with many villagers. Dinner ended, and seeing all the new faces was exciting. I'm back in my little house on my bed, with the homesickness I felt earlier seeping back into my heart. I debate if I want to read all the letters in hopes of mending this feeling of longing. I see Doratea's letter poking out of my messenger bag. I'm too hot to sleep—I snatch the letter and tear open the envelope.

Dearest Tessa,

We miss you beyond words and to the moon and back again. I don't like writing letters as a rule. I have to set an example since this was my idea.

You were my first child in a way, opening the hearts of many people in our group of friends. Our time together inspired me to have a family. I have to give your mother credit for sharing you and her ideas and perspectives with me. I became a mentor to you—a second mother in some ways and certainly a friend. I ended up on a pedestal I might not deserve. Remember that I am a Leo—headstrong and fiery at best, stubborn and selfish at worst. The idea of writing letters to you has prompted me to review my longtime relationship with your mother and open up some valuable understanding for you and me. I don't think we ever told you this story.

Viva and I met saving a dog from drowning in 1964. We were in our early teens. The dog, a big Irish setter, was trapped in a canal hung up in some branches at the edge where the water met the bank. The canal was full from recent heavy rain; the current was moving fast. The dog was exhausted from fighting the current.

I saw Viva at the edge of the canal trying to reach the dog, and I ran down yelling, "Be careful! You'll fall in too!" The rushing water was so loud she didn't hear me, so I went closer until she saw I was there. She wore a long scarf looped over her leather belt as a colorful accessory, or so I thought. She tied a sturdy knot, attaching the scarf like a rope onto her belt and loopholes and handed the towline up to me, motioning that she was going in the water. I knew that I should hold on to the fabric. She went in nearly to her waist, untangled the dog from the branches, and grabbed its collar. I held on and pulled her back to the edge where she let the dog go. He ran off, relieved, and Viva and I embraced.

From that day on, there was no shortage of drama between us. We continued to rescue each other over the years.

As you know, my heritage of Spanish and Kiowa Indian often brought discrimination our way. My mother died when I was seven years old, and you have met my siblings over the years. My father did very well with managing farm equipment, although he struggled with bigotry as a businessman. He respected and loved Mother Soil, yet he was *so* not a farmer He made sure we were educated and also given a hefty dose of common sense—and morals. Morality was critical to him; however, people can be cruel, and even my father couldn't protect himself or us from prejudice at all times.

After our mother passed away, our grandmothers were our female role models. Our father promised we would have everything we needed or wanted. We lived a privileged life until we were teenagers, with plenty of tradition and consistency carried over from his Native American heritage. Nothing stood in my way of fantasizing becoming a beauty queen or a quarterback's girlfriend. I was soon to realize the lack of respect white people had for us "red-skinned" humans. Then I met Viva.

Although your mother and I went to the same school, we had never spoken to one another until that remarkable day when we saved the dog's life together. Viva seemed not to care about social status, which in high school was my main course of study. She was an awkward, mysterious girl who many ignored. We were both minorities in our own skin: she awkward, me native.

Before the dog incident, I didn't take notice of her, even though her height and posture made her stand out in the crowd, and her odd combination of clothes often caught other people's attention. After saving the life of Red, as I came to call the dog, I noticed her bravery out of the corner of my eye. If anyone was being made fun of or ridiculed, she came to their defense. The rest of the time, she kept to herself. Eventually, I started to give her attention at school, and our friendship blossomed.

Viva was from a blended family of many brothers and two sisters. I hardly knew her sisters because one was already in college, and her younger sister had gotten pregnant and was out of the house by the time we became friends. Your grandmother, Marme, welcomed me easily. She eventually started calling me Dot, an endearment short for daughter.

I visited your grandparents even when Viva wasn't there, and Marme would treat me like a blossoming adult, not a teenager. She valued my curiosity and willingness to ask questions about the meanings of words and classical musicians I knew little to almost nothing about. We smoked cigarettes while we pored over the latest *Vogue* or *Look* magazines. She talked with me about adult things like film, dance, and art, even Edgar Cayce—subjects not integrated into discussion in my Native American household.

Your Marme allowed me intellectual and spiritual notice. She had style, humor, and intelligence, and she fascinated me. As a role model, she offered perspective different from my grandmothers—she served as my empress and trustworthy friend. I came to be considered part of the family. This was an honor because even though my Spanish/Indian heritage gave me a sense of love, I needed another family dynamic to shape my confidence.

I had sex with guys who were often attracted to Viva. I was willing to make myself available to them; Viva was not sexually active until she was twenty. She was more inclined to write and establish herself as a beatnik poet. She would have been a great folk singer too. I could lure a guy in a heartbeat. The sensual power I possessed intimidated Viva; she remained a virgin and awkward out of preference. Many times things became difficult for her because of how I chose to handle men. She would always say she didn't mind when she would find out that I slept with someone she had a crush on. I knew she struggled with feeling betrayed. I can see now she never failed to put me first, just as *I* put myself first.

Your mother had a strangeness that repelled some and attracted many. The most striking thing about her was her ability to look beneath the surface of things to what she called "the tapestry." I think she was soul-searching; at the time no one recognized that as an endowment.

Marme was her protector, alter ego, and they were both ahead of their time, unique and unconventional. I'm sure Viva's strength came from a sturdiness she developed with her brothers, Marme, and KW.

Though I could see and admire Viva's devotion to doing the right thing, we had different attitudes and priorities. We both moved to Aspen, where Viva's family had spent time over the years we were growing up. On the one hand, Aspen was the essence of beauty, with athleticism and design as its structure. The place was also constructed around a drug culture that ended up ruling supreme, rotting friendships, and ruining lives.

Aspen had barely 1,500 residents, so Viva and I could quickly hook up with the right (or the wrong) crowd. When I chose drugs over her, she threatened to leave and return to Santa Fe with or without me. Although my friendship with Viva had included plenty of arguments over the years—the standard things young women argue about—that was the first time we ever fought about ethics and priorities.

Viva stayed in Aspen. Her loyalty was in giving me the space to wallow in my preferences, which often didn't include her. She went to bat for me, lied for me. She even stood in front of the bright red Volkswagen my father rebuilt when one of my boyfriends threatened to smash the car to smithereens out of jealousy. I had left town with one of his friends to go on a road trip to see a concert. Viva stood with her legs planted wide on the shoulder of the road in front of my house, her arms crossed defiantly on her chest, willing to be run down to save my car. My boyfriend backed off, cursing her and me, and drove away. When I came up for air, I finally recognized Viva's love, devotion, and loyalty.

Our circle of friends in Aspen regarded Viva as someone who could take anything in stride. Most didn't know about her ideas and beliefs; some thought of her as naïve. She believed strongly in her interior constructs so that no matter what happened she could keep herself safe in her version of reality.

Then came Flynn. When Viva got together with him, I realized that she had been so forgiving of my shenanigans with men because she was waiting for the *right* man and could easily give me the space to try all the *wrong* men. Viva had only one serious boyfriend in college before she met Flynn. She moved into Flynn's little cabin pretty soon after they met. She beamed with even more light than usual. She had waited for love while I had been trying to corner a relationship. Even after a year together, Viva and Flynn were devoted. They shared like no two people I have ever seen or known. Then hell crashed into their idyll.

Flynn fell in a climbing accident and died. He was gone in an instant, and your mother's psyche fell with him. The heart inside of her cracked as his absence haunted her. I hadn't a clue how to care for her, nor did anyone else. Death was something none of us had yet experienced. I didn't see Viva for a year afterward. She told me years later that she felt his death was her fault.

As time passed, her acrimonious affect—all that inner turmoil she wore on the surface—turned to a soft quietude when she met Fabian and her four precious little children. They had shown up just in the nick of time. Fabian's intellectual prowess and artistic abilities, combined with the light of her four children who ignited a new fire in Viva and reminded her to be present, was like a fairy tale come true. She threw herself into a dedicated friendship with all of them, and I went on adventures away from Viva. No matter how many separations and crossovers Viva's friendships had, I knew that she and I would sporadically come back together.

Viva eventually went on an adventure herself, sailing on a trimaran with the intention of going around the world. She and the crew ended up in Tahiti after a fierce, difficult sail. They lost their motor and their easting winds, which placed them in the doldrums for days. Apparently, at one time they were circled by sharks.

Your father, Declan, was a part of the crew, and they ended up in a relationship. Viva returned to Santa Fe, where your grandparents lived, and your father followed her. She became pregnant with you, and she and Declan decided to marry. I was a bridesmaid, along with Flicka, Fabian, Hazel, and other friends. We wore retro dresses from the forties at your mother's insistence. We looked classy and beautiful. I felt like I too was holding a child's life in my hands when your mother was pregnant with you.

I lived with your parents for a while, and we became closer than ever. Viva and I ate the same foods, read the same books, and did the same exercise routine, usually together. I went to Lamaze classes with her and Declan. The three of us did everything to prepare for your birth, and from teething rings to clothing, everything had to be perfect. When you arrived, of course, I was named your godmother. I lived in a guest house just over an adobe wall so I saw you and Viva daily, and she shared you with me. You became mine too. In hindsight, I realize how generous Viva was sharing you with me.

Your mother was an exemplar for her contemporaries. She studied homeopathic medicine, herbs, and nutrition that would give you the best chance at life. She refused to have you or your siblings vaccinated.

I learned a great deal from her, and to this day I have never given her credit. Neither of us knew anyone well who had given birth at home or fought against doing the expected.

Viva didn't want to marry until you were born, to make certain that she and Declan were compatible, but your grandfather, KW, persuaded her to make the conventional choice and marry. This was the only time I remember her conforming, and she did so because of you. She was generous with everyone and everything—with you, her friends, money, ideas, belongings, and hospitality. She had no boundaries.

I took plenty of wrong turns in my life, and Viva called me on them every time. I resented her, but I owe her a lot for who I've become. I disappointed Viva at times.

Your mother and I have issues regarding our past that were never reconciled, and now remembering and processing seem too arduous. We have settled into our lives and have moved into a convenient and somewhat distant respect. The circumstances with my son Patrick's diabetes and Xavier becoming a paraplegic presented heart-wrenching circumstances, which led us in different directions. What we have in common is loving and mothering our children. I am grateful that my children consider you their sister.

This rambling letter feels like a purging. I think this is why I was so insistent we all write our feelings, secret reflections. I needed to come clean with the hovering impulse of the unsaid.

What a life you have before you, my darling Teca. I keep thinking you are out on one of your short adventures and will be coming through my door soon. Making Christmas cookies this year is going to be dreadful without you—a tradition you and I started when you were three years old, before Kaitlyn, Patrick, and Lucas were born. For a while, I thought you were going to be my only child.

I'm excited to hear more about your colleagues, Tonga, and the monarchy. You will always have my deepest love and respect for your courage and willingness to be daring. I love you to the moon.

—Doratea

I knew my mother and Doratea shared a past full of contentments, complexities, and controversies. I appreciate her giving me details of my mother in a more positive perspective. Sometimes she had judged my mother's choices, especially when I went to her with my complaints. Life experiences seemed to have damaged parts of their loyalty as they lost respect for one another when their life agendas, personalities, priorities, and experiences were left behind without examination. Frankly, they don't seem to have much in common anymore outside of their children.

Doratea's honesty encourages all kinds of curiosity and a need to investigate and talk deeply with my mother, Marme, and godmother. I want them to reunite in confidences and talk through secrets, strengths, and flaws. I would like to have known all these women when they were young. I hope to bridge the histories, see the distant closeness, and mend the harm that can happen through misunderstandings.

The air is still hot and heavy tonight. I want to sleep and dream of how to inspire sifting through the lives of my tribe and myself while making a difference in this village.

Tu'anuku

Dreaming through traditional remnants
crossing paths of friendships
Signposts

Tu'anuku receives me.
Women gather with food in their hands.
Children envelope inside curiosity and caution

Plans develop
Tender roots
New holds
Jigsaw puzzles in my entryway.

Steamy browns and greens
Cars as artwork
Crowds of pigs.

Chapter Four
TU'ANUKU

I felt even better this morning. Doratea's letter helped me to be more accepting of my mother's ambiguity. A good night's sleep can throw off a weepy mood for me. I wake up early here with the dawn, and the sunrise feels like pure promise.

While I made my morning tea, one of the village kids appeared with an invitation. Late that afternoon, there would be a kava ceremony. I was invited to pour. All that I knew about kava came from reading bottle labels in health food stores back home: a "natural relaxant" for "clarity and focus." I learned that kava is a root of a plant in the pepper family and is indigenous to islands of the South Pacific. The people here have used the drink for centuries. This was exciting for me.

That same day, I met with some of the older kids to talk about plans for a library in the future. I also helped youngsters put together a jigsaw puzzle. I was distracted as I imagined what the kava ceremony might entail.

Later that afternoon, I led some students on an expedition to pick up trash. We made a game out of separating plastic, Styrofoam, bottles, and cans from each other. I thought how the trash doesn't seem to bother the villagers. I came up with a theory, which helped me feel less disgusted. These islands have been inhabited for thousands of years. The inhabitants of these islands were accustomed to fruits, vegetable husks, coconuts, and shells blended in with the landscape.

Then along came the 20th century with new materials that don't automatically turn into compost. Now we have plastic, Styrofoam, aluminum, and glass. The islanders were introduced to these new elements and continued to throw everything over their shoulders the way they always have—and gradually got used to seeing the two types of materials mixed. Now that most of the trash is the non-biodegradable kind, they don't see it as an eyesore but just an ordinary part of the environment.

I began thinking about why I'm here and what my Peace Corps mission actually means. Whatever we do has to be helpful. That's the key word: *not* impose foreign values, rather assist however I can with necessary knowledge to make life more practical and functional.

I know the missionaries who got here long before the Peace Corps thought they were "helping." They imposed an odd kind of prudery on these island people. During training, we were told to dress modestly: shirts that covered our shoulders and shorts that weren't too short. Even when we go swimming, we're expected to uphold these requirements, which takes some adjusting. In this tropical place, short shorts and a halter-top would have been my clothing of choice. However, this lingering effect of a foreign culture has been around for enough generations to be deeply felt, and in order to show respect, we need to comply. No open displays of affection between boys and girls are allowed either.

I also learned that young unmarried women—like me—are not allowed to go into the "bush." This kind of message obviously intrigued me. I was drawn to what lived in the bush. The young men could go without an escort—not the young women. Certainly they could not go together without an adult. The modest clothing, I could live with because the men dress that way too; however, the business about the bush was hard for me to accept. The boys were allowed adventure and freedom—not the girls.

I *hate* being told I can't do something because I'm female. Here I am, an athlete and an outdoor adventurer, and I can't go exploring because of some silly, forced, sexist rule made because of religion. So far, I've kept my mouth shut, the same way I did when they killed the piglets. I'm a guest, I remind myself. I'm not here to shape things to my preferences. I'm here to help and follow the customs. I am, after all, supposed to use my moral and spiritual discipline to lead by example.

I don't mean this in some vague way. I chose to devote my spiritual self to Buddhist philosophy with a beautiful refuge ceremony almost six years ago at a temple in Santa Fe, when I was barely eighteen. Oddly, that was the same day my brother Xavier was injured. During that ceremony, I knelt, and a lama snipped a lock of my hair while I pledged to help relieve the suffering of all living beings with compassion and empathy. My prayer had ended with these words:

May all beings throughout infinite space reap the benefits of my living in accord with the precepts. May I become a fully enlightened Bodhisattva for the benefit of all.

That Buddhist prayer had a way of putting things back into focus whenever I felt doubt, fear, loneliness, or impatience—another way of reminding myself: *I'm here to help by example.*

This isn't the first time I've found myself far away from home and bewildered by what I see. When I graduated from high school, my family gave me a trip to Tibet, India, and Nepal so I could learn more about Buddhism and herbal medicine. I chose to trek to Nepal, a very poor third-world country with Buddhism and Hinduism as philosophical traditions. The people were generous and friendly, and I saw things that shocked me. I met a woman whose eleven-year-old daughter had been sold into sexual slavery, and I learned about women being doused with kerosene and set on fire after giving birth to baby girls. I saw an infant girl being fed a thin mix of white flour and water instead of milk because the parents believed milk was wasted on a baby girl. The baby was skinny, wretched, and cried all the time. She was punished for being born female. How could this be? Where was the compassion of Buddhism? I had what you might call a crisis of faith and conviction.

I dug down into Buddhist teaching. There are three great ages in Buddhism. In the first, the thousand years after the death of the

Buddha, the teachings were intact and humming. This was a golden age when Buddhists were able to accept the teachings, practice them, and spread them. After a thousand years, though, things started to run down, and corruption prevailed for a thousand years following. The teachings were still true and valid, but people became less and less able to follow them. A little was lost with each generation. After that, the beginning of the third thousand years comes. This is known as the Age of the Decline of the Law. Very few people, almost none, are practicing the original teachings. They go through the motions without any spirit, and Buddhism weakens and fades. This happens until a "new" Buddha comes along sometime in the distant future and refreshes the teachings.

We are in that age right now. That's when it's up to the Bodhisattvas—those who have achieved enlightenment and could, if they wanted, get off the wheel of life and not reincarnate again—to keep the teachings alive. They vow to keep reincarnating throughout this long, long age to help every living thing move toward enlightenment and freedom from rebirth. I know I'm no Bodhisattva. I *am* here to make a difference.

As the kids and I picked up many bags of trash, separated them out, and raked and cleaned the places where the trash had been, people began to smile. They looked a little puzzled, but nobody's feelings seemed to be hurt. The trash mattered to no one. Now that it was gone, they started to understand how well-off they were.

The children enjoyed cleaning up the garbage, and they ran around energetically tackling piles of trash. They caught on right away how to separate the materials, and they came to me with things in their hands—a headless doll, a shoe, a broken toy—to ask where each should go if they weren't sure.

After our workday, the kids and I rolled around on the ground, wrestling and playing. The children are beautiful, full of affection and joy, their little bodies vibrant with health and energy.

In the early evening, Hakalo, one of the boys from last night's piglet presentation in my hut, came to take me to the kava ceremony. He told me the Tongan word for the person who pours: *Tou'a*, an old word with a sound I liked. I dressed up a little—a nice sarong-type skirt, my best long-sleeved white shirt, and a flower behind my ear. I pictured Viva standing behind me, smoothing my hair, arranging the flower just so, her head tipped to one side while smiling.

My mother is a lot taller than I am. Most people eventually get to be taller than their mothers, but not me. I'm fully grown, and Viva still towers over me. She refers to me as "small and mighty."

"I'm your little *tou'a*, Mother," I said to her in my mind and imagined her cool hands on the sides of my face.

I expected some sort of special ceremonial hut for the kava ceremony, but Hakalo took me to an ordinary little house. He told me this was *faikava*, an informal, friendly gathering. I saw a plaid sofa and some plastic chairs in the living room, all shoved aside to make room for pillows and mats on the floor. People came in: Atiata, Lio, other boys and men. All males, I realized—no women at all, only me. I heard the tinny sound of a cheering crowd and a sports announcer. A TV in the corner broadcasted a rugby game from New Zealand.

Tongan men take up a lot of room. They are stocky, massive, and strong, descendants of warriors. Their size is impressive, and when they're all together indoors, they fill the space completely. Sweat, big white teeth, enormous hands and feet—their masculine aura was overwhelming in the ordinary-sized parlor.

I'm used to feeling small. I'm only 5 feet 2 inches tall. I'm strong. I can hike all day, swim furiously without even breathing hard, shoot the rapids in a raft, kick a soccer ball down the field and through the goalposts, and ski from the top of a mountain to the bottom without stopping.

One of the men at the ceremony had a guitar, and I wanted to teach him some new chords. I remained ready to learn how to serve the kava. On a low table was a bowl of soupy, greenish liquid with a ladle and a stack of coconut shell cups. Behind the table was a cushion where I was to sit. The men arranged themselves in a jagged circle on the floor, either cross-legged or leaning on pillows. Hakalo introduced me. The men were shy but friendly. Even though they smiled and acted polite, we all knew that somebody new was in their midst. I had the feeling that they were going to be on their best behavior for my sake.

I recognized some of the men, but not all of them. Atiata, Hakalo, and Lio sat near me. All the places seemed to be taken up. I counted seventeen men and boys, seventeen cups. That was when I realized that there was no cup for me. I would pour, but I wouldn't drink. *Maybe,* I thought, *it's just some formality. The one who pours isn't supposed to drink.* Was I supposed to be honored by being allowed to pour for a bunch of men and not allowed to drink like some kind of glorified waitress? My rebellious spirit contemplated using the ladle for a cup and taking a big drink of the stuff. That's as far as that impulse went. I was a newcomer in a foreign, different world.

The men were kind, sweet, in fact. Speaking of sweet, I wondered where was Tatafu? Did some other obligation keep him from being here? I'd find out later. I poured. The cups were passed hand to hand, and I soon had confirmation I wasn't going to be invited to partake. The man with the guitar strummed chords while the others talked and a few smoked cigarettes. They spoke in English and Tongan. The talk was banal—rugby scores, the weather, the fishing.

The sounds of the game went on steadily in the background, catching their attention whenever the crowd cheered or the announcer got excited over something. The men would stop talking, gaze at the TV, then talk again.

They seemed self-conscious in front of me, shooting me shy glances, then taking refuge in what was really a boring conversation. Not much happened until the game ended. There were some shouts and cheers along with the muffled sounds of the television set. Somebody turned off the TV then, at last, and the man with the guitar started singing. Everyone joined in, and the small room was quickly filled with rich harmonies.

I had heard a lot of Tongan singing before, but not in such a small space. The music is compelling, tuneful and complex, people singing different melody lines that weave in and out of one another in a kind of call and response. There are wonderful key and rhythm changes. The singers get involved, tipping their heads back and closing their eyes as they warmed up their voices and burst into a beautiful melody. I closed my eyes and let the songs engulf me, knowing they were probably hundreds of years old, predating the sailing ships that arrived here bearing Europeans. These were 21st-century men. The music pouring out of them was ancient and vividly alive, a total antidote to the television and the humdrum boring conversation. Whenever people sing together, there is cooperation and fellowship. The Tongan singing brought an unusually powerful feeling of something I cannot describe.

They sang for at least an hour. In between songs, they laughed, smoked, and cracked jokes. I couldn't tell if the kava or the music had made everyone relaxed and genial, almost goofy. The feeling was contagious, for sure, and my annoyance at the talk, the rugby, and not being invited to drink took a backseat to the pleasure of the singing reverberating in my head. The ceremony, which, except for the singing, seemed to me more like a frat party minus the alcohol, broke up and drifted apart after dark.

I asked Lio and Hakalo about Tatafu. Was he off somewhere? Busy? I felt a pang of wanting to be with my brothers. I had a constant stirring of thoughts in my head, musings of rewriting my family history and being a better role model for those closest to me. I had exposed my brothers and myself to alcohol, pot, and independence too soon, too young. I hope I can introduce them to better things now. I wished they were here with me to experience the diverse culture.

I was jostled back to the present moment, again wondering where my new friend Tatafu might be.

"He's at home," the men said.

"Why wasn't he at the kava ceremony?"

They didn't answer me right away. They looked at each other and spoke a few quick undecipherable words in Tongan. Lio said I should ask Tatafu when I see him.

"And why couldn't I drink kava? Because I'm a woman?" I asked. "I want to know what the kava root offers."

"Women sometimes drink kava privately though not at the official men's gatherings and ceremonies."

"I want to try some," I said, feeling a little rash as I spoke the words. As we were walking back to my house, the darkness gave me more nerve than I might have had if we were having the conversation in broad daylight. "It looks like fun. And I'm curious." I thought carefully about my next words. "Where I come from, women are free to do anything men do. We don't have separate rules. At least, not anymore."

"Tessa," said Hakalo, "we can drink kava together one night at your house if you want to try it."

"Yes, with you and the guys as well as Lina," I said.

I felt good. I asked myself if I was imposing my cultural values on them. Young people everywhere have one big thing in common: They like rebelling and bending the rules. These guys are no different.

A couple of days later, we sat on the floor of my tropical shack: me, Lina, Lio, Atiata, Tatafu, and Hakalo. Candles and lanterns cast a dreamy glow in the room, illuminating everyone's faces. Piglet slept in my lap. We were having our own ceremony.

I got out a jigsaw puzzle of a mountain desert scene so we could piece together an ongoing project with others in the village who might want to participate. I had drunk a couple of cups of kava and found the brew slightly bitter, just like every herbal concoction I'd ever consumed. My mother had me drink herbal combinations my entire life. Ten minutes later, the kava brought a gentle elation that seemed to reduce my anxieties.

Viva. I wondered what she was doing at that exact moment, thousands of miles away from me. My head and heart worked in tandem, and I felt like a strong, clear radio transmitter as I tried to think of my mother in that very instant. I looked into a candle flame on the table nearby and beamed a message directly to her as my new friends began working on the puzzle. I sent no words, just my face and my love. I did a little calculating: Midnight in Tonga meant my mother would be still asleep in New Mexico, not yet starting the day we'd just finished. I'd pop right into whatever dream she was having. Surprise, Mom!

I couldn't be sure I felt anything other than the fun and fellowship of being with this bunch in the sweet island night, the windows open, the candles and lanterns inviting us to talk, laugh, and assemble a puzzle together. This entire experience was a comfort. I asked the others about their earliest memories as little children.

Lio remembered taking his first steps, back and forth between his parents. Lina remembered somebody taking her picture when she was three or four years old. Hakalo remembered standing in a garden of brilliant flowers when he was three, and Atiata said he remembered lying in his cradle before he could even walk, with the faces of his big sisters looking down at him, and they were tickling him. I told them that I remember being born. A lot of people say they remember their birth; however, they can't give any proof. I can.

I told my friends my story: Once when I was very young, around seven, I told my mother that I remembered her talking to me as I was getting born, coaxing me. When I said this, she looked at me for a moment, then asked, "And what did I say to you?"

I answered, "You said, 'Come on out, I'll keep you warm and cozy and wet just the way you are now. You'll hardly know the difference, except there'll be light and more voices. You'll go right into a nice warm bath where you can splash around and get used to things.'"

My mother told me that was what she said and exactly how the world was when I came from her protective womb. There were soft voices and dim lighting. My body was immediately submerged in warm water. I recall the entirely new sensations of light and motion startling me a little, yet because of the bath, I felt calm and content. I feel the memory of serenity this moment.

My friends looked at me with envy and disbelief. I could see that they were wondering if they relaxed enough and let their memories roll back, back, back, that maybe they'd remember being born too.

I realized that Tatafu had said nothing. He sat next to me. I could feel the heat from his skin, and I also felt a deep inward reflecting coming off him. My head was a clear transmitter and also a receiver.

"What about you?" I asked him.

He turned to me, smiled, and shrugged. "I am the youngest of thirteen children. I remember nothing. Nothing at all."

Stages of Love

*Is freedom the only pursuit
finite from the dark void?
Listening moist birth
rejuvenates blood desire
blind as the light ever more we speak
in tongues of timelessness?
Wandering without clocks
having no pain as hands click; reversing the lies.
Immersed in the currentless water, we flower.
What better a pillow to flood our dreams
with than illusions
colliding with visitors
bearing pollen we sneeze around the harmless bank of fruition?
Is a vision meant to reverse and lap up a cycle for intent?
The imprint will satisfy the man's desire.
Flashing light burns streaks of lit adrenaline.
Persistence drifts into tones of sand.
Splendor breaking through flow,
like anger never wanting to stop the rush.
Grace steps up to beckon peace between the taste
Of a bouquet eaten with the eyes.
The outburst is pardoned
and quickly shelved as another simple mistake.*

Chapter Five
MARME

I was cloaked in the schoolchildren and my new friends—planting a garden, going to church, teaching soccer. The many duties lessened my pining for my family. Tonight, though, that yearning returned.

Earlier, I finally got around to unpacking everything I brought to Tonga and came upon a velvet satchel containing a strand of pearls and the letter Marme gave me the day I left on my trek to Nepal, and two old photographs of her with Zo and Avna.

My eyes watered when I unfolded the letter and began to read again. She was my confidant, protector, mentor, and spiritual guide. She shared elaborate knowledge and deep love with me. Our closeness was probably from another lifetime, as she had suggested on several occasions during my life with her. I even miss her slovenly handwriting. She died unexpectedly five days after my birthday last year.

She supposedly had a heart attack or pulmonary embolism after having sex with KW. Apparently, they had awakened at dawn, had coffee, and when Marme complained about a pain in her leg, they went back to their cozy bed. KW said they had sex. (Of course, I wondered about that because he was ninety-four, but he is a Scorpio.) He dozed off, and when he woke up an hour or so later, she was dead.

The family was unprepared for the death of our dependable matriarch. Viva especially wanted to pamper Marme and have private time with her. She was, after all, nine years younger than KW. She had the omniscient talent of pretending everything would unfold in due time, a great pretender and a vehicle of endless forgiveness and love.

In a way, I was upset that Marme procrastinated and hadn't been able to visit with Viva about her heritage. I am missing unrevealed historical information. Marme had grown weary from the misrepresentation of family, secrets, lies, hardships, and the inability to unravel the keepsakes of historical events. I'm certain that her exit, on a certain level, could be considered cowardly and timely.

I happened to receive a book of Rudyard Kipling's poems from Marme on the very day she died, March 25, 2005. She had flagged a particular poem titled "If." I read that poem at her memorial.

My grandmother's handwriting is on the envelope of her letter. The letter is dated March 20, 2005.

My Darling, My Tessa,

As we both are turning another page in our lives, I am moved by your strength, courage, and willingness to go on yet another adventure. I think everyone in the family is living vicariously through you—for obvious reasons. The poise, perseverance, and patience you have displayed with me influenced me to become a better woman. I am flabbergasted by how much I have learned from you and how much we've shared with each other, our most intimate stories.

And then there is the whole idea of humanity, which I never considered until you became a humanitarian. I stand corrected: You were born a humanitarian, and I got to observe you filling in and flushing out what matters. I learned how to bow because of you.

When I was younger, I had a very inflated view of myself because I was a surprise child. I was seventeen years younger than my sister, and everyone coddled me. And then, all at once, my lifestyle was pulled out from under me because of my choices. I felt as if I had been burned to the ground, and lo and behold I was able to rise like a phoenix.

Nothing in my imagination could ever replace someone as decent, compassionate, sensitive, and meaningful as you. I think you inherited that from your mother and your biological grandmother. I fear you have become a vessel for my personal weaknesses, and I apologize for that.

I haven't had the nerve to tell your mother the truth: I have been so afraid of her feeling second best, unloved, left behind, or resentful. I worried: What if she rejected me, turned from me because I never told her the truth? I was unable to risk losing her. And yet, like you, she is the vital, vibrant victory of the unspoken mystery of my life.

As you know, this wasn't my secret alone. Viva belongs to so many people, yet she is always hanging by a thread or by her fingernails or walking a tightrope. Her birth was not an accident, and yet it became an anachronism.

I have wanted so much to be candid. Being truthful in the moment is easy for me. Being honest has always been a jambalaya of subterfuge.

You hold the vision story passed through our tribe. I intend to convey this story to Viva before I die. I want her to know how important she is as a catalyst, a matriarch, a mother, and a master of everything. I plan to tell her tomorrow how deeply I love her and if I can collect enough chutzpah when I am with her, it will pour from me how I admire her, and this will empower her.

I want her to live like you live, fearless, as if you will never die. I am finally able to merge my regrets with my gratitude, and I want you, above all others, to know where I find myself in this mix of joy and pain called life.

We have spoken about my affluent upbringing, and I had always thought myself infallible—until my first trip to Europe and the incredible people and experiences that were delivered to me on a platter, reflecting my naïveté. That's when I met my best friends, Avna and Zo, who are actually your biological grandparents.

I loved them and still love them to this day the same way I

love you, your mother, and your siblings. We share a strong bond that has nothing to do with blood. By the grace of circumstances, we came into one another's orbit when Avna and Zo entrusted Viva's upbringing to me and KW. I was pushed toward a deeper seeking, a remembered record of my own universal grain.

After you return from this journey, we will talk more about me sitting down with Viva and disclosing her birthright. I am afraid of her reaction.

For now, remember me always,

—Marme

I read Marme's letter over and over. I traced my finger along her craggy handwriting, trying to get a feel for her. She is still a treasure in my life. She suffered inwardly over choices she made more than sixty-five years before. She hid her sadness and secrets behind her love. I regarded her as a teacher. She created her own suffering, blaming KW for never learning to be emotionally intelligent and a viable mooring.

Marme's letter reminded me of the day she first tearfully told me of Avna and Zo. That was a lot for such a young girl to be burdened with. I've borne the weight of the responsibility of this secret ever since.

She was such a developed woman intellectually and spiritually, yet she held on to her guilt. She was generous, tolerant, and patient, and she shared wisdom and knowledge with me when she was alive.

However, she did a disservice to my mother and me by sharing her indiscretions with me and not with my mother. I felt a knot in my heart remembering that I am probably the only person Marme confided in regarding Viva's true parentage. I want to believe she would have soon been strong enough to tell Viva the whole story, had she not died.

I carefully put the letter away, wishing I could tell Marme how her words have strengthened me. I also wished I could have been more honest with her about meeting her responsibilities and resolve.

I think of Marme when I see the patriarchy here and how the men turn to their older sisters for guidance. She spent her life with my grandfather. living under a patriarchy of one. KW and their children were all she had.

I curl up on my bed and try to fall asleep; however, the thoughts of my beloved family members living with so much pain their entire lives keeps me awake. I toss and turn, hoping that I'm not too tired to face what tomorrow brings.

Drifting

*Sleeping softly as I
care and feed angels
in my dreams,
Wondering and wanting
Fleeting moments
Days incomplete
Unfinished
Until they run into beginning again.
The trail is wet and narrow,
Reaching for signs and directions
Answers.
Foggy moods invent new light,
Surrounded
By tiny indiscernible voices
Music making melodious
Completeness leaves visible whirls,
Plentiful and gripped with slipperiness.*

Chapter Six
GRANDFATHER

I didn't sleep well. I woke up way too early this morning before the sun rose and was still bothered by the thoughts of my dear Marme. I wish she could've stayed with me a little longer. I pray the pain could have been lifted from her heart. Perhaps that is what death is: a release from the suffering. I hope so.

Teaching today was difficult. I don't want my memories of where I come from to hinder my experience here. Mustering the strength needed to separate is a struggle. Luckily, the children are good distractions. They giggle and climb on top of one another, harboring an insatiable curiosity about what I know and what they will learn from me.

Teaching is a rewarding endeavor, and I remember when I was in school for my teaching degree. I would act as a shadow teacher at various schools in Santa Fe. If I were a shadow nurse or engineer, all the professionals would simply have me observe and offer information and respond to my questions because they knew I was only there to experience and learn. When I was in the school system, the children were vibrant, curious, and in wonder of me as a new, interesting person in their midst. This fosters satisfying interaction, and it's the reason I became a teacher.

The weather was hot and humid today. Every now and then I

catch myself missing the dry heat of New Mexico. Humidity and I are not compatible. I'm trying to adapt to the intensity of the moisture. All the Tongans act so comfortable in the dampness. I suppose that makes sense because that's all they know. The stickiness in the air was not helping my fatigue.

Hakalo and Lina walked up to me smiling as I entered Heamasi's house with the greeting, "*Fefe haki.*"

"Still adjusting?" grinned Lina, noticing my tired eyes and slow movements.

"*Sai pe,*" I replied, "just fine."

Lina handed me a plate of food, and we sat and chomped down on the seafood. Eating fish so regularly is definitely an adjustment. I'm a fairly liberal eater and have never seen the point in making a fuss over food. I never felt inclined to eat seafood in a landlocked, desert state. Eating sushi in New Mexico seemed like a bad idea so far from the ocean. I reserved eating fish for when I was visiting the sea. The time was upon me.

Lio joined us at the table, and he and Lina began talking in Tongan. I assumed they were greeting one another as they were both smiling the entire time. I've noticed that Tongans are often smiling.

If Jazie were here, she would definitely be making snarky comments about whether the Tongans know how to do anything else besides smile. "All the smiling is just creepy," she might say. A slight grin formed on my face as I ruminated on Jazie and her brutal honesty.

"What are you smiling about?" asked Lio, obviously smiling too.

I looked up, and Jazie disappeared from my thoughts. I thought about Lio, Lina, and Hakalo, how their dark skin contrasts with my lighter skin. Lina's black, wavy hair was scrunched up in a bun, and her hazel eyes pierce in contrast to most of the dark brown eyes on the others. She is slender, athletic, and pretty.

Hakalo and Lio look like most Tongan men—solid, robust, and unbelievably strong. Xavier used to pride himself on being the tallest in our family; he was almost six feet tall at sixteen years old. He dominated us at arm wrestling, challenging anyone and everyone in his free time. Hakalo and Lio would probably crush

Xavier's arm-wrestling confidence. Hakalo is the oldest; he seems to be in his thirties, but in Tonga you are considered a youth until you marry. I caught his eye, and he asked me for my thoughts.

"I was just thinking about my sister," I replied.

"You have a sister?" Hakalo asked, curious. His face is full and chubby, compared to Lio's chiseled jawline. They both have warm, chocolate-brown eyes. I stared into their faces, looking for camaraderie.

"I do," I responded. "She is younger and taller than me."

The three of them looked at me, waiting for me to say more. I thought about sharing more about Jazie, but I went back to eating my food. They shrugged off the momentary silence and went back to chomping and talking.

I noticed that Atiata and Tatafu were not at the dinner table. When I was done with my meal, I walked outside and there was still no sign of them.

Lio ran to me. "Tessa! I almost forgot! Here's a letter for you. The Peace Corps officer dropped it off today. I told him I'd give it to you."

"Thank you," I replied.

We smiled and wished each other a good night.

I walked back to my house, and the children from school accompanied me. They played as we walked, then dispersed when I reached my front door. I take comfort in how people appear willing to provide me company so I'm not lonely whenever I walk.

I flopped on my bed and checked to see who the letter was from and was stunned to see the name. Too wild—a letter from my grandfather, Kenneth Wayne Prater, KW, or "K-Dub," as he was called. Two days ago, I pulled out Marme's letter from my home stuff, and today a letter arrived from KW. BIG surprise! He has written me short notes on special occasions, but until today, no long letter.

He was crushed that I was leaving to come to Tonga, although he tried to act stoic and said he was too old for me to be leaving him. I saw tears on his face the last time we were together. Although my grandfather was chronically pissed with my parents and often insulted my mother in front of me, I loved him. I knew he was troubled from a long, complicated life.

Before I left, I asked him to tell me what he remembered about his life before Viva. He balked and made some sarcastic remarks, and that was the end of the matter, or so I believed. Now, look—an actual letter from him! My elderly grandpapa wrote to me! He comes from strong stock and might live forever. My father says he's lived so long because he is a feisty curmudgeon.

Coincidently, the lesson in school today for the Tongan children was about ancestry. Here in Tonga, ancestors don't seem to go back further than when the missionaries arrived. That's when their time began. My family's time began in the 1940s, or was that when our time ended?

From my spot on my bed, I glance at the room to check on the ten people on the floor in the breezeway of my house, continuing the puzzle composition. I'm pleased that they have entertained themselves even without me. I'll read my grandpa's letter now.

Dear Tessa,

You have always been an unwavering pillar of patience, weathering my doubts and complaints with grace. Amidst my vulnerability, feelings of abandonment, and the perplexity of your departure to a distant and unfamiliar land, so much remained unspoken between us. This year has exacted its toll, with the loss of your dear Marme, your decision to join the Peace Corps, and the ceaseless tide of changes. Time seemed to slip away faster than anticipated, and now, at the age of ninety-five, I find myself physically strong yet emotionally fragile.

The night before Ruth died, she revealed that she had shared our secrets—a glimpse into our complex past and Vivian's true lineage. I chastised her for burdening you with such weight at a tender age, but she believed that someone needed to bear witness. Sometimes, truth can be callous, and I have been guilty of evading, denying, and revising our history. My longing for a sense of belonging encompasses all of you. You and your mother and grandmother are the epitome of strength and remarkable women. In my heart, Viva is mine, as I played a role in raising her alongside Marme and the rest of the children. Regardless of my actions, I am prouder of your mother than any of my other offspring. She possesses a fierce determination and boundless compassion that I deeply respect and admire.

I have resolved to sit down with her on Valentine's Day and reveal the unvarnished truth of her extraordinary existence. As I write this to you, I contemplate the best approach, practicing while pacing and tending to household projects. These moments of reflection and planning are when I am at my finest.

To paraphrase Mark Twain, two of the most important days in our lives are the day we are born and the day we find out why.

I am certain I will live until your return, and in the meantime, please write to me and share your experiences, thoughts, and emotions about the village. Be patient with this old man as I eagerly await your correspondence.

—Grandfather

I was driven to respond right away. I'm fascinated by the delivery of his truth.

My Dearest Grandfather,

I am utterly astonished by the profound impact of your recent letter. The moment I delivered my swearing-in speech, just a few weeks ago, invoking Gandhi's timeless words, "May we all be the change we wish to see in the world," I felt a surge of purpose. Little did I know that your letter would solidify that possibility in my eyes, transforming you from as you reference a mere "old man" to the valiant warrior king of our family. Your words have left an indelible mark on my heart as to the possibility of change.

I am deeply grateful for the honesty, unwavering devotion, and attention to detail. Your long and eventful life has demanded an extraordinary level of fortitude, adaptability, and responsibility. I can only imagine the changes you have experienced over living almost 100 years. I look forward to celebrating your 100th birthday with you. You will live a long time. Today, I humbly bow to you, not only as my grandfather but as the epitome of strength and resilience.

As I stand here, honored to be your granddaughter, I understand that I am not only a recipient of your boundless love but also the torchbearer of remarkable lineage from a mandala of people. I vow never to forget the profound impact you have had on my life and that of my siblings. You have loved us unconditionally, and for that, I offer my deepest reverence.

Grandpa, I am in gratitude and admiration. Your unwavering presence in my life is a beacon of light and a source of security. I am forever grateful to be your legacy and your spokesperson.

With eternal love and gratitude,

Your granddaughter,

—Tessa

The image of what family is supposed to be allows ideals to drift through loving nostalgia of my grandparents. Now I see that my grandparents loved each of us differently, wholesomely, and deeply, constantly adapting, overcoming, and improvising. Waves of amazement fill me. They knew none of us grandkids had a drop of their blood in our veins. Yet they loved us wholeheartedly in our innocence.

I'm realizing attachment is the investment we make in each other. Energy, time, and effort shared is our bond. Bond is thicker than blood. I imagine how challenging this must have been for our rascally KW with his generation of denial, yet he is always there for us. The amount of devotion necessary to provide and protect Marme, Viva, and all of us kids inspires me to yield all of this to Viva. I want so dearly to move in truth and intimacy with my mother.

I understand Grandfather's rapacious need because life is unknowable until you get to the end, and he is so close to death and probably afraid.

I trust that he is on his own journey. I'm a part of his family so I plan to comfort him with a Bardo Prayer when he dies to assist with his safe passage.

Secret Places

Sound the sight of remainders
Spills of the river converge downstream.
Attuned to the current of the rushing passage
Access granted through a path of fallen rocks.
Larger design of nature opens
Traces of another lifetime chiseled
Crumbling the mind.
Sun rising through other doorways…
Cracks of light open nostalgic relics of atoms.
Mirror expands the dominance through the natural vortex.
Wrapping around inseparability…Mother Nature
Reflection…walk me toward the light.

Chapter Seven
MARKS OF THE VILLAGE

This morning the principal of the school, Sione, always with a cigarette hanging from his mouth, started hitting a child. She was a little girl, no more than eight years old. I have a temper that I've learned to control, yet it took all my self-discipline not to rush over and knock his hand away from the child.

Instead, I approached Sione calmly and asked him to stop. He did, though he gave me a puzzled look. Their custom here is to discipline children with corporal punishment. This is impossible for me to accept. I can't change my feelings. The necessary adjustments are endless in this country. What would I have done if he refused to stop?

The hierarchy here is patriarchal. The men are the decision-makers. The Kingdom of Tonga is one of the few monarchies left in the world. Tonga relies on cultivation and farming. Women cannot own land, yet they are responsible for growing and marketing the produce.

I am told that the father or husband makes the decisions in the family group. If there is a quandary and he wants another opinion, he defers to his oldest sister. A force that lives below the surface here feels untamed. Some things make sense and much is unsettling. I sometimes feel like I am becoming a behavioral scientist as I observe this village in comparison to my family.

Just an hour ago, we all finished playing a game of soccer. Nearly everyone had gone home for his or her family meal. Before long, only Lina, Atiata, Tatafu, and I were left. Tatafu started walking out to the end of the jetty and began tossing rocks into the sea. Atiata gave me a funny look as we began to follow Tatafu. Atiata scrunched up one side of his face and shook his head.

"What's up?" I asked.

He said Tatafu wanted to confess. I didn't understand what that meant. Atiata made the sign of hush with his finger, then he yelled out to Tatafu as a warning that we were approaching and then he wandered off. When Tatafu didn't move, Lina sat down on one side of him, and I sat on the other. We each grabbed a handful of rocks and began throwing and skimming the water with them like I used to do with my siblings.

I decided to break the silence. "You're very quiet tonight, Tatafu."

"Because lot to say."

"I'm all ears."

He looked puzzled, reached over to pull the hair off my ear, and smiled.

"It means I want to listen," I chuckled.

His smile vanished, and he looked back at the sea and threw a pebble. We sat for a while as I gave him the chance to talk if he wanted to. When I decided he probably wouldn't talk after all, I moved to stand, but Tatafu grabbed my arm and kept me seated. Lina encouraged him in Tongan to speak English.

"Please...I not so good." He brushed Lina's hand off his shoulders and bowed his head down.

Lina and I looked at each other. "What are you talking about?" I asked.

Tatafu took a deep breath and glanced at us. "I born with no father," he whispered.

I could see that he was biting his lip. "I remember nothing. I remember everything," he said.

I could feel myself turning more serious. The smiles were gone.

A lump formed in my throat. Whatever Tatafu was trying to communicate was traumatic. Lina stiffened at the sound of Tatafu's voice. Her eyes anxiously gazed into mine. I didn't know what she was trying to tell me.

Time passed slowly as the three of us sat there. I think all of us were busy thinking. Tatafu didn't speak another word. I became overwhelmed by the serious silence. The tension in the hot night air grew thicker and thicker. My heart beat faster. The nerves boiled inside me. I had to slide myself off the jetty and slip into the water before I melted.

I swam slowly and quietly toward the moonlight. I wondered what Tatafu was thinking. Thoughts about what had happened to him sank me further in the water. Perhaps the water would dissolve this anxiety. My head went under, and my mind suddenly switched to a memory of a full moon night in France, during a visit Jazie and I made with our mother to visit her friend Reen, an Italian woman with three children.

The common denominators between them were eccentricity, art, and willfulness. Reen's husband and Viva shared the same birthday—a sign that they were destined to be friends. Viva became a sort of mentor for Reen.

We were on the Mediterranean Sea that night in the south of France in a village called Ramatuelle. Viva, Reen, and I went swimming in the moonlight with me in the lead. Viva said that we were having a rite of passage ceremony for me beginning my menses. I was almost fourteen. What a night—such a romantic experience. My mother had a hard time keeping up with me and Reen. We kept swimming, trying to reach the moon.

I was forced back into the moment as I heard my Tongan friends breathing behind me and whispering to one another. Tatafu and Lina told me they'd never gone swimming in the moonlight before. We swam a short distance, then returned to the jetty and climbed up on the rocks. I watched Tatafu resume his position on the jetty. Lina joined him.

Tatafu was different from the other Tongans in the village. Everyone is happy here, sometimes too happy. Tatafu is sensitive and cautious. He looks at the ground more than the others. Perhaps not all Tongans are happy. Maybe more of them are like Tatafu, who have guilt and shame rammed down their throats from superstition and religion.

I let Lina and Tatafu sit together in their silence as I walked over to Atiata. Sitting down next to him, I was able to see their silhouettes against the moonlit sea. Atiata leaned over to me and started quietly talking as we both looked at the two of them. "Tatafu understands English, but he is self-conscious about speaking. He is embarrassed about his pronunciation. He is older than me and knows more, and he keeps his feelings hidden. It's hard when you feel strongly and you cannot convey your perception of things."

"He seems sad," I replied.

Atiata nodded, then looked at the ocean, sitting quietly for a few minutes. I wondered if Atiata was debating whether or not to tell me the source of Tatafu's discomfort. After a short time, he stood and walked over to Tatafu, and they began speaking in Tongan. I sat there with my curiosity getting the best of me. My mind switched to thinking about the fact that Atiata is Mormon, and he will soon leave the country on a mission. In order to have the privilege to travel, Tongans must be in command of the English language; this is why his English is fluent.

Atiata walked back to me. He didn't look up. He sat down and looked very seriously at me before he began speaking. "Tatafu's story is not private. Many people in the village talk behind his back about what happened."

"Why?"

"Because he's different. They like him because he is a strong rugby player for them, but before no one interacted with him. He was considered an outcast."

"What happened that made him an outcast?" My eyes grew bigger, and my voice softened to a whisper. I became nervous that someone might hear us talking about Tatafu's story.

Atiata sighed, pinched the bridge of his nose, and furrowed his brows. "Tatafu's father is not his father. He doesn't know who his father is. No one does."

I perked up my head. "Is that why no one likes him? Because he doesn't have a father?"

Atiata raised his voice a little. "It might be okay not to have a father in the United States; in Tonga, it's simply not acceptable."

I think my ignorance annoyed him. "I...I," my voice stuttered. "I'm sorry." I could feel my face turning red. Tatafu cannot possibly be the only one in Tonga who has secrets about his birth.

Atiata looked over to Tatafu, who stared at the ocean. He seemed completely detached. I sat there and held my knees close to my chest, trying to forgive myself for making a statement of mockery. Atiata glanced down at me and chuckled.

"No, I'm sorry. Talking about this is hard for me too. I know of Tatafu's agony. He has shared his insecurities with me. Most Tongans don't discuss feelings."

My head lowered, and I thought about my own mother's secrets and how people gossiped about her atypical, eccentric lifestyle. I thought about my brother Xavier and his disabilities. I thought about my family and wondered why chaos is such a prominent, almost necessary, part of our life. Atiata scooted closer to me and dropped his head to my level before he began speaking.

"Tatafu's mother, Malia, was abused terribly by her husband. He would go out drinking with buddies and return home only to blame her for all his grief. He would punch her and knock her down. He broke a chair on her back once. Then one day, Malia left on a ferry to go to Nuku'alofa. She took her two daughters with her and lived with one of her sisters in the capital city for a few years. When she returned to Tu'anuku, she brought back a son."

Atiata paused and looked over at Tatafu. I glanced toward him as well. Tatafu, Atiata told me, never learned any details about his mother's life in Nuku'alofa. She returned to her abusive husband in Tu'anuku when Tatafu was two years old. Villagers noticed immediately the toddler boy she had trailing behind her. They all knew she didn't leave pregnant and that she only took her daughters.

"Of course, people started to talk," said Atiata. "The people talk about how her son doesn't look like her husband, yet they don't talk about how abused she was."

I squinted my eyes, trying to understand. "Why do you think that is?"

"That's a messy situation. You as an American aren't going to understand."

"Well…" I stopped myself before possibly uttering another insult. I gulped down my words. "So what else happened?"

Atiata looked at me. "Everyone knew that his mother was hiding something. People were disgusted with her because she didn't look remorseful about what she did. Her husband beat her more. But she wouldn't talk, and that enraged him. My mother, Voni, walked by their house to eavesdrop on what was happening, just like everyone else did. But Malia never talked about the other man. Everyone remembers her walking around with Tatafu holding her skirt and stumbling while she smiled distantly. She's never told Tatafu who his father is, which makes her even more peculiar. I don't think she knows how hard this is on him. Eventually, the husband left the village."

I thought about the sense of unknowing, especially when you don't know the person who was the other half in the essential process of giving life to you. Looking toward the jetty, I saw Tatafu burying his head in his arms. Lina was nowhere to be seen. I shifted my gaze to Atiata, who closed his eyes and sighed heavily.

Untucking my legs from underneath me, I walked out to the jetty again. Tatafu's back was heaving. I placed my hand on his shoulder and knelt beside him. He lifted his chin and exposed the tears streaming down his face. His gaze never met mine. I didn't know what to say, so I hugged him, and he cried harder. I felt him take a deep breath, and he held onto me as we stood.

"No identity," he spoke brokenly.

"You're Tatafu," I replied tenderly.

"No," he said, wiping his eyes. "No father. No birth certificate. No identity."

Suddenly, Lina's eyes were visible in the water from the moonlight shining on them. I looked at her as Tatafu confessed. She stared back at me, and while Tatafu cried, she sank her head back into the water.

Tatafu and his story have stuck in my mind. I haven't seen him for two days. I saw Atiata after school today, but he turned when he saw me and scurried away. Like anywhere, people have their secrets.

Seems as if Tongans are more private than many others I have run across. How very interesting that Tatafu has divulged some very emotional stuff to me. Even Atiata has a hard time talking about Tatafu's situation, but he is right: This really seems like a confession for Tatafu. He must be tired of hiding and sense that I will not judge him—a liberation and maybe a calling out for help.

Tatafu came to visit this afternoon. He knocked on my door and handed me a basket of fruit. Lio and Lina were with him. Tongans are rarely alone. I couldn't help myself and gave him a big, friendly hug and did the same with the others. I was so glad to see them and that Tatafu was not going to hide from me. Tatafu looked me straight in the eye.

"Tessa, now you know my shame."

I put my hand on his shoulder, such a solid thing. "Shame is not who you are, Tatafu. You don't have to be ashamed with me."

"Too kind," he whispered. "Too kind."

I sensed an acceptance this time. I walked over to the CD player and put on Bob Marley. The four of us headed out to the back porch. Lio took out his machete and opened a coconut. The afternoon was great. We sat and listened to songs and ate fruit, happily getting our fingers sticky. We didn't talk much; rather, we swayed to the music and smiled at each other.

We tossed pieces of mango into the air, trying to catch them in our mouths. It was one of those times where I felt happy and liberated. This is what I want to pass on to others. Aren't we all granted the right to feel happiness?

We eventually began working on the jigsaw puzzle in the breezeway as we hovered our heads and eyes over the pieces, trying to fit them into the scene. So far, we had gotten to a small portion of the lake below the Maroon Bells in Aspen. I had explained the beauty of the area to them, and they were excited to begin the mountain scene.

"You know," I began, "whatever choices our mothers and fathers made shouldn't affect the here and now. I mean, how can what they did make us who we are?"

Tatafu met his eyes to mine. "What do you mean?"

"What your mother did shouldn't affect how people treat you.

You are your own person. You do not have to carry your parents into your persona."

"Tessa," he began, leaving my glance. "I don't understand what you are saying."

"Okay, I know that getting others to see you as your own person, someone who is not at fault for what happened, is hard. You don't have to believe what they say. It's not fair that they treat you differently because of your parents' choices."

Lio and Lina stayed silent and concentrated on the puzzle pieces.

Tatafu's eyes closed. "It's different for me."

"What do you mean it's different?" I asked.

"Because you don't know." His voice rose slightly.

"Tatafu, I see how others look at you when we're walking. Please don't let them make you think you are someone other than who you are. You can't—"

"Don't understand!" Tatafu shot up in a standing position and whipped his eyes to mine.

I sat still at the sudden noise he made. My temper got the best of me. "Yes, I do!"

"How?" He was upset.

I thought about telling him all my stories, my family, my fears, everything. "Because of the choices my grandmother and my mother made that brought a lot of grief!"

He gave me a curious look, like he was waiting for me to say more. I didn't. I sank back to the floor and stared blankly at the puzzle as if the pieces could give me words of wisdom. Lina put her hand on my wrist.

"Hey," Tatafu whispered.

I kept my head looking straight down. I closed my eyes. "I'm sorry. I want to help you go beyond gossip." I rolled my head to look at him when he repeated his words. I squinted, trying to figure out what he was saying. He looked at me knowingly. His gaze was kind and perceptive. What does he think?

He smiled and laid back down. "It's okay."

We all remained silent. I forgot that the music was still playing.

Soon enough, we returned to swaying to the songs. Our snippy minute dissolved entirely.

I looked over at him. "Why did you want me to know that about you?"

He shrugged. "I don't know."

"I'm glad we're friends."

The sun was starting to lower, and our evening meal was being prepared. We all stood and walked through the village, gathering Atiata, Hakalo, and others for a friendly game of soccer down at the wharf.

"I want new food," he said. "Sometimes."

"Really?"

Tatafu scrunched his face and shrugged. "New place too."

He was curious about what life was like elsewhere. I wondered if he had a natural hunger to travel to other places. If so, I understood. I wanted to experience a new place, something new, another culture. New food too, I guess.

"Where would you like to go?" I asked.

"New Zealand, the States," he replied innocently.

"Why those places?"

He chuckled. "I don't know. Looks nice. You from States."

I nodded.

"Is..." he began slowly. "Your family in States?"

"Yes," I replied. I thought carefully about what I said next. "I have two brothers and a sister."

"Do they play sports like you?"

"Kind of. One of my brothers is in a wheelchair."

"He can't walk?"

My eyes looked to the ground. "No."

Tatafu grew silent. "Sorry."

Telling him this information about my family history made me feel vulnerable. I've told others about Xavier before, yet telling Tatafu seemed more intense, more exposed, almost strange.

We arrived at the open space at the wharf and began our soccer game with me explaining the rules. I wondered what kind of food Tatafu wanted to try while I took the ball down to the imaginary goal surrounded by my new friends, hovering to try and take the ball from me.

I was in the mood for a green chile burrito. My mouth curled into a smile thinking about Tatafu eating New Mexican food. Suddenly, Hakalo got the ball and began to turn the ball around to his team's goal on the opposite end. After an hour of playing, we all went to Lio's house for dinner with his family. We sat down and began eating.

Atiata sat beside me. "Hey," he said.

"Now you're talking to me?" I teased.

"Whatever," he replied with a smirk. "Busy days. There's always something to do."

I didn't comment.

Dinner was a blur of laughter, jokes, and each other's daily accounts. I felt good practicing my Tongan with the friends I made here. Once we were all filled with food and fun, I stood up to walk home.

Tatafu stood up too and said, "I walk you home."

We strolled through the evening air, not saying much. Tatafu is such a good guy. I am glad he has chosen me to unload some of his grief. He is shy but brave. He must feel that he can trust me.

When we arrived at my house, I invited him in but he declined. Then he stood facing me, his gaze far beyond me, over my shoulder and out to the universe.

"Tatafu, do you think you could find your father?"

"Maybe not alive."

"Maybe, but you need to know."

"Why know?"

I surprised myself by tapping my finger on Tatafu's chest where his heart was surely pounding. "You know why."

His eyes met mine then, and he frowned.

"Maybe hurt more to know father."

"Maybe this, maybe that. That's always the way it is. Maybe you know I'm right."

"Maybe I do." He tapped himself on his chest with his finger, smiled, turned, and was gone.

If

BY RUDYARD KIPLING

If you can keep your head when all about you
Are losing theirs and blaming you;
If you can trust yourself when all men doubt you,
But make allowance for their doubting too:
If you can wait and not be tired by waiting,
Or, being lied about, don't deal in lies,
Or being hated don't give way to hating,
And yet don't look too good, nor talk too wise;
If you can dream—and not make dreams your master;
If you can think—and not make thoughts your aim,
If you can meet with Triumph and Disaster
And treat those two impostors just the same:
If you can bear to hear the truth you've spoken
Twisted by knaves to make a trap for fools,
Or watch the things you gave your life to, broken,
And stoop and build 'em up with worn-out tools;
If you can make one heap of all your winnings
And risk your wealth on one turn of pitch-and-toss,
And lose, and start again at your beginnings
And never breathe a word about your loss:
If you can force your heart and nerve and sinew
To serve your turn long after they are gone,
And so hold on when there is nothing in you
Except the Will, which says to them: "Hold on!"
If you can talk with crowds and keep your virtue,
Or walk with Kings—nor lose the common touch,
If neither foes nor loving friends can hurt you,
If all men count with you, but none too much:
If you can fill the unforgiving minute
With sixty seconds' worth of distance run,
Yours is the Earth and everything that's in it,
And—which is more—you'll be a Man, my son!

Chapter Eight
XAVIER

After Tatafu left that evening, I entered my house, lit a candle, and cozied up on my bed. I glanced over at my bedside table and saw the letters waiting to be read. Xavier's letter was on top. His moniker for me is Teca, and I traced the word with my finger.

I remember wanting to read all my family's writings during the flight; however, I felt I needed to get to know my new colleagues first. I didn't want the confusion of this new life experience to be laced with the emotions of separation.

As I reached for the papers I had stacked on my makeshift nightstand, I thought about Marme burning her journals in the backyard one summer night. Once that happened, Viva wanted to burn her journals too.

I would never burn my journals. I think it's rather important to have life documented somehow. I picked up the next envelope.

> Teca,
>
> When I thought of a personal letter to you about my memories of our childhood, our relationship, the grownups, everything became emotional, raw. So much got stirred up. I decided to make this an essay assignment in the third person so we can remember

together. Think of this letter as a way you and I can be close and relive events without too much emotion.

I was born seventeen months after my sister Tessa. I call her my Irish twin, though the rule is twelve months. She claims to remember her own birth and also recalls being agitated about mine. She has a clear memory of me on the floor as our mother was changing my diaper. When Viva's back was turned, Tessa stood on my chest, testing my durability as a magic carpet ride, presaging moments when I might vanish or be crushed. That I survived her flattening ceremony made her appreciate me more than she cared to admit.

My first memories are on Palace Avenue—a brick house with a pitched roof in the middle of flat-roofed adobe-style buildings. There were often rose petals on the floor, odd art hanging like bats, and sweet smells of incense and oils. There were shrines and altars in all sorts of places throughout the house and a carpeted ladder to a secret kingdom above the kitchen that we'd climb up and down like cats. We dressed up and performed plays, which never lacked in fun or inspiration.

Concepcion, our nanny from Guatemala, lived with us. She had a magical air. Her clothes were a riot of colors. She was barely taller than we were, and she didn't scold. She tied bright woven shawls around our backs so that we could carry our baby brother, Indigo, papoose-style.

At our Santa Fe Southside Compound, we had a go-cart, a trampoline, and motorcycles—and constant attention from the grown-ups. Friends loved coming to our house, but to spend the night meant you had to eat broccoli, seaweed, and tofu for breakfast. We had a blonde Spaniard macrobiotic cook in those days who came to live with us. She took some of the load off my mother, as we were a handful and a full house.

We shared a property line with the Santa Fe Country Club, located essentially in our backyard. At Easter, Viva gave us ducklings instead of candy. We would carry the animals with us to the country club ponds and then go jimmy the candy vending machines. The Santa Fe Country Club was not so much an exclusive haven for the privileged by way of money, but rather an *inclu-*

sive oasis of the blessed by way of location. We could get hamburgers there and French fries and hot dogs—very exciting for kids raised on a strict macrobiotic diet.

We went swimming and learned to play golf and tennis. Viva was there with us most of the time, being friendly with the other mothers. That's where I met Crockett Bodelson, a towheaded, blue-eyed kid. I felt instantly connected with him, even before I learned that we shared a birthday, August 21, a year apart. The shared birthday deepened our camaraderie and made our friendship seem predestined. Indeed, years later Crockett would witness the fateful event that changed my life forever, which I might not have survived had he not been there.

Our father, Declan, was not an artist, rather a businessman who traveled often and sometimes worked behind the house in a studio garage—supposedly refinishing furniture. He had a cool 1967 Toyota Land Cruiser, which was so much fun to drive with him. Tessa and I would pretend we were Ninja Turtles trying to save the world in the backseat with the roll bar.

One day while waiting in the car, I found a bag of money under the seat and stuffed the hundred-dollar bills in my pockets. I must have forgotten to close the bag because soon, when we were driving, the money was flying out the back of the Toyota and into the air like confetti. I watched until my dad stopped and jumped from the car, seriously agitated, and picked up the bills all over the road. We actually had a good laugh. I was surprised I didn't get into any trouble.

I attended a Catholic school for seventh grade. The next level of fun began there, and my business enterprises flourished. Like in many middle and high schools, we were given lunch cards. They cost $50 and were good for ten lunches. *Well,* I thought, *why pay $50 for a lunch card when it's just a thick piece of construction paper?* The voice that spurred me to replicate these lunch cards on my own (and sell them for half the price) *may* have been the same one that told me to jimmy the machines at the country club—criminal tendencies to some, but I prefer to think of these escapades as entrepreneurship, not to mention the money I was making for countless Santa Fe school children. If a kid's parents give him or her $50 for a lunch card, and the kid comes home with a lunch card, all's well. If the kid really spent $25 on that lunch card and kept the other $25 to take a crush to the movies, everyone's happy. I was making money and so were some other of my peers in a true trickle-down economy. Money trickled down to us kids from the school, our parents, and the food distributors. The idea of a bunch of middle schoolers making a few extra dollars off that crowd was sweet.

Because the middle-school lunch card scam was a success, I decided to go bigger in high school. After all, what's the point of getting older if your business doesn't expand? The next logical step, now that kids were more interested in beer than movie money, was to make fake IDs. I was pretty good at it, and my price was $50—very fair. In those days, all a person had to do was pull back the laminate and alter the print underneath, then replace the laminate. Easy. Any kid who had purchased two lunch cards from me in middle school had saved enough to buy a fake ID from me in high school.

Unfortunately, my scheme was found out. Viva was pretty furious. She grounded me, not only for the fake ID scheme but also for neglecting my chores and getting an F in French. Viva and Jazie were going to Aspen to visit Francis and Indigo. I managed to charm Viva into letting me stay in Santa Fe with our dad, Declan, who I knew would not enforce my sentence as strictly as she would. Tessa was occupied with a ceremony taking refuge in Buddhism. I look back on that day, April 11, 1999, as the time when Tessa went one way with her life, and I went exactly the opposite.

It was no trouble at all to convince Declan to lay off the grounding and let me attend a party with my friend Crockett. I was driving the Toyota Land Cruiser Crockett's dad had bought for him only a week before. We had taken off the hard top to Crockett's new ride earlier that day, but his dad had made us put it back on. In our haste, we'd failed to secure all the bolts. Around 11 p.m., Crockett was pretty high, and we had to be home for his dad's curfew. I didn't feel drunk, just excited, so we designated me the most sober driver.

I was driving pretty fast around corners on the dirt road when the tires caught in the gravel on the shoulder of the road, and I lost control of the car. I was wearing my seatbelt and so was Crockett, but there was a slight tear in the fabric of mine. The Land Cruiser rolled, the top leaving the body of the car. As I was flying amongst the debris, I could only think of Tessa and me watching *The Wizard of Oz* scene when Dorothy whirls in the tornado. I was lost in flight and almost dreaming. But then I was thrown smack on my back, hard, and everything was dark. I thought I was having a nightmare. Then I heard Crockett threatening to kiss me if I didn't open my eyes. I smelled and felt his gingery beer breath and opened my eyes.

He grabbed my arm to help me up. I had no feeling in my chest or in my legs, just dead weight. I couldn't get myself to pull up on his arm. I was scared. I told him to run for help. Crockett must have been gone twenty minutes or so. A young guy named Jeremy arrived on the scene first. He was an EMT and was called to the scene because he lived close by. He tried to comfort me when I saw the spinning red and blue lights of an ambulance pierce the desert darkness, and then I heard voices on a walkie-talkie and saw people scurrying around me.

They were extremely cautious moving me. I knew things were serious. It seemed to take hours to get me to the hospital. Then they had to airlift me to Albuquerque on a flight-for-life helicopter. I couldn't feel anything but my arms. I thought I was dying because of the commotion, intensity of voices, and feeling of urgency.

After that night in 1999, my previous life faded away. The doctors told me that my body was paralyzed from the chest down. My mind couldn't comprehend. In the days that followed, I became a child again, infantile, weak, vulnerable. I would lie awake and remember summer evening fires we built behind our house…now wishing *I* would catch fire and burn away like a marshmallow held over the flame.

There is poetic justice in the stripping away of my previous infallibility, conceit, popularity, good looks, and charm. Humility was forced upon me. Though many things were taken, many have been given in return. I am grateful my mother didn't take me seriously when, in the midst of my desperation, I asked her to smother me with a pillow. The way I get to live today, courageously and committed to the possibility of unlimited connectedness, is a gift. I take nothing for granted. I am alive and grateful, having surrendered to reality after six years in a wheelchair.

Okay, now I want to get personal with you, Teca. Forget the essay.

I know a little about our grandmother Marme's history. I know you had her confidence. I wish I would have listened or had interest in her stories. Most of what I've surmised came from my clever way of eavesdropping. I never had a shortage of creativity. She has a son from a marriage that ended in disaster. She was cast out, never to see her son again. Same with KW.

They must have had a torrid affair—nothing too out of the ordinary today, but a real scandal in high social circles in the late 1940s. They came to live in Santa Fe as exiles. Our mother was the real scandal. If Marme hadn't become pregnant with Viva, surely the affair would have run its course and their lives would have been unaffected.

"If" is too big a word for most stories. *If* the top of the Land Cruiser had been attached properly, *if* the seatbelt wasn't torn, *if* I hadn't been drinking and firing up my teenage hormones. I could have gone to "if" after my accident, could have stayed in a dreamy story about mistakes I made, about who I even was—a typical self-absorbed male living in a culture that rewards the most self-absorbed. It's ironic that the prize for being at the top of the pecking order drives more self-absorption.

Marme's fall from grace is something I have experienced. The next day after falling and the next day and the next, there is nothing to stop the falling. When I was ready, when I stopped wishing everything would end, when I reached the bottom, my parents were there. You were there. You gave me comfort and assured me life was a possibility. You stayed close. Viva was devoted to my care and rehabilitation. I don't know what Marme went through in her past, but I'll bet having her child taken from her was devastating, especially because it was a result of her choices. And now I too know the loss of something I had taken for granted.

I know I've still got some attitudes, especially with the family. We are a bunch of characters who are each unique, close, and dynamic, but we tend to get wrapped up in stories. I tried self-pity for a while. You wouldn't have it, Teca. You became my captain, and now you steer the vessel for our family.

I don't have to imagine how Marme felt about how she changed the course of her life with one impulsive act. I *know*, better than anyone else in the family, exactly how that feels. Maybe even more than she did.

I needed to review these memories and thoughts. Thanks for encouraging all of us, Teca. I love you, miss you, and feel excited for you.

—X

Reading Xavier's missive has torn my emotions. I'm unsettled with guilty memories. A flood comes over me. I remember when my brothers inspired me to draw because of the adventures and celebrations we had together. I wanted to halt time and document our lives with lines, shapes, and colors. One of my favorite things to do was to draw their faces and expressions while we joined forces in the escapades of the outdoors. Athleticism and blood connected all three of us. We were all soccer players, and our sister, Jazie, eventually became a soccer player too. She, however, was more feminine than me and wanted to be a ballerina, at least for a while.

I wanted to set an example for my siblings with everything that mattered. I made too many mistakes eventually and fell off my self-designed pedestal. I regret that I lost the way and got attracted to a different frequency. I made mistakes with my choices of exercising independence while trying drugs, alcohol, and a bad attitude. Eventually, I chose the right path, yet for a while I played around with being ordinary.

Xavier and I partied together, and we dragged our little brother, Indigo, down with us. Instead of protecting him, we exposed him to the wrong things. I have regrets. April 11, 1999, was a day of horrible, conflicting emotions. On the day of Xavier's injury, I had committed myself to a Buddhist spiritual and moral discipline and spiritual peace.

To be honest, I felt a lot of disappointment and jealousy. When Xavier was injured, I was only a month from graduating high school and had planned to go to college at the University of Puget Sound in Washington State. The entire family was in a panic. Because of Xavier's injury and the state of his body, my college plans were derailed. With the help of my godmother, Doratea, and her husband, I applied to the university lottery program in the state of New Mexico and had to go to college at the University of New Mexico.

I was sorry for X's accident and admittedly became resentful about what I had to give up for him. I learned to live each day deliberately, and because of his injury I decided I wanted to be a doctor. I did my senior project on his spinal cord injury, stoically I might add.

I had missed the last few weeks of high school because I was afraid he would die. Our parents were drowning in despair. He was in the ICU for quite a while and had his spine rebuilt from his hipbone. The time was devastating and stressful.

After his surgery, Xavier began a new life in his wheelchair while the rest of the family slipped into chaos. To the outside world, we upheld the image that we were creating our own shelter from the storm—a façade of resilience.

Indigo's Lament

The fury melts away.
Spontaneity comes in waves.
Rolling with his vulnerability,
sensitivity brings the room to tears.
Then uproarious laughter.
Loss for him is profound
a mass of moving sadness.
Grief and ache come
over his world.
He is broken.

She was hard to remember,
impossible to forget,
gone in a heartbeat,
swallowed away,
leaving a wound,
which may never heal.
Redemption proves
empirically to exist.
He feels more singular now that she is gone,
and he will eliminate resistance, always reaching for relief.

Chapter Nine
INDIGO

I lie in bed, trying to calm my mind from digesting Xavier's report. His written pages rest on my legs. I think about how he has probably forgotten what that feels like—something resting on his legs. I am uncomfortable remembering how I reacted to his accident and rehabilitation. My jealousy and resentfulness still trouble me. I cared undeniably, but I struggled that we were all so focused on him.

I stare up at the ceiling. Turning my head back to the bed table, I see my name typed on an envelope from Indigo. I wonder if I should read his letter now or wait until tomorrow. My hand reaches for the papers before I decide. Our dear Indigo. He calls Viva MOMA (Mother Of Many Assets). He coins acronyms often. His acronym for Tessa is Trust Everything See Sustainability Abound. A little smile forms on my face when I think about his brilliance and his rants.

> Dear Tessa,
> Kaitlyn is typing this for me because my handwriting is for shit, and I am in one of my fast-paced moods. She is one of the few people who can follow my thoughts and is a fast typist. Kaitlyn has had some caffeine so she can keep up with my thoughts. So here goes my letter for you.

Some of my first memories as a child are centered around our grandparents. They were both always around. I obsessed about them dying. I made up dioramas in the yard under the ash tree, where I covered piles of weavings and sweaters with sheets, which became their dead bodies. I didn't tell anyone that was what I was doing, especially when I crawled under and pretended I was dead myself. I am telling you this now because I want you to understand me.

One time I actually fell asleep under those coverings, pretending to be dead. When I woke up, I was so disconnected that I thought I *had* died and gone to heaven. You and Xavier came out to the graveyard I had invented in my head. You had to pinch and tickle me to convince me I was still alive.

Along the same lines, when my hamster died and we put his little body in a hole in the yard and covered him with dirt, I felt myself there in the hole with him.

When I was diagnosed with ADHD, Viva said that the acronym stands for Attention Dialed into a Higher Dimension. I am Indigo. This nickname was always Viva's endearment for me. I am her indigo child, which means that I possess special, sometimes supernatural abilities, according to her.

A few folks have even described me as manic depressive or bipolar. As you know that is now my diagnosis, with schizo affective disorder tagged on to the end.

Indigo child is an easy way of saying I'm strange and on the spectrum. There've been too many times when I find out only too late that I've gone on some wild ramble, then my obsession turns to blame or anger.

I have to find a way to hook up with discipline to harness my mind. The snakes in my head will pounce on a subject, then leap from one possibility to another—a proliferation of emotion to speech, with a myriad reflection of what-ifs.

Isn't death simply a failure, or at best a sacrifice, to time? There's never been enough time. This too shall pass, but what's the hurry? Loss is just a stepping-stone to sacrifice and makes a stone of the heart. I create ramparts to keep myself safe and trick fate. I know you would say "count the days rather than be crushed by them."

Sure, grandparents are taken away, parents are taken away, but where does the eye of God gaze? Is there even a God? Is God just a figure of speech? Can we keep everybody and everything alive just because *we* are still alive? Who will we become after we are gone? All these ideas populate my mind and emotional body.

After Xavier's accident, we were all changed. We *tried* to build again—unable to be the way we once were. We're like a house compound with different wings built ten and twenty years apart—a home that has rough patches and issues that looks authentic and resolved from the outside.

I always question why Xavier's accident had to happen. We are a cracked vessel—unable to ever be completely repaired again into a whole vessel.

I tried to learn routine from Francis. His routine gave him—and sometimes us—a feeling of safety and moment-by-moment authenticity. Routine gives a sense of control. You trick yourself into thinking you know everything. Routine helps people like me, yet things can look shiny on the surface but be rotten underneath. I have to keep noticing when I do things frantically, compulsively. I get too tired and feel desperate, wondering, is this really my job? I sense the scatter coming into focus.

I tend to get friendly with girls who have crushes on me. I like the way they display their kindness in the form of sensuality. Sometimes those relationships become dead ends because they constantly require more refined reactions. I have to react to women and give energetic boundaries even though often I have no idea what I'm doing, like I'm a junky who needs his drugs. I love what women offer me, yet sometimes I'm uncomfortable being the target of their wounds.

When the building of defense sinks in, you must cop to your faults, which is what I'm doing here sharing my manic thoughts with you. Why are we so afraid to look at ourselves? Because we're intimate with the bully inside, we realize he doesn't serve us. He brandishes his slingshot and covets our lunch money. All negativity is caused by accumulation of psychological time and denial or the present unease as in anxiety, tension, and stress. We put the power of us investing in ourselves on the back burner.

I see the characters surrounding me. I wonder, am I being codependent or am I really invested in what other people are thinking and feeling? It's like the masks we wear. I like to think I'm empathic; I don't really know where I end and others begin. I intellectually evaluate myself while withdrawing or restoring others. I don't *suffer* from insanity; I enjoy every minute of it.

And so here we are, holistically charmed by the parts of ourselves that are like this big cup with a mommy and daddy on it, filled with mountains in front of landscapes, like the scenery in New Mexico when you're driving down roads with Spanish and Native names. Where do we go from here?

Can we make sense of how the saturated nutrients of life communicate with our cells, all systems functioning optimally? That goes directly to the blood. This slippery living-kit makes so much sense and then suddenly makes no sense at all.

And then I ask a question: How small a part of life is taken up by meaningful moments, and then those moments are over before they start? To even cast a light on the future? Then a silence comes, which can be deafening. The thoughts held so clearly in the mind's eye start fading like a dream. Good thoughts fade, then comes a mind-fuck in which I exaggerate things. Memories expand and loom until I become a victim of my own reality. They seem so visible, like that hall of mirrors—an expansive form of self-centeredness.

Things lost have bitter or better fear of hope. Tears come from feeling out of control. Hope comes from abrupt stops and starts in our relationship with something outside ourselves. How secure is the platform on which I am building my thoughts? Can we all savor while we see and understand the experiences of life? Right now I can only think of *savvy, savor, satyr*. Truth can produce a pseudo-seeing, things of enduring worth bring to mind elation, exhibitionism. There are principles of the spirit, heart, mind, body. I guess the most important is reviving a sense of humor. Yang is talking; yin is listening. The body's health depends on how we adjust the energy that flows through our minds and our hearts.

In thinking thoughts, sometimes I am painting and other times I am throwing paint at the wall. The context, the adjustable, and the unknown—the more you ingest, the more you excrete. Parameters. Perhaps eating protein causes the body to excrete something and provokes the heart to regenerate. How am I to know for sure?

April 11, 1999. Eleven is one-to-one scale spiritual teacher as Moma says. There are nine elevens in ninety-nine. I'll call it multiplicity. My life has been about studying chaos in order to think about how to get rid of the compelling madness. Response to crisis is absorbed differently between people. The real evil on earth is the irrational racism from brutes who have the mentality and determination to make others feel lesser or vulnerable. We can level ourselves, physically or metaphorically; the world has a way of allowing us to concede to the inner turmoil. Then there's that part of the adrenaline rush that likes watching you falter as you flee into an emotional destruction, knowing that you have to pull yourself out as quickly as possible, not allowing the baggage to weigh more than your consciousness. I wonder if what you want is what defines you. It's like uttering the caw of a bird inside your torso, crowing the need to be watered and tended to, like a garden.

When I was ten, I went camping in Chaco Canyon, New Mexico. That was May of 1996. Viva disappeared from her assigned tent late in the evening. I was woken by a medicine guide, scaring the wits out of me, and I couldn't find Mom. The adrenaline pulsed through my small body, holding me captive to fear. Viva was nowhere to be found. The inconvenience of her disappearance in my time of need put a wash of chemical overload onto my brain.

At night, we are all strangers—even to ourselves. The stimulation pushed an overflow of tears out of my eyes, mouth, and nose. The aching in my bowels was so intense I felt as if my digestive tract would explode. A swirling complication of synesthesia affected the chemicals in my brain permanently. When you change the way you look at something, the way it looks changes. Thusly, if you deconstruct things too far you won't find your way back. Sufficiency is what is most important. Abundance is excess. Not all things can be resolved. Some things must be endured. And none of us are immune to prejudice.

Can I maintain my self-recognition without having to name experiences with reactions? I cannot control my own behavior easily. This I know. How can I expect to change others' reactions? Moma says the desire to change someone's behavior is referred to as "fantasy bonding." I still seek permanent healing for the world and then maybe I can calm down.

And you, my sister, *are* changing the world. You are a magician, and you inspire me when I pay attention. Remember how my hamster escaped, and we found him, having injured himself the way hamsters do. He had a long cut on his hide and was bleeding. You stayed calm. You went and got Viva's sewing box. While I held the hamster, your hands worked like a surgeon's as you sewed up the small rodent's wound. That hamster lived another year, probably the equivalent of twenty human years. That was when I saw that you have the touch. You are a healer, and I could always, always trust you—even when I couldn't trust myself.

I cannot journey into my own soul. I'm afraid of what I might find.

We all miss your guiding light. Moma and I feel your presence, though. You know as well as anyone how much I can feel—probably too much, and you know I love you.

—The wild one, Indigo

I can see the spark of madness in Indigo, coupled with his extreme brilliance. Experts say people on the spectrum can often amaze us if given the proper support from family and professionals.

Indigo is the most sensitive person in our family. He doesn't hide his feelings. His writing lets me see that he is trying to make sense of his pain and chip away at the culminated ideas. I can see through his flesh and blood into his mind. He's like an unfolding season.

Yet none of us wants to have ownership of his feelings because we cannot keep up with his mind. He is a Pisces, the most sensitive sign of the zodiac. He reaches for new ideas with energy and lightness, yet pain comes from simply having to inhabit his body. The database inside his head doesn't sequence because he can access too much of his brain. I wish he could be a spiritual leader and harness everything he wrote into a sensible conversation of blessings—rather than disjointed manic depression.

Sometimes I feel as if *I'm* mentally ill because of my deep need to analyze things. I see in my little brother's writing that he could go either way right now. He's young enough to do something positive, and he's defiant enough to end up in jail. He has no filter and often says the wrong thing at the wrong time. He gives his girlfriends too much information. Then he's sad when he feels they've stolen ideas, things, contacts, or friends from him.

I worry about his self-medication. I know that he likes to get high. Now that he lives in Los Angeles, he's going to be exposed to a myriad of chaotic lifestyles. I spent a few days with him and Xavier before departing with my colleagues of Peace Corps Group 70 for the Kingdom of Tonga. I noticed he appreciated the naturalness of my philosophy: cooking, caring, and meditating with him.

He wants to be remembered, known, special, and rich, and I think he feels an extra pressure because of his learning challenges. Or are they abilities that people have a hard time accepting? Jazie, Kaitlyn, and I have done his homework since he was in junior high school. He doesn't learn like regular kids. He's spirited and obstinate and needs to be reined in. I have to continue to provide confidence for him.

At this moment, I want to collect Indigo and sign up for an Outward Bound course with him, put him on the river, and teach him how to meditate every day. I want to allow him to recognize that these things will always be higher ground than copping dope and acting like a high roller. I want to guard, defend, and cherish his soul. I don't want him to stumble on the spiky, scary, gangster lifestyle. He's witty, intelligent, silly, stupid, scared, and high-strung. My first commitment after this assignment in Tonga will be to take him on a vision quest.

Indigo is the one in my family for whom I have the most concern, with me being away for two years. If only I could put a spell on him to keep him out of the clutches of the vipers until I can get back to him. Indigo is convinced his mother and fathers led him into his scrambled vision. He won't latch on to anything because he so strongly feels the confusion that Viva, Francis, and Declan unknowingly presented to him. He has to hold *someone* responsible.

We all want Indigo to be comfortable in his own skin and learn to format the brooding duplicity inside his mind. He has to find a way to replace blame of others and keep his cracked vessel intact, through which he can see a smidgen of light at times. My eyes sting from his brilliance and his sadness. Everything and anything flows through his head—and therefore mine.

I can't keep up with thoughts of repairing my family's woes, especially my siblings'. I want to sleep. I reach over to turn off the light. I glance down and see Jazie's handwriting. Her letter will be soothing and perhaps bring me to sleep—rather than obsessive thinking.

Jazie

Is this bonding as I dance to reggae?
I cannot study without music and my phone.
They are my best friends presently.
What is the premise?
When things move too fast, I get edgy.
Certain skills I must learn, such as patience.
Has existence rented space from me?
I have to invent words and sometimes turn nouns into verbs.
Stunning sounds solicit my attention.
This might be a good time to hold my hand, Mother.

Chapter Ten
JAZIE

Oh, Jasmine. Her name is simple and sweet and means exactly what you might think: fragrant flower. When I take her letter from the envelope, I get a little whiff of floral fragrance. I'm so tired, but I need to read what my sister feels.

> My sister Tessa,
>
> When I was born, the cord was wrapped around my neck twice—just like Xavier. You probably recall this story. Suddenly, the midwife had to plow through all the tension and disagreements that she had with our mother, begging her to listen so that I wouldn't suffocate. This was the first argument I had with Viva, me telling her: "Listen to the midwife, or I'll be born dead."
>
> We still hash out our differences to this day. We're both willful. She had to stop pushing, and that's not easy for her. She likes to be in charge inside her queendom, and she usually has no idea how imperious she can be. She sticks her own ideas into our lives with insistence.
>
> I like my name, Jazie. I'm only referred to as Jasmine when a grown-up is in reprimand mode. You've been a grownup to me, until recently. Thanks for confiding in me before you left and letting me be your best friend and equal.

I'm proud to say we were all born at home, and we were fed a "balanced" diet, with grains, the occasional fish, but no sugar. I remember our friends thought our diet was strange. They didn't like spending the night because they might have kale salad or turnips for breakfast.

I think people were jealous of our lifestyle and our kooky parents. Viva wakes up, belts her nightgown with a concha belt, throws on a sweater, and looks fashionable. Our dads were mysterious and very involved in our lives. Walking down the street with Viva and Marme gave me a feeling of prominence because people knew who they were and wanted to engage with all of us. With their fashionable attire coupled with spirituality, liveliness, and intrigue, we stood out as a cooperative.

Anyway, I came out alright. I have a different spin on the happenings in our lives because I am the youngest. There were too many men in Viva's life, including our two fathers, all her brothers, and now *our* brothers. Her search for the ideal man will be her ongoing quest. We've had to live through the unresolve between all our supposed role models—nothing but "power plays," an ironic nod to her last name, Powers. I'm thankful for you, Tess.

We as a family had our share of hardships and trials. Some were almost too much to believe. We are a vulnerable, colorful family. The memories incite exaggerated feelings. I like to think that you and I are the reasonable ones who keep things level. You've taught me how to separate emotion from logic.

Viva is whatever she thinks she is in the moment, a chameleon. I'm beginning to appreciate how she exposed us to healthy eating, meditation, bodywork, acupuncture, and spirituality. Her fantasies and efforts are ours and have proven to be useful. She still irritates me, thinking she will always have the last word and be right.

Remember when Marme and KW used to take us to the mall and fast-food restaurants on occasion? How they wanted us to keep that to ourselves? That's what grandparents are for: giving to those deprived of sugar, fast food, and television.

Viva lives in denial, have you noticed? She thought of herself as spiritual and level-headed. She was self-absorbed, annoying, and bossy. She rearranged our furniture way too many times. We heard over and over again that "the house is symbolic of the psyche"—so why the hell was she constantly moving through time and space like an untamed mustang? She meant well, but life was all about Viva's world. To be kind, I'd call her eccentric. Tessa, you and Xavier kept our mother in check. Indigo, however, became the burr in her saddle. And I was cared for by all of you. I'm not sure how I would have turned out if my parents had been left to their own devices.

We were all loved, yet too much happened in our lives too fast with many coincidences and extra imbalance. The grown-ups lacked consistency, communication, and a united front—prizing egos over everything—Declan wanting to be relevant, Francis demanding control, Viva insisting on respect as the director of operations. The grown-ups were confusing, including our grandparents.

Viva still says our grouping of family is karmic. What does that mean exactly? She comes out with these proclamations that we're all supposed to understand without any questions. She says karma in Sanskrit means "action," and it's not that we came into the world with bad karma, but choices we make in this life shape us. Fair enough. She tells me I chose her as a mother, that we all did, and that Declan and Francis are part of the arrangements made in the celestial waiting room.

I say that's bullshit. I have a weird feeling about Viva. She's all otherworldly. I blurt out my truth and then try to pull back by using the expression, "just kidding," when I insult someone, which I hope softens the blow of my observant honesty.

When I was young, I adored our grandparents. As I grew older, I realized something wasn't quite right with them either. Grandpa was constantly at odds with mom, Francis, and Declan. "At odds" seems to be a common theme of our whole family. Grandpa is sad and crabby, but I love him, and I know you love him too. One of my favorite pastimes was to watch him dig postholes for fencing, dividing up the property when he got mad at one thing or another. He'd cuss, and I'd try to calm him down and remind him that I loved him. After all, he did take me to Taco Bell.

Honestly, I didn't know what the hell "taking refuge" meant. Viva told me that you were making a commitment to compassion. I still didn't understand. All I knew was that I loved you and you loved me, and frankly I liked you a whole lot better than I liked Viva (just kidding).

One particular date, April 11, was a pivotal point in all our lives. Viva and I were in Aspen. I was so excited to see Dad and Indigo, mostly because Viva was dating another man I didn't like —none of us liked him—ten years younger than her and an asshole. We exhausted ourselves skiing that day. I remember being cozy in bed after story time, and then in the middle of the night, there was a phone call.

I was scared. I didn't know exactly what was going on—didn't understand the concepts of injury or death. All I knew was that something was terribly wrong and that Xavier was in serious trouble.

That's when our life took a sharp turn with no warning. Xavier was no longer throwing me up in the air, and I was no longer the center of attention. Everyone focused on Xavier. I became the mascot everybody turned to when confusion and indecision overcame them—maybe my practical nature and level emotions were their refuge. I felt sorry for Xavier. I felt sorry for the whole family. The accident completely disrupted our lives. I was bounced around between our grandparents and friends while Viva slept at the hospital with Xavier, who was hanging onto life by a thread. I remember you were our rock, a picture of functionality, staying with Mom at the hospital and even pulling yourself together enough to finish high school.

I felt like I lost my childhood and had to become more serious and helpful. I was jealous of all the attention Xavier got. Viva was learning how to care for him and us. She would make his tea and toast and serve it to him in the front seat of the car. He always got to ride up front. It was like he was having breakfast in bed. I thought that was unfair. Now I understand that Viva was learning to manage our new situation. Preparing Xavier for a day was a struggle and required team effort. We were all on a learning curve. There wasn't enough time to get him up, dressed, fed, in his chair, and out the door. I knew I wasn't getting enough attention. And I couldn't see a good enough reason for Xavier to have breakfast in the car with Viva's special treatment while the rest of us had our breakfast at the table. I thought that was unnecessary. I lost my special position in the family, and I was slow to readjust.

Pretty much everyone started acting out their pain and frustration in different ways, including you, who decided you'd better go to Nepal. You thought you were going to some la-la Buddha land, but I think that part of the world was tremendously shocking for you. After your trek from India to Nepal, you talked about poverty and the undervaluing of girls and young women—how they would be the first to go if something had to be given up. The family would sell a girl before selling their sacred cow.

Xavier's rehab and reintroduction to life were impressive. There was so much hurt. The wound went deep inside all of us. In all the messed-up ways we reacted, we were lucky to have each other. Declan thought Viva would go back to him, and everything would be all right. Everyone went back to living together in the Southside Compound again—grandparents next door, dads weaving in and out of our lives. Francis would come out on the weekends; Declan was erratic with his appearances.

Viva was back, and so were we. Instead of living at the various places she had chosen to live because of whatever man she was with, we were all together again. I didn't understand what all those men wanted from her and all the antagonizing that happened back and forth. She seemed like an accumulation of irregular features, men, and occurrences.

At the Southside Compound, the grown-ups came together out of necessity for the essential focus on healing Xavier. We were in crisis! I understood that in Viva's almighty, resilient, compassionate rationale, she just wanted to take care of her children. I yearned for some sort of resolution to an ongoing tangled thread of relationships. I wondered what a more traditional partnership would do under these circumstances.

Though our nontraditional life was okay, I wondered if there was a way to have what Viva had *without* the dysfunction. Our old home movies show a happy, playful family that looked eccentric but well-adjusted from the outside. Generally, home movies portray the positive aspects of family life. When I watch those movies now, the sentimentality and the unsettled disturbances are visible to me.

Looking back, I think we were all trying to reboot our lives so we could feel like we were starting fresh and new. We did, and the trajectory was very different than it might have been. Our new family plan was a business arrangement for supporting Xavier's recovery.

I was proud that Xavier eventually wanted independence and to learn to live his own life. He went to California for college and became a film sound mixer and engineer, a job he could do easily from his wheelchair.

I'm so glad that I have the chance to unload all this on you without judgment. You probably know most of what I've written, but being up front with you gives me a good feeling. Let us know how you're doing out there in the boonies.

Love ya.

—Jaz

Beautiful, blunt Jazie. A smile folds on my face thinking about how I miss her. I have all my siblings' writings around me on the bed. The papers become my blanket. I miss them. I miss home. But I remind myself that I wanted and needed to leave. My eyelids are too heavy to clean up the handwritten papers. I turn off the light and try to go to sleep with their written voices lying on top of me.

Woman

The woman tried to love him,
hold influence in his life.
His stubbornness and fear
Discouraged her prominence.
She is the unseen hidden bones that give him shape.
Infrastructure.
Her emotions, natural vulnerabilities,
and wild swing of expression were not available to him.
He passively
inflicted pain, trying to break her spirit,
forcing her to access invaluable reserves.
He refused to pay her tribute.

Chapter Eleven
ENIGMA

My spirit was exhausted as I pushed through my day. The things my siblings wrote activated memories, and recollecting demanded my attention. I am a work in progress, and I'm trying to leave behind my family complexities.

I felt slightly guilty leaving my family, the ghosts and resentments aside. I wanted to breathe and live my own life. I've learned not to let myself feel responsible for matters beyond my control. A family system is laced with issues that are influenced by uncertain pending of histories. Is the past for persevering, changing, or detaching? The patterns are often too much to bear.

I long to be home. I want to be rid of the flutter through my head and heart. I have good and bad memories, like I suppose everyone has. To me, family isn't about biology; it's about loyalty.

I promised myself before coming to Tuʻanuku that I wouldn't let my personal history taint my experience here. I want this journey to be separate from all that I've known, a new undertaking, yet I also wish I had someone around who knew my history.

I think about how Tatafu let Atiata tell me his history and did not tell me himself. No one here in the village knows my story. It's nice to be incognito, yet I want someone to know I am trying to separate from my family myth. I am a contradiction.

For the past twenty-four hours, I've felt as if Tatafu is making an effort to offer me his honesty. Tongans do not gift you with material possessions; they gift with food. They don't cling onto material things; they like to weave their memories into the crafts they create with palm leaves, which have aliveness much like the utilitarian things Native Americans made, which have now become collectors' items worldwide.

Here I am in Tu'anuku for less than a month, and I am involved in a compelling hidden family saga. I am accustomed to drama and complexity, although I *crave* simplicity and ease. I wonder if there is any way to live by breathing into the day without bringing up wasted past conflicts. Some story forever follows each of us around, suppressed and deniable, then leaping out with force into our heads.

Tatafu knows intuitively I am receptive to communication, and perhaps this is why he wants to express his pain of shame and unburden the cultural stigma. I'm surprised that Tatafu is opening up to me. I want to inspire him to be himself, free of the sordid grappling of religious judgment.

This morning my heart ached for him as though my own father were missing, not his. There are no letters in my colorful woven bag from my fathers. Where are they? I love the male energy and have always had ideal visions of what the father-daughter relationship would be like. My fathers love me, without a doubt. They didn't feel comfortable divulging or discussing flimsy emotions. They preferred talking about sports and intellectual topics of the world.

My relationship with my fathers was filled with care, and they were anchors for me, yet the emotional component of the male gender is often difficult to comprehend. I hoped to see that this would be different in Tonga, in this country so far away. The emotional literacy that most females hold available to them is not a written doctrine to the men. Instead, women's emotions often make males feel vulnerable and defensive.

As the daydreams washed over me, I floated through my routine as a teacher at the Tu'anuku primary school. I've decided to do an art project with the kids soon. I have a children's book about sharks that explains how important they are to the ecosystem. I'll give the kids construction paper to make shark masks.

I mentioned the project idea for my class to Tatafu and my other friends, hoping to enlist their help. They nodded and smiled, eerily advised not to do any work on Sunday. Sundays are inactive days. Working, swimming, going into the bush, and such are prohibited by Tongan tradition. Tatafu said that if you engage in any prohibited activities on Sunday, a shark would eat you because you're not resting. I unintentionally giggled, then noticed that he was serious.

In Tonga, church services are not only available Sundays but daily.

I felt like seeing my piglet. Pigs are like dogs in Tonga. Instead of roaming mutts, trotting pigs and piglets wander all over the place.

I walked next door and gave a holler toward Atiata's gate. After a moment, Atiata called out, "Come in, Tessa!"

When I reached the house, no one was there, so I yelled a big hello.

"Hello, Tessa!" Atiata's voice came again, with no visual of Atiata. Then I heard him laugh, and I looked up to see him at the top of a coconut palm tree. He threw down a few coconuts, then he grabbed hold of the tree and walked backward down to just above my head and jumped, landing right in front of me.

"You have to teach me how to do that, Atiata!"

"Best to learn when you are little. Hard for grown-ups," he said with a smile.

Atiata took me to the edge of the bush across from the house where the sow was busy nursing my piglet and his siblings. I call my little piglet, Suey. I told Suey that no one was going to eat him. He smiled his little piglet smile. Atiata and I sat on a fallen palm tree and watched the pig family.

Atiata looked over and said in a more-than-all-knowing tone, "Just like people: The babies are always cute, and the grown-ups aren't as attractive."

We laughed and then we sat quietly for what must have been fifteen or twenty minutes. When Atiata spoke, I was startled. "Tessa, I have a confession to make too."

"Must be something about me that attracts truth telling."

Atiata has a funny mannerism when he's trying to figure something out; he puts his little finger in his ear and shakes it vigorously.

Maybe he's stirring up his thoughts so the right words in English will come out of his mouth. "That might be true," he said. "Probably because we've not ever had a Westerner in our village, and we all want you to see us as we really are, not how we pretend to be."

"I've always wondered why people pretend," I said.

"Yeah." His finger was back in his ear.

"So, Atiata, confess."

He probed one ear then switched to the other. "Tessa, I didn't lie to you, but I didn't tell you the truth." Sometimes after he shakes his ear, he actually turns his head to one side and shakes it without the finger. This really looks like he is trying to empty something out of his head. I realize this is his nervous habit.

"You're going to tell me the truth now, though, aren't you?"

"Yes, I am." Then Atiata didn't say a word for another five minutes. Patience is a real virtue in Tonga. "I told you Tatafu has never known who his father is. The truth is my parents learned *where* he is." He looked at me like he was expecting the worst. I waited. "Apolosi, my father, met Tatafu's real father while in Nuku'alofa at the Mormon church there. Tatafu's father *supposedly* joined the Mormon church not too long ago, and my father overheard him mention someone named Malia who lives in Tu'anuku. I heard my parents talking about this when my father returned. My father said Tatafu's father didn't seem serious about the Mormon church. My father also said that his face looked similar to Tatafu's. I started thinking hard about what my father said, and I figured it had to be true. He doesn't lie."

The wheels spun in my mind. "Atiata, why didn't you tell Tatafu this? How long have you known?"

"What if I'm wrong? This is very serious, and I couldn't just tell someone else in the village. I've known for some weeks. The excitement of your arrival made me forget problems. Tongans talk in secret. We don't try to solve these kinds of issues. My parents haven't even told anyone because it is considered to be bad luck to get involved with Malia's unusualness."

"And yet you think this is my business to know?"

"Tatafu is my good friend, and I can tell he feels ignored and unimportant. He carries sadness. We Tongans help with fixing everyday necessities, not personal problems. We avoid and ignore such things. I know you are different and understand. I've seen how you look at him and try to communicate."

"Well?"

"Well," he sighed as though preparing for what to say next. "Maybe this is your opportunity to help Tatafu unburden his shame. Why do you think he told you about his story? Tatafu won't admit that he wants your help. He's nervous. This is a big deal, Tessa. He wants this judgment to end, but he won't listen to us because we don't understand like you do. He wants to listen and learn from you to have more intelligence in his world."

"What makes you think I can handle this?" My heart pounded.

Atiata stared into my eyes. "Because you are foreign and smart."

Both of us sat quietly, ruminating on what was just discussed.

This is my chance to make a difference in someone's life, I thought. *Whether this change will be positive or negative, I'm not sure. I think Tatafu is pained by his mother's affair. He said that with no father, he has no identity.* I thought about the impact of giving someone his identity. My heart warmed.

I rubbed my temples, thinking about what I'm getting myself into. "Okay." My voice was quiet. "Where do I start?"

"I think Tatafu's father's name is Koloa. The last I heard my parents talking about him, he was in Neiafu. I'm not sure if he's still there, but it's a start."

I'm trying to adjust to the cultural differences. My confusion morphed into an understanding and acceptance of his actions. Life here in Tonga is full of gossip. An immense amount of hesitation wards off the truth. I've noticed that the villagers like to know what's happening with everyone but prefer to act like they are at a distance. They're stubborn, private, curious, and nosey. They are like my own family.

I wouldn't leave Atiata without making him promise to talk to Tatafu with me. I asked him how we should tell him.

"You tell him, Tessa. I will be with you."

"Will he understand? You know, since his English is—"

"He has been speaking English with me a lot. He wants to learn the language. He understands most words, but he is sometimes too shy to speak."

"You can make sure he understands in Tongan too. Where do you think Tatafu might be? I think we should find him now."

"Now?"

"Why should we keep this from him? This needs to be talked about with him and then he can choose how he wants to go forward. This is what we call *logical* in English."

Saturday morning became Saturday afternoon. Atiata followed me as I paced, thinking about where to start. I figured I should tell Tatafu's mother what we were going to do. Not only did this seem polite, I also thought we should have her permission because this was *her* privacy, *her* secret life. This family struggle is not my business. I had to consider the mother, the wisdom keeper. She might have good reasons why she has not shared this information.

"Where does Malia live?" I asked Atiata as we made our way to the road.

He looked a little shocked when I mentioned her name. "She lives with her sister, Lekeleka. Her husband, Makoh, is nice enough to let Malia live on their plot of land after Malia's husband left her and her daughters. You can imagine the looks Makoh got when villagers found out he was letting Malia live with him. They said it was bad luck. I don't think he minds the extra company. Makoh is a very kind man." Atiata paused after he said this, acknowledging this kindness was something new. He cleared his throat. "They live at the house down below." He pointed left at a fork in the road.

We made our way down the path.

I saw Tatafu's mother hanging out clean, colorful sheets when we got to the house. Her dark, small, round figure stood out; she could barely reach the clothesline. Her face was concentrated on hanging the sheets correctly so they didn't drag on the ground, and her eyes looked determined as we approached. I realized this would be the first time I've been physically close to Malia. Before I'd only seen her walking away. She doesn't interact much with the others; she lets them know that she's there by taking walks.

When Malia saw us, she smiled and kept working. Her face is lovely—a pained beauty. I helped Malia hold and pinch the sheets. I wondered how to ask her. Should I be blunt or careful with my words?

I chose to be direct. "Malia," I began. "Tatafu's father is in Neiafu."

Atiata translated. Malia smiled and shook her head from side to side, which in Tonga means *yes*.

I knew she would like my bluntness. "Have you seen him recently?"

Malia kept smiling and spoke for a while, shaking her head a little now and then. Her voice was smooth and light. When Atiata translated, he only told me, "Yes." He whispered to me after Malia was done speaking, "I don't think she's seen him recently. I think she's just agreeing that yes she has seen him."

"What else did she say?"

"She said Koloa is a fine man. She respects him."

"Really? Tell Malia that we are going to tell Tatafu who his father is."

"Well, that's what else she said. She thinks it's time for Tatafu to meet him. But she knows that he needs to do this only when he's ready."

"Can you ask her if it's okay for us to tell Tatafu about Koloa, his father, being in Neiafu and how we want Tatafu to meet him? Explain this is about his self-preservation and self-esteem."

"Tessa, I don't know what those words mean, so I can't translate into Tongan."

Atiata and Malia started speaking in Tongan. She glanced over at me and smiled casually. I wondered what her smile meant. Her white teeth glowed against her dark skin.

Malia gently grinned and said, "*Malo.*"

I could tell that this was a gift for her. I can't imagine what this weight would've felt like for all those years. I wanted to alleviate the burden for Tatafu and his mother.

When we left Malia, she was sitting in the shade on a chair, fanning herself and still smiling. She's small, so her feet didn't touch the ground. I bowed to her as I backed away from the house. I wanted her to know I felt compassion for what she's gone through.

Instinctive

Accomplishment in a village
No power tools.
Leaders emerge from circumstances.
How far will any of us go
To make life "better" for another?
What do people want?
Who is asking?
Questions of authority
order of politeness
wrapped around
curious quests.
Hearth of suffering sways
Leaning into others.
Adapting and striving…
framework of respect.
Not receding too much.
Instrumental movement
stimulates obvious resources,
reclaiming personal wealth.

Chapter Twelve
STIGMAS

Before leaving Malia, we asked her where Tatafu might be. She said he was probably in the bush. Tatafu was never given a plot of land like other male villagers here. Atiata told me as we walked that this was so because he had no father here in the village. Also, Tatafu's eldest brother decided not to be generous in giving him land. Similarly, Tatafu hadn't been at the kava ceremony because he simply wasn't allowed due to his rank in the village.

Atiata's family allows Tatafu to work on their land so he can grow fruits, coconut, and taro to take home to his mother and sisters. Even though Atiata's parents know the troubled history, they're still kind to help. Atiata's family is proof to me that people can be genuinely good with no ulterior motives.

As we got closer to the bush, I didn't hesitate to head for the trees. But then I remembered the taboo about women in the bush. I asked Atiata how he felt about taking me there.

"No one will disrespect you, so no one will question me for respecting your wishes. You make us all more brave, Tessa."

Maybe I *was* being brave. Having a father and a mother was a given for me. My parents were not considered conventional. "Normal" is an overused word that has a meaning no one understands anymore. I have two fathers in my life. Tatafu didn't have a father, and this greatly affected him.

As we walked, Hakalo, Lio, and Lina appeared as we passed their houses. They started following Atiata and me. I barely noticed them join us. Soon we were a group, and Atiata took the secret path into the bush. Girls aren't allowed to go in unless their father or family elder is with them, and today I had Atiata, who is only a friend. We were on a mission to find Tatafu. So maybe this instance was okay.

When we found Tatafu clearing away jungle for a new planting patch, he was surprised to see all of us. As I prepared to talk, Hakalo, Lio, and Lina made no move to leave. This is so typically Tongan that a group of people would quietly observe a serious exchange. Atiata immediately suggested the others move to gather taro root.

I got right to the point. "Tatafu, your father is in Neiafu. Atiata knows who he is. Even your mother knows he is there. I think your mother would encourage you to go and meet with him. I believe the time has come for you to receive closure."

Tatafu kept hacking away with his machete as if he couldn't hear me.

"Tatafu?" I asked.

He hacked harder and harder and kept silent. I sat down in the nearby shade and waited. He finally stopped with the machete, burying the blade in the stump of a tree. By the time he sat down next to me, he seemed calmer. I called on my patience. I thought Tatafu would take a while before speaking. But he surprised me.

"Tessa," he began, "you come to our village, help school, help clean up trash, help tend gardens, help everything, and help me. You speak. I listen. You say to me, person is person, not made by mother's history, father's history, any history. You are Tessa. I am Tatafu. Father is father." He wiped what I thought was sweat from his face. "Father's story can be my story one day. Today no. If one day father comes, says, 'Hello, I am your father,' then I say 'Hello, I am your son.' Until then, I only me, and this is good enough."

I was stunned. I looked over and Atiata and the others were no longer there. We were alone. I couldn't speak, even if I had words to say. I felt a lump in my throat. This time I was the one who sat, elbows on knees, gazing into the jungle surrounding me. I know some time passed, because when Tatafu stood up and retrieved the machete, his shadow was long.

Then I spoke, the words tumbling out of me. I told Tatafu he had just now impressed me with his attitude. He was expanding possibilities; I wondered if he understood, so I rephrased and said that he was growing himself as a man and a *human*. What he had just told me stood out like a star leading a pilgrim to a holy site.

Tatafu looked at me with wide eyes not knowing how to respond. My face was ecstatic because of his words. I could feel the adrenaline rushing through me.

I looked around and remembered that I was in the forbidden bush. "Tatafu, here I am in the bush!"

"Easy," he said.

"Can we go farther?"

Tatafu playfully grinned, forgetting the intensity of the moment. He waved his machete in the air and started running. I ran after him. I was in the prohibited bush, and this was maybe the only chance I would have to explore what was here. We ran for ten or fifteen minutes; the running became a game of jumping over tree roots, taro, passion fruit, and flowers. Tatafu was much better at this than I was.

He had to wait for me a couple of times. I was shocked seeing him run up a coconut tree so fast that I stopped in my tracks. I had never seen anyone do such a feat. He ran up, dropped a couple of coconuts, climbed back down, took the machete, stripped the outer layer, cracked the coconut, and handed it to me to drink. Refreshment could not be any better.

We began to run again and headed down a sharp incline, both shrieking and laughing and paying very close attention to our steps. Suddenly, we broke through some vines and plants with huge scratchy, aromatic leaves. I saw a pool of clear water fed by a waterfall. The sound made by this little cascade stayed just there in that shady nook. The jungle canopy was complete; no sunlight entered. We both walked right into the pool. Kneeling, the water was just to our chins.

Tatafu spoke first. "To me, this is sacred spot. I come here all my life. When trouble, I come here. When receive good gifts, I come here say thank you. I come here to pray."

"Tatafu, your English is very good. I thought you couldn't speak so well."

"I make Atiata practice with me. Lazy time over." We laughed.

The water was a comfortable temperature. I could feel little fish nibbling around my legs. Occasionally, a ray of sunlight pierced the green ceiling, illuminating the wet air full of insects. I felt like the Earth itself had finally welcomed me to Tonga and the bush.

Tatafu spoke, his voice soft like the water babbling behind him. "Tessa, you came to Tuʻanuku and teach me. I have no care now how people think me this, me that. I have always made way by work, by rugby, by friends. You help. I give up worry. I give up sorry. I give up how maybe should be. I do not hate man who made me. I must understand. I felt the pain now need to understand. Understand will be good. Maybe I learn love." Tatafu looked up to the canopy and swayed his hands in the water. He tipped his head down to me, and his eyes squinted, trying to adjust to the darkness. "Someday," he smiled. "Life will be better."

"You are my teacher too, Tatafu," I said, scooting closer to him so he could hear what I had to say. "I am so surprised by your thoughts and your heart. I believe that in order to help anyone, I first have to help myself. You thank me, and I thank you. I thank you for being a man who will take care of himself. You have shown me great strength."

As I said this, a ray of sunlight snuck through the canopy and hit Tatafu on the forehead. He closed his eyes and smiled in the warmth.

"Life can be difficult until we transcend it," I said.

Tatafu, with his eyes still closed, furrowed his eyebrows when he heard the word *transcend*.

I smiled at him. "It means to excel, to be better."

He opened his eyes and looked into mine. "How be better at life?"

I gazed into the water. "Not sure…"

Then laughter and the swish-swish sound of humans in the bush roared over the little waterfall, giggling Tongan words I didn't know. I was curious who was coming. Then I looked around and glanced at Tatafu with worried eyes that we were to be found out and I'd get in trouble. He responded with the same look, and both of us quickly stood up out of the water, getting ready to make a sprint for the trees.

Suddenly, from somewhere in the deep green that surrounded us, a familiar laughing voice and body flew through the plants and splashed in the water. Atiata was now dousing himself in the water. Lina, Lio, and Hakalo, quick behind him, immersed their bodies in the crisp pool. When they all jumped up and reached their arms high, I recovered with applause and laughter. Tatafu got back in the water and made huge splashes with his hands. Everyone was giggly and goofy.

As we lingered in the pool with small conversations, something washed over me, and I felt like I was speaking Tongan. I could understand most of their words and let the thoughts I wanted to say flow out of my mouth. They all looked at me as if, like Tatafu, I had been practicing behind their backs and suddenly was fluent. The water, air, smells, sounds, and friends all cleansed my brain of always thinking in English. I thought about my brain and about my mind. My brain is a storehouse of facts and information, and my mind emanates from my heart and connects me with everything outside of my body.

I tried to say this, with some pointing at my head and at my heart and some grand gestures signifying the universe and smaller gestures indicating books, words, and thoughts. Atiata helped me out, finding the Tongan words that were closest to what he thought I was trying to say.

Our brains are machines that can be very powerful, but our minds and our hearts can play tricks on us. I pointed all around while explaining. I believe the mind will live on after our bodies are gone. Perhaps our bodies will be reincarnated and manifest differently, with mind and heart as one.

They didn't immediately understand *reincarnate*, but once the meaning became clear, they liked the idea better than heaven and hell. Another chance, and another, and another to *get it right!*

Lina said, "Tessa, no way Tongans reincarnate! Don't care if get it right!"

More laughter, then splashing began. Atiata climbed out of the pool and took another running leap to cannonball again. The rest of the time became a bit riotous. I can't remember the last time I laughed so much. Hakalo and Lio lounged in the water.

When we finally sat quietly at the edge of the pool, the sun was getting low. My brain came up with a thought: *This whole afternoon was a prohibited affair!* I stuttered to Tatafu about this, and he replied, "We all human, Tessa. Even Tonga change some day."

As we walked back to the village, everyone was quiet, no words exchanged. I could barely remember that Tatafu had shown me the strength of his mind by acknowledging his father and standing apart from him at the same time. He had been preparing his whole life for *this* afternoon. Something that had been dammed up in him was gone. I felt great peace and gratitude that I was allowed to be a part of this. What a mysterious world.

King

*Far away, and so close
the tender sight, sight of being tender as kindness
glimmered in his eyes . . . he wanted to show himself . . .
to leave no misinterpretation undone, unwound. And she,
robed in the once-right of authority he held,
once wound and weighted her: yet he sat, sometimes,
intimidated by the notice she took in from him, from
others. Falling into a chain of attachment
she began to love him, for the way his rigidity softened.
Sight tendered, turned stone to velvet
he sat sometimes and noticed the kindness in her eyes.
She watched him be king.*

Chapter Thirteen
ADOPTED

Tatafu's mother, Malia, is an interesting woman. You'd think she would want to be left alone after all she's gone through. Instead, she walks around the village with a smile on her face. She attends choir practice and eats and brings food sometimes. Every now and then, others will look at her with odd looks.

I tried to imagine how she felt, returning to the village with a baby who did not belong to her husband. She had been gone for years, and the courage and personal authority she must have summoned in herself to return is incomprehensible to me. I've occasionally met people like that—the ones who break the rules but are somehow immune to the disapproval of society that would make anybody else creep around in shame.

Two of Malia's daughters were a few years older than Tatafu; both were married and lived in the village. I don't see Tatafu's sisters around the village as much as I see his mother.

An idea started to form in my head. I kept this to myself for a short while, reflecting about the different angles. I wanted Tatafu's sisters to help me find his real father. I knew that Koloa was in Neiafu. I was unsure what we were going to do once we got there—hound him to meet his long-lost son? Logistics needed to be figured out.

I was walking back from the school when I ran into Lina. I've seen Lina talk with Malia on occasion, and they've been friendly from what I could interpret. I asked Lina if she knew anything about Tatafu's sisters—or even just one of them.

"Dafotilia, Tatafu's oldest sister, likes to keep to herself and her family, nothing wrong in that," said Lina. "She's just quiet and shy, and Tattia is private."

I wondered if their shyness came from how the village reacted when Malia returned. Dafotilia and Tattia were just girls when they witnessed how their mother was treated. The girls loved their mother, and seeing her disrespected undoubtedly upset and confused them. I speculated if they were worried that they would be abused by men in their future.

"Do you talk to them?" I asked Lina.

"Of course," she chuckled. "They're my friends and very kind to me, so I'm kind to them."

"Could you introduce me?"

"Yes. I'm actually going over to Dafotilia's place right now if you want to join me," Lina said.

Dafotilia. I liked the sound of her name. Lina and I walked to my place so I could drop off my school supplies and change my clothes. I decided to take my piglet Suey with me as a sort of cultural icebreaker. I tied a bow under his chin. I dressed even more modestly than usual; I wore a long wraparound skirt and a long-sleeved blouse. I put a flower behind my ear. Lina and I set out.

Dafotilia had two small children, a boy and a girl, and they were thrilled with Suey, squealing and chasing him about. Dafotilia looked a lot like her mother. She was friendly, though slightly wary and formal—not because I was an outsider, but because she seemed to know that I was there to ask about Tatafu, I felt. I guess our friendship was known around the village.

I wasn't really there to ask about Tatafu. I wanted to know about Tatafu's *father*—who he was and how I might find him. I knew my plan was sort of crazy. I had the feeling that maybe things weren't as complicated as people might think.

We chatted for a while about the work I wanted to do in the village, the school repairs, *sima vies* (water tanks), gutters, library. We stumbled with our two different languages. She asked me about where I came from and if there was a lot of snow there. She was especially interested in hearing about snow—she'd seen pictures of snow and images of people with what she called "planks" on their feet. This was perfect! Snow is something I know plenty about. I told her that I was a skier and did my best to imitate a graceful zoom down a snowy mountain. There I was on flat ground in the tropics in my flowered skirt, imaginary ski poles in my hands, bent forward, pretending to "shush" from side to side. That got her laughing, and she relaxed a lot. I told her that everyone in my family skied, including my fathers.

She caught that plural: Fathers. "How many fathers do you have?" she asked.

"Just two," I said. "And they are good friends," I quickly added.

"Not jealous? No fighting?"

"Well," I said. "They have their disagreements sometimes, but they are friends first."

"Your mother has children with both of them?"

"Yes," I said. I explained as best I could in Tongan and English. "And we children don't even think about which father is our 'real' father because we have been raised by both of them."

"Tatafu has two fathers," she said. "There is no friendship between them."

I said nothing at first, acted casual, though I was excited at the turn of our conversation. I scratched Suey's back with a stick. "Maybe that could change," I said.

"No, no, impossible," she said.

"Do you remember Tatafu's other father?" I asked, casually.

"I was very young," she said. "I remember him. Tatafu does not. He was a baby when we came back here."

"Was he a nice man?"

"Nice, very…how do you say?" She twirled her hand next to her head, tugging and looping a piece of her hair.

"Dreamy?" I asked, making a guess.

"Yes!" she said. "Head in the clouds! Did not like to work. He wanted to sing his thoughts. Mama liked him, and she became frustrated. Never enough money. Always singing, playing his guitar.

Sometimes made a little bit of money that way, playing in bars and clubs, but never steady. That's why she came back. Three little children to feed."

"Tatafu's father is a singer?"

"He calls himself King Koloa."

I wanted to go to Neiafu and find him. I'd need most of the day because I wanted to go to the library in Neiafu too. I was curious to see what a Tongan library looked like, what kind of books were lining the walls. I hoped to talk to the librarian and find out if maybe the Neiafu library was interested in seeding the library I wanted to start in Tu'anuku. Did they have books they might want to donate? Did they have advice? My plan was to get to town early in the day, so that I, as an unescorted woman, would not draw attention. Daytime and sunshine equate to innocence.

I caught a ride the very next day with the Peace Corps staffer, Lepa, who brings me my mail and supplies every ten days. He would return me to the village in the evening. This was perfect, allowing an entire day to investigate and learn. Before Lepa arrived early that morning, I left Suey in the care of Atiata's little sister, Lifi. I told her he liked to be scratched behind the ears and that she shouldn't let him wander out of her yard. I had painted my name on his back in red fruit juice, and I told Lifi that she could decorate him with more if she wanted. She laughed with delight. I knew he'd be safe in her care.

The ride from the village to Neifau made me angry about the laziness within the passing villages. The morning sun was golden and slanted through my eyes, which were not growing accustomed to litter and lack of care for the earth. My original shock had subsided. I was not as startled now that I have settled on the conditions of the country. The trash became a natural part of the scenery now, and the beauty of the vegetation dominated. I didn't react as frantically inside myself at the trash we passed as I had previously.

The older Tongan man of fifty-six driving me told me in Tongan that he had lived in Neiafu all his life. I was full of questions through our entire trip to Neiafu. Did he like music? Were there places in town where a person could hear some good singing and maybe some guitar playing? Would I be able to walk there from the library?

"Walk anywhere in Neiafu," he said with pride. "Little big town. Plenty of music. Don't go to Vava'u Club near post office."

"Why not?"

"A men's club started by old German back in 1875."

"Am I not allowed?" I asked, a little indignantly.

"You *are* allowed, but you will not like the place: pool tables, waiters in uniforms, mosquitoes. No music."

"Mosquitoes?" I asked. "You mean…" And I slapped my arm in demonstration.

He laughed. "No. Not that kind of mosquito. Girls. Lots of makeup, hang around the bar, get men to buy expensive drinks."

"Where I come from, they're called 'B-girls,'" I laughed. He didn't understand, so I shifted the subject. "Where else, aside from the Vava'u Club?"

He thought for a moment.

"Tonga Bob's," he said. "Fun place. Wednesday night Fakaleiti Night."

"Faka…?"

"Fakaleiti, men who dress like women."

There is a tradition in Tonga that goes back a long time. Our Peace Corps group learned of this in our Tongan cultural training: boys raised as girls in families where there weren't enough girls. They were taught domestic customs, such as sewing, cooking, and childcare. Some of them grew up to be gay; others carried on as males. I knew it was a whole subculture, accepted at large—oddly conservative in its own way and definitely not to be mistaken for the Western version of cross-dressing and rebellious gender politics.

This was fascinating to me. I knew I couldn't stay too late; maybe I could catch a glimpse of one of the lady-men. Fakaleiti sounded to me like "fuck a lady." How ironic.

I enjoyed riding into Neiafu with an adventure pending. I'd passed through only briefly on my way to the village, and the postal carrier was right: It's not a city, by my assessment, but definitely larger than Tu'anuku, with flowers, churches, colorful houses, and views of boats in the harbor at every turn. He made a point of driving me past the police station, so I'd know it was in the neighborhood near the post office and the library.

He dropped me near the library, and I began walking. I was only about a block from the main wharf, the big vegetable market, and the road that went along the edge of the harbor. He said he'd be able to give me a ride back at 7 p.m., when he'd be making his deliveries along the return route.

I went to the library first. I found out that the queen's niece is responsible for this library, which pleased me. I was relieved to know that women were of some standing here and could achieve good things, even if they are royalty.

I've always loved the smell of books. There was a smell today of fresh paint too, which I've also always liked. The combination of the harbor breeze coming through the open windows and the smells of books and fresh paint put me in a cheerful, hopeful mood.

I greeted the librarian, an enormous woman who had a big smile. I told her I was with the Peace Corps and hoping to start a library in Tuʻanuku. This made her very happy, and she showed me all around the building.

I saw a whole section of paperback and hardcover novels that looked as if tourists had left them behind in their hotel rooms. There was also a pretty big history section and a set of the *Encyclopedia Britannica*. There were maps, many books of photography on Tonga and other South Pacific islands, what looked like old dusty logbooks from ships, and an entire section devoted to religion—bibles, many Books of Mormon, and hymnals.

The librarian said she would be happy to set aside donated books that they didn't need and eventually share them with Tuʻanuku once the library was organized. I was grateful—my trip into town was already worthwhile.

I told the librarian I wanted to get some lunch where there was, hopefully, live music and asked if she had heard of a singer named King Koloa.

"King Koloa!" she said and rolled her eyes. "Very handsome man. Beautiful voice. Sings at Tonga Bob's."

Tonga Bob's. That made two votes.

"Handsome, eh?" I asked.

"Ladies love him." She laughed. "So do the Fakaleiti." And she did a funny little dance with one hand on her hip, fluttering her eyelashes.

"What's his real name, this King Koloa?" I asked.

She shrugged. "That's the only name he has. Says he's a real king. Sings about how to be a king. Nobody knows any other name for him!"

Well, this was intriguing. I asked for directions to Tonga Bob's, which she said was just a few blocks away. She also mentioned that the place was owned by a New Zealand expat.

I had no problem finding Tonga Bob's. The double doors stood open. I could see a bar inside; a few people drank beer in the cool, dark interior. There was a dance floor, a little stage, microphones, amplifiers, and shimmery curtains to the rear of the stage. The bartender was a white guy with a scraggly beard and reddish hair. Could this be Tonga Bob? I approached. He smiled.

"What'll it be, love?" he asked, friendly, looking me over. A definite Kiwi accent. "You must be one of the new Peace Corps volunteers. Haven't seen you before. Now a new round of helpers has arrived."

Although I rarely drink alcohol, I decided to order a beer. I didn't have to drink the whole thing. I was obscurely cheered and thirsty because of the heat, humidity, and anticipation. I had questions to ask and wanted to be sociable. There were hardly any other customers at this time of day, so he put my glass in front of me, filled one for himself, and leaned on the counter.

"You're American," he said and raised his glass in a toast. "I was there once—took a boat ride up the Mississippi from New Orleans to Natchez."

"Well, you're ahead of me. I've never been to Natchez nor up the Mississippi. But I've been to Nepal and India, and now I'm here!" We clinked glasses. I looked around. "When does the music start?"

"Nine o'clock. Karaoke starts at seven. Gets the crowd warmed up. It's dress-up night tonight."

"You mean the Fakaleiti, right?"

"Right," he said. "Things get wild and crazy! Some of these

lady-men can really belt out a song! You should stick around for the show."

"So," I ventured, "no King Koloa tonight?"

"Not tonight." He looked at me with playful curiosity. "How do you know about King?"

"Somebody in the village mentioned him." This was the truth, of course.

"You come here to see him?" he smiled.

My cheeks flushed. I knew I was blushing. I'd been caught—quite obviously.

"Relax," he chuckled. "Everyone wants to see him."

He took a long swig of his beer and picked up a clunky old rotary phone, watching me as he dialed three numbers. Then he said something in Tongan. I caught a few words—"pretty girl" among them.

"You're in luck," he said. "The king is awake, has had his coffee, and is on his way over here to meet you. And he's bringing his guitar."

We chatted for no more than five minutes before a man came through the door, carrying a guitar case. The man I assumed was Tonga Bob turned to me.

"I didn't ask your name," he said.

"My name's Tessa," I said and put out my hand. Bob shook my hand. He turned to the man with the guitar. "Tessa, meet King Koloa."

I watched my own small hand vanish entirely in King Koloa's huge one. His hand was warm and dry, and he had a gentle touch. He smiled down at me from where he was standing. He was much taller and more massive than Tatafu, but the resemblance was startling. From that moment, I had no doubt I stood before Tatafu's biological father.

"Tessa, Tessa," he said in a melodious voice. "I am so, so happy to meet you. We all travel great distances and know not who or what we might meet along the way, but we know sweetness when we find it, and the magic that flows like the currents of the sea!"

Another person appeared from the shadows near the stage, wearing a long shiny dress split up the side so that his leg flashed when he walked, with eye makeup and black hair pulled back and piled atop his head in a shiny knot. He also wore dangly earrings and lipstick. He was as massive as King Koloa, but with feminine mannerisms.

"Hello, King! I heard your voice!"

They kissed, lightly and platonically, while I stood there in wonder.

"Tessa," said Tonga Bob, "this is Falala."

Falala turned to me. I had already put out my hand, but he ignored it, pulling me into a warm, perfumed, two-armed embrace. The top of my head barely came up to his collarbone. I lingered in the embrace for a few heartbeats, thoroughly enjoying it, feeling a sort of mother-father love enveloping me.

"So little!" he exclaimed, looking at me. "But so mighty!"

I blushed.

King Koloa took out his guitar, plunked himself onto a bar stool and began to strum. Tonga Bob leaned back comfortably, sipping his beer, and Falala began to sway as King Koloa started to croon a wordless melody. He had announced that the song title was "Makai," which means "toward the sea." His voice was rich and smooth, climbing up and down the scales as he warmed up, eyes closed. His voice conjured pictures in my head: sea-going canoes paddled by strong brown men, ocean winds, vast distances.

When Koloa began to sing words, they were in Tongan, and Falala hummed and swayed and gave me a running translation about the movement of the sea in splendid waves.

"This is a ballad of green and lovely Tofua, which once spouted fire and where no man lived…where there was fire, there is now cool, deep, cold water…a god named Tafakula had stopped the flowing fire and turned it into beautiful water…and Tafakula dwelled there as a mortal man, so much did he love his island and his lake…and he sang of its beauty, hoping that the wind would carry his song and bring others to the island…so lovely was his singing that people heard it on the wind and came in their boats from other islands to live with Tafakula…they made him their king and lived there for many generations in peace and happiness, with Tafakula's sons and the sons of those sons reigning as beloved kings...but a warlike man was born among them after many peaceful centuries, and declared himself the true king, King Manu, and went to the other side of the island with his followers and declared a new kingdom, a true kingdom...the kingdom toward the sea.

"These were not peaceful people like Tafakula's people; they did not welcome visitors from strange lands. One day from a high lookout, they saw a boat approaching... They beat their drums in warning, telling the warriors to gather on the beach... On the other side of the island, Tafakula's people heard the drums too, and fearing trouble, they set out as quickly as they could... When they arrived at the beach, King Manu's warriors had killed a man, a strange pale man. They had killed him with stones and clubs, and there were more strange men who they were going to kill as well, but Tafakula's great-great-great-great-grandson, King Koloa, intervened, drove off King Manu's warriors, and welcomed the white men from across the sea. The pallid men had a chief among them; William was his name, with eyes as strange and blue as the sea itself. These foreigners stayed, rested, and gathered food and then set out to sea and never were seen again.

"For more centuries, King Koloa's people lived on Tofua with Koloa's sons and sons of sons, all named Koloa, as their kings...but King Manu's sons and sons of sons on the other side of the island never left them alone... They had tasted war and blood and loved it so much that they killed every living thing they encountered...and so the descendants of Tafakula, now King Koloa's people, left the island in many boats and found another island, where they lived in peace for many more generations, until the world caught up with them and carried them farther and farther. One among them today is still a peacemaker, truly descended from King Tafakula, and his name is King Koloa the Ninth, and he sings for you this song!"

King Koloa and Falala then let their voices weave in and out of one another in a soaring harmony. I thought of sea birds circling, riding a thermal draft up and up into the boundless sky. I was utterly transported, almost in a trance, the two voices at such close range enveloping me, carrying me to the sound of my brothers' voices harmonizing. The song ended with a fancy little flourish of the guitar strings. Tonga Bob and I clapped spontaneously while King Koloa raised Falala's hand theatrically, like an Italian tenor onstage with his duet partner, and then bowed deeply.

"That was lovely," I said.

"You know," said Tonga Bob, gesturing toward Tatafu's father, "the king here is true to his ancestor. He's a genuine peacemaker. Puts his money where his mouth is, as you Americans like to say."

Tonga Bob then told me a remarkable story about how King Koloa had been in the capital city, Nuku'alofa, the year before, when there had been dangerous unrest. Three thousand civil servants had gone on strike, angry because of pay raises given to a top few elite civil servants while the majority received no such raise.

"A bunch of those pissed-off civil servants burned one of King Tupou's houses there. There was a mob forming, wanting to burn and destroy more of Tupou's estate. This guy here," he said, gesturing toward Tatafu's father, "went among them, without fear, spoke to them, soothed them, told them he understood their grievances, and said that a new Tonga was coming soon—that their king was a very old man and would soon pass to his reward, that the new king, his son, was ready to make reforms, and they just had to be patient a little bit longer. They calmed down, they went home, and at least on that night, nothing else got burned, no one hurt, no property damaged."

I'd heard about the strike in our Peace Corps training on the current state of the country's political scene. I knew that there was a major movement in Tonga to remake the kingdom into a democracy and that things had been tense. The king was almost eighty-eight years old, and big changes were expected after his passing. As in other traditional monarchies, there were plenty of loyalists, faithful to the old system, and there were also people who were sick of monarchy and eager to move on.

Tonga Bob had me come around the counter and look at a newspaper clipping stapled to the wall near the telephone: a story with a photo of King Koloa, shaking hands with another man, one of the leaders of a contingent of strikers. The story said that Koloa played an impromptu concert in a park that evening, singing until midnight, promoting peace and calm. The caption beneath the photo read, "King of Peacemakers."

I stayed at the bar for another hour or so, enjoying what felt like one of the best days of my life. I sang along with Falala, King Koloa, and Tonga Bob. I taught them a couple of songs from home—an old folk song my father had taught me, "If I Had a Hammer," which they absolutely loved, and a couple of rock songs from my teen years.

When it was time for me to go, King Koloa looked at me. I thought I saw a shadow of sadness pass across his face. In the next moment, he smiled.

"You will travel so, so far," he said. "You have only just begun. Your heart contains the whole world."

Walking back to the library, I was dazed by the sunshine after the indoor shade of Tonga Bob's and what I had just experienced. I was excited, too—the name of the island in King Koloa's song, Tofua, was a real place, one that I remembered from my Peace Corps studies of Tonga.

"Oh, yes," said the librarian after I got there and had asked her about Tofua. She took a volume of the *Britannica* from the shelf, flipped through the pages, and laid the open book before me.

There it was: the astounding story of the almost perfectly circular island, once a volcano but now with a huge freshwater lake in its center, like the hole in a doughnut. I looked at the aerial photo. King Koloa's song had told of the god Tafakula, before he became a mortal man, and how he transformed the flowing lava into beautiful water. The part that just about blew my mind was that King Koloa's song had told of strange, pale men landing on the island, bad King Manu's warriors killing one of them, and that the name of the pale men's chief with the strange sea-colored eyes was William.

The encyclopedia read, "In 1789, Captain William Bligh of the *HMS Bounty* had been set adrift in a lifeboat by mutineers led by Fletcher Christian. Bligh and about eighteen crewmen loyal to him landed on the shore of Tofua. There they were attacked by hostile inhabitants, and one among them was stoned to death. The rest of them escaped, went further along the shore of Tofua, sheltered in a cave while they gathered provisions, and then set off again."

King Koloa's song, though half mythical, was also half historical truth. I had no doubt that he was a true descendant of the king of Tofua, that in that sense he was actually descended from a once-royal line, and that he had a right to his name.

What this meant, of course, was that Tatafu, an illegitimate outcast, was in fact a *prince*. More important, though, were the truths about his father: that he lived up to his name and that he brought peace to troubled people through his artistry.

I'd make sure Tatafu knows who his father is and who he *himself* is. Even if he never told a soul, he could carry the knowledge in his heart and hold his head high.

I could hardly wait to get back to the village. I made my way to the Peace Corps office to find Lepa with the Peace Corps van. He handed me an envelope, and I saw Viva's handwriting. I thought about reading her letter right away but decided I needed my mind to be focused on Tatafu. He was my priority today.

Life

Happens
When you sit so still
Only your heart moves.
Staring
Into the screen of life
At petals
Blown in from the garden,
You overlook the living.
Poised in irresistible resistance,
The result of forces
Beyond even your own control.
You hardly notice being caught, then released
Into the moon's eclipse.
While safety's at stake,
Erogenous tones
Plunder the equilibrium of fire,
Cultivating a season's opportunity
Embers banked for another day.

Chapter Fourteen
VIVA

I got back to Tu'anuku as the sun set. Nighttime engulfed the village. I was too tired to attend dinner, so I walked back to my house, intending to prepare for sleep. While walking, I reached in my bag and felt my mother's letter. I thought about trying to find Tatafu and tell him all that I've discovered about his father. Before I could make a decision, I saw Atiata pacing at my front door, holding Suey.

"Tessa," he turned and walked my way. "Where were you today? I came home to find my little sister watching your piglet. She told me you went to Neiafu. Where did you go?" He glanced over his shoulder and checked around us. "Did you—were you gone because of Tatafu's father?" he asked quietly.

"Yes, Atiata, and I met him," I whispered with composed excitement. "I met Koloa. He's a singer. He's living and working in Neiafu!"

Atiata's mouth fell open in astonishment. Suey slipped from his hands and went trotting behind the house. "That's great, Tessa! And all on your own," he said smiling. Both of us stood there taking in what I had said. Tatafu's father became a reality rather than just a story. He had a life. He was alive.

"So did you..." Atiata began, "you know, tell him about Tatafu?"

"I didn't," I admitted. "I didn't even ask him about Malia."

Atiata looked at me with confusion. "Why?"

"Because I feel the choice of what happens now is for Tatafu to make." I breathed in deeply then exhaled. "We need to think about how to approach the subject with Tatafu. I wonder if it might be best for you and your father to talk with him. I'll see you in the morning after church, and we can make a plan."

"We could meet with him and tell him together," suggested Atiata. "Until tomorrow, my friend."

"Perhaps," I replied.

We said goodnight and then I walked into my house. Exhaustion was setting in, and my body felt weary as I got closer to the bed. I was grateful that the hour was late enough that no one would come to my door expecting to sit in the breezeway and work on the jigsaw puzzle. I washed my face and hands with cool water, not having the strength nor patience to warm the water for a serious cleanse.

Then I unwrapped Viva's letter from the envelope, noticing her handwriting and drawings. Suddenly, I wasn't tired because I was instantly carried home to the sound of my mother's voice.

> My Amazing Courageous Child,
>
> The day after you departed, I began wearing the sanguine cape you brought me from Nepal. The color of the cape reminds me of the first chakra that symbolizes the connection we have to our tribe, our family. You and your siblings are my blood, my kingdom. The thoughts crowding my mind right now are from a vast array of amends, awareness, and sentimentality. I write the way I draw and paint: in splotches, segments, and inspired spurts. I'm pleased to have this opportunity to be thoughtful and reflective with you, although I wish I were drinking tea with you and able to gaze into your eyes.
>
> I want to relegate to you a many-roomed house, which is symbolic of the psyche and therefore will reveal history. Our house has been regularly divided in the past, which creates weakness and fracture. Nevertheless, I receive strength from loving you and your

siblings. I am astonished by all of you and constantly trying to find ways to improve our lives—the internal review board that swirls around me. I aim for improvement, which might enable you to work with me as one of my guides.

I imagine this letter to be an exchange of information being tracked from lifetimes before, a record housed in the filing system of the universe. I think you are old enough for me to admit aloud my inadequacies. I don't want to sound detached, ridiculous, or absurd. I have made time to contemplate and marvel over you since you were born. I wanted to feel safe, so I set up a fortress of people as layspotters to work with me because I had doubts about my capabilities as a woman, a mother, a provider, and a teacher.

The question to contemplate with our association: Were you children my destiny, or are we together because of physics, atoms, and molecules? The inclusion rallies to recruit that which is nonphysical to physical, if only I could actually remember another lifetime like you remember your birth. We are a constellation, however this came to be. And so, here we are, advancing in the family myth because of you. My parents, your grandparents, did their best to make a life for me and my siblings. We were all children pieced together after random acts of passion, also known as thoughtless, impractical, and irresponsible when considering birth control, timing, and finances.

I think I'm a sum of my memories. The myth and habits were passed to me, and I became a breeder like Marme. With each generation, there is hope for improvement and change. I recall your grandmother saying to me, "Viva, in life one door opens, and another one closes. But it's hell in the hallway." I've spent time in that hallway.

All of you children were allowed to live in a protected fantasy life for a while, and I truly believe this encouraged creativity and safety. I wanted to do a better job than my mother, but fantasy, friends, and fairies were a part of our protection as well. Marme insisted we were bohemian, exotic, and special, so we ran with terminal uniqueness. Lacking boundaries or ordinary atmospheres, things were discombobulating and lurking below the surface, like the raw underbelly of an animal.

Our house wasn't like anyone else's because Marme had a style that defied convention, especially in the stodgy 1950s. In our neighborhood where no one was yet collecting art, we had a jade-tumbled fireplace with a copper hood in the middle of a scored concrete floor with curved built-in planters around the edge of the room. These housed so much foliage that even the ponies and the geese felt comfortable in the house. The space seemed huge with high-pitched ceilings and a freestanding divider encasing a colorful stained-glass window.

We were a blended family of nine children, and I was the middle child who played many different roles. That is your heritage from my DNA, and I know less than you do about your fathers' upbringings. When you return from your assignment in Tonga, let's research and find out all the details we can before you marry and have children. I know you started the process and I want to help you complete the task. We will go see my half-brother David because he has done some investigating into your grandfather's heritage. I wish that I had paid attention when you were eager to research the family ancestry last year.

Sometimes I feel as if my family walked off with my skin, because I have such a promiscuous appetite in regard to expectation. I continue to be the guardian of the language of day glitter, even though the invisible wounds are lurking. I don't want you ever to feel wounded or unworthy, and I believe my unresolved wounds kept me from being all I could be as a mother. My accumulation of irregular features and obsequious and conciliatory tactics allow people to be curious about me. After a period of time, an opinion is established, and folks either like me or they don't. There is no gray area.

You, however, attract everyone with your consistent good intentions and efforts. I admire you. I haven't taken the time to make certain you know the respect I have for you. Just because I don't live by what I say doesn't mean that what I say has no value. Blended families are often affected by disappointment, competition, cruelty, and misunderstanding. The innocence and love dissipate all too soon when people are inhospitable toward one another.

I am only as good of a mother as you children believe I am. I know some things about me have disappointed you. I am still trying to make progress before I die so you have no resentments to carry into your future from your family myth. You will be a better mother than me.

A strong mentor protects the birthing of the leader within all of us. You struggle to cultivate peace while investigating, watching, and listening. Utilize the vision inside the chrysalis of the cocoon. We don't live like a caterpillar twice. We don't go back, although I have been known to do the same thing over and over, hoping for different results.

I admire how you challenge power and then give that power to others. You were born a humanist.

Out of my eight siblings, I only fraternize with and vaguely know two of them. You, your sister, and your brothers have such a bond. I was close with all my younger siblings when we were growing up, especially Tony. His ski accident, when he was under my supervision, was the first critical shock. He was twelve, and the swollen knee was on top of a serious bone infection, osteomyelitis. His leg was amputated on April 11, 1968. Thirty-one years later, on the exact same date, Xavier was in his car accident that would leave him a paraplegic. The synchronicity is interesting.

I think I have a better understanding of the word "karma." I believe female intuition is like a muscle, surrendering, contracting and then relaxing, and then the energy in the muscle changes course. Love is the fascia of a woman's world, the connective tissue.

I watch you give voice to the voiceless with amazing sincerity; your efforts magnify possibilities in the world. Love is infinitely more durable than hate. Marme once said to me, "You can lead a human to knowledge, but you can't make him think." Emotional intelligence is the most important ingredient for success, and we often learn more from our mistakes than our successes. Of course, it's important to have an intellect as well as emotional literacy. You have gone beyond your parents' abilities to communicate, both with your thoughts and feelings

So here I am entering my second Saturn return, which will

move me into my sage-ing years soon. I want you youngsters around me. I was upset that you chose to apply for the Peace Corps and be assigned in a country so far away.

I am so impressed with all you have accomplished in twenty-four years; you've done more than most manage in a lifetime. You achieve and follow through, while I just dabble. You are capable, strong, resilient, defiant, intelligent, and magnificent. I want you to come home, my darling child. I am aware of my misgivings, mistakes, and wrongdoings. Please forgive me. We have tried to do better than our parents, and you children can do better than we have done.

The questions you might ask yourself are: What is the specter of this family? Are we culpable as we retrench and deepen? Can the emotional deficit that tends to corrupt be interpreted as a genetic predisposition? Is it possible your parents can grow into better people? Did you have to separate yourself from us so you could make sense of who you are?

I don't suppose any of us are meant to stand alone, heal alone, nor love alone. I believe in tenderness and adoration too, honey. All of you children taught me to love on a grand scale that surpasses any other goals I might have previously thought important.

I hope you will enjoy yourself as your eyes widen with experience and you discover something in yourself, the landscape, the culture, or your friends. You are my daughter, my beautiful and courageous girl. Pay attention, be mindful to all that is around you, and continue to share with me through your letters, calls, and emails. To say that I miss you is an understatement. In the meantime, live, my child. You are my teacher.

All the love in my heart and more,
—Moma

I feel my eyes water while reading her words, recognizing I am transcending my resentments, sympathy, and secrets. She and my grandmother have carried their families as best they could, against the odds of a family that binds you like a noose. The decisions you make as a woman, mother, wife, and confidante often discourage respect, acknowledgement, and trust. I see how mothers are in precarious positions daily to satisfy the audience they have before them.

Knowledge is power, yet also a burden. Things often fall and are built again emotionally, and the mother is generally responsible for silently or openly suffusing relief. They hope to make life exuberant and emergent in the stream of a family dynamic. The whole of life can be turned over quickly as with Tatafu's mother, my mother, and probably their mothers, a chain formed from generation to generation. The women are often responsible for inspiring change and an interlacing world of networks for opportunity.

I'm gone for two years, carrying with me an untold story that belongs to Marme, Viva, and now me. When Marme first shared particulars with me, I felt a sense of honor, yet now I feel burdened. Viva cherished the final days that I spent with her. Reading her letter reestablishes a respect and insight into her nature and nurturing of those she loves. I shake and dislodge myself from my family myth and uncover Tatafu's story as a discipline to lead and reflect on my own family mystery.

The subtle unseen energies shine as a device that can take thought and transcend matter while I make excuses for investigating someone's life. My position as a woman allows me to openly communicate in a way of life drawing. Life is not a template; it's nonlinear. This experience I've had with Tatafu and his father reminds me of my own father and how he understood so little about his own parents' relationship and history. He refused to talk about his feelings. They were estranged and my father felt abandoned by his mother, even though his own father gave him to his parents because he was too busy to care for my dad himself. He too was looking for love but was unsure of what in fact the word *love* meant.

Is this what everyone strives for: intimate communication and a partner who can accept and understand your journey? What does partnership entail to keep people united? And why is partnership important? I understand that women need men to propagate, but is there any such thing as a perfect relationship? Are we supposed to accept things with alacrity as if everyone is interested in finding the answers.

I come to this under-sourced country with my modern views. I see that even here the stigmas of attraction, gratification, and lust take up residence as a necessity. Can we intuit conclusions by not having an explanation? The sensitivity that surrounds cultural contrast sets me in motion of forgiveness, understanding, and hopefully acceptance. Xavier's adapting to being wheelchair-bound, Indigo's other worldly perceptions, Jazie's determination—each of us has a unique strength.

Although I feel a sense of freedom, I miss everyone: my parents, siblings, friends, and my dog, Kalu, for all the right reasons. Mysteries are the universal system of survival and then we evolve. The journey here with the Peace Corps is to experiment with actualizing visions through other people's eyes, allowing me to be freed from resentment and my analytical need to make sense of my family and to concentrate on what matters in this village for the next two years. A notoriety surrounds me because of experiences, in part due to the yearning. I hope to join some fragmented pieces together inside Tu'anuku. In my estimation, it's a blueprint for a story with a combination of choices for success.

I'll have a good sleep tonight. I feel an unraveling taking place for me to come face-to-face with the agreeable temperament that lives inside of me. I want to be as cheerful and positive as possible, knowing there will be occasional bad moods plunging into my psyche. I'll get over those hurdles because this is a human condition, and I am not alone. Neither is Tatafu.

I was late to church this morning, which is silly because the building is practically out my front door and across the road. I got lost in my dreams and fell into a deep rest I desperately needed. When I awakened, I threw on my clothes and did my ablutions in record time.

I entered the church too late to join Tatafu, Lina, Lio, and Hakalo singing with seven other Tongans. Their voices sounded particularly magnificent this morning, and I was thrilled to be observing rather than participating. The unanimity blasted before my eyes, and I felt the frequency of their voices in my bones.

After church, there were probably fifteen people on the floor in the breezeway of my hut house, continuing to work on the jigsaw puzzle. I asked Tatafu to join me outside on the porch with Lina and Atiata. I blurted out to Tatafu that I met his father in Neiafu. He looked perplexed and stunned, and then Atiata started speaking to him quickly in Tongan, faster than ever, and I couldn't follow the conversation because of the quickness of words I haven't heard before.

Lina took me to the edge of the property and pointed to the waves lifting with the wind. Two wind surfers bounced on the sea in their rigs, which was a surprise. That was the first time since I have been here that I have seen anything other than fishing boats and the passenger ferry going back and forth from the main island and an occasional yacht. Lina told me this is the time the mother whales come to migrate and give birth to their calves en route to New Zealand.

"The wind surfers need to be careful," she said.

Tatafu and Atiata eventually came to stand beside us and watch the ocean activity. Tatafu turned and said, *"Malo aupito"* to me, which is "thank you" in Tongan. Atiata said the two of them will go to town with Atiata's father, Apolosi, to meet Koloa next week. I felt a sense of relief.

The four of us walked out of my yard with my piglet over to the town officer Heamasi's house for a Sunday feast. I felt relieved, accomplished, and comfortable—the most relaxed since I have been in the Kingdom of Tonga. Life is good, and although my piglet is not a perfect replacement for my dog Kalu, he plays the understudy for now. Dogs are a rarity here; pigs are the large commodity and cause a lot of damage to the landscape. I have to reinforce my fence to keep the pigs from ravaging my garden and yard. I will teach my little piglet better manners.

After the Sunday dinner, I started preparing supplies to make shark masks with my students in school the next day. I'll start the construction of a good fence for my piglet tomorrow morning.

Drowning

Upside down, shimmering
Water pools below.
Immersing into coldness,
Racing thoughts forming
Tumbling words.
Hands reach for me.
Tears stream my cheeks.
Rivers running through me…
Carry me downstream.
Finding a branch to grab
And cling,
I float furiously by
Suddenly safe.
Circling right side up with life,
The journey stretching before me,
Laughing under water, coming up for air,
Healing from the drench
Resting.
After a while, I walk around,
Remembering I had once
Learned to move with
the current.

Chapter Fifteen
THE TRANSMISSION

"The Trouble with Truth" was coming through my little radio, broadcasting from New Zealand. I didn't even know the radio was on or able to tune into a station. I thought of my mother—how she is such a revisionist, mixing, exaggerating, and missing the truth. Beliefs are mental concepts invested with a truth claim. I gathered the seven letters in front of me, testimonials of the principle players, an amazing story about a family trying to unite in private and public matters with various beliefs.

Being in Tonga has helped me to reassess my relationships and remove the attachments to whomever I thought we were. It's crazy how little say we get in the biggest transitions of our lives. Floating free is scary.

This is my sixteenth day in the village, late nighttime here. In New Mexico, it's still yesterday and four hours earlier. I feel the frequency of my extended family all around me. They inhabit my thoughts, and I can actually see them. They have appeared almost like a council out of their letters, spinning halos around my head—mother, siblings, grandparents, godmother. (The fathers are the only ones who haven't written.) I've read and reread the paintings of confessionals, linking a chain called family. What was hidden in plain sight is in this little house with me now.

What was obscured is Marme's self-effacing regret and KW's accountability and perseverance. What is with me now is Marme's adoration and KW's devotion; she was his only true friend. I am aware of Viva's fear that the karmic wheel might keep turning, dictating sacrifice without renewal, and she only knows what she has lived with, not without.

I made a good choice volunteering for the Peace Corps and being assigned far away from my story—past, present, and future. I can't do anything about decisions my loved ones have made or will make. This is my fable. Later I'll cherish the unhinged condition of slowly leading myself into the world outside my family, a surge I chose to make as much for them as for myself.

I wonder if I'm depending on myself to be the heroine, to save them from themselves and their propensity to repeat a self-propelled momentum. The circular snake biting its own tail is a primordial ouroboros present in my life. The effect starts at one end of the spectrum (we all must go through the experience of where we came from) and cycles to the opposite (flying completely out of that universe). I want both.

The word *privilege* comes to mind as I look to this village as a library to store away previous views of who we each are in my family—who the family is, as a whole, unequivocally unique, as is this small village. I want to heal sadness. My mother says I am empathetic, and I can feel a melancholy in this village hidden thinly behind eyes. I have been led here to grow myself. I am reminded of my siblings in my friendships developing here, who look to me for guidance, each of them forging their own way, knowing or unaware of their inner guidance. I am searching and experimenting with independence.

February 1, 2006, I walked down the village road to school with my trusty journal in hand. The day before, after church, the children and I spent the day going in and out of buildings while dodging the rain; we were trying to do an arts-and-crafts project. During this time of the year, the whales migrate through Tonga and head toward their breeding grounds. This is always exciting because from the beach you'll see the whales shoot water out of their air holes.

The children were eager to do the project so we spent the day making whale, dolphin, and shark masks. Their families brought fruit and hung out with us, and everyone was smiling and laughing. We constructed the art while I told my students about ecosystems and ocean life. The kids had a blast. I told the children to bring their masks to school so we could play with them some more and speak about them in English.

Later that day, I had a soccer game down at the wharf with other young adults from teens to my age. My heart felt enlightened. I thought about Tatafu and how peace is gradually penetrating his own human ecosystem. During the morning, Atiata mentioned to me how upraised Tatafu seems. He said Tatafu's confidence boost has been noticeable.

Atiata and Tatafu are planning a trip to Neiafu to meet Koloa. I asked Tatafu if he wants to reconnect with his father and told him that the relationship might take some time to build into comfort, patience, and plenty of understanding. Koloa might not want to recognize himself as Tatafu's father immediately. Or Koloa might not believe Tatafu.

Either way, Tatafu and I had a long talk after choir practice the other day. The entire time we talked, he looked composed and wise —as though he knew how to handle himself.

"Don't know what will happen. Just want to see Koloa. Might not say who I am," Tatafu said.

Atiata and I talked after he and Tatafu discussed their plan to go to Neiafu. Atiata said that Tatafu mainly wanted to see what Koloa looks like. "I think that Tatafu wants to take things slow. He's not sure if he wants Koloa in his life. To be honest, simply knowing that you went through all this trouble for him is really all he needs. He struggles in understanding that people care about him. But you showed him that you cared. That's what makes him the happiest," said Atiata.

His words stuck in my mind, and I smiled, knowing that I possibly positively inspired a change of attitude in someone's life.

I am now sitting here in my school with two of my other teachers, listening to the radio program for teachers before school starts.

The radio program tells all the teachers in the country which lesson to teach when. I'm bored right now, and I feel like falling asleep. The school overlooks the sea, which is beautiful, and palm trees sway in the wind as the rain comes and goes today. The ocean looks busy today; small waves bounce off each other and all around.

Sione, the principal, sits on top of the table cross-legged, smoking a cigarette. My Tongan language teacher is heavyset and built like a rock. She looks strong and dignified with her graying hair pulled back and her formal black clothes.

We've had rain almost every day this week—not the kind of rain that we get in the high desert, but rain that comes down all day and night, like waves of water splashing the ground. All the water tanks are full and running strong.

Now that Tatafu has reached his resolution and is content, I'm remembering all my other projects I want to accomplish. The library for the village is definitely the top project that I want to work on now. I never realized how much I took libraries for granted until I started teaching in Tu'anuku, where there's no library for the school or students. This makes lessons a little bit difficult because the resources are so limited. If we had a library, we would be able to teach the children so much more because we would have books, content, and possibly even computers available.

While trying to listen to the radio broadcast, I sketched out different floor plans for how the library should look. Shelves and a whole lot of books—the more I sketch and plan, the more I realized how big this project is. I knew I would have to enlist help. I wanted to take a trip back to Neiafu and revisit the librarian I met there. Perhaps she would be willing to spend a day here in Tu'anuku to create a design. I'll have to ask Hakalo, Lina, Lio, Atiata, and Tatafu to start collecting materials.

After the radio broadcast ended, the children started to swarm in through the school doors. And what do you know? They remembered to wear their masks! They pretended to swim as they took their seats. Seeing the children try to talk through their masks was hilarious.

The entire class was a bowl of giggles today. The children

started playing a game of whales versus sharks. When we took a break and went outside for a short time, the sun was shining. The children started chasing me, and I playfully ran from them, trying to avoid the childish shark, dolphin, and whale bites. Then school was over. It would soon be time for the soccer game.

Déjà Vu

Lapses, time
Broken blowing parts
Breath becomes the width of spiritual growth.
Desires scream messages
To packages of wounds.
Shadow stars resolve fear
Before the neutral eye
Words slide through time,
Creating stories.
Come with me now
For a deep swim and a long
Flight through sight of an expansive sky.

Ascension

The water was beautiful that day. I felt perfect. When I jumped off the jetty, the rush of air cooled my sweaty skin, and when I hit the water feet-first I plunged down, in a rush of bubbles and momentary muffled quiet, then shot back up toward the sun. I broke the surface and was back in the world of air, light, happy voices, the vigorous splashing of the other swimmers.

My competitive spirit took over, and I swam hard and fast toward the open sea. My body obeyed my every command. I felt as if I could swim the entire ocean if I had to, and I savored the integrated rhythm of strokes, breaths, and kicks.

I fantasized that I lived in the sea, that I was some sort of sea creature, that I swam alongside dolphins, rocketing through the water and leaping up into the air for the sheer mad joy of ability.

I thought of my dog, my beloved Kalu. He loved to swim too, and he loved to jump. I wanted him there in the fantasy. I imagined him swimming alongside me, streaking through the water, the two of us side by side, the way we used to run together along trails, for miles, so full of life and strength that we couldn't run out of breath no matter how hard we tried.

Maybe Kalu's asleep right now, on the other side of the world, and having dreams of me, I thought.

I always knew what time it was back home, without even thinking. Late afternoon here in Tonga meant late evening of the day before in New Mexico. Kalu could easily be asleep and dreaming. My mother probably was not sleeping, not quite yet, though she'd be getting ready. I could feel her thinking of me. And I thought about how she would tease us with her saying, "Let be, be finale of seem, the only emperor is the emperor of ice cream." I learned in my late teens this was a line from a poem by Wallace Stevens. We loved ice cream, and we would say that to coax one or both of our dads into making ice cream on special occasions when we were all together. I came to understand how pertinent the line from that poem was to our family.

While I swam, I had a pleasant, vivid image of my Viva, a cup of tea in her hand, looking serious as she leaned toward a book of photographs on the table.

I'll be in her dreams too, I thought.

What a day I'd had. Images from our adventure in the bush played in my head as I swam. These excellent people, my island family: Lina, Lio, Atiata, Tatafu, and Hakalo, in the water with me now. Because of them, my homesickness was not exactly gone but softened, not the awful empty pang I'd initially felt. I could feel my parents, siblings, and extended family all relaxing, everybody calm, knowing that our reunion, when it came, would be sweet. I still have eighteen months remaining here, and by then I'll be a changed woman.

I stopped, treaded water, and caught my breath. I was startled to see how far from the shore I had swum. People on the jetty and the beach were tiny, distant.

The sun went behind a cloud, dimming the brightness of the day in a brief instant, and I felt a momentary shadow of the familiar old loneliness pass over me, out here by myself in the deep water, far from shore, far from home.

Where was everybody? In the next instant, the full brilliant sun was back, the shadow was gone, and there was Tatafu, catching up to me! The others were way behind him. I'd certainly won this impromptu race! I'd shown them what a girl could do!

"Fakavavevave!" I shouted to Tatafu. *Hurry up!*

I could see that he was swimming hard, but he didn't seem to be getting any closer. The sight was almost comical. I thought of a time when I was little and my mother and I walked the wrong way on an escalator, just for fun. There we were, climbing the moving stairs, but staying in the same place, like magic. She held my hand while we climbed, and we laughed like two children, one of them very small and the other really tall.

I thought of my dad. He'd meet Tatafu someday, and they would like each other right away. I imagined the three of us swimming together. My father loves being on the water.

When I was first born, my parents put me in a Leboyer bath and then weeks later placed me in a small freshwater pool, and I swam like a fish naturally. They felt completely safe watching me glide smoothly while enveloped in the water. I can actually remember their faces and smiles as they watched me swim like a minnow. My mother told me when her water broke before my birth, it tasted just like the ocean, so she knew we must all come from the sea.

I could see Tatafu's shoulders, the water sliding off his brown skin in a beautiful silvery cascade, his muscles working under the shimmery glint. I tasted the salty sea on my lips, felt the sun on my head, heard happy shouts. Suddenly, something bumped me under the water. A piling from an old pier? A sunken boat? A dolphin?

"*Tessa!*" my mother's voice screamed inside me as plain as if she were in the water next to me. I had a vision of her standing abruptly, her knee knocking the underside of the table, and her cup of tea spilling. Then I felt a wave of pressure as something big pushed the water against me. In the next moment, I heard my own voice, screaming, startling me, filling the world: *SHARK!*

Then I was looking up from below at the surface of the water as I was pulled down. I saw the pale, distant, distorted disc of the sun, a froth of bubbles, my flailing arms and hands. Then I was released and rose, trying to kick my legs, but feeling strange, able to move only my left leg. I heard my own voice again the instant I was back up in the air, screaming, not under my control at all, seeming to belong to somebody else: *HELP ME!*

Tatafu was there in the next moment. His face was a mask of fear.

Help me! Help me! I heard myself cry, and my arms wrapped around his neck. The froth of the seawater around us as we struggled was the wrong color—red.

Calm down! Be quiet, I tried to tell the screaming voice. *You're being ridiculous! A little bit of blood, and you freak out. You're scaring Tatafu out of his wits and everybody else too.*

"You're okay; you're okay," Tatafu said, but his face said something different. His face frightened me. "Hold on; hold on," he said, and then he screamed in Tongan, in a voice that must have carried for miles: *HELP US! HELP US!*

Tatafu's cry sent a current through my arms that made them tighten around him on their own, as if they had a will separate from mine, as if they were alive in some way independent of me. My voice screamed along with his, but I couldn't seem to get any pressure or volume.

My arms felt the life in Tatafu's body as he turned and swam, the surging flowing power of his life, but then Tatafu and I were sinking, and I thought, *Poor Tatafu, he must think I'm trying to drown him. I'll just let go and start swimming on my own.* And I gently loosened my grip.

I was happy to see my friends Lio and Hakalo joining us, but I was unhappy to see their faces looking so grim and frightened and to hear the sharpness in their voices as they all talked at once in Tongan, too fast for me to understand, just a flow of breathless, urgent, shouted syllables and consonants.

I was put on Lio's back, and I tried to help, tried to put my arms around Lio's neck, but everything seemed slippery and dreamy, and I couldn't get a grip. I felt hands on me, trying to keep me from sliding off, and I lay on Lio's back and looked over his shoulder down into the deep, deep water and thought, *How cozy, how inviting. I could just swim down there and join the other sea creatures, and everything would be fine.*

Then I felt myself being rolled and rearranged so that I looked up at the sky, and I thought the clouds looked cozy and inviting too and that I could fly up there and join the gliding, soaring birds. I had a brief vision of all life, including the life of the creature that had pulled me under the water, as infinitely flowing and intertwined, a vast multidimensional web of exquisite sensitivity, and I knew in that moment that no life anywhere on the earth, from a single cell on the bottom of the sea to a bull elephant on the African savannah, could exist without some awareness of every other living thing in the world, however faint, tiny, or distant. In that moment, I understood that my mother was, quite literally, there with me.

Tessa, she said sharply. *Tessa, stop this right now. Don't leave me.*

I'll never leave you, Mother. I looked up at the sky. *I couldn't possibly leave you. If I could make you understand that you and I will not be parted, we were together even before I was born through you, we are those twin particles they talk about in physics. No matter where in the universe the particles are, what one experiences, so does the other, no time, no space. I think the Buddhists were all-knowing of this concept. I take refuge in the Buddha. I take refuge in the Dharma. I take refuge in the Sangha. May all beings throughout infinite space reap the benefits of my living in accord with the precepts, all beings through infinite space, all beings, all beings, all beings... The caverns of consciousness make me feel as if a screenplay of our lives is being written.*

My powerful wings carried me up on a current of air. I had only to make the slightest twitch, the tiniest adjustment of muscle and sinew, to tilt, glide, and climb with accuracy. I banked, circled, descended toward the interesting scene below, the people struggling in the water, the man in the canoe pulling up alongside them. They shouted, they nearly tipped the canoe over as they pushed and heaved a body up out of the water, the man in the canoe perilously standing up, grabbing the arms, dragging the body over the gunwale, stumbling backward. The body was torn, terribly damaged.

Ah, I thought, *I recognize that body. It was once mine.* I felt sad for the body, bleeding and injured, and I watched the man in the canoe try to bind the terrible gaping wound, I knew the body felt no pain. I felt much sadder for the young men in the water, pulsing and alive, their fear rising from them to the heavens.

I ascended and made another wide circuit. I scanned the surface of the water and saw that the young men need not fear. The shark was moving away from them, already far, far away, swimming fast, moving on toward the open sea.

I knew that the shark was as innocent as a lamb in a meadow, that it had no malice and was only doing what nature had designed a shark to do. The rain started then, dappling the surface of the sea and pelting my wings.

I circled back. I watched the people on the beach surge like a tide toward the canoe when it approached the shore. I watched them swarm over the body in the boat, and watched as that body was borne toward a car, heard the shouting and panic and rising prayers, watched patterns form and dissipate as people surged around the car and then stepped back out of the way and dropped to their knees and bowed their heads in prayer.

The word had spread through the village, and everyone came to the road and sat on each side in the rain as is the custom if someone from the royal family dies. As the car began to move up the incline to meet the road, they watched the vehicle drive away from the village. Some of them ran after the car for a short distance until they too dropped to their knees with the other villagers.

The body in the car still breathed. I could feel every breath as I felt every stroke of my wings. I flew along above the car, wanting badly to let all the sad, crying, praying people lining the road know that all was well. I knew that this was impossible, that they were enclosed for now in the immediate tragedy in front of their eyes and senses. I kept flying, following the car as it bounced along the road in the rain, feeling the affirmations and concern, taking them in, savoring them, so rich, so real, and when the moment came, I knew the body in the car had breathed its last breath. I rose, full of strength, banked, and turned, like an eagle heading out across the sky to travel home.

Prologue

by Fabian Bardot, late February 2006

Never was there so blithe a spirit as Vivian Powers when we met back in 1971. She flitted, floated, and ruled the world around her from some sweet perch up off the ground.

Viva's perch, specifically, was the loft above her shop—one Aspen Mercantile, or more fittingly Aspen *Mercurial* because the merchandise was wildly eclectic. She bought suitably bizarre embroidery from me, shirts blazoned with, say, Adam and a Botticelli-esque Eve stitched in. My subject matter hasn't changed a whit, I'm afraid, although perhaps I'm more confident with my artistry after many years.

Viva breathed confidence like oxygen, or so it seemed. Life was good for her, give or take a wayward boyfriend or two or a night on the town gone astray. Life was good for all her friends—each and every one. Aspen was full of vibrant characters, many whose real names were unknown with monikers "Cotton," "Gloves," "Yum Yum," "Craven," "Ant," "Fanucane," and "Flicka." Viva thought them swell.

I had four children in tow. I had previously discovered Aspen as a little known Shangri-La through a boyfriend. Eventually, I herded us there so that the children would be raised in haute hippie style, scampering like Heidi's goats in alpine high meadows. Viva was indispensable to us. We all tribed up, became one family, as it were. We settled into Neverland. It occurred to Viva then to replicate the type, determined to have her own four children when chance arose. I admit to being proud that my motherhood was an inspiration to her.

I think it was in 1975 or 1976, Viva sailed to Tahiti, and I packed my girls up and left paradise for Mill Valley, California. Paradise, by then, had put up traffic signs. Viva needed an adventure, and I needed to get a job, as my father once again reminded me. Eventually, maybe in 1977, Viva returned to her other stomping ground, Santa Fe, and took up motherhood. We maintained our friendship, traveling between Aspen, Santa Fe, and California.

Tessa was the first child, blood of sweet Declan the sailor who'd captained that Tahiti trimaran and our Viva, who, ever the confident hostess, fussed about serving tea to her attendants while she gave birth. One of my daughters was there, and she swears this is true.

Tessa's soul did not replicate that of her mother. I knew her as akin to the sort of mythological or religious character who closes herself up in order to search for deep truths, to commune quietly with water and earth, fire, and air. I felt deeply, even frantically, when last I saw Tessa that someone should direct her to a convent, that she should be a nun, that there had been some misunderstanding in the direction she'd been shown when she'd turned to mountains and whitewater. I thought she needed instead a protected place. That hadn't yet dawned on her.

Tessa chose the Peace Corps. She was an idealist, and the Corps offered purpose, a way to channel her innate dedication. And thereon hangs the tale, which, as I write this in late winter 2006, has turned dark, dark as the deep sea.

PART II
Shattered Vessel

Narrated by
Viva

Chapter Sixteen
FRAGILE PARTS

All the family is in the white van—the bread truck my brothers used for gigs when they were a jazz band. I am driving, paying more attention to what everyone else is doing. Tessa is the only one who seems focused. She sits beside me and has a map unfolded on her lap, which is upside-down. Her brothers X and Indigo are playing music in the back of the van while Jazie is dancing in her seat with two little boys. Everyone is joyful. Tessa then turns upside-down to read the map, and her brothers move up to the front and try to set her right side up. As I try to understand how that is possible, Jazie takes one of the babies in the van by the arm. As one of the babies tries to climb into my lap, she yells at me, "Mom! Slow down! Keep your eyes on the road. Don't you hear the siren?" I look at the road and see there is a tunnel ahead. I hear the siren sounds close, too close to us. The sound is an excruciating, shrill ringing coming from the core of me. And I awaken.

I switch on the light beside my bed; the clock reads 2:22 a.m. The siren has turned into the telephone ringing, ringing. *2:22 a.m!* I want to move quickly when I realize Tessa is calling from Tonga. The phone keeps ringing. I try to stand, but my legs are heavy, I can barely lift them off the bed as if they were made of concrete. I drag my body down the short hallway, and the 2:22 on the clock seems to be a neon sign in front of me.

My legs must be asleep, numb. I can only inch along. The hallway seems endless, the walls filled with framed family photos begin to close in on me. I smell a pulsating, plastered moisture. When I finally reach the desk in the kitchen, the phone is not in its cradle. The continued ringing disorients my sense of management. I hit the speaker button and hear a man's voice with a harsh quality to the tone and a distinct, Latino accent. I remember his name clearly. He says, "My name is Gaddi Vasquez. I head up the Peace Corps in Washington, DC."

A percolating screeching begins to swirl inside my gut. Mr. Vasquez asks, "Is there someone in the house with you?"

"Why are you calling me at this hour?"

Jazie has the phone in her hand as she walks toward me from her room. Suddenly, she sounds official in her phrasing. "I'm here," said her serious voice. "I'm Tessa's sister, Jazie." She becomes an interpreter, while words between them turn into a foreign language I am unable to hear or understand.

I know he is telling Jazie that Tessa has been hurt. The sound of ocean waves all around me drowns out his voice. I can see Jazie, but I can't reach her. Her eyes have enlarged by three times, her lips are quivering, and there is a red ring around her mouth, made redder by the paleness of the rest of her face.

"Hello, Jazie?" Mr. Vasquez's voice sounds like fingernails going down a chalkboard.

"Hello," Jazie finally whispers and closes her mouth. She shuts her eyes too, tightly.

Mr. Vasquez's voice sounds ugly and comes through the speakerphone and the handset simultaneously. I am afraid of what he is going to say, and I want Jazie to hang up to protect her from the voice. She turned sixteen years old only ten days ago, yet in the moment she looks to be five years old. My arms are around her now, the two of us alone with a strange voice. I try to speak, I have no sound coming out of my mouth.

He mentions the police and then the word "water."

The current of the ocean gives way to the siren.

The ringing is insistent.

I feel as if we are drowning, and I am grateful in the moment to be swallowed by the wave so the water will take away the noise. How can we keep breathing without more air? Our breaths stop and bodies coil into tumbleweeds, spinning like a storm in the ocean. My arms embrace Jazie tightly. We rock and cling to one another as we seem to be falling...and suddenly, we are aware that Tessa has been swallowed by death. I now think of my other children, the boys, Xavier and Indigo. My mind is aggravated with thoughts. I think I am screaming.

Suddenly, policemen come to be standing in the entryway. Declan walks in behind them. I am forced to envision others who might soon walk through the front door. I dial the phone and call Francis. I tell him in monotone what has happened and immediately hear the weeping in his voice. He tells me that he'll call the boys in California. He promises to come from Aspen immediately and send the boys to me as soon as possible.

Am I dreaming or waking from a nightmare? There is only a demanding presence that has no name except Life, unless that name is Death, Grief. Birth and death are bookends for the human contract.

I suddenly remember my water breaking before Tessa was born, tasting the salt, and then submerging her in a Leboyer bath so that she wouldn't be shocked coming out of water into such a dry, expansive world and climate. When she was born, I really didn't know what I was going to do with such a little, precious life form. I remember my mother and Doratea there with us. I watched them look at each other so peacefully. They connected immediately as if they were the same ancient souls beneath different skin textures.

Thirty-six hours of wakefulness now. I try to rest my eyes without falling asleep, and then the dream from before returns.

I am back in the van, and this time I'm spinning. I reach out my left hand and grasp the right hand of my mother. My right hand holds Tessa's. We spin together at the center of a vortex. I feel the urgency of Marme's authority enter me and immediately move through my body and pass into Tessa. Tessa seems to be chasing after Marme. She has something important to discuss with her. I am between them. Suddenly, Marme follows Tessa, keeping an eye on her—not an eye for safety nor one that is hopeful, but rather an eye of fascination. She seems to be taking instruction from Tessa, studying how she can be steadily herself.

Tessa slips out of the circle while she spins, then rights herself quickly.

Marme laughs each time this happens, then spins faster and cranes her neck as if to get a closer look. The forces of this spinning—centrifugal and centripetal at the same time—take me apart and then put me back together. Am I the person who these two women have created from before? I was sure that just a short time ago I had disappeared and reappeared as another me who had no certainty, no self apart from them.

I grip their hands more tightly and feel as if I have squeezed right through them. There is no sense of touch—nor sight of them. They have disappeared, and all the other children in the van are left with me, along with the little babies who are now comfortably in my lap.

A sharp screech of a crow lifts me from the dream. I hear the clamoring of voices in the great room of the house. There seem to be many voices in the house who remember Tessa. She is dominant in her absence. Doratea enters the room, her mouth trembling as she comes closer. I turn my hand over onto hers and hold tightly. "Remember the Native American prayer my grandfather taught us, Viva? Tessa is rooted in the earth and in us. We do not die, we remain as energy in the wind, rain, birds, and stars."

A soft knock at the door, Declan's head appears, a white wall behind his head, framing a photo of Tessa. She is eight or nine years old, carving the eyes of a pumpkin for Halloween, and behind her is a banner that says, *Dia de los Muertos*, the Day of the Dead. I can't separate Declan's head from the pumpkin: All four eyes are hollow, and his hair becomes the shadow of the pumpkin on the herb patch where Tessa sat.

I am still clutching Doratea's hand. I can't remember the prayer we said over and over again when we were young: the sun, earth, and sky, the moon circulating, the water coming to us for good maybe. I can't remember anything because I haven't slept or eaten much. I just want my child in my arms. "I have to take a break. I am going to take Kalu for a walk."

"Fabian called from the airport," Declan announces. "She'll be here in an hour. And Betsy tonight."

Alice is one of my goddaughters and along with her three younger sisters, daughters of Fabian. I am relieved to hear that Fabian and the girls will be arriving. My friend Flicka and I helped Fabian raise her daughters. She was a single mother, and her daughters needed various facets of attention, protection, and support. They were magical, fun, and easy to entertain. We became a tribe of women with lots of flattering followers wandering into our circle. Not one man stayed around or felt inclined to help us raise the girls. Being the object of a man's desire is not practical or convenient—unless you are focused on the whole package, and we were a package deal.

I had sworn never to have children after growing up with too many siblings and watching Marme struggle. I didn't think mothering was my calling, but time with these girls eventually rearranged my priorities. The girls taught me the skills of loving.

"Declan!" Something, some force I still seek on occasion, propels me across the room to the door where Declan is ready to escape. I embrace him, and we enclose ourselves in the tightest, most sincere hug that has ever existed between us. We weep together. There is no emotional flexibility inside our canister, and we are in this moment owned by our shared grief.

Memories can't be trusted. Without memories, how would we grow ourselves and become someone whole? I am Tessa's mother, the one she fled to when she needed to feel cozy. I was the one she struck out from, refused to follow, and reflected reversely. I presented a model or a value, and she examined my flaws, tolerated me, and also realized she did not want to follow in my footsteps. She loved me as her mother, yet did not respect me as a woman. She saw me as reckless, boundary-less, and undefined.

Now, as everyone who comes to the house is full of their own loss, I wish I was strong enough to bear their sadness. Memories are shadows falling on me, and I want to be the lone mother, a female wolf limping through the terrain, burned by the sun and the disease of loss. I feel I am on the fringe of being a victim.

When the shadow appears, I hope rain starts and washes my body into a river. I'll float far away and back to being with Tessa so we can reexamine my choices. She is my teacher now.

I feel Tessa's hand on my shoulder, and her breath is warm down my neck. I can smell her breath as she whispers to me, "Mother, try to remember this isn't about you. You are not the only one who is going to miss me. I have left something of myself behind, even though I've gone away and you can't see me. You can be more helpful if you let go of your self-pity and set an example."

My mind relaxes into her voice. I can feel a drift, the first drugs of calm that my body had produced in days. Tessa is right there, watching me falter. She says, "Before it's time to leave, there is no going, and when it's time to leave, there is no staying."

Fabian arrives with her daughters, Flicka too. Flicka and I met in New York on the street when I was modeling cowboy boots for the Stitching Horse on 64th and Lexington. She was taller than I—at least six foot one—black as night, the whites of her eyes and teeth were almost day-glow. She waited and watched, and we went for tea and became fast friends. Flicka slips quietly into the room. Declan leaves us. I notice the strong face she had put on. Her counterfeit strength and certainty encourage me to believe for a moment that life will go on. I pretend they are making sense to me. Flicka wants to see the other children. I reel backward into the silent perfection of the past, so noisy with life.

I close my eyes, and 2:22 is burned into the dark walls of my eyelids. I try to change the numbers—2:21 or 2:30—but I am unable to control the image of the numbers. The number two has a duality, which I cannot escape—the feminine, soothing and balancing the hard number one of a man. My father was one by himself and stiffly suited to ruling all the other numbers because he came first; so, my mother made me promise to never let a man rule, belittle, or scorn me.

"Men are meant to protect and provide. Women inspire. Emotional literacy is far more important than money and intellect," she said.

But men have ruled societies, households, and women for centuries. Even as I left one man for another and then that one for yet another, there was an authority in them that I could not, cannot, dodge.

Tessa taught me the softness of two, as she and I curled our hair at midnight on full moons when we were together. She was born on a full moon. We were bolstering the feminine, placing ourselves on altars to worship pagan origins. I learned that two is the woman, complete, and one is what we couldn't understand alone. We reach for the other: the parent, the child, the brother, the sister, the friend, the lover, the stranger who came as one and became two by our side.

My beta mind begins to move to alpha, and I drift into my parallel reality.

Now Tessa is on the floor of the bread truck. Jazie is sitting on her lap, and on Jazie's lap sits one of the young boys. He is small, a perfect image, an avatar. He is steering the van by telepathy.

I sit beside them. I am fascinated as I absorb them into my psyche. They bounce and laugh on the bumpy road. Dust comes through the windows. The road becomes a rhythm of laughs and rough bumps.

We enter a tunnel, and Tessa takes the driver's seat, lights flash, and we descend into the darkness of a canyon. When we come out the other side, the van is caught up high in a tree's limbs. Our bodies are hanging upside-down. Men come and quickly build a rickety scaffold with ramparts from the rocky outcrop, providing temporary stability, which keeps us from falling. I remember from before that Marme was trying to convey a message about the men in our lives. Somehow the men, along with Xavier and Indigo, get us safely back into the van.

As we get out of the van, Tessa takes my hand. "Mom, I am a terrible driver. That will never happen again. Before I drive in the future, I will take lessons."

I pull myself out of the dream, going from three to being one on my own, here in this moment. People are coming to pay respects from all over the country, all over the world. Here we are in Santa Fe, New Mexico, a place people visit for the expansiveness and to get lost and be anonymous.

I've driven these streets for decades, and I still take a turn that makes me take another turn and another to get to my destination. Santa Fe is not a grid; there is no significant organization.

Life also is not a grid, more like a painting, a canvas where a soul has no tether, rather color and strokes. You can either create a mooring or fly independently. You can be at home with being lost— as long as there is calm somewhere inside and you relinquish fear.

Everyone who comes to the house has that look about them: Their eyes are clouded by pain, not knowing where to find relief, yet I can feel a sense of freedom from their souls. Intimacy and imagination are the sanctuaries.

We all look for signs of Tessa, and I start to sense she has joined us. Although we feel helpless and hindered by loss, we have another contrasting feeling of rhythm while we chant together and use our breath to calm the aggravation in our minds, focusing on the exhale while promoting the humming up and down our spines. Sound is a manifestation of everything. I can feel Tessa in my spine, the thrum of her wrapping energy consolidated into a package of her twenty-four years. We are tying a ribbon around her life.

I have to excuse myself because I am weary, wanting to rest because the thoughts start up again. I retreat to my room and curl up in the fetal shape on my bed and try not to feel sorry and pathetic.

Marme spoons behind me with her body. Tessa in front of me. I feel safe, and comfort surrounds me with their bodies as I go dreaming. There I am, between them, found. Tessa squirms like a fish, and I hold on tighter. Familiar voices want to distract me. They whisper loudly, filling my head. Suddenly, they become the sound of water lapping all around me. The water is warm. I taste salt as Tessa floats away.

I swim with Tessa in Tonga, far from the jetty. I am concerned that we are too far out into the bay, I see others' body forms, and I calm a little. Tessa is a stronger swimmer than me, so I try to pace myself. The water is the same temperature as our bodies, and we can only feel the motion of strokes pushing a vibrational field away from us. I focus on circles moving from my arms, and I try to find Tessa with my next movement and realize that she is no longer in my sight. She must be diving. Her breath can hold for long waits under water, unlike mine. I breathe deeply and turn my body downward into the water. I see Xavier, Indigo, and Doratea's son, their godbrother Patrick, on the shoreline.

A dark shape moves quickly below me. "I am here, darling." My arm is around Tessa now, and suddenly we are calm. But the water is red—and warmer.

And then I hear her say, "A shark, Mama."

And I say, "I know. Just let me hold you."

"Viva, it's me, Flicka." She is staring at me, with the brilliant white of her eyes and teeth in contrast to her black skin. She looks at me with sudden concern. Immediately, I feel the need to tell what I had dreamed. Tessa is circling, trying to message with us. I feel her. I begin to explain this to Flicka.

"I was just in the water with her, swimming, talking, noticing, participating."

Flicka's eyes soften, and she smiles while tears fall down her black cheeks like crystals.

"I was there with her. Everything was clear: the water, the sky." I close my eyes, hold Flicka's hand, and notice how warm her hands feel. "I had been there with Tessa. Her leg was gone. I knew. We spoke softly. Tessa whispered. She was close, and at the same time she seemed to be flying away like a bird."

How many hours or days has it been since Tessa died? Death carves holes in your life like moths eat through wool and cashmere. Yet life and death are so mixed up together. My boys, Xavier and Indigo, and Doratea's boy, Patrick, are sleeping in my room on day beds. They are gracious, patient, and tender. I wish they didn't have to endure this terrible emptiness and that I could take better care of them.

Patrick stays close to the boys because he wants to comfort himself and them. The girls stick close to the fathers. Doratea stays with her husband, Nigel. Flicka and Fabian greet, comfort, and talk to people as they arrive.

I am incapable of assisting. Anguish is magnified by visitations from the dead when I drift: thoughts, hallucinations, dreams. We all witness the same sun coming and passing, the sun is without warmth, a faint light swallowed by clouds. How many pairs of arms have held us? How many times have these children cried?

I fall back into the place behind my eyelids, and Flynn, the love of my life, appears. I ask him how many days we have to wait for her body to arrive. I go to Flynn because I'm comfortable with the invisible particulars he offers to me. I wonder if I have idealized his power of making suggestions, passing with him through the shadows of mountains stained with his blood. He wants me to look at the blood as symbolic. I remind him of our precious child Kapira, whose blood was warm for only a few days. Flynn and Kapira are both also dead. She had been my first child who left me to the death dreams. He laughs when I say "a few."

"A day doesn't make it less of a lifetime, Viva. Your memories are more dependable than this present moment."

"Why do the strong, young, and best of my life go first?" I ask him.

"Perhaps the gods are not ready for you, Viva."

I laugh. "You've gone to the macrocosm, Flynn. I am left to stumble through regrets chasing after you, Kapira, Marme, and Tessa. One day, I'll catch up to you nonphysical beings. I wish you would put a sturdy guide in front of me to direct me in these matters."

I feel fortunate to have Flynn communicating with me. I question whether I am capable of seeing through the veil, or if this is of my grief. I feel more anger than self-righteousness. Then, as quickly, I feel grateful—for the presence of my dead man conversing with me, protecting me from myself.

Flynn walks away with Tessa. I watch them, reassured that they are together at least so she has his guidance, making things up as they go along. Or is this me making things up? I want to believe he is helping her. After all, Tessa and Kapira share the same birthday, March 20, the vernal equinox.

I notice their bodies turn to cloudy air with very sharp-looking angular edges, then a distant image. Flynn's dark hair blonde, Tessa's blonde hair dark, and both of their tan skins light. I ask Flynn if he is a shaman now, and Tessa answers from the ethers. They are no longer visible. "Mom, being a shaman is no big deal. Everyone has the capacity to reach into the other side. You are consumed with labels. Attachments."

Doratea's voice takes me away from them and back into the room as she asks the boys if they want something to eat.

"I'm sorry. I can't swallow food," Patrick whispers.

"Tessa just scolded me," Xavier claims as he wakes from sleep.

These shifts are not what I would choose. I look to find a thread, as if I were trying to connect my chakras. I search for Tessa, and instantly, I find her. I feel her arm around my waist, her hair, just below my nose, smelling sweetly of mint. I recall making an infusion from the fresh mint we harvested, and I see her head in my hands under the waterspout as I wash her thick strawberry-blonde hair. She luxuriates in the smell, the soaking, the touch.

"Mom, you're kind to take the time to wash my hair in the sink. I'll never forget my hair being washed by you."

These memories feel dangerous as if I will never be able to function in a traditional human way. I feel a shroud, a voice, a certainty. Tessa's death is my companion and stern master. What I know and what I feel are debating the meaning of memories. Somehow, Tessa had become one of those few whose intention was to question, moving beyond change to action. I want the trauma to stop. I grow to hate the enduring passing of time. I drift off, drugged by scarcity.

Marme and I are hitchhiking. We are arguing about where we should go. People are after us who want to kill us. She says we need to be in disguise, and then no one will know who we are. I say there is nothing wrong with who we are; we only need to get a ride.

The bread truck rolls up and stops, making a horrendous belching noise. We step up into the creaky van. Marme is wearing a mask and tells the driver to step aside. I wonder if she has a driver's license. A raucous game is being played in the back of the truck, which smells of fresh bread.

Marme explains that the bread truck is a metaphor; bread is the staff of life. The van is like our bodies, a vehicle that carries us where we are going. The large truck transports the whole family. This is symbolic. She explains that different people driving the van indicates that we go where the driver needs to take us for the lessons that must be learned.

Fabian has placed her hand on me gently, waking me from the dream. Someone is always pulling me out of this parallel reality. I want to keep hiding in my subconscious. Tessa resides vividly in our shared psyche. I see her there clearly; she is tangible.

I ask Fabian if someone is slipping morphine into my food. She seems nervous, and I begin to weep because I was serious. She promises that no one is medicating me. But why would she tell me if they were? I allow for the possibility that my body is producing morphine as a device to protect me. Fabian agrees that is much more likely. I tell her that I feel like I did after Tessa was born, unsure of my abilities to take care of her, and now I'm lost to know how to care for her in her death, especially when I'm conscious.

Fabian responds, "I understand all of your sentiments."

"No, you don't understand, Fabian! Only in the agony of parting do I look into the depths of love. You think you know what I am feeling. You have no clue." Circumstances jump me through reactions. The only relief is to find a good memory. In Greek, *Tessa* means fourth child, and spelled backward, *Asset*. She was the first-born of these four children. I didn't know what the name Tessa meant when I named her. Marme was the one who found the meaning. In fact, Marme wanted me to name her "Caress" because her sweet tender, teeny, beautiful, innocent, squishable body made you feel like you wanted to smother her with caressing.

I somehow was drawn to "Tessa." One of the reasons was that one of Marme's good friends was named Tessie Twibell. She looked like a fairy nymph and wore high heels and unusual clothing. She spoke to me as if I were all knowing and understood. I was taken with her as a child and observed her magical transparent quality. She was a seer and planted the seed in me as time being a scarce commodity.

Declan and Francis have been greeting and visiting with people. I wonder how they manage to host the stream of consoling friends and acquaintances? Declan talks to the Peace Corps people; Francis stays very close to the children. Xavier and Jazie appear calm while giving people information as they learn more. Indigo plans glass-blowing with the Brodsky boys for Tessa's urns. I am barely able to be in the front room for more than ten minutes.

Fabian has finished a drawing of Tessa for the memorial program. She has perfectly captured Tessa's spirit. I want to feel pleased with the drawing and be courteous and appreciative. Watching Fabian draw magnifies our loss, as we await the arrival of Tessa's body from Tonga.

I ask myself why we didn't go to Tonga and get her body ourselves? What good will the body do us now anyway? Tessa's soul is a good reason to stay present and awake. Her body, ah! Her strong precious body that she didn't always enjoy inhabiting. This body will soon be cremated. Is that the right thing to do, to burn her? Will her spirit and soul survive?

She fills this room right now. She is able to be as tall as she always wanted to be. She seems to be filling all the people she loved with continuity. I want to give everyone some of her things. I can hear her saying to me, "Mother, the best things in life aren't things."

I reach for justification. Or contemplative resolution? I have a flashback of the Peace Corps director telling us of Tessa's death. This has never happened; therefore, it cannot be a memory. I am the child, and she is the teacher with lessons I don't wish to learn, the ones about impermanence.

I start to doze off again, and my mind shuts down. I can feel only the magic of Christmas, of candles in paper bags, snow and a horse-drawn wagon, straw, and hot cider. KW, Marme, Declan, Francis, Tess, Xavier, Indigo, and baby Jazie circle the plaza with carols blasting from singing voices and loudspeakers from the stage under the gazebo. Marme is responsible for this lineage, history, festivities, and celebrations. Tessa is wearing her elf costume, holding Jazie in her arms. Xavier sits beside her, dressed in cowboy attire. Marme is proud; she takes care of us all with her shine.

That Christmas, Tessa told Xavier that she remembered being born. Yesterday, he asked me if I thought she actually did remember her birth. I can't answer his question. All I can think about is that she is dead.

Can you tell me about the Bardo? The place after death before your next birth? We have started the prayer to make the transition easier for you. Does the in-between exist? Is your consciousness not connected to a physical body as we were taught in Tibetan Buddhism? Can you see us? What do you think of what has happened? Did you know you were on a short timeline?

I hear her voice, *"Mom, I can see all of you, sometimes clearly. Other times you are in a fog. Death is not the absence of life, but life amplified. You have to be careful. Remember that actions are susceptible to unconscious impulses."*

And I respond, *"Careful of what, Tess?"*

I open my eyes, and my head is pounding in resounding pulsations of thick, sloshy red liquid. The emotion is ferocious, like an injection of poison right behind my eyes, giving a presence of something dreadful, impossible, unchangeable.

Doratea appears before me with her long, beautiful, wavy, black hair. She is suspended in the air, inhabiting her lingering body. She lies down beside me, fixing the blanket on top of us, meshing us together with her arms as we both lie weeping.

"Is it possible, Doratea, that you can take me back into the dream I was having with Marme and Tessa?" I ask.

"Yes, let me go with you." Doratea softly touches my hand. "I call on the cosmic forces to send me a vessel that will carry two." Together we had been one perfect mother, the chocolate and vanilla, black and white, yin and yang. I am Anglo, and she is Kiowa. Her history can be traced through ritual and through her father's, grandfathers', and great-grandfathers' history through many generations of living in the Americas. She was the first one to share Native American ritual with us. This is what drew her and Marme to one another: They had the common denominator of a practice, a centerpiece of faith, without religious dogma, suspended to great creation, earth, sun, moon, sky, and water. I want to hold her children and my children in my arms. We are so fortunate to have her in our lives.

Doratea's stare penetrates deep into my soul by way of my lungs, and I breathe deeply to absorb her knowingness. I feel my lungs fill with air as I gasp and beg for water, and my body protracts. Fear fixes upon our eyes. She reaches for water and pulls me up and guides me through slow swallows.

Last Night's Dream

Small primal imprint,
A child who stabilized the woman,
the principal chunk of me
gathering a mechanism that turned
my flaws to strength, fortitude.
I look through her photographs now,
an ancestor who holds placement steady.
Her face so knowing.
I am afraid to be without her.
She was the glue that held us together.

Chapter Seventeen
THE TRIBE GATHERS

Nothing prepares a parent for the death of a child. Everything is complete—then suddenly, the vessel shatters. Although Chinese wisdom says the destiny of all glass is to break, not yet, not now. I cannot embrace the granite hard reality of my Tessa's death, phoned to me from the other side of the world. Merciful Universe, I am cleft open, as if the ocean has left its floor, laying bare all her secrets.

We are burdened with the impossible imposition of sorting the details after a death. I am not wired for this. Without my people—my family, my friends, my children, my tribe—who flooded around me to manage the details, I would be less than a wisp of unrecognizable existence scattered on the vast ocean without a vessel.

In my dream world, everything is an effort; steps are stumbles.

I was beside Flynn at sunrise. The last crescent moon had just come up and looked dangerous outside my bedroom window. I felt steady though as I looked at the children, sleeping as if they were babies. I knew I was in between sleep and wakefulness. I was in between worlds with another reality from before. Flynn and I were here now, his hair a shining silver. He usually stayed the age he was when he died; he has changed to be my age now. We were walking slowly in an immense throng of people—had to be in India or somewhere in Asia. Many voices were barking and whistling and singing. Even so, Flynn and I spoke softly to each other, engaged in a conversation about the men and the children in my life. What kind of choice was involved? He wanted to know. I tried to tell him, but he disagreed. He wouldn't tell me what he thought and kept urging me to be completely candid. His voice was comforting. Our arms were linked, and I leaned into him.

"You are the only one I ever chose." This is what I kept telling him.

"I'm not sure you even chose me," he said. "You've chosen me ever since I left, of course you've idealized me. I've now become an archetype. And remember you were young, fearful, impressionable, and willful—all the things that you are ultimately working to shed." Flynn's voice was a blanket around me. "And then Kapira got to come through you."

I'm suddenly shaken from my conversation with Flynn as I hear Fabian's voice in the distance, and then Doratea comes for me. There are too many people in the great room. Fabian feels this is important: Alice is making everyone comfortable, and the people glance at me as they try to stay focused on Fabian and her daughters. She begins to speak, validating our longtime friendship and insisting that this is necessary. She is giving an introduction.

"We will all see with Viva's eyes now to remember Tessa through her siblings and all the young people of the world, who continue to be the largest, most important resource we have."

I listen to the echoes of Fabian's voice and then return to my sanctuary and curl up in my covers. The aching inside of me brings on obsessive thoughts. Why am I still alive and why is my ninety-seven-year-old father, who has been a curmudgeon most of his life, still alive? Why is young, precious, beautiful, giving, magnificent Tessa gone? The caving-in of the tragic reality suffocates me with a continuous torture. I feel betrayed by Tessa's death. This is out of a natural order, a long, cruel road to navigate.

In the late afternoon, the Peace Corps regional director, Sharon, arrived from Dallas. The shell of my body was trying to register what was happening. I was trying to be present, to hear what she had to tell us. I noticed how every one of us was in shock and floating in and out of paying attention. My house was headquarters for the frequent briefings and updates. Doratea and her husband, Nigel, listened and watched as Sharon described how Tessa had gone swimming after playing soccer with the village youth. She had formed a team nine days prior, and they had a routine of going in the ocean after their game—Tessa especially, to get her exercise. She swam out into the bay, where the shark attacked, with four young adults swimming after her. They saw what was happening and bravely tried to save her, knowing that the shark might very well still be close. Tessa died soon after they got her to shore. Sharon cried as she told us.

My close friend Hazel stayed in the house with us. Emotional upheaval circulated in my suspended body, and my legs were still sore, not quite as crippling as the night before but obviously afflicted with the tension and my deep energetic connection with Tessa. I still felt Tessa's presence. I could smell her breath and feel her feet molded atop mine, just the way she'd placed them when she was a little girl.

Tessa had spent the night before leaving for California to be with her brothers for a visit. She wore a Victorian nightgown of mine. Tessa, Jazie, and I cuddled up in bed together, and I remember the smell of Tessa's breath on me while she slept so deeply. I looked at them both sleeping and wished I could keep her from leaving us the next day. A few days later, she would rendezvous with her soon-to-be colleagues comprising Group 70. They would be off to the Kingdom of Tonga and an adventure.

Sadness and despair were like a documentary, looping through my mind. I kept hearing Tessa scream with fear when the shark struck her. I could feel her clutching me while trying to stay in this world.

In the night when I couldn't sleep, Hazel got up and read to me, turned on NPR, made tea—to no avail. Nothing could soothe me. I could only obsess about knowing Tessa was leaving the physical and might make her spirit known to me.

One moment there is a surging of possibility, then everything tips over. The lights turn off, and everything goes dark. In the time my heart could beat, life changed for me, my family, and friends.

The next morning, Tessa's fragrance seeped into the dawn along with the daylight. I hadn't slept deeply, and I didn't know if I would ever be able to sleep again. I had been anxious for the Peace Corps woman to arrive again that day.

Doratea and Nigel were in the kitchen, and Nigel was trying to balance his own emotions by making lists of what we needed to know. Declan stood out in the driveway on his cell phone, his stance unsteady, his shoulders drooping.

I can't remember eating or drinking. The intensity of despair not lifting hovered over us unremittingly like a harness. Nigel kept direct eye contact with me, telling me what he felt was necessary for us to ask the Peace Corps woman. I couldn't believe how he could keep his focus. He was right: Discombobulated as we were, we needed to have the facts.

When Sharon returned, I was on the phone with the Peace Corps director of special services. He briefed me on the recent events in Tonga regarding Tessa's death.

The moments ran together, accelerated and changed gears constantly. My heart was caught between desperate, stunned, deep sorrow and the desire to try to take care of everyone.

Tessa had taken refuge in Buddhism as a moral discipline and maintained her faith by embracing pieces of all religious beliefs that made sense to her. Buddhism was her anchor. For her to have a Buddhist practice was the integration of compassion and empathy into her lifestyle. She respected all sentient beings and was frustrated with the historical religious wars.

Many of my friends, who became Tessa's friends, were part of the Santa Fe Buddhist community. Hazel, being part of Thubten Norbu Ling's (Land of the Jewel of Buddha) teachings, sponsors a medicine Buddha Puja, a purification ceremony for a deceased person that enables them to journey through the bardo unhampered and with a clear consciousness.

On the evening before the puja, my brother Daniel; his wife, Flavia; and their son, Lucas, came from New York. Hazel, Fabian, Mary, and Flicka prepared the calming, soothing ceremony and made us all feel like we were doing something useful to take special care of Tessa.

By 7 p.m., we were all with Hazel's Sangha, our family and friends reciting the Buddhist prayers necessary for Tessa to be reborn. Each day we prayed to add another layer of protection, for

Tessa and for us. A constant flow of friends started filtering in and out of the house.

I was unable to speak on the phone because I was too heartbroken. Declan, Francis, Doratea, and Nigel handled the communication. I kept waiting to see how the tragedy was going to register in my heart and body. The phone rang incessantly, and extended family took charge of answering, preparing food, arranging flowers, everything. I was capable only of listening and following suggestions from others.

Tessa's former boyfriend had begun working on a website to honor her. News of her death echoed out of Santa Fe, all over the country and world. The media called constantly, and Nigel had all of the calls forwarded to his office to be handled there. Doratea enlisted a support system for her and her children's needs. Everyone tried to keep busy and distracted, damming back the pain that threatened to engulf us. Francis, Declan, Xavier, and Indigo distracted themselves with constant duties.

Declan's eyes were red as a bloodhound's from lack of sleep. Occasionally, he would lie on the couch in my living room and snore for a while, a sound which, in the past, irritated the hell out of me but now had become almost melodious and welcome. When I found him resting, I covered him gently with a blanket. He was tired, incredibly lonely for his daughter, and fearful of a future without her.

My niece Nicole kept phone contact with the Peace Corps office and finally made her way to Santa Fe. She and I had been separated for a long time, too far away emotionally and geographically, and we had lost touch. Now our lives had changed irreparably, and we knew we must make ourselves closer and better to honor Tessa. We felt an unspoken knowingness about leaving behind the negative, separating dynamic. The energy of collective consciousness and compassion built a foundation, a sort of lily pad on which we could step together and rest our weight, a seemingly delicate structure but strong enough to allow us each to persevere. Like me, and with me, Nicole wanted to keep Tessa's memory alive.

Truckloads of flowers began to arrive, and I was overwhelmed by the thoughtfulness, generosity, and fragrance. My goddaughter

Mary arranged an altar in the corner of the great room, and others hurriedly made floral arrangements, searching cupboards for containers. We received large bouquets of white lilies, white roses, and white peonies from all over the world. Fabian's youngest daughter, who couldn't be in attendance, added the siblings' ages together and sent eighty-four roses of flower power in their honor. Alice was called to slip a single white lily on my night table, an intimate dear gesture, hoping the fragrance would assist me to sleep or sweeten a quiet moment.

I had a notion to walk from the house to the ski basin road with Tessa's dog, Kalu. Hazel, Tessa's boyfriend, and I met at the head of Tessa's favorite trail, the wind whipping like ocean waves, as if Tessa's wild spirit were surrounding us out of the sea. We kept talking, processing her death. The thought of Tessa still being with us in spirit was more touchable than the finality of death.

On this pilgrimage we had fashioned, although I still had trouble moving my legs, I was determined to walk the entire 3.5-mile trail. Hazel noticed I was struggling and suggested I find a walking stick. I looked in the woods, and magically I spotted a stick of the perfect size and height. I turned to Hazel and mentioned that Tessa must have been attacked in the legs by the shark because of the way my legs were throbbing, twitching, and cramping. As we finished the hike, Kalu put his feet on my chest, and I wondered if he knew his lovely master was not to be seen again.

After we returned home, I actually fell into a deep sleep. I think the mountain air and hiking helped me to rest my body and prepare for reality.

I was awakened by a vaguely familiar male voice in the great room. I stood on my shaky legs and went to find his voice. Jack Silverman sat surrounded by all my women friends; my daughter, Jazie; Doratea's daughter, Kaitlyn; and my goddaughters, Mary and Alice. He was engaging them in the story of meeting us in Aspen and his observations of us over the past thirty years. He is explaining to Jazie and the others how he is at least ten years our senior—except for Fabian, who is approximately his age. Fabian detests speaking of age so she pretends she is our age. Silverman explains his fascination when we all relocated to Aspen in the early 1970s. He is telling the girls tales:

"I had started collecting American Indian artifacts and rugs, and I opened a museum called the Silverman Museum in Aspen. I not only had art, I had drugs to share, and eventually my museum hosted an evening event at least once a week. The guys in town referred to these women sitting here and including your mother, Jazie, as the A team. They represented a mix of heritage, looks, interests, knowledge, beauty, and most importantly innocence. They dressed in vintage clothes when they paraded around town for gatherings, and during the days their athletic wear and abilities were noticed. They had pizazz, a pastiche. Do you know what that word means? They were a form or motif taken from different sources. They understood loyalty, camaraderie, motivation, and creativity in a very unique way.

"In the 1970s, the Aspen drug culture was fueling all sorts of possibilities, and all hell broke loose. Mary and Alice were little kids in those days. Do you remember me, girls? They were a family of women, and they took care of you first before indulging in drugs, men, or parties."

I was concerned what he might divulge to the children when Flicka stood up and acknowledged my presence. Silverman, Fabian, Doratea, and Hazel also stood as if a ghost has entered the room. Jazie, Kaitlyn, Mary, and Alice remained seated and watched with intrigue. Silverman composed himself and said something to the effect of how beautiful, caring, and talented we are. He kept talking of our personal challenges in perpetuity: Flicka had an autistic son who has seizures. Doratea had a diabetic child, Fabian's girls being mistreated by one of her boyfriends. Reen had two boys she raised on her own. Xavier being a paraplegic, and now Tessa dying by a shark attack. Why have these things happened to all of you?

I was wondering what he was talking about my goddaughters being mistreated. Fabian left the room. Mary was obviously feeling vulnerable, exposed, and Jazie, Patrick, and Kaitlyn looked uneasy. I wanted to protect them and me from the conversation. Flicka moved fast in Fabian's direction. I heard them raising their voices on the other side of the house. Silverman appeared manic and otherwise occupied with accidental confrontation. I apparently knew nothing about this particular thread of suffering that also runs through our lives.

Flicka came back down the hallway. "I apologize for blowing my stack; you have been deprived of vital content involving the girls."

"Perhaps this is the time for us to process," I said.

Silverman, in his manliness, suggested we have a heart-to-heart in a few days. I wanted to understand how he was cognizant of personal things about the girls. How is he privy to information about them that I don't know?

The sensitivity and quiet inside the house suddenly had an inhospitable vibe. The underbelly of oversight was glaring. I suggested we all sit down together, read the Bardo Prayer and breathe to calm down. The more I wanted answers, the less I could see. We sat in front of the altar and followed the lines on the papers with the prayer. Silverman joined us.

Tessa's body was to arrive today. Most of the men were at the airport to receive the casket and bring her to the mortuary. Her Buddhist Sangha met us there so Doratea and I could help anoint her body in saffron. Tessa's siblings and friends stayed with her body all night, singing and talking to her spirit. They dressed warmly because they kept her body cool in the refrigerated chapel. The sweetness of them staying with her, singing, drumming, and talking was especially poignant for them. Indigo stayed all night, greeting and ushering people in and out through the evening until the morning.

The lama arrived mid-morning and began with prayers. Tessa's closest extended family were invited to view her body, speak, listen, pray, and watch her be cremated.

Bear Witness

Wanton feelings.
Symbolic quality.
Cremation is easier
to remember and explain, especially
when making an elegy.
Catholic trappings, most intimate.
The sensual
aspect of death interests me.
The swerve of word becomes
dynamic, and then permission is granted
for the icons and saints
to bear blank eye witness
to the radioactive components.
Poetic impulse,
noticing the lipstick smeared glass,
contagious with fragile entertainment.
I haven't seen the pall bearers' gloves
or the inception of death being so much life.
Undeniable, uneaten feelings have symbolic quality.

Chapter Eighteen
BEARING WITNESS

Eleven days have passed since Tessa died. I still waver between constant emotional upheaval and being overwhelmed with necessary plans to be made. I am the last to enter the beautiful St. Francis auditorium connected to the fine arts museum with my nephew, Brendan. He is tall and handsome, and he holds my arm securely as he takes me down the aisle. I notice the old corbels and the hand-hewned beams and latillas, uneven adobe walls, and old Spanish wooden pews.

I am flabbergasted by the number of people outside the auditorium, in the gardens, and inside the hall. I see the stage, filled with tropical and domestic flowers, and I smell the fragrances of different incense. I notice huge Buddhas and a slideshow with pictures of Tessa with our extended family. I can hear everyone breathing.

People turn while I float down the aisle, as if I were soon to be married. I hear Sarah K. strumming her four-string guitar, singing a song that she wrote, "What Matters."

I see Roshi Joan Halifax, who organized the memorial, standing beautifully poised as a leader and caretaker. She shines with assurance and truth. I distract myself and recall when I first met her in the late 1970s. She was an anthropologist and already an activist, and she taught me to meditate properly, engaging in contemplation to promote personal growth. She is now a religious leader of a group of Zen Buddhists, a roshi, a wonderful woman, and my friend. She managed to enlist a rabbi, a Catholic priest, a Native American elder, and a minister from the Church of Religious Science to attend this ceremony. We decided to include several different representations of spiritual paths to honor Tessa's desire for peace among all people, regardless of gender, race, or creed.

How can all memories come so fast as I am approaching the front of the auditorium? This good memory of my connection with Joan is the scribe keeping me upright.

Roshi Joan guided me in with her eyes as she appeared to be floating an inch above the floor, taller than the others on the stage with her, who all stood like statues. I could hear Roshi Joan's breathing, like an iron lung hooked into a stage speaker. I felt unsteady yet tried to appear strong and stoic. I wanted to drop to my knees and sob, and the roshi's eyes kept coaxing me to continue upright with strong strides. I must hold myself together. I was meant to be exemplary, the mother, the person in charge, the spokesperson for my children. Yet I realized Roshi Joan was my focal point, my conduit. I kept moving forward steadily.

I was seated between Francis and Declan. Francis held an urn in his lap, and Declan took my hand. Eventually Declan moved to the podium and began to speak, introducing all of the people of religion who suddenly came alive on the stage. The ceremony began with the roshi explaining the Bardo Prayer, and we all recited the prayer together in unison three times.

Oh, Tessa, do not be afraid of what surrounds you.

Recognize all appearances to be a manifestation of your own luminous mind.

Your life in this existence is over.

Do not be afraid to leave and continue on.

Now is not the time for regrets or to recapture that which has been left behind.

Your friends and family are saying goodbye, so that you may find peace and calm in a new existence.

Do not cling to the memory of this life, which is fraught with suffering.
The body which you inhabited will be no more.
With a mind calm and free of fear, enter a state of happiness in a new embodiment.
Recognize that all appearances you experience, whether frightful or serene, are the nature of your own basic luminosity.
Do not cling to illusion for it is illusion which surrounds you at this time.
Nothing is ever lost. We will meet again, we pray, in better circumstances.
Say goodbye to this world, your friends, and family.
Let the love of your friends and family guide you to a better rebirth.
Concentrate on all that surrounds you as the play of emptiness and awareness. Without clinging to this life, or fear of what is to come, enter into the light which is the basic wisdom and clarity of your own mind.

The power inside the auditorium, as well as outside where the overflow of people watched on large screens, exuded a feeling of extreme connectivity. In the moment, we were the most powerful community that ever existed. The wholeness was seen and felt, the majestic holding of a ritual for someone not forgotten.

As Roshi Joan explained to me, death is a high frequency. She teaches facing death with courage at her residence and Zendo. Suddenly I was inspired to believe this was Tessa's time. As the Dalai Lama said, and as Roshi Joan reminded us after saying the Bardo Prayer, "Some people, sweet and attractive, strong and healthy, happen to die young. They are masters in disguise, teaching us about impermanence."

A few days later, I sat alone on my window-seat in the soft light of the coming dawn, my journal in my lap.

The memorial was done, a fleeting reflection that soothed us in our shared loss, now once again the raw reality of her physical absence and other-form presence around me both stings and settles my sanity. I was reflecting on the days ago exchange with Silverman and the girls.

My blank book sat in front of me on my lap; imagined filled-in pages are covered with a fresh start. How do I begin? How do I start without my daughter? Tessa would want her family to inspire one another, to give of ourselves the way she was willing to do. Many of us left to take on the tasks of reaching out and bringing our world up to a better standard with compassion and respect. The question is: Will we be able to work toward a goal?

I was bemused by how efficiently loss opens us up without regard to what else is going on. The people who showed up, family, close friends, and even acquaintances from the past and present, responded outside of normal structures. Some left important temporal events to be here to honor Tessa and express how much she meant to them. The acknowledgment of her existence was immense.

Flicka came to talk to me about Fabian and things I didn't want to know.

"Listen, Viva, we need to discuss the accusations against Fabian's boyfriend, now husband. Are you actually telling me that you didn't know the asshole tried to molest our girls when he was younger and a junkie?"

"I did not know that, Flicka."

"Are you really that oblivious and ignorant, Viva?"

"Fabian never shared that with me."

"Of course not. She is not only good at embroidering on cloth; she embroiders the truth dexterously."

"And what do you want me to do, Flicka?"

"Tell her you know she's an aberrant revisionist, a fraud. This is the time to confront her. She might listen to you now that we have all lost Tessa."

All the people who live somewhere else have returned home. Their accolades during the sacred events of the memorial, cremation, and honoring were heartfelt and spilling over with appreciation and sincerity. Several good friends have chosen to come later, knowing the measured sorrow ebbs and flows. Time does not heal the loss; you simply long for acceptance.

I was with my Jazie and the trusted close companions, devoid of the coverings and beliefs that protected me while Tessa was alive. Life was now too garish and jarringly insensitive for my heart and soul. Things that I tolerated or did not consider offensive now unnerved me to devastation. I was cloistered in my house, surrounded by Tessa's beautiful artwork, gathered from individuals to whom she gifted them, and her portfolio, which has taken on new meaning and has been framed to preserve her strokes.

Jazie went back to school today. Fabian and the girls are leaving tomorrow. I confronted Fabian about her husband, and she went into a fury, packed her bags, and left for a hotel. I asked her to explain, and she told me the girls made up those lies about him. She is small in stature, a good writer, a painter, opinionated, and a snob. I have always looked up to her, admired and respected her. In that moment, I saw she was afraid of growing old and being alone so she was willing to overlook her husband's indecent indiscretions.

I wanted her to leave my house. I didn't say that, yet when the taxi came, I was glad she was gone. The girls returned an hour later, and I told them Fabian has gone to a hotel. They sat with me and told me the truth. They stayed the night with me, and the following day Declan took them to the airport. I was now solo with Jazie for the next weeks.

My eyes rested on the altar created for Tessa, which had been illumined with candles since we received the grievous news, adorned with images of her at various points in her life, mementoes from loved ones, and flowers. I considered the choices Tessa made, the people and events that shaped her and that ultimately brought her to the moment that ended her physical life. I was filled with gratitude for the precious time we had together. I will treasure all those moments for as long as I live.

I believe Tessa's life and death have placed a unique perspective for each of us who knew her. She followed her heart while watching and checking her intentions, questioning her dedication, and choosing to give of herself in hopes of living the higher principles of consideration. When I reflect on my observations of her, I see she was leading herself to follow the indicators of goodness.

Life is a struggle when we are surrounded by people who contradict themselves. Tessa gave of herself as honestly and purely as possible, embracing and analyzing her own mistakes, refinement above the mundane. Her momentum was not a path for the timid, fearful, or egotistical. She found her path of determination, empathy, and compassion in the life of saints and seekers, heroes and heroines, willing to show up with their precious lives and say, "I've grown from my past indiscretions, and I want to give back this way."

I contemplated crises that brought me to recapitulation, consideration, quietude, with deep desire to make sense of death before I too leave this world. We come into the world with pure essence, and we formulate our departure by our choices. My family has been through a multifaceted, complicated life, connecting us by fate. We are a clan. The attitude in regard to experiences gives me the knowledge that the children are my heart, and death is a shadow of birth.

I've had the sensation of no skin with a gaping, uncontained, obvious wound. I struggle to be actively busy as another day persists, and scar tissue begins covering up the wound.

Tessa's birthday was yesterday, the vernal equinox, first day of spring, the day her Buddhist Bardo Prayers ended. One auspicious, beautiful day, her colleagues put together a race up at Ski Santa Fe, the Tessa Ascension Race, one that continued for years to come. The tenderness of this day was evident.

At the top of the quad chair lift at Ski Santa Fe, a trail drops down into Aspen Vista. Tessa, her dog, and her friends enjoyed navigating that trail at the end of each winter. Although the trail was unmarked, years after she died, the Forest Service agreed to mark it TR 381, which is the month and year Tessa was born. The entrance of the trail is off of the road that leads to the ski basin, and you can find a placard. Eventually, we began to maintain this trail with **REI** and volunteers.

I tried to spend the day as Tessa would have: a yoga class, acupuncture, fasting. I stayed off the phone and computer. Declan, Jazie, and I had dinner with Doratea's extended family up at the ski area.

Sometimes during the day yesterday, I embraced the reality of not seeing Tessa again. Marme and I had a tradition that I gave her a gift on my birthday, to honor her for birthing me. Tessa, as my oldest child, carried on the tradition. She always wrote a beautiful poem and made drawings for her gifts, and now I realize how fortunate I am to have the house filled with her artwork, with journals of her secrets and poetry close by for moments of reflection. Tessa's legacy is immense—such profusion, so much to be thankful for. I try to keep that in perspective.

Alerted yesterday by a friend to go outside and look west as the sun went down, I saw Venus and the slender crescent moon beaming together through the glow of sunset, uniquely and beautifully close tonight as well. And on March 15, a new green comet, Tessa's favorite color, was discovered in the southern hemisphere—the Lovejoy Comet, another perfectly timed heavenly event. That was Tessa's gift to me this year.

Though I have no previous experience, I've decided to interview family and friends for a documentary. This is a way for everyone to process, and so whenever friends or family come to the house, I find my way into interviews. I set aside my fatigue, nutrition, and daily routine. My priority is to take care of others and supply a safe haven for anyone who might be desperate to sort through their feelings about the loss of Tessa. I know all the projects we are diving into help us maintain some continuity.

The gaping hole that I woke up with has somehow been stitched together, and I am reminded of my purpose as a woman, a mother, and a guide.

Nietzsche said that you cannot fly into flying—you must stand, walk, climb, and dance into life. Tessa maintained an artistry of patience, knowing she would eventually learn to fly. She did not hinder her direction; she left behind craving immediate gratification.

The sharp clarity with which she is remembered by her siblings, family, and colleagues is in essence powerful, the recognition possessing an attachment worthy of purpose and direction. This young woman left a legacy while touching people, some of whom never knew her, carrying energy in a collective heart. She was a conduit. The human species has the ability to reflect on major forms of care—the love that holds the atom together.

The discontent and despair in Tessa's loss has acquainted many of us with despair, a natural reaction to moving closer to freedom, away from sadness and heartache. Parents do not ever want to see their children go before them.

Tessa died in the service of her family, country, and world.

When Tessa joined the Peace Corps, she took her whole family with her on some level because of our closeness.

President Kennedy said it takes one person to make a difference in the world. Tessa had already made an impact in several countries: the United States, Mexico, Tonga, and Nepal, to name a few. She started a ripple effect for the change she wanted to see in the world. My only choice now is to follow the path she traveled.

Eyes of a Goat

I feel like my life is marked by departure.
There is a seam between worlds.
Comfortable with loving generously,
life becomes a soft barrage of impressions
feeling like dream residue…
I am not a regular girl,
and sometimes I'm a woman.
So yes, I am reaching for safety.
I have worn certain capacities threadbare in myself.
I know those layers of my world.
Rapture gets aroused, and difficult
details materialize.
Tessa emerges in me each day.
She is vital, lively.
You only die when people forget about you.
Her balm arises in me sometimes,
the way we describe
how chocolate
tasted in our mouths,
the melody of her voice.
It's not about sadness anymore,
but rather me finally growing into acceptance.

Chapter Nineteen
EYES OF A GOAT

Before Tessa committed to her Peace Corps assignment, she was living and farming in Las Trampas, New Mexico, with two young men she had known most of her life. Their younger sister, Felicja, had been away at college. She returned in May after her final exams, four months after Tessa's death, and when she arrived on my doorstep, I embraced her. As we visited, Felicja shared sentiments, tears, and stories of her time on the farm. I handed her a story that Tessa had written. Felicja asked me to read the story aloud to her.

> For some time now, I have thought, "What the heck am I doing here?" Can you relate to thinking you really don't belong in this century of fast-moving technology, or even belonging to this planet? These seem to be questions I have in common with many a country folk. However, I am here, and here is a small story about how I came back to earth.
>
> I have been an outdoor enthusiast, skiing, playing soccer, kayaking, rafting, climbing, biking. I eventually realized this was my forever. I worked as a guide and ski patrol person and really felt in my element, yet something was missing. My mind was clearing, my heart light and free, being in the outdoor entertainment business. I wanted something more, closer to the basics of human-

ity. I went searching back in time for a simple life with my reading and studying. I found the knowledge outside my backdoor in our family garden.

I then noticed some of my acquaintances from childhood were at our local farmers market selling vegetables at a small stand. I asked them if I could participate as an intern on their small family-owned farm! They welcomed me readily. Two days later, I started driving up to their farm an hour plus outside Santa Fe. I remembered on the drive having dreams as a child of working with animals and growing things, and it came true. I practiced as a child, caring for our dogs, geese, and kittens. I watered the garden with my younger brother, and we pretended we were farmers.

After a week of driving back and forth, I was invited to live up there in the main house. In simple rural life, I have learned what really matters and the importance of patience in growing and the changing seasons. You must have patience in relationships and life. I was unable to find patience consistently until I became a farmer.

Working on the land gives a sense of peace and contentment. I have found that slowing down and getting back to basics (food, clothing, shelter) have made my life simple, free, and a learning process.

A viable life in the form of earth providing high-quality nourishment to family and community feels rewarding. I believe connecting with sun, earth, moon, and water—with less dependence on television, cars, pavement, cell phones, and out-of-control consumer culture—can open our hearts to healing ourselves and the planet. In my opinion, growing gardens, harvesting your own food, and spending more time at home can keep life simple and is a great step in healing relationships.

After all, this is what our ancestors did—grow food. Living on this farm and learning skills that help sustain our lives has provided so much self-confidence, love, and healing for me, and I have been given means to take a step back from our fast-paced society.

We all have a ton of healing to do in one way or another. I feel blessed to have the opportunity to share how living a life on land close to our Mother Soil has drastically changed my perspective.

"Grow your own," I say. Make a difference toward a healthy planet. I support the environment with educating myself continually about sustainable living. I am attracted to like-minded people.
    —Tessa, 2004

Felicja and I both cried. She and Tessa had developed a kinship living at Gemini Farms—farming, traveling, talking, sharing. Tessa had been a mentor, a friend, a sister, a guide. Because Felicja was away at college when Tessa died and unable to come home, she was surrounded by friends who didn't know Tessa, who could not fathom the impact her death had on so many. Felicja hadn't yet taken time to grieve.

Needing a distraction, we got in the car and went downtown to walk around the plaza to shop and find a place for tea. En route, we came upon a pretty, curly-headed, expressive lady on the side of the road shouting, "Viva! Viva!" I realized I was acquainted with her. Caught off guard, I pulled over quickly, not certain if her desperate vibration came from excitement or terror. Sara Rose was her name—someone I knew casually.

Sara Rose cried breathlessly, "Viva! Do you know anyone who owns a goat in this area? There is a black-and-white goat on the loose! It appeared out of nowhere," she continued, with frenzied details. "I heard a bell, and out my window I saw a black-and-white animal flash past. At first, I thought it was a small cow. Upon closer inspection, I realized it was a goat. Three women were trailing behind the goat. I followed through an alleyway into Mrs. Baca's casita. The door was ajar, so the goat wandered right in, sat down on the floor in front of the fireplace as if she belonged there, and won't budge."

We were the right people to flag down. Tessa had been in charge of the goats at Gemini Farms up at Las Trampas two years earlier. Swiftly I turned to Felicja, referencing her as the nearest person available to a "goat lady." She broke into laughter.

We decided to investigate and drove to the address Sara Rose gave us, pursuing the wandering doe. Our mission was unclear: Were we on a quick shopping spree as before? Or were we turning our attention to the goat caper? Were we on course or diverting from the plan?

When we passed the address on a one-way street, we elected to keep driving, maintaining our original purpose. The evening light was turning to sunset, transforming from late afternoon to night. Felicja was still laughing about the "goat lady" comment.

Suddenly, an overwhelming sadness gripped my gut, rising around my heart, burning my throat. I remembered why I was with Felicja: I have known her since she was a young girl, and now at barely twenty-one years old, she had become a close companion by a twist of fate. Loss changes relationships.

Felicja and I were both intent on returning to the street where the goat was last spotted. We combed the area on foot, trying to find someone involved with the black-and-white creature. A woman appeared out of a dirt alleyway and led us back to where the goat was corralled inside adobe walls, coaxed out of Mrs. Baca's casita and allowing herself to be admired in the cool sunlight. Someone across the way had called animal control, and Mrs. Baca phoned the livestock people, who said when the goat was picked up, it would be slaughtered if not claimed in twenty-four hours—with a large fine for the owner. Felicja lost her composure. She phoned her brothers at the farm, asking if they would take another goat. As the brothers were telling her they could not manage it, I was wondering if any of this was our business, even as thickly involved as we were.

I looked into the goat's eyes. They were very pretty, sort of a greenish-blue, and at the same time strange, with horizontal, rectangular pupils. The eyes popped right into my own. The doe looked at me as if she knew exactly who I was.

Felicja wanted to return to my house to make flyers and put them up all over, trying to find the owner before the authorities arrived. I couldn't go with her because all I could think about was the bread truck in my dreams. I felt as if I were spiraling down into a rabbit hole, where grief waited to pounce on me. For a moment, I thought I was walking out of my body, going several directions: worried about Felicja and the goat, knowing I needed to get home to my safety net. I dropped Felicja at the house so she could print out flyers, then practically ran to my bed. By the time I went back out into the great room, Felicja had disappeared.

The neighbor phoned me to find out what was going on because the goat was nowhere to be found. Suddenly, she saw Felicja walking down the road, with the goat and a guy, looking perfectly nonchalant, as if they were simply taking their goat out for a walk. Relieved that Felicja found the owner of the goat, I went on about my business, the story over and done.

I learned later that Felicja had been in a panic because my printer wouldn't work. She ran a few blocks down to Coronado Street where a friend, Ibrahim, lived with his father. The two of them couldn't get a word in edgewise as she went on about the poor goat, her concern and her enthusiastic gibberish filling up the house.

Finally, Ibrahim interrupted and explained the goat was theirs. They were planning to roast her for a party that very evening, and of course, Felicja was invited to the party. Ibrahim's father, as is custom, had gone out to ask the goat's permission for the evening's feast, but the goat, apparently not comfortable with the plan, ran away in search of greener pastures.

Felicja was taken aback as she realized she was about to reunite the lost goat with her executioners. Ibrahim followed Felicja down the block to retrieve the goat.

We attended the party that evening, not just for posterity's sake but also to make sure they didn't kill the goat. When I wandered out back to converse with the doe, who was tied up in front of a small yurt, Felicja, trailing in all her organic grace less than an inch behind me, stooped down to the goat. The goat looked at us with the same deep recognition in her exotic eyes, and Felicja quickly named her Selfie.

Two days later, when Jazie returned after being gone all summer, I heard a voice echoing in my driveway. Jazie and I quickly ran to the porch to find a woman, goat in tow—she got away again. I gave Jazie a quick summary of the story and asked if she would walk the goat back over to Ibrahim's house. She didn't even hesitate. Jazie and the goat strolled off as if they were old friends.

In some spiritual traditions, a person's soul can float in and out of animals after death. That goat, meeting so many people Tessa was close to, bringing us together in all different configurations: Isn't it possible this was Tessa's way of reminding us to stay connected to one another?

Why a goat? This animal is the vehicle of Garwai Nagpo, a sworn protector of Tibetan Buddhism, a spiritual discipline to which Tessa was drawn. Her experience at Gemini Farms, where she often played her flute for the goats in the early morning, links her more closely to the creatures. And goat clues abound in Tonga. Lydia, a Peace Corps colleague of Tessa's, told me of a goat tethered outside the Seventh Day Adventist school in Neiafu, where she taught. The last few times Tessa visited, she took water to the goat and spent time with him. In fact, the last time Lydia saw Tessa, she was contemplating getting a goat for herself. Did Tessa's soul fulfill that wish?

When, that October, the family visited Tessa's adopted home of Tuʻanuku, Jazie bonded with Tatafu, who tried to save Tessa in the water, who brought her body back to shore and was with her in her moment of death. One day when he tried to draw an animal for Jazie, his artistic skills and broken English inadequate, he led her outside to a pen where a mother goat and her baby were tethered. He was so proud to share them with her, and tender, as if it were his own child. Was that Tessa's spirit, too, through the intimate experience of death, still nurturing her sacred animal? The circular thread of the goat's path that Santa Fe summer day—almost a mandala—led us down a string of clues, establishing a memory and a quest for the future.

The endeavors that we participate in give us ways to regain wholeness. Tessa is our guide. We never have to let her vanish, and she is kept alive by an audible texture, the story-telling gravitating toward a link. She is vision in my dreams, reminding me of a tree with deep roots and the branches growing from the trunk of her. A constant gnawing and struggle into being completely, utterly, incandescently productive is the spark that keeps us going. There is something to be said of drinking from light that quenched her thirst; her love is friendship on fire. We will always carry a spiritual torch in her honor, and I will try to activate my potential and goals in her honor. That is my job as her mother.

No sooner do you take a breath when something else reminds you about impermanence. On September 23, 2006, the daughter of my Tibetan teacher, Bhakha Tulku, died in a helicopter accident in Northeastern Nepal. I began my studies with Bhakha Tulku in October 2002, and Tessa with her teacher Gangteng Tulku in 1999, where he gave her a Dharma name—Yeshe Drolma. She shared that name with Bhakha Tulku's daughter—Yeshe Choden Lama.

The Tibetan community worldwide was profoundly impacted by the tragedy of Yeshe's death, a powerful lesson in the fragility of life. Yeshe, Tessa, and I then had a new golden thread of connection between us—both sad and profound. Their lives wove a pattern of selfless service to all beings and concern for the environment. The life and death of these two beautiful young women provided me with the inspiration to hold the highest motivation in all that I do. Nothing insulates any of us from death. I hoped that their commitment to protecting the earth, the environment, natural resources, and the underserved would be carried forward by everyone whose lives they touched.

The news about Yeshe was an obvious sting, and our family began preparing for our journey to Tonga.

Barely Holding

Barely holding
Cordless stretched across the Pacific

Cascading through life's mystery

Relations altered, unity embraced
Her presence recognized as part of the folklore

Messages repeating
Skydiving birds perform for the leftover angels

The encore of her vision keepers
Sustain the motion mandala

Revived for another glance, cozying up to rest
Under the heart of Creation
Seeing a glimpse of what her legacy will become.

Chapter Twenty
TONGA WELCOMES US

On October 17, 2006, we left for the Kingdom of Tonga in the South Pacific, losing a day after crossing the International Date Line. Our group consisted of Doratea, Jazie, Declan, and me. We flew into Nuku'alofa Tongatapu, the capital city.

In 2006, the entire island held three-fourths of the population of the Kingdom of Tonga—an estimated 75,000 people. The airport was small, and we were detained in customs, with the doors opening and closing, people entering and exiting.

From photos, I recognized two of Tessa's colleagues outside the doors, Sarah Cha and Anne Marie. David Wyler, the Peace Corps business manager, was with them to give us an official welcome. I raised my hand for them to see, and they immediately knew who we were. Tears gathered in my gut and throat; anticipation of being face-to-face with Tessa's friends gave me a sense of camaraderie and healing.

We had finally come to Tonga. I felt in the moment a question: Why hadn't we come to be with them when Tessa died? Why did the Peace Corps keep us distanced from these islands?

We were taken by taxi to our hotel, the Waterfront. The official Peace Corps car followed behind. The fragrance of South Pacific exotic flowers was overpowered by car exhaust.

I noticed tall marigold bushes lining the walk of the hotel—not the low marigold plants I am used to seeing along vegetable gardens to keep the pests away. The marigolds were swarmed by scads of black butterflies with white polka dots.

About a month and a half before, in Santa Fe, Jazie and I had been gifted an angel reading. The woman, not knowing any details except that Tessa had died, talked to us on the front porch of our house. She said that Tessa's symbol was the butterfly or hummingbird. I said oh, no, her symbol is a heart as I pointed to the green heart tattooed on my right wrist. It was the same as the one Tessa had tattooed on her right wrist to remind herself how much she was loved and continues to be loved. The woman who was doing the reading showed us that the heart was shaped like a butterfly or hummingbird, and she recommended I should be mindful of Tessa's spirit when I see these symbols. That gave me three symbols to remember Tessa by, as if we would ever forget her. The polka-dotted butterflies were swarming as if they too were still in mourning and dressed appropriately in her honor.

The hotel, perhaps six to eight rooms in size, had a feel of the southern United States. The halls were wide. Upstairs, our family kept the doors to our rooms open, like we were visiting cousins.

We had brought along a bag of gifts to share, and we unpacked those immediately for Sarah Cha and Anne Marie. They picked out a few things for themselves and organized piles for Tessa's first home-stay family, Komoto and his family of girls. Anne Marie had been Tessa's roommate there. We would see Komoto, who was the talking chief for the king, and his family at some point during this visit.

We had afternoon tea at the Peace Corps office, where we were embraced with sincerity and purposefulness by the staff, consisting mostly of Tongans, eight trainees who had known Tessa personally, and a few who knew her only by reputation.

A man named Jim Russell was acting as the temporary country director. Jim began the reception with a heartfelt welcome and remembrance of Tessa, commonly known in the Tongan culture as a *fakamalo*, an acknowledgment or speech of gratitude. Then each person introduced themselves and explained how they were connected to Tessa. The people were sincere, and the ritual was very emotional and touching. Everyone expressed how being in our presence had reactivated the difficulty of losing Tessa.

I was moved by the continual conversation and loveliness with which all these people had grown to care for my daughter in such a short time. She made a long, lasting impression in this building.

We spent several hours there, sharing and interweaving all of our memories. The Tongans, particularly the men, were stoic yet sensitive and respectful. We had brought a montage video of Tessa's life to view with all of them. There was footage of Tessa's memorial collaged with photos of her Peace Corps family.

After leaving the Peace Corps offices, Doratea, Jazie, Declan, and I spent the evening reflecting on the intensity of the day, the necessity of the trip, and the journey still ahead. We would leave the following day for Vava'u, the island where Tessa lived in the village of Tu'anuku.

For the first time since arriving, I noticed the weather—mild, warmish, windy, springlike. Despite the heat, we all wore black out of respect for our Tessa and also because of the recent death of the king. We would continue to dress accordingly.

The next morning, I spent time getting to know Sarah Cha, one of Tessa's closest friends from training. She is Korean although she was raised in the United States. She traveled with us to Vava'u and spent the next ten days weaving us amongst their friends in the villages where they all lived at various home-stays. It was a bittersweet adventure.

After the short flight to Vava'u, we were met by Dan and Heather Equinoss, Ryan Smith, and Scott Ralston—all colleagues of Tessa in Peace Corps Group 70.

Mafu, the local Tongan coordinator for the volunteers in Vava'u, was there to receive us as well. He had driven Tessa to her village when she was placed in Tu'anuku, and he was present when she organized her first village meeting, where she introduced her ideas and goals and asked the villagers what they wanted for the village. Apparently, she wasted no time integrating herself into their lives, and Mafu expressed that he witnessed her capabilities and dedication firsthand.

A meeting was organized for family and friends. We stayed in a small hotel known as the Hilltop located atop the town of Neiafu. A long community table sat at the entrance to the hotel's reception area, a large open veranda living room, with views to the ocean and the village below. The owners and staff were welcoming. Tessa's friends and colleagues surrounded the table.

We also met a carpenter from the village and Tessa's counterpart, Pungatoa, and his wife, Asena. Each Peace Corps volunteer worked with a counterpart, a professional Tongan with whom the volunteer shared skills, building a foundation that could be continued after the volunteer left the site. Pungatoa served as the conduit between the villagers and Tessa.

At the time of Tessa's death, her project was to build a village library. In her absence, the work continued with enthusiasm. Mafu and Pungatoa told us that the library would be finished before we left. They were excited, happy to be doing something in Tessa's honor and pleased to be actualizing Tessa's project. Mafu, Ryan, and Scott had been in the planning stages for several weeks and had secured books from other resources. Dan and Heather lived on Lifuka in the Ha'apai group and brought seven boxes of excess books from their public library, and Anne Marie in Tongatapu planned to send up four more boxes from Nuku'alofa, a good start for a library collection. Pungatoa was due to start work on Monday morning in Tu'anuku. Doratea and Declan purchased supplies and paid the carpenter.

On Tuesday, we would go to the village to see the school, the library plot, and Tessa's house.

Our hotel overlooked the Bay of Refuge. There's a huge Catholic church below and a beach peppered with small beach houses.

The wind was whipping that morning, surprisingly cool as it blew across the deep, cold water of the Tongan Trench in October 2006, eight months from Tessa's death.

First thing the next morning, we went to *maketi* (Saturday market). Thanks to the experienced Peace Corps volunteers, Heather, Dan, and Sarah, we procured food for dinner. As we meandered through Neiafu, we encountered Heather and Dan's host mother, Pina, who lives in the village where all of their host families lived during volunteer training. Tessa and the others spent several weeks training in the village of Taoa. When we saw Pina at the market, she invited us to lunch. After the invitation, she quickly walked all of us over to the store where Solome, Tessa's host mother, worked, then took me inside and introduced me to Solome, who seemed a little awkward and emotional. Solome was unaware that Tessa's family had arrived in Neiafu. Our eyes filled with tears, while we embraced across a counter. I wanted to stay there, hold her, touch the woman whose roof my daughter lived under for a time.

Out of respect for Solome's job, we left quickly. We would see her again on Sunday in the town when we would accompany Sarah Cha, Dan, Heather, and Scott and meet all of the people these young adults had lived amongst.

As we departed the store, a reporter from a Tongan newspaper and radio station approached us. He wanted to have a quick interview with us. He explained how important it was for the Tongan people to know about our arrival on the island. Sarah Cha was concerned whether I was comfortable with this and asked my permission before allowing him to talk any further. I said I was fine, and I gave him the requested information:

> "After going to the village of Tuʻanuku and dressing ourselves in the raw emotion of stepping into an unknown culture, the reality wrapped us in the intimacy of Tessa's last pilgrimage. She had immediately brought her integrity, intention, and sincerity to the village. As far as the villagers were concerned, she was like a native. The day after Tessa had arrived at her site, she had gone to every house and personally introduced herself to each family—60 different households of 362 people."

Pina was a gracious host. Within a few moments, she had planned lunch for us with Sarah Cha and Tessa's host mothers, so we could all congregate together the following day, Sunday, a day devoted to church. We would attend church in the town, then meet at Pina's house for lunch with everyone.

The next morning, we entered the village of Taoa in a van with a driver who would be our escort while we were on the island. Mafu was our guide, and Dan, Heather, Sarah, Scott, and Ryan were our entourage. Our family was still dressed in black, and the Peace Corps volunteers were dressed in their Sunday clothes—also black. The villagers in church were waiting for us to arrive to begin the sermon.

The religion was Free Wesleyan, Methodist. I wasn't sure if this was the only church in this village. The entire village seemed to be there. We sat in front of the volunteers, in a different pew.

Solome had seen us arrive and rose to join us. Her eyes never left mine as she approached, a layer of tears covering her eyes like sheer gossamer cloth. I really didn't want to cry, but my tears were difficult to contain given the ever-present emotions surrounding daily occurrences, one seeming to tag immediately onto the other. Sometimes, my reserve seemed full enough to maintain, yet other times I wanted to drop to my knees on the ground, the floor, the beach, wherever I was at the moment. I somehow kept from breaking apart.

We sat all in a row. Solome clutched my arm, and Mafu and Mana stood on each side of the pew as if to protect us. The sermon began. The minister sat high on a huge pulpit carved of unique wood that looked like it belonged in a building one hundred times the size of the church. The minister was proud to be perched high above his congregation.

When the minister finished his sermon, singing began. Melodious voices contained within the dark-haired, dark-skinned, dark-eyed people filled the church. The a cappella tones were rich, loud, and vibrational. Tears streamed down my face, and I looked toward Jazie, who was stoic as usual, squeezing her hands tightly on the pew in front of her. Then I looked at Doratea next to her, who was as wet-faced as I was. We faced forward, trying to stay in the moment.

When the minister asked Declan and me to address the village, Mafu translated my English into Tongan as I thanked them for receiving us so warmly and allowing us to participate in their Sunday ritual. I was on automatic pilot, so speaking to the congregation was easy. I wasn't sure if there were 75 people in that church or 200, but I was comforted knowing we were surrounded by people who had spent time with our daughter.

After the church service, a receiving line formed as if we were attending a wedding. The people seemed honored to view us face-to-face and touch us. All of them knew Tessa.

Next we meandered down the village road to Pina's house, flanked by Pina's children and other people who were invited for the *kaipola* (feast). Pina's house was filled with furniture lining the walls, almost like a clubhouse, with artificial flowers draped throughout.

This I could not understand: Tongans have fresh flowers growing everywhere, yet they all, not just Pina, love artificial flowers. Perhaps they find artificial flowers are easier to take care of, and they do not have to watch them die. The people collect very few material possessions.

The feast was quite an experience. Pina, Solome, and Kalo, Sarah Cha's host mother, were responsible for preparing all the food. The serving dishes were wrapped in cellophane, piled on top of each other on a long banquet-style table set out on the patio, much like Christmas gifts piled under a tree. There was an array of foods—sweet potatoes, Taro root, a pile of bodiless fish heads with bulging eyes, sweet-and-sour this and sweet-and-sour that could be chicken, could be fish, could be dog (yes, they do eat dog meat in Tonga)—all surrounding a baby pig in the center of the table.

The extended family was proud to gift us in their most natural way of gifting—with food. We were gracious, yet also apprehensive. I think we were all feeling like no one would notice what we ate because there were so many of us. The Tongan tradition is for people of status like us to eat first. (They thought of us as dignitaries.) They sat on their mats and watched us eat. They did not eat with us. This custom was so awkward. It also allowed them to see everything we put on our plates. Mafu and his brother, being Tongans, and the Peace Corps volunteers, having grown used to this food over the last year, explained to us what each dish was as we served ourselves.

The baby pig in the center of the table was disconcerting. What we all wondered most was which dishes might contain dog meat. This first Tongan feast was breaking us in for what might come our way in the weeks ahead. The assemblage of food and having to eat with people staring at us made for a truly unusual experience; however, we saw beauty in the proud faces of the women who watched as we consumed. Before we began eating, villagers made *fakamalos* (prayers) from around the table, lots of touching words and remembrances of our Tessa from Mafu, Dan, Ryan, Pina, and me.

I wondered about Tessa's first Tongan feast, how she must have felt much the same way we were feeling. That made it easier to eat the unusual food. I ate pig skin at the insistence of Sarah Cha, who told me that I would like the taste. Jazie ate mostly fruit and experimented with only a couple of things. The entire meal was surreal.

Heather presented a collage she had made of pictures of the volunteers doing traditional village tasks. The host mothers were taken with the photos and the way Heather had so artistically portrayed their several weeks living amongst them.

> Jazie's diary entry:
> This is meaningful for me, significant. Part of me didn't want to come. I knew I would be hesitant, uncomfortable, shy. My mother finds significance in every little thing. She thinks Tessa is trying to give her messages. She annoys me at times. I worry about Declan. Mom is more resilient, and she's also fragile. We are all sad in different ways

On Monday, we visited some sights on the island of Vava'u. The first was 'Ene'io Beach, which is frequented by many people, and the Matoto Cliffs. A botanical garden is close by. The trip by van was almost like bushwhacking on foot as we drove past the garden and made our ascent to the cliffs. Scott encouraged us to take the adventure, as his village of Tu'anekivale is near the cliffs. He visits the cliffs regularly.

Our arrival at the top was beyond spectacular, with the deep waves of the wide-open sea accumulating, creating an expanding aquamarine display of crashing waves dancing in splendor on the rocks below. We were high above on the edge, watching the performance with the wind threatening to throw us from the cliffs down several hundred feet to the beautiful dramatic sea. We could feel the spray of the waves as if they were only ten feet below.

The Tongan legend associated with the cliffs and the beach says that Tuʻimatoto, a good spirit that protects the village of Tuʻanekivale, lives on these cliffs. The myth suggests he was tempted by an evil female spirit until he acquiesced. He made love with her continually until she turned to stone. ʻEneʻio was born from this coupling and became a beautiful young woman. The myth says that a Samoan man tried to take her from her father, Tuʻimatoto. To protect her from this Samoan, Tuʻimatoto sent her to the moon. On full moon nights, the reflection of the moon on the waters below the cliffs looks like a woman swimming out to the sea. If any noise is made on the cliffs as the moon rises, dark clouds cover the moon, and you might miss seeing the magnificent sight.

Leaving the cliffs was difficult because the beauty held our attention, and we were all silent as we descended back to the main road. I can imagine this view held Tessa in awe as well.

We spent the remainder of the afternoon visiting sites of different projects that are assisting the people of Tonga. One of these was the Ministry of Agriculture's compound in Vavaʻu. The ministry runs a Woman's Training Center there for Tongan women who want to enhance their lives, creating products from native materials, including coconuts, plantains, and tropical flowers. Everywhere we went, the people remembered Tessa and knew we were her family.

We rested a few hours after this adventure, then went to Ryan's house in Vavu'u for a potluck organized by the Peace Corps volunteers. The food at the potluck was the best food we'd had since arriving in Tonga. We also viewed a plaque Tessa's friends had made for her that would be placed at the library. It was made of granite, with a poem Tessa recited as a child at the Waldorf School inscribed and the heart Zia symbol she designed with her brother engraved in gold lettering. The plaque was very nice, and Tessa's friends were proud to present it to Tessa's library.

Meeting the Shark

In your honor, poems and songs are written.
Heart messages are heard.
My own is torn, yet still
slapped with ambiguity.
Customs are followed here.
They remember you as the world has noticed you.
Knowledge with estimated value
Spoken stories differ from village to village.
You were revised within dimensions of culture.
Respect, achievement gathered for you,
with the royalty and the commoners'
methodical devotion in place.

Chapter Twenty-One
MEETING THE SHARK

Tuesday, October 24, 2006, we arrived in the village of Tuʻanuku—a group of ten, traveling as if we were a squadron looking for refuge. I remembered that the day was my father's ninety-eighth birthday.

Tessa was accepting and patient with KW because he was the elder, and she enjoyed the history he was willing to share with her. I distracted myself with these memories as deliberately as Tessa's colleagues distracted us with explanations of village customs. We were close to the scene of Tessa's demise, and sadness seeped into my body. Tessa's colleagues kept close to each one of us like soft cushions: Sarah, Scott, Ryan, Dan, and Heather, also Mafu and Mana. They knew we were uneasy.

Arriving at the government primary school in Tuʻanuku, where Tessa was to be a teacher for two years, was like walking into a fog. The yard where the children gathered seemed almost in another dimension. My heart thumping, I walked toward Tevita, the principal, and Asena, who was there on behalf of her husband, Pungatoa (Tessa's counterpart). Declan, talking with Asena and the contractor, stepped into the small building that would become Tessa's library. The five people who had been working on the building stopped, giving us a moment to equip ourselves for all the different happenings. Doratea was trying to take everything in stride—children, teachers, workers.

Then a young man appeared: Tatafu, who went to and stayed with Tessa after the shark had attacked her. He refused to leave her alone and probably hoped he could bring her to safety and save the life of my child. I could hardly breathe.

I scanned the yard for Jazie. She was nowhere to be seen. I felt panicked without her in my sight. Tatafu was suddenly in front of me as if he floated over the open yard. His eyes filled with tears. I wanted to hold him, but I had to find Jazie before I could dedicate myself to the exchange between us. In that moment, I wasn't sure what to do or how I felt. He was stiff, and I needed contact with Jazie's body—shoulder, legs, some part of her. Doratea walked toward me and let me know Jazie was behind the van, sobbing.

Doratea stayed with Tatafu as I went to comfort Jazie. She started walking in circles, unable to compose herself. Her behavior reminded me of her father's. He too would pace around in a circular motion when grief arose. We humans do peculiar movements with our bodies when in fear. This was the first time I'd seen Jazie sob in public since March, though I often heard her cry quietly in the privacy of her own room at home. I felt helpless because Jazie is not one to cuddle up in my arms for security; she has to come to her own consoling methods. My first instinct was to put my arms around her and put her in my lap like I did when she was a child.

Jazie was being confronted with the reality of her sister's death. Scott sat and talked with her until she wiped her tears and stood, ready to face the squad. The young children gathered around us, and of course, Jazie was a fascination—blonde, blue eyes, fair white skin, and most interesting for the little girls, tall. Jazie tried hard to pull herself together and joined Heather in a game of circle ball.

I wanted so much to hold Jazie. I knew she would not allow this. This was not what she wanted from me at that moment. Jazie does not like to be out of control; she prefers to gather her own wits to the best of her ability in her own way. Unconsciously this is how she protects both of us from vulnerability and open public displays of emotion. She is developing an air of dignity.

After an hour, we bid Tatafu goodbye and walked from the

school to Tessa's house. Declan was moving slowly behind. Sarah Cha, Dan, Scott, and Ryan sat on a bench in front of the town hall across from Tessa's house, allowing us time to be together as a family. Declan caught up, and we circled the house with Jazie, Doratea, and Heather. A woman appeared to unlock the door. No one had been in Tessa's house since her death. Her Tongan name, spelled *Tesa*, was written on the salt frosting from the sea in a couple of places on the windows.

The house was small, and I saw a wooden bed still remained with her heart signature in black marker. I walked out of the house across the road to sit on the cement slab and cry. I too was overcome with emotion. Doratea followed behind me, holding me. I wanted to go to the wharf where Tessa had last been on land. The struggle inside was like none other I have experienced. I knew everyone was suffering. Being close to the event was like being smashed to smithereens, yet at the same time, the visual gave a sense of calm.

We walked through town and descended the hill to the wharf and soccer field. We could see that the dark blue water was very deep. An island across the channel looked deceptively nearby, and Scott told us that's where he suspected Tessa was trying to swim when she died. Sailboats were passing by, and a man nearby worked on a small Tongan fishing boat as we all went out to the wharf and sat in a circle. Each of us said an acknowledgment and took a bit of Tessa's ashes from the lightweight wooden vessel that contained them. The wind was blowing toward shore, so we climbed down to the water to release her ashes from our fingertips. We planned to spread most of her ashes later, in the spot where the shark attacked her. That we would do by boat.

I walked up the road with Scott as he told me about a kava ceremony he attended in his village a week before our arrival. The men in his kava circle wanted to talk about our visit because they knew Scott would be spending time with Tessa's family. A Tongan man, who is sixty-three and was raised in Australia, told Scott that it had been said that the graveyard on the way down to the wharf has a spirit who had fallen in love with Tessa and wanted to keep her close to him and his family because she was such a good person. Her goodness prompted the attachment. Those who believe this feel this is why she died off that wharf, one of several Tongan theories we heard about her death.

We delved deep into Tessa's life in Tonga, sometimes intentionally, and at other times serendipitously. Many peculiarities still eluded us, but with the company of her friends, each day and experience intertwined to create a vivid tapestry. From the moment we set foot in the Kingdom of Tonga, I tried to walk in Tessa's shoes. I visualized her journey—arriving in Tonga, taking the small aircraft to Vava'u, navigating the Peace Corps offices, interacting with the locals, tasting the cuisine, feeling the water, and enjoying every nuanced experience. I was captivated, imagining the stark contrast she must have felt compared to her earlier life.

The owner of the hotel had prepared for us a sail on the Hilltop's catamaran. The owner's sister was there, and she explained that she heard the news of Tessa's death when she visited her brother earlier in the year. She remembered seeing the Peace Corps volunteers coming into Nuku'alofa for Tessa's memorial service, and she shared with me that she was very affected by the loss without even knowing Tessa personally. "There was so much energy circling around the islands in relation to your Tessa's death," she said.

Our family, Tessa's colleagues, the owner of the hotel, his sister, and her son joined us on the catamaran. The captain, a Tongan Peace Corps staffer named Lepa, sailed us to the spot where Tessa died. The wind was perfect, and we spotted the wharf where we had stood in circle just the day before. Lepa pulled in the sail and circled back to the place we were meant to be. He knew the exact spot Tessa died.

One of the colleagues pointed out the Pulupaki, the ferry that only moved between islands once a week, crossing the lagoon before us as it had done just before Tessa was attacked. We all stood quiet, shocked, watching the boat as Tessa must have done. Once again, I am framed in time, I thought, in her last moments here in these waters, as if the Pulupaki had been there especially to ferry Tessa to her next life couldn't have been more perfectly scripted.

Coconut leaf baskets held flowers. We gathered at the bow of the boat; Sarah Cha and Heather were at the tip of each of the hulls with Jazie, throwing the flowers as offerings. We sprinkled her ashes, like golden flakes, into Mother Ocean.

The sparkling water, shimmering with symbolism and beauty, perfectly complemented our heartfelt intentions during the ritual. I deeply wished that all who cherished Tessa could have stood beside us, absorbing the profound ambiance and unity of that moment. We journeyed to a serene, untouched island, leapt from the boat with gleeful abandon, and swam with fervent energy—living the adventures just as Tessa would have, had she been there beside us.

Before leaving the Kingdom of Tonga, my thoughts lingered on Komoto and his family. His role as the king's talking chief demanded his dedication to the royal family. To meet with Komoto during this mourning period, we relied on Tessa's colleagues to tactfully navigate official channels. We held off on making plans until we received word from the palace.

Our days were mostly spent at the Vava'u Peace Corps office, where we organized books for the library and connected with Tessa's Peace Corps colleagues.

Scott lived on Vava'u and had previously been a Peace Corps volunteer in Mongolia and in Arizona on the Apache Indian reservation. He was in Tonga for his third, and probably last, service in the Peace Corps. As he told of his time there, I realized how experiences can vary, even among people in the same country. Scott lived in Tu'anekivale, teaching at the elementary school. When the lord of the village lost the title of Tu'imatoto because he married a commoner, the position was bestowed on Scott. This meant Scott was considered royalty and could not fraternize with the villagers. He was now considered important. He was called Matoto. Only two people in his village knew his birth name. The villagers prepared and brought him food from a different family every week. He worked at his school about four hours a day, teaching English to grades one through six.

He lived in a cinderblock house with few windows. It looked like a homeless shelter and turned into a wading pool when it rained. On several occasions, he had been stuck inside when the door swelled.

People didn't often visit Scott at the house, and when they

invited him for dinner, he would go to their houses. They gave him food to take back to his house. His accidental position set him up for loneliness. Scott thought he was perhaps given the title to make up for his *fakaofa* (pathetic or sad) house. He liked Tonga, especially the sites around his village, and he was having a pretty good experience—except he got lonely sometimes. He spent as much time as he could with us, and his presence was helpful in completing the circle of Tessa's friends. He told me he considered Tessa one of the best friends he'd ever had—and also one of the best people he'd ever known.

Sarah Cha shared with us her placement on the island of 'Eua, which is a little southeast of the main island of Tongatapu. She had to ride a ferry between islands if she wanted to go to the main town. Her village was very rural, and she lived on the school campus. Her house was small and quaint. She was generally happy there and had a great supervisor who supported her well, which was a main factor in her satisfaction regarding her site.

'Eua is very hilly, and Sarah did not live near a beach, but good hiking spots were close by. She joked that she was "addicted" to Coca-Cola, though she only drank it when she was in town. She spent a lot of time with Tessa during training because they lived in the same village, and they became close friends. As evidenced by the Coca-Cola, Sarah was very different from Tessa, especially regarding food and exercise. She mentioned that Tessa would encourage her to go running—or walking, in Sarah's case—with another colleague, Louise, during training. Sarah was an absolute asset for all of us while we were in Tonga—darling, sincere, and considerate—and a wonderful companion. She had great respect for Tessa's ideals, and she appreciated that Tessa accepted her just the way she was.

Then there was Ryan Smith, who lived in Neiafu. He was an ex-college football player from Pittsburgh and lived just on the outskirts of town, working at the school that was Tessa's original site before she requested a change to a more rural area. Because Ryan didn't have a village, he didn't get the community experience that everyone else got. He was okay with that, especially because he didn't have random people coming up to his house all the time, though he did occasionally have pigs, chickens, and cows that he didn't own coming into his yard. He called himself a city boy and liked to go into Neiafu to meet all the expats.

Ryan also volunteered at the Vava'u High School and sometimes his electricity was out because the school had not paid the bill. When the electricity was out, the water didn't work either, which was a drag because Sarah Cha, Heather, Dan, and Scott were all staying with him while we were visiting.

Ryan hosted most of the Peace Corps functions at his house, including the potluck held in our honor. He had the nicest, biggest house among the volunteers in Tonga. Ryan had been working hard with Mafu to bring the library project to fruition.

Dan and Heather lived in Ha'apai, which is the smallest island group by land mass in Tonga and sits between Tongatapu and Vava'u. Although we weren't able to see their beach house on our visit, they showed us pictures, with the beach just footsteps from their door. They lived in a compound where the school was located, which was a common living situation for volunteers who are teachers. Dan and Heather were both teachers before joining the Peace Corps.

Although Dan and Heather were disappointed with their Peace Corps experience on many levels, they made the best of their situation and created work for themselves in Pangai, the village where they lived. Dan, who went to Tonga to teach the teachers how to be more effective in the classroom, was very frustrated to find that the Tongans are basically uninspired when it comes to teaching.

Heather faced another challenge at her school—severe corporal punishment, which she had been working hard to mitigate without seeing much change. Tessa had a strong issue about this as well. The intense punishment deeply affected Heather—and also Dan. In the face of what they could not change, they immersed themselves in other projects, including a public library and a small Tongan museum that was previously run by another *palagi* (Western) woman, who had recently passed away.

Dan and Heather stayed longer in Tonga than they expected, partly because they wanted to meet us and express their close feelings for Tessa. Disillusioned by Peace Corps' policies, they planned to leave the agency the following January after only one year of service, mainly due to the way the Peace Corps handled the volunteers when Tessa died. The agency expected the volunteers to grieve in a limited amount of time and then get back to work.

As I got to know all of Tessa's colleagues, I felt I would have close relationships with all of them for the rest of my life. Their integrity, kindness, and honesty were exactly the sort of traits Tessa was attracted to. I will always remember them.

Jazie's diary entry:

October 29, 2006, Tu'anuku

Mom and I sleep in the same room. She had a small cot brought in so I could have my own bed. I am covered with a mosquito net. I read my book *Memoirs of a Geisha*. I have to do a report for English, but truthfully, I like the diversion. The past two years, I started calling mom Viva. She began ignoring us kids when we called her Mom because we were exclaiming a complaint, need, or demand. Since Tessa died, she responds to Mother. It pisses her off when I call her Viva, and I like to annoy her.

I've enjoyed all the Peace Corps friends, Tessa's group. They respected and liked her so much. I feel sorry for Scott Ralston in a way. I don't know exactly why—his house, the village, his loneliness. He is the boyfriend of Valerie. I haven't met her yet. She lives in the capital city Tongatapu. We will see her on the way out of Tonga. I hope she is nice to Scott. The way he describes their relationship sounds a little iffy.

I am trying to be patient. Mom tries to explain things to me, but Tessa wrote me private information that is between sisters. I have talked a little with Sarah and Heather about Tessa's romantic interests and if she had a crush on Tatafu.

I had a bond with Tessa that no one else shared. Mom and Doratea seem to do well, and they both can be irritating with their spin on things. Mom does a lot of the public speaking for us, and I don't know how she does it without crying.

I am protective of Declan just because I am. He has a hard time in different ways. I keep him occupied in conversation the way I do with KW. I know how to deal with him and my grandpa. I miss Gabe and my girlfriends. I am glad that I came. I think it would have been good for the boys to be here and Doratea's kids, Kaitlyn, Patrick, and Lucas.

The food is awful here, and the culture is way different.

I miss Tessa.

My (Viva) journal entry:

Interesting observations about Tonga: Pigs run around here like dogs. There are very few dogs, and I think dog meat might be considered a delicacy, but there's no open discussion about eating dog because of how beloved dogs are as pets internationally. The air is filled with exhaust from cars.

Tongan women love to have their pictures taken. There are rites of passage with the teeth of young girls around fifteen or sixteen: They get gold inlaid on their front teeth, shaped in the letter L. I really don't understand this custom. First of all, it's a waste of money. And why the heck do they think that looks attractive? I mean, come on, they claim poverty here.

Jazie has been more flexible than usual, and I think she's really enjoying the different experiences. I have to hand it to her: She has been through too much for a girl her age. The experience will be one she will not forget; this is true for all of us.

Although we have walked the same roads in Tonga, have seen the same ocean, have met the same villagers, and have heard the same sermon on Sunday morning, each of us will remember this journey in our unique way. While some of the memories will be similar, we all have different ones because of our individual personal relationships with Tessa, my daughter, Declan's daughter, Jazie's sister, Doratea's godchild.

Mana, our driver, came for us in his van by 9:30 on the day of the library's opening and dedication. The Peace Corps family had left with Mafu an hour ahead of us to finish shelving the books and help the villagers prepare for the ceremonies. When we arrived in the schoolyard, the adults, youth, and children were awaiting us. The magnitude of the greeting, the preparation and care, was obviously a collaboration of the entirety of Tu'anuku. The villagers were so grateful that the library was complete.

A large open canopy tent was erected to protect us from the bright sunshine and possible rain, depending on the weather spirits. The poles of the canopy were wrapped in pandan leaves and woven mats covered the grass. Chairs were set up for our group, and the village elders (all men) were in a circle formation, anticipating Declan and the other men to join them for a kava ceremony.

Although women traditionally do not participate in the kava circles, because of the special circumstances, they included all of us. The kava tradition is considered an honorable gesture, a way of welcoming us to their community. Ryan told us that this was a re-enactment of the way they received Tessa on the day she arrived. Tatafu was now indoctrinated into the kava group. He was considered a hero in the village and perhaps throughout the Kingdom of Tonga. He was in charge of the ritual. We all sat before the elders, who passed us kava in coconut bowls. I could see in Jazie's face that she was nervous about how the kava was going to taste. We drank quickly, in one gulp, as instructed.

When the sharing of kava was finished, we were led back under the canopy to our chairs in the front row. Tessa's Peace Corps family sat in the next row, and the elders surrounded us from behind. Children ages four to ten sat dressed in uniforms, the girls in red and white and the boys in tan and white. The women, men, and young adults wore black with *ta'ovalas (*woven skirts), wrapped and cinched. Two Tongan reporters and photographers were present to cover the story.

There was a hymn, an opening prayer, and a welcoming address by the head teacher, or what we would refer to as the present principal, Tevita. Declan and I held each other's hands as we cut the white-and-red ribbon draped across the green door: the red ribbon symbolizing the blood of Christ and the white ribbon for intent or purity.

We were all mesmerized, Doratea beside me, Jazie, and Declan.

The library—barely the size of a large living room at home, but huge for the village—had become a reality.

Tessa's name appeared at the top of the building: "Tessa Marie Horan" painted in a green crescent, with "Library" forming a straight line under her name. The door trim was painted in the same green, Tessa's favorite color. The memorial plaque dedicated to Tessa by her Peace Corps friends was held in a cement slab right in front of the library to keep it contained and visible.

The stillness of the stares from the youngsters as I took in all the visuals was hypnotic, their dark skin, hair, and eyes contrasted with our fair skin and light eyes. The scene was poignant and revealing, as always when we were grouped with the native peoples. Having a library in their village was considered a special privilege. Tessa saw the need for this upon her arrival and made a commitment to herself to improve their quality of life through learning. And now her library is the legacy she left behind, the chronicles rich and meaningful.

We were asked as a family to approach the front of the library and assist Tatafu in planting two heilala bushes. Apparently the flowers from these bushes were used only to make *kahoas* (flower necklaces) for the royal family. Tatafu had already dug the holes where they would go, and he handed the bushes to us. Jazie helped Tatafu plant one, and Doratea and I helped with the other, and then Declan shoveled the earth to fill the holes. All the children lit candles for Tessa and then began singing a song composed by a village man named Vava, who lived across the street from Tessa. The song was melodious and beautiful, bringing all of us to tears. The girls proceeded to do a little dance they had choreographed while they sang. The performance was absolutely precious.

We later joined in a feast that the village women had prepared in our honor, with fresh lobsters and shellfish accompanying the regular staples. We sat on the veranda as the elders came and joined us. The women and children waited to eat until we finished, as was the custom, which made it difficult for me to enjoy eating, although I did manage to quickly rip the shell off the lobster tail because I knew the lobster would be valuable protein and taste good.

Asena spoke at a podium and then she introduced Tatafu. He

spoke in Tongan because he did not have a command of the English language. (I later came to find out that he totally understood English, yet he was embarrassed to try and speak it.) Mafu translated his address to us. Tears dripped down Tatafu's face as he spoke. The immensity of his emotion communicated how difficult the loss of Tessa was for him.

Tatafu described trying to rescue Tessa, his fear, and his caring for her. He also mentioned that Tessa frequently swam out in the lagoon by herself. He spoke of how important it was for him to swim to her even though he was frightened for his own life. The entire village was weeping as he spoke—as were we. The day activated the memory of her loss, but it also established what a huge piece of history she had become for the village and the country.

Next the villagers presented gifts to all of us. We didn't know quite how to receive the generosity. They honored Tessa and her family, as well as for constructing the library for the village.

When we were asked to speak, I spoke as a representative for Tessa's extended family and friends. I told them of the collective of people who had donated funds to build the library.

Tessa had a whole life with the village in a very short time. They were witness to her incredible capabilities and organizational skills. I thanked them for the day of celebration and tenderness. Jazie, Doratea, and Declan presented the gifts that we had brought to the community. Doratea gave Tatafu a bear fetish carving made by a native American friend, symbolizing courage and strength. He was most appreciative, as were all the other people we gifted. The ceremony came to a close.

Scott walked over to all the children, dressed in black, with his light complexion aglow as if he were an angel. The children gathered around him. I have no idea what possessed him to organize a choir. He got all of them shouting Tessa's name in unison. They would pull him in close to them and catch their breath, then he would flail his arms to the sky, and they would scream out her name —again and again. Many photographs were taken, and the day lives in all of us as a sacred memory.

Many of the village youth gathered inside the library to utilize some of the art supplies. Jazie wanted the village children to draw—

her way of communicating with them. Jazie would use this for her own art class project—to illustrate her trip through drawings. As they all sat in the library, Tatafu stayed close to her, communicating as best he could in his broken English. Tatafu drew some sort of animal, unable to explain what it was supposed to be. He got frustrated and gestured to Jazie. She followed him to the back of the school, where there was a makeshift pen, holding a mother goat and her kid. Tatafu was so proud to show her the baby goat, as if it was his own child. Somehow, this experience brought an ease of communication between the two of them. Jazie had studied him since they first met, and with her close observation, she began to sense his need to communicate with her. The baby goat was a conduit for their communication and a way for Tatafu to show his tender side.

Tessa left Santa Fe for the Peace Corps in October 2005, and there we were, in October 2006, almost a year later, celebrating her life, her death, her vision, her memory in their village.

Faction

Crossing over acquaintances
Signposts of curious plans
Sorting village systems
Seeing through to
The backs of their eyes
Piglets as pets, dogs few or hidden
Broken cars become foliage sculpture
Food as currency
Intensions revealed cautiously
Alarmed only when there is no rain
Or a cyclone comes upon them.

Chapter Twenty-Two
A ROYAL WELCOME

The night after the inauguration of the library, I could hardly sleep. The sounds I heard outside were memorable and seemed to have a sequence: pigs squealing, crickets singing. I finally fell asleep after replaying the day in my mind, then I was awakened at 5 a.m. as the routine drumming started, acting as an alarm and reminder for the townspeople to get up for church. I focused on Jazie's melodious breathing, just short of snoring, as a hypnotic way to take myself back to sleep. The blending of the various noises made me feel as if I were swaying in a hammock up above the village.

In Tonga, I woke every morning around 6:30 and walked up to the veranda to do the Five Rites (Tibetan exercises). Declan usually walked in around 6:45 after being down at the Catholic Church to listen to the singing in person. We could hear the voices carry all the way up to the Hilltop. Declan had been reading *Shantaram* and told me about what was happening in the book.

That morning, at 7:15, I went down for Doratea, who was always up early to write in her journal. I woke Jazie and then we all met on the veranda for breakfast. We were usually out and on our walk by 9:30 or in the van with Mana, our driver. This was the morning routine, all of us together because our purpose was the same. I began to better understand the saying "parting is such sweet sorrow" as I noticed so many details in our routine as our departure grew imminent.

On Sunday, we went to church in Tuʻanuku, attending the service across from Tessa's house. Out of courtesy, Tessa had alternated going to each of the three churches in the village. They appreciated her thoughtfulness and really liked that she went to church so often.

The day was another incredible experience, wrapping our lives around the love we had for Tessa. A small lunch was prepared for us by Asena and some village women at Tessa's house before we went to the top of the road to get our last glimpse of the library. I walked with Pungatoa, Tessa's Tongan counterpart, to meet the woman who wove the *taʻoavala* the village had given me. The woven wrap was made from bark of the kuta tree, which grows only in Tuʻanuku. People familiar with *taʻovalas* could tell that mine came from Tuʻanuku because of the pink cast to the tree bark. I wore it over my black clothes, as was the custom when one is in mourning. The black clothes combined with being wrapped in a woven mat on the humid Tongan days was rather hot.

Later that day, we left Tuʻanuku for Toao, the village where Tessa did her home stay, and had a midday feast with Solome and her family. Then we all went to the outdoor market where Primrose, who knew Tessa personally, had a concession where he sold his handmade crafts. He was what they call *fakaleiti*, or "like a lady."

Primrose gave us several different crafts, one of which I thought was a grass skirt. Then I was told it was actually a *taʻovala* for a commoner. We had been dividing all the Tongan gifts amongst us. Doratea kept this one for her collection of crafts.

"Oh, thanks, Viva, you gave me the commoner's wrap," she joked. Back in Santa Fe, she is far from a commoner, but for the next twenty-four hours until we spoke with the palace, Doratea continued this funny dialogue.

On Sunday night, we went to dinner at a restaurant, all of us extremely tired, with anticipation of our departure the next day lingering in the air.

We were due to return the next morning to Nukuʻalofa to be with Sarah Cha and Ann Marie and hopefully to meet Valerie, the new Peace Corps director. We would also meet with the royals and Komoto's family.

Doratea, who was not feeling great, decided to go back to her room because she was restless, tired of waiting, and had a severe ache in her gut. The service in the restaurant was slow. Declan, who had stayed behind at the Hilltop, phoned the restaurant to let us know that Lina, her family, and Tatafu were with him at the hotel.

In a gentlemanly fashion, the restaurant owner quickly drove Jazie and me to the Hilltop so we could say our goodbyes to Tatafu, Lina, and her family. By the time we arrived, Declan had been visiting with them for an hour. Tatafu was outside, pacing, seeming rudderless. I guessed he was waiting until Jazie and I got there before going inside.

When we arrived, the family presented us with more gifts, weavings that Lina, her mother, and sisters had made in honor of Tessa, their way of recognizing our family by continuing to give of their craft. They stayed with us until nearly midnight.

The next morning, we were meant to arise by 5:30 a.m. Mana, who was now our friend, would be coming for us at dawn.

Emotions are the only real immediate response to events. They are the truth before our brains start thinking. Leaving Vava'u was heart-wrenching for all of us. Our plane was due to leave at 8 a.m. We arrived at the airport at 7:15, and the pilot decided that because everyone who had reserved seats on the small plane was there, we would leave at 7:30.

We flew over, watching for the freshwater lake and Tu'anuku. The vast ocean surrounding the village and Vava'u was almost like a warm blanket. Leaving our newfound community and comfort below, we arrived in Nuku'alofa at 9 a.m. and drove to our bed and breakfast, where we got settled. Sarah and Ann Marie came for us by noon.

We walked to the Peace Corps office and gave staffers Tasi, Taua, and Paea Native American fetishes. We had given all the pallbearers from Tessa's memorial fetishes, honoring them with our traditional New Mexico gifts, which symbolize protection. We did not stay long at the office because the staff was busy with the new training group, Group 72, which had arrived two days earlier.

We had the opportunity to meet a few of the kids, a very young group, thirteen single females and one married couple. One of those new people would be working in Tuʻanuku at the end of the training, heading up the Tessa Horan Library. We planned to have some contact with her, and we were eager to know who would have the desire and qualities to live in such a rural setting. I was sure she would be honored to continue the work that Tessa started. She would have huge shoes to fill. I wondered if she would get to live in Tessa's house.

We had lunch at a restaurant called Friend's, which was owned and run by a Westernized Tongan man. The place had an American flair, and the food varied between Tongan and Western.

I had spoken on the phone with Rosemund, the spokesperson for the royal family. We were to be received by the current crown prince and his wife, Princess Nanasi, at 4 p.m. at their personal residence. When we entered the grounds, we saw guards dressed in camouflage. They approached the van as Sarah Cha and Ann Marie got out to wrap us in our *taʻovalas*. After the crown prince and his wife received us, we visited and presented them with a Nambe heart bowl made from eight metal alloys with the major component being aluminum. Some of the craftsman who make the bowls are from the Nambe Pueblo near Santa Fe. They are made in sand molds and are one of a kind. We chose a heart shape for the royal family in appreciation of what they had done to honor Tessa.

We also presented them with a Tongan armband from the 1940s, which had been given to Doratea by someone in Santa Fe who wanted the artifact returned to the kingdom in Tessa's honor. When I mentioned to the crown prince that Tessa's godmother was waiting in the car with her colleagues, he had juice and potato chips taken to them. I expected that he would invite all of them in, but apparently that was not the protocol.

We expected to be with the crown prince and princess for fifteen minutes, but we stayed forty-five minutes. The prince and Declan spoke about sailing. He told Declan he would like to get a sailboat, but his wife wanted to build a house in Neiafu. Princess Nanasi asked Jazie questions, and we spoke about shark habits and why the shark may have been watching Tessa's patterns. The prince had been an officer in the navy when he was younger, and he had told the princess when Tessa died that it is likely the shark had been picking up on Tessa's daily swimming habits and finally made the attack. I actually find it fascinating that there are so many opinions, stories, and myths about why and how Tessa died. The crown prince and his wife said they were grateful to have met us. Because this was our last day in Tonga, we planned to spend it with Tessa's colleagues instead.

Valerie was another one of Tessa's friends. We didn't get to meet her upon our arrival because she was teaching school, but we later got to spend some time at her house, watching a slideshow of Tessa. Valerie's house was comfortable, and she even had a cozy bed with a coverlet that Princess Nanasi had given her after the king's death.

In Tonga, there is a custom that after a head of a family dies, female members of the family have their hair cut. Long, dark, beautiful hair is a status symbol in Tonga, and the cutting of the hair is a tradition that has nothing to do with economic position. Rather it is associated with humbling yourself in honor of the head of the family. Someone other than a family member must do the cutting, and in the case of a king's death, it cannot be a commoner.

Peace Corps workers are an elite group in Tonga and are certainly not considered commoners, although they live humbly in villages. Valerie was asked to cut Princess Nanasi's hair, and afterward, the princess gave Valerie a beautiful pink-and-white quilted bed covering.

That afternoon, I was so tired I took a lie-down on Valerie's bed for a half-hour nap underneath the coverlet. It seemed so appropriate because I had just come from a visit with the princess.

Around 6 p.m., we all left Valerie's house together—Sarah Cha, Ann Marie, Valerie, Declan, Doratea, Jazie, and me—to have dinner with Komoto and his family. These people were Tessa's first introduction to Tongan family life. We had been unable to see them when we first arrived because of the time we needed to spend with the Peace Corps staff. Tessa had lived with this family for two weeks when she first arrived in Tonga. There were six girls: Tuki, Lia, Mele, Voni and 'Ema (who were twins), and Lifi. There was also one boy, Siaosi, but we did not meet him because he had recently joined the army.

The king had died just before our visit. Komoto, as talking chief for the kings of Tonga, was expected during mourning to live on palace grounds with his wife, Sia, who assisted him by cooking or taking care of other details. After 100 days, the mourning would be lifted. In the meantime, Komoto had been given permission by the new king to go home and spend time with us.

We walked to 'Ahua, the village where Komoto lived with grandparents next door and various family members in close proximity. The family gathered in Komoto's front yard in a line as if we were visiting dignitaries. Everyone spoke English fairly well, except the grandparents and Komoto's wife. The daughters dressed rather fashionably, and they were extremely excited to be with us.

Komoto's house was very humble, yet there was a lively comfort inside. In typical Tongan style, their front room was filled with different pieces of furniture, covered with colorful cloth, blankets, or tapestries. We sat in the living room, visiting, talking, and taking pictures, then presented Komoto with a silver-and-turquoise bolo tie and Sia with posole, a beautiful scarf, a Virgin Mary figure, and various other little mementos.

Ann Marie presented a basket of clothing we had brought for the girls. She and Sarah had put it all together so the sisters could share. In turn, they presented Declan, Jazie, Doratea, and me with beautiful tapa cloth and T-shirts. The setting was very comfortable, and we felt casual tenderness, as if we were having a rendezvous with longtime friends. When we went back out to the front of the house to fill our plates with food, they allowed us to go first before joining us. This was a more relaxing atmosphere than we had previously experienced.

Komoto's family was more Westernized than others we had met. The sisters were attentive toward Jazie. They wanted to continually have their pictures taken with her. The five unmarried sisters joked about marrying Xavier or Indigo. The whole night was great for Jazie. She was the center of attention and enjoyed being with the sisters immensely.

After we had been there several hours, Komoto and his sister

Noku piled all of us into two vans and took us on a half-hour drive back to our bed and breakfast in Nuku'alofa. Komoto insisted that they take us to the airport. Our visit to Tonga was almost at an end.

On our last evening with Komoto, he and his wife, sister, daughters, and grandsons all shuttled us to the airport. They loved Tessa enough to embrace us as family. Komoto held each of us girls around the shoulders for several minutes, moving back and forth between Doratea, Jazie, and me. His daughters and sister, all very physical people, continually wanted to touch and hold us. His wife, Sia, was more reserved, like the matriarch she is. They really care for Tessa's memory and for us. Their frequency holds an obvious energetic jolt in our hearts. Forgetting them is not an option.

The chain of events was like system sequencing, an unforgettable journey that will live in all of us for the rest of our lives. The time we spent in Tonga has taken us to a new stage in the healing process.

"Tessa inspired others to excel," Sarah Cha said, and her colleagues agreed. This made Tessa a leader in their eyes. She continues to remind people here of their own potential.

By now, Jazie was tired of being in Tonga and looking forward to being home. She said, "I need to get out of these clothes, and the first thing I will do is go to Whole Foods and get some vegetable sushi and a smoothie. Santa Fe, here I come."

The flight from Tonga to Los Angeles put me to sleep. Our plane was late departing. Jazie had put on her pajama pants and slippers while we waited in Samoa, and on the plane, she was curled up so close to me she was almost in my lap. I adored having her so close. We went through two security checks in Samoa because there seemed to be political unrest there.

I felt odd, as if I had left Tessa behind in Tonga.

Her spirit came so alive to me while we were there, as we transitioned in and out of her life, people, and visions. Our journey was a rich, powerful experience. I look forward to sharing with Xavier and Indigo all the encounters, sentiments, and values that rekindled the spirit of a human being turned to history: a woman who will be remembered as a part of the Tongan culture. Just like us, they will never forget her. She is conspicuous in her absence.

Transition

Slivers of polished time
pale peach sky
amidst stark horizons
tugging memories
sugar skulls, ornaments, affirmations
cookies, herbs
fragrances.
Lay lines of gaiety surface.
The puppy arrives,
easily evoked on
holidays and solstice assemblage
floating serial of Buddhist rituals
stirs of merged reunion.

Chapter Twenty-Three
MANNEQUIN

We returned to the United States on *Dia de los Muertos*. This happened to be the same day Tessa left California with her new colleagues in 2005. There will forever be connections with numbers, people, and stories—Tessa's folklore.

Halloween, Thanksgiving, and Christmas were always important holidays for our family. Every Halloween, Doratea and I dressed all the children and ourselves with a theme and went to dinner and divine candy collecting, which the children enjoyed. That was the one time of year they could have sugar without me objecting. We had such splendid times during the holidays when the kids were young, with Tessa and her cousin Nicole taking charge of the decorating and planning.

Having lots of children makes for a great parenting strategy because the older siblings help take care of the younger ones. When there is only one child, you have to be everything in one person—mother, friend, playmate—which seems to be harder.

The holidays had begun: Xavier and Indigo came home from California for Christmas with their dog, Harper, who was a puppy. We thought the Christmas cheer would be distracting, but memories of Tessa's leading her siblings in decorating the tree brought back memories. The children became terribly saddened and wanted to stop decorating and reminiscing after we began. I was heartbroken, watching them try diligently to keep lighthearted.

This is when Tessa's death returned to once again take a toll on us as a family. I stayed close to home with the puppy, Harper. The children went out to see friends at the festivities of a New Mexico Christmas. The *luminarias* and *farolitos* are always an inspiration of light.

I started interviewing the children, extended family, and friends to create a documentary about Tessa. The family took on another project, this one to accumulate and frame Tessa's artwork. Songs were written; tributes were made.

When the one-year anniversary of Tessa's death came, we gathered in her memory. The time seemed scarce, as if only weeks had passed. We decided to plan an exhibit of her artwork in my house on her birthday.

At that time, I could only go out of the house for necessity. I preferred being home unless we were doing service work in the community. Even then, I looked forward to returning to my house and being close to Tessa's things, the altar, the garden.

Tessa's Buddhist teacher Rinpoche Gangteng Tulku came to his temple in the states for his annual visit, and Doratea and I were invited to meet him. The American temple built in his honor in Crestone, Colorado, is called Yeshe Khorlo. I was able to meet with him and talk about Tessa's death

"There is no birth and death," he said. "It's just about coming and going, Viva. Being and not being."

In the temple, there was a *Drubchen* (a traditional meditation) of *Vajrakilaya* (the wrathful side of the deity *Vajrapani*). Rinpoche is the exceedingly secret raiser of life force and explained to us that in acknowledging *Vajrakilaya* one can cut through obstacles, sufferings, and resentments. This is a practice for accomplished Tibetan Buddhists, which I am not. However, I was invited to attend, and it was a great honor to be in the presence of so many of those who were.

A *Drubchen* involves ten days of praying twenty-four hours a day. This does not mean a person has to stay up twenty-four hours because everyone takes shifts, so there is always someone in the temple praying. People from Tessa's *Sangha* (a group of people who study dharma [teachings] together) were in attendance.

This was the first time that Rinpoche had done a *Drubchen* in our country, and the prayer was really meant for the entire United States. Everyone who attended the teaching, approximately 100 of us, worked daily to spread affirmations throughout in a spiritual frequency. We prayed for all the people in this country to be protected, blessed, and moved toward enlightenment. The teachings transmitted from the monks, lamas, and kaempos (the scholarly form of lamas) include the knowledge that only our species has the energy field central channel, which runs up from our tailbone to our crown (known to many as electromagnetic fields or chakras). This main energy field is flanked by two side channels. Other animals, beings such as bugs, and plants do not have this central line. This main energy field makes humans capable of moving toward enlightenment.

I was in Crestone for the last four of the ten days, and it was quite an auspicious, inspiring event. I had never met Tessa's teacher before. The year she died, I had gone to a White Tara empowerment, a guided meditation (Tara is an enlightened female being), intended to bring great fortune and fight contagious disease and ignorance. I felt it necessary to embrace this unique opportunity.

There were dancers there from Bhutan, and on the closing day of the ceremonies, right before the long-life empowerment, they did several dances, including a bardo dance and a cremation dance. Doratea came up for the last day of the ceremony, and it was an amazing experience for both of us.

Magnetic Pull

Rich blood swaths amongst us,
traipsing through chakras.
Commence from the tailbone,
ascending upward.
Motion and pause with each hue.
Red turns orange with procession,
where health and creativity lie.
Pigments thread to a yellow tone,
Pushing through solar plexus disk.
Energizing self-esteem,
bursting of green wheel
indicate compassion.
Passing to midnight blue
adds to the throat chakra
to soothe harsh sounds.
Let us be impeccable in our words.
Perseverance of restraint,
and the lavender halo
appears like a crown,
spinning between our eyes,
gentle sharp edges
circle spacious soft
log for the Akashic records.

Chapter Twenty-Four
PEACE BY PIECE

I encouraged everyone who visited to express and palpate their emotional mind and be candid on video. Xavier and Indigo suggested we compile the interviews into a documentary. The name we chose for the documentary was *Peace by Piece*. Busy McCarroll, a well-known Santa Fe musician, and her husband, Baird, recorded songs in their studio written by various local songwriters and musicians. Busy herself wrote the theme song "Peace by Piece" to honor Tessa.

Xavier wrote and performed his song entitled "Teca," which was an opportunity for him to allow his voice to soar with sincerity and without modesty. Tessa's cousin Lucas wrote a song for her called "A Notch in My Heart."

The event proved to be sensational with live performances and a collection of voices that set the stage for exhilarating performances.

The film's music propelled us into the ritual of a common defense against the stern master of death. Then patterns started bubbling to the top, as if we had found a natural spring mineral bath underneath a calm, pure current of water.

We passed through the first-year anniversary of Tessa's death on February 1, then Heart Day (Valentine's Day), when many of us decided to get the tattoo that Tessa envisioned on her wrist—a heart taking off from the Zia sun symbol, adding a wave for the water element and a star for the sky. Eventually, many would all bear her insignia on their bodies.

On February 27, the front page of the paper announced that a young woman from New Mexico, Ashlee Pfaff, had been killed by a wild animal at the Denver Zoo. The circumstances were all too familiar.

I called Declan and told him we had to go and be with her family, who lived in Bernalillo. I phoned the Pfaffs a week after their daughter had passed and asked if Declan and I could go be with them, and I explained that we too had lost our daughter to a wild animal. As I was speaking on the phone with Janice, Ashlee's mother, something in her voice seemed familiar. I recognized the tone of despair I know all too well.

Janice and her husband were willing to receive us in their home. When we walked in the door, I fell into the woman's arms, and Declan held the husband as if we were long-lost friends. The hours we spent with them were like a salve and gave a sense of relief. We asked questions that no one else had the nerve to ask them: What happened? Did you see her body? Did she look peaceful? Are you afraid to live without her? What do you want? Do you want to cry? Do you want to be alone? The Pfaffs were grateful to have their feelings validated by our questions.

Parents can have a unique connection when they have lost a child. You're not afraid to be intimate or receptive. I'm not sure if that's because Santa Fe is considered an energy vortex or because of the willingness to seek support. Yet that has been my experience with people who gather and share their grief. The loss of a child is insurmountable and dismantles your life to such an extent that you must remind yourself you are not the only person who has ever felt this broken.

Declan and I shared with the Pfaffs that we had made a documentary with interviews of our children and Tessa's friends. We suggested it might be helpful for them to come and be around all of us for a preview. We hoped perhaps they could be inspired by our creative endeavor to do something in honor of their daughter.

When Tessa had died after being attacked by a wild animal, it would have been helpful to our family to talk to people who had a similar experience. Although the Pfaffs' daughter had passed so recently, they were very receptive to visiting and viewing the documentary at the cinema cafe. I felt it might be a way for them to start approaching and accepting intimacy with death, which has taken a great deal of time for our extended family—and the process seems to be ongoing.

Janice and Norman Pfaff were brave to attend, having lost their daughter only six weeks earlier. When they walked in the door of the theater, Janice asked me if Tessa had ever attended public school, and I said yes, actually, she had left the Waldorf school to attend Sweeney Elementary because she wanted to be a cheerleader.

"Viva, I was Tessa's fifth-grade teacher."

Stunning coincidences synchronize the merging of lives at the most unexpected times. All I wanted to do was grab onto this woman, lie down in a soft bed, hold her in my arms, and cry.

How we managed to remain stoic enough to watch musicians surrounded by all those people baffles me to this day and brings up contrasting emotions. The Pfaffs' daughter and Tessa had their own relationship, and Ashlee had become Tessa's mentor for cheerleading and soccer. All I could think about was how to have more time with Janice Pfaff. I wanted her to be my sister, my friend, my mentor, my confidante. Suddenly, there was too much between us—yet also not enough.

The evening was very charged with emotions, appreciation, and community. When Xavier rolled out onto stage in his wheelchair and grabbed the microphone and the pianist started to play the melody of his song, Busy McCarroll and Sarah K joined him on stage. Busy with a six-string guitar and Sarah K with her four-string stood like pillars on either side of Xavier as he sang his song. His voice hummed with the perfection of his lyrics, and the audience was transfixed. We were all inside of every word, and it seemed as if the guitar strings tugged at every heart in the room, the piano clipped to every ear. Of course, tears streamed down my face, and as I looked around, I saw that everyone near me was crying too.

Next, Busy sang the song she had written "Peace by Piece,"

which was all about Tessa, and Xavier and Sarah K harmonized with her. Martha Reich, another singer songwriter, joined them on stage with her guitar and sang her song entitled "Song for Tessa," another lovely experience of Tessa. Everyone who viewed the film that evening was awed by the united frequency.

I had no way of tracking my next right move. I could only think about the effect of all the congruities, groupings of people, and memories that actually belonged to Tessa. How did I miss noticing that Janice Pfaff had been Tessa's teacher? I must have known her and gone to conferences with her. I know that I went to basketball games to watch Tessa jump on the shoulders of other cheerleaders and do amazing feats, yet I could not recall the actual players.

I questioned myself: Am I still in shock? Was my memory taken hostage because there were too many other notions I had to cram into my new psyche? Bewilderment, confusion, and facts became a swirl, and I realized it didn't actually matter. We were all doing the best we could.

The grand finale of the evening was the recitation of a poem written by Sunny Redmond, a family friend. She wrote the poem in honor of Tessa, Xavier, Indigo, and Jazie. It was a beautiful way to end a poignant evening.

She Was Always There
BY SUNNY REDMOND

As I became aware / She was always there.
The cadence of her voice / Her ear as close as it could get.
Deeply listening / Wondering / Who we would be for each other.
Her bright eyes and smile / Lips pressing her first kiss / And the laughter that followed.
I watched as she wove us all together / Holding my hand / We matched in heart and mind.
She was always there / Part of my world / My past and my future.
Witness to possibilities. / Supporter of dreams.
Leaping in the faith that sustained her / And all of us to a place where I could not follow
Till my time is correct and Everything changed forever,
I am listening to understand. / Why.
Gathering to help each other / Holding our disbelief and longing,
Honoring the light that she had lit,
Burning even brighter / Because we needed it to.
And to carry the flame forward / In love and respect for all.
In the loss and longing / We all see, feel the place / Where she was always there.
Now we must do that piece, finding our way. / For ourselves, for each other / For the world.
In her leaving / She left a trail to follow. / In our own ways
Which, grows us all / More fully present / As community, family, and world
Uniting in life / What was transformed in death / A legacy of kindness.
She was always there / And continues to be / Though in different form.
Her soul's alchemy / Transforming the physical
Her golden essence / A glistening reminder / Of dreams and possibilities / And bright hopes for the future, the transcendence of form.

Chapter Twenty-Five
SHE WAS ALWAYS THERE

In 2007, Jazie's graduation from high school on June 18 was marked by *Saga Dawa*, the month-long period of Buddha's enlightenment some 2,500 years ago. If one is virtuous during this interval, it is magnified by 1,000 times. That was a good omen for Jazie's future.

The students were restless because the administration decided they were not allowed to have the usual celebratory extras that seem to accompany graduation, such as colorful beach balls and humorously decorated caps. Naturally, the beach balls and plastic monkeys appeared in the thin, sun-warmed air anyway, leaving the faculty up in arms. In the end, all the students managed to get through their expressions of excitement and graduate.

Francis, Declan, Indigo, Doratea, Nigel, and their kids, my sister April and her daughter Katy, and of course Gabe, Jazie's boyfriend, were all there to witness this pivotal time in Jazie's life. The family continued to be a source of interest and excitement.

My sister April had attended every one of my children's graduations. She is on the spectrum yet did her best to traverse through her days. I remember writing at the time:

> Visiting us is like traveling to another dimension for her. She soaks it all in like a sponge, yet the knowledge and color are only tempo-

rary, like a fix. She is in awe of the way we live and the continued strong friendships that surround us. She dips into the sensation while she's here, and I am more than glad to be able to share. She thinks she wants a life like mine. Somehow just being my sister is not enough for her. The only way I know how to take care of her is by allowing her to feel a part of something—the many facets.

Jazie's graduation luncheon was a remarkable experience. She had her own ideas of how she wanted the décor and the seating, and she planned the event with our family friends. They gave me instructions. We were honoring Jazie's aliveness!

The three of us made the party favors—matchbook shrine boxes covered with tiny Mexican playing cards and eternal light candles tied with heart fortunes. Making fifty handcrafted gifts for the family and friends in attendance was an absolute breeze. Jazie loved the artistic party favors because they were reminiscent of the art projects she had done with Tessa.

We transformed the living room into a more radiant interior than we had been living in previously. We adorned six tables with apricot-and-plum tablecloths and alternating colored napkins. Around the perimeter of the living room and porch were coral roses mixed with brilliant orange sunflowers and day lilies, an array and cacophony of uplifting exuberance. The house and its display flowed surprisingly well given the large number of sit-down luncheon guests. The display began at the entrance with huge vases of curly willow, stargazer lilies, and gladiolas. The prominent vases invited the guests through our large front door, which is decorated with a carved Buddha. A welcoming box of wheat grass grown especially for the occasion greeted guests immediately after they entered. Bamboo sticks with decorative letters on their tops sat comfortably in the wheat grass and spelled out the words "Welcome" and "Congratulations Jazie."

The graduate was honored, recognized, and praised while beaming with pride as she stood looking delicate and lovely in the midst of the aesthetic, colorful surroundings. A spiritual energy permeated the room.

As the party began, a bright yellow bird flew into the living room, quietly soaring above the beautiful people and décor. At one point, the bird flew onto the tear-shaped, enamel bowl I made for my mother when I was a kid, which rests upon an eight-inch Buddha sculpture. After a minute or so, it flew off and knocked the precariously balanced bowl into the kitchen sink.

The color and size of the bird, as well as how calm and comfortable it seemed amongst forty-five humans, led everyone to believe the bird was a domesticated canary. I am sure the bird came for the party. Fifteen minutes after the special bird's arrival, I reached over to Jazie and said, "Tessa wanted to be with you on your graduation day, and she has found her way to you in the form of a bird—most appropriate."

Our *Peace by Piece* film was shown at a local movie theater during the Independent Film Fest. I asked the manager if he would allow us to show Jazie's eighteenth birthday/graduation video beforehand. Before long she will be the matriarch of the family. Jazie narrated the film in a voice that resonates wiser and more at ease than her age would suggest. Everyone in the audience was impressed, and Francis was extremely proud of her. The last few months had been totally focused on Jazie, and her appreciation showed in her eyes and proud yet humble smile.

Since Xavier's injury and Tessa's death, much of Jazie's childhood was stripped from her. She was introduced to her personal strength through the challenge of so much grief. Jazie is a stoic and impressive young adult, and narrating the documentary was not an easy task because she rebuffs the idea of being center stage.

During and after Jazie's graduation, she came into her own identity. What was once indicative of a family under struggle had now come to represent her own self-esteem, and one could see in her posture that she felt productive. She had the time and energy to make decisions for her own life, and the elders appreciated this obvious fact. In truth, all the disruptions had been a nuisance, and she moved through an ocean of tears to separate herself. Although she knew we would always be near, she wanted to experience something new and different. I saw in her a maturity that came from her starts, stops, and stumbles. Now she was writing her own story.

As Halloween approached, I gathered a few of my close lady

friends. We mixed Marme's and Tessa's ashes together in whatever drink suited us. Hazel mixed it into her wine. Doratea and I made smoothies. Suzanne had come to visit from New York, and she wanted her ashes in a cup of soup. This was our way of beginning our tribute to the dead, as *Dia de los Muertos* was only four days away.

Jazie came up the ladder to the attic to find us and was absolutely disgusted that we were ingesting our dead relatives. She wanted no part of the ceremony, saying boldly, "I think I'll go have some turnips and do my college applications while you cannibals consume the remnants of the dead."

The next family enterprise became an active strategy. Tessa was a minimalist and never approved of my collecting clothes, things, and paintings. I remember once she reminded Marme and me after her travels in the third world how often Americans are disliked because of our capitalism, consumerism, and covetousness.

Tessa enjoyed coming home and borrowing my clothes and sleeping in my nightgowns. She rarely wanted to own anything except her outdoor gear and suitable clothing for her life. She took only what she needed, which was fine by me because she asked for so little compared with other children.

After Tessa's death, I wanted to stop clinging to my possessions and decided to have an estate sale, sell the house, and found a charity organization in her name, Tessa Foundation.

That year, our Christmas was supposed to be simple. On Christmas Eve, we went to Chimayo, a small town north of Santa Fe, which is a pilgrimage destination. We took gifts, food, and a Christmas tree for a young mother and her two children, who were living in a garage. She was from a family of addicts. Her husband was in jail for dealing heroin. She told us her grandparents had used and sold heroin as had her parents. Addiction was pervasive and passed down through generations. She was not a user, and she hoped her two girls would not have a destiny of drug use. She wanted to break the cycle.

After Christmas eve day in Chimayo, our family joined together for dinner. Xavier sat at one end of the table, and I the other as I caught his eyes. He was handsome and capable. I was reminded of his disability, pain, and emptiness without his body and his Irish twin sister, Tessa.

Indigo looked at me soon after that thought, saying "Hey, Viva, do you want to talk more about going to Nepal and seeing what that other nonprofit is doing with the money we gave them for the kiosk in the middle of Kathmandu? Have you researched that woman Sajita who Tessa met during her trek?"

Then Jazie piped up and reminded me that she's doing a semester abroad, "Remember that I'm going to be leaving for Spain before my birthday. Maybe you and Indigo can go to Nepal while I'm away."

After Christmas, Xavier and Indigo went back to California, and I began to plan for the months ahead. Jazie went to Spain, and I made travel arrangements for Indigo and me to go to Kathmandu in March.

Poverty

Widening stimulation,
stringing impossible cultural goals,
bubbling as if inside a busy arcade
tinker toys bound only for a museum.
Raw ambit quickens
generating sadness.
We are surrounded by too much.
Electrical restrictions limit warm water and light.
Inside accomplished duties
of poverty seen on every shoulder of a district,
coaxing crowded views that flicker.

Chapter Twenty-Six
TESSA AND THE TRAVELLERS

I've always been intrigued by British spellings, like two Ls in "travellers."

On February 24, 2008, Xavier and his team of eight won the Oscar for sound editing and mixing on *Bourne Ultimatum*. Just the day before, Xavier's team had won a Golden Reel award at the Motion Picture Sound Editing Awards, where they were up for awards for nominations for both *American Gangster* and *Bourne Ultimatum*. *Bourne Ultimatum* won.

When I am afraid, I move in and out of being connected to my physical body. My family and I kept ourselves busy, diverting attention from the muscle memory imprinted in our bodies of something missing: our daughter, our sister, our friend. We wanted to believe we were a regular family, rather than people who had been changed through continual shocks. We built bridges across the caverns of loss.

I was making plans to follow Tessa's trails through her world with intention. Indigo and I planned an expedition to Nepal to meet people with whom Tessa had formed previous relationships when she had trekked there in 1999. We were in the initial stages of applying for a 501(c)(3), which is required to establish a charitable organization. We continued to map the groundwork for the Tessa Foundation.

Indigo and I left in March of 2010. We flew into Bangkok and had several hours' layover. Indigo and I were wrapped in the security of each other when we arrived in Kathmandu. The reality of being somewhere too foreign and not even close to what Indigo was expecting set our mission on a zooming pace. Indigo shared his sister's legacy with anyone who would listen. Being somewhere that had been so important to Tessa grounded him.

Richard, an American who ran a nongovernmental organization, or NGO, collected us at the airport, and we were to stay with him. Our family and friends had given $10,000 for a tourist coffeeshop kiosk that Tessa had envisioned during her trek to Nepal. The kiosk was to be a place for tourists who might want to integrate and help the impoverished Nepali people.

Richard strapped our luggage to the top of the vehicle, and off we went off into the heavy traffic, plenitude of people, exhaust, pollution, poverty, and children sniffing glue. The culture shock was dramatic. We were acutely aware of the contrast from our lifestyle to that of this third world surrounding us on every street corner.

Richard drove us to his home. The household included Richard's girlfriend, Devna; her children; and two of her cousins as well as a few other young people who were there to experience the culture through volunteer work. Indigo and I were surprised by the location of the house—Maharajgunj, which was apparently where the kiosk was located. The neighborhood was gated and locked at night. We had expected the coffeeshop kiosk to be in the middle of Kathmandu so as to be accessible to tourists.

One night, we walked with Richard and his girlfriend to have dinner. It was a dangerous walk through the narrow streets, dodging unruly drivers.

Richard's volunteers invited Indigo to go out on the town for Saint Patrick's Day. He chose to stay close by me instead because he knew that was what I wanted. Kathmandu is truly crazy, crowded, and wild outside the gates of our billet.

This morning, the milkman just arrived with two tin cans of

fresh milk. How cool. There is only electricity four hours a day here. I had a cold sponge bath that was raised to tepid when one of the girls in the house brought me a kettle of hot water. I gave the extra hot water to Indigo for his Nepali shower. Indigo was absorbed in a book and blown away by our surroundings. I think he was expecting green tropical rice paddies, and he was surprised by the reality.

On our first day in Nepal, we visited a safe house for disabled girls, Kopan monastery, Eido Tamang's house (Ngima), and the Saving Women Foundation's women's shelter. Indigo and I were adapting, overcoming, and improvising routinely. We were a united front.

The first door we walked through to the safe house, which Richard called Tessa's *niwas* in Sukedhara—this translates as "no water," and there had been no water for over five months here. The air was filled with exhaust from the cars, cooking odors, and kerosene fires. The six girls in the safe house were all disabled in some way: two dwarfs, one with a mental disability since she killed her child, her sister with a deformed right hand, and the youngest in the house with such a severe facial deformity that she was hard to look at for any length of time. Indigo and I visited with them for about a half hour.

The safe house where they lived belonged to a previous ambassador to Pakistan, so the furnishings and decor were rather plush for the third world. Indigo asked me what "third world" meant. I responded, "underdeveloped and poverty stricken." We later learned that this was Richard's residence before he hooked up with his girlfriend, Devna. She did not want to live in this area, first of all because she is a Brahman and second because the district had no water at all.

Indigo was quiet and astonished as we were introduced to the disabled girls in the safe house. Devna and Richard were with us, of course. There was no way we could get around all these different districts without them, and they introduced us to the basics of Kathmandu protocol. Whether we could adapt to getting around on our own remained to be seen. It was an intense state of affairs.

Then we continued on to Eido's house, which is close to Kopan

Monastery in Sukedhara. I had met Eido originally through Tessa when he came to the United States to be the gardener at the Upaya Zen Center in Santa Fe where Roshi Joan Halifax resides. He had invited us to his home before we left the United States. His eighteen-year-old daughter lives in Santa Fe with a family and goes to the community college.

Richard and Devna walked us to Eido's house, which took more than two hours across several districts of the city. We could only have tea there because we had a late lunch appointment with the Saving Women Foundation. Eido called for a cab to take us there because we were running so late.

Truthfully, I felt safer in that city walking than driving, and often it was faster. Navigating streets in a car was like being inside of a pinball machine with cars going every direction. There didn't seem to be rhyme, reason, or any kind of order to the streets, especially if someone had died, and suddenly streets were filled with people, flowers, and ceremonies in honor of the dead. Planning to be somewhere at 1 p.m. doesn't mean you'll arrive on time because of the happenstance rituals that might be taking place in the streets along the way.

During our visit to Nepal, Indigo protected me and provided a sense of safety for us both while at the same time twisting us into various configurations with his manic observations. We rendezvoused with Sajita Sharma, the founder and director of the Saving Women Foundation—an NGO supporting marginalized women and children in Nepal—and three of her colleagues at Mike's, an American restaurant where ex-pats hang out for breakfast. This is where Tessa had met Sajita. After our late lunch, we went to Sajita's office to be recognized in a Hindu blessing. Then we learned about Sajita's history with human rights, the abuse of women and children in Nepal, and how she and Tessa had crossed paths.

When Indigo and I were asked to introduce ourselves, I lost my composure as I spoke of Tessa and her siblings. Indigo put his arm around me and took over. The sensory overload was overcoming both of us, and we would cover for each other. I was continually surprised by Indigo's demeanor and his ability to communicate despite diversity, poverty, pollution, and oppression.

Sajita showed us a slideshow that chronicled oppression and the foundation's housing, school, learning center, weaving center, and beautiful kitchen, all impressive and inspirational. After our lunch, Indigo and I returned to Richard's volunteer center to have dinner with a British woman and a Canadian man who finance health clinics in other areas of Nepal. Indigo was too exhausted to visit or eat. I had a short conversation with the people.

Indigo was not sleeping well. He has anxiety, which was exacerbated by challenges adapting to the Nepali lifestyle. He also had the responsibility of making sure we didn't get side-swiped in the crazy streets.

"If anything were to happen to me, Mom, I can't imagine what Dad would do to you," he said.

During our time in Kathmandu, I began to have different experiences in the same surroundings when I was sleeping and dreaming. I started to latch onto certain recurring elements that would connect me to people—a long, large, oval table made of brilliant cherry wood, outside on a veranda. The table seemed to be symbolic, and the dream would always have familiar or interesting people. The landscape would also vary. I was tired after supposedly sleeping as if living two separate lives. I wondered if the parallel life was because I was outside my comfort zone. I admit I was apprehensive about the surroundings; therefore my psyche would grab onto a safe environment.

The attendees would visit, share food, or discuss and consider opportunities both tangible and ethereal, political, intellectual, spiritual, emotional. I thought about the white bread truck that was in my parallel reality for weeks after Tessa died, a duly noted urgency to hold on to life and acceptance. And now I have a parallel reality, oddly grounding and connecting the table as a place to break bread, share ideas, and be productive. This form of lucid dreaming is instrumental in allowing me to breathe into a space of strength and notice the large concepts, such as courage.

Indigo and I decided to conference with Sajita and her

colleagues about the possibility of moving these girls to her shelter during our visit. Sajita's and my plan was to move the disabled girls from Tessa's *niwas* to the Saving Women Foundation women's shelter because they needed more attention and socialization. There were already 100 women at the shelter. Sajita was willing to take the disabled girls because they have a new building, financed by a private donor, which was just completed in December. She says that each girl will cost around $800 a year, and she will guarantee that they have a nice cozy bed with a comforter and pillow and three meals a day, and they will learn a trade depending on their disability.

Unfortunately, in Nepalese culture, female children are undervalued and thought to be inferior, and they are the property of their fathers and later their husbands. They are often considered to be financial burdens because their families must supply a dowry in order for them to marry. If a woman has a disability, she has little chance of survival unless she has a very loving family. This mystifies me when every one of us is born from the basic human female form.

These six disabled girls did not have any support, so they've basically been shut-ins all this time. Although they had a roof over their heads and food to eat, the NGO will give them a chance at socialization as well as more attention than they've ever had in their lives.

We traveled with Sajita to Bakhtapur, a quiet, unique, artistic village with a plaza for craftspeople. Sajita wanted to take Indigo and me to see some important historical sites.

Kathmandu is plundered by the residue from civil war, exhaust, cooking fires, trash burning, poverty, and overpopulation. The physical and emotional overload of poverty hovers on every corner. The women wear their *kurtas* (dresses/skirts) with pride; their children often beg on the streets. The saving grace and distractions are the rituals, celebrations, and prayers of Hinduism and Buddhism. The two devotions give an element of confidence and an infusion of hope; however, the disciplines of supposed moral and spiritual practice does not protect from abuse.

We moved from Richard and Devna's house to Eido's house at his insistence. Being with him, his wife, children, and relatives gave us the chance to understand the life of a sufficient Nepali family. Thirty people lived in their house, which is typical of a Nepali family. They made the remainder of our visit vital, rewarding, and successful.

Eido and two friends had founded the Dawa Hostel, a haven for abandoned children in Kathmandu, where Indigo and I spent a great deal of time. There were twenty children living there, ages five to twelve. I taught yoga and applied essential oils, Indigo helped teach them English, and we both did art, music, and garden projects with and for the children. They were fascinated with Indigo's wavy mop of hair, his clothes, attitude, and height. They followed him around as if he was their guru.

One day, Eido, Indigo, and I planned to meet Sajita for a meal in the district where her Saving Women Foundation office was located. While we waited for Sajita, we investigated the area, drank tea, and wandered in and out of spice shops, smelling the various concoctions.

I noticed Indigo had strayed across the way and was talking to a young Nepali fellow. The next thing I knew, Indigo took off his T-shirt, which was covered with images of guns and a bright red heart, and handed the shirt to the stranger. Indigo and Xavier often wear shirts with controversial messages in regard to religious dogma, weapons, and politics.

The young Nepali man was good-looking, despite the cigarette hanging out of his mouth. Indigo waved at me across the street so I joined them and then the three of us sat at a table drinking tea. The conversation between the two young men grew quickly familiar; Indigo was almost talking in a Nepali accent in broken English, and they shared details the way women in the United States do, exchanging nuances and personal material in a heartbeat.

I was amazed by their association, as if they were hungry for friendship. I knew by the way Indigo was directing and conversing that he was digging for valuable information about local youth and their culture. Indigo has a knack for inspiring people to reveal their secrets.

As I walked back up the street for a few moments to let Sajita know where we were, I saw her standing in front of her office. She immediately alerted me that the young man Indigo was talking to was undesirable—from a family that dealt on the black market in arms, drugs, and people. Naturally, I went into alarm mode and rushed back to get Indigo away from the situation. He instead coaxed me into sitting down, put his hand on my leg, and asked this fellow, whose name was Rama, when they could meet again.

Rama wanted to know more about what we were doing in Kathmandu, and I explained that in honor of Indigo's sister we were trying to help women and children who had been abused. He cryptically divulged that his family was involved in trafficking guns, drugs, and people, explaining that he had learned the trade through his parents and grandparents. He acted as if he was a proud child prodigy.

Indigo said to him, "Rama, I like to make money, and I've bought and sold some marijuana, but selling people is considered slavery and abuse where I come from. We regard people as precious, not chattel. How would you like to be kidnapped, sold, and used for things you were too young or unwilling to do? My sister came to Nepal on a trek a few years ago to study Buddhism and healing herbs and watched young girls being sold into slavery. She was shocked that people were so poor they would sell their daughters because they were undervalued. Just think about this, Rama. My mom and I want to rescue them from people like your family."

Rama responded, "What is that word 'chattel'? You want to buy some girls?"

"No, Rama, I want you to give us some, help save their lives, and give them the chance to do something they might choose," I snapped back.

"Well, women aren't meant to choose," Rama said.

Indigo, in his inimitable style, started shucking and jiving with Rama to calm the rising tension. Suddenly, Rama offered to sell us six young women.

Indigo responded, "Rama, how about I trade you all of my American clothes, belongings, and books?"

I was physically ill, scared, not knowing what was going to happen.

Indigo held my hand as he said to Rama, "Hey, I'll be back with you, brother, in a couple of hours and bring you some clothes."

I was in a panic as we walked back to Sajita's office and shared with her what had transpired. She could not believe that Rama had divulged to Indigo what his family business entailed.

Indigo explained, "I don't know how this all came so fast and furious. I think it's because of my T-shirt and Western style. He is basically a nice guy who works in a family business. He doesn't really understand the destruction connected to it. I know the feeling of wanting to be a hotshot."

Indigo was still without a shirt. Sajita quickly found a *kurta* (loose, collarless shirt) in the office he could wear temporarily.

Next, we had to figure out how to get back across Kathmandu and gather Indigo's clothes. He was determined to trade all his belongings to rescue some lives. Sajita was willing to house and care for any women we could save from abuse. She was nervous about Rama's family knowing we were involved with her. We had to be cautious, and Indigo was fearless. He wanted to do something meaningful in honor of his sister and himself.

We enlisted Eido, who had no idea what was going on, to pick us up in his van so we could get Indigo's suitcase.

By the grace of circumstances, all came together. Indigo took his clothes, belongings, and books to Rama by himself. Eido and I waited on the street with the van.

Two hours later, Indigo stepped out from the alcove with three young girls. We watched as Indigo walked toward us and shuffled them into the van. In some Nepali dialect, Eido told them to duck down and stay low. I gestured with my hands and got down on the floor with them. The girls were frightened, not knowing what might be in store. We hoped we weren't being followed or watched. The next thing I knew, Eido was driving us outside of Kathmandu to the Saving Women Foundation shelter. Indigo and I were in absolute shock at what had just happened. When the girls met Sajita and she spoke with them in a language they understood, you could see hope in their eyes and faces.

Sajita is a Brahman, the highest caste in Nepal, while Eido is of the Tamang, the lowest caste. Despite this gulf between them, they became well acquainted because of their personal missions to help save people. Eido had his hostel and Sajita her foundation, and their work had a similar dedication and focus. Eido was also an organic gardener, and Sajita had a gentleman on her staff who headed up her agricultural programs. Eido and this fellow had already talked about building raised beds on the site of the Saving Women Foundation. The women we had just rescued could learn sustainable horticulture.

Indigo told me that in addition to his clothing he also had given Rama his good watch, his gold bracelet, and a charm necklace I had given him for Christmas.

Eido got some new clothing for Indigo. His wardrobe was so different, Indigo looked like a holy man. Indigo began to enjoy his simple attire as we traversed the Kathmandu area. We were constantly reminded of why we had come: to follow Tessa's trail to to support efforts to reduce the starvation, loneliness, devaluation, and abandonment that are integral parts of life for most Nepali people.

During our stay in Nepal, we were fortunate to be under the tutelage of Sajita and Eido. They both had witnessed this suffering and were passionately committed to bringing about change in their country. The three young women in the van with us that day were now in the best of hands.

I remember thinking, *We have done something of service. So unexpected, eventful, and amazing. This is what Tessa was about. Her legacy, the Tessa Foundation has begun.*

That night, I dream I meet Rama's family and talk to them about human trafficking. *They are trying to be communicative, and they are frustrated because they don't understand why I think I have the right to talk with them as if I know them. Rama's mother gives me food and puts a* bindi *(red paint) between my eyes. I am at the oval table, and my children are there and ask me with their eyes to stop talking to Rama's parents. Indigo invites them to leave after the father says no when Rama wants to stay visiting with us. They all leave the veranda.*

Tessa's birthday was approaching, March 20, the first day of spring. As usual since her death, her colleagues back home in Santa Fe, along with family and friends, would be up on the mountain at

Ski Santa Fe celebrating the Tessa Ascension Race. This would be the third anniversary of the event. Indigo and I, however, went with Eido to Namo Buddha, a sacred Buddhist pilgrimage site outside of Kathmandu, for a blessing with a Nepali Lama and a butter lamp ceremony in Tessa's honor.

Near the Namo Buddha is a cave, a sacred site where legend tells of a prince 6,000 years ago who encountered a weak, starving tigress and her five cubs. The prince realized that six beings were about to starve to death. He dripped blood from his fingertips into her mouth and then he cut flanks from his right hip with his knife to feed her and her cubs. He cut away his own flesh until he died. Because he saved the life of this family, he became an avatar reincarnated into an awakened one known as Buddha. This process of returning back to earth after death in another form is reincarnation. His willingness to give his body to the tigress and her cubs was an extraordinary act of intuitive intention.

Eido wanted to do a remembrance ceremony of Tessa at this site because of the significance of her being killed by a wild animal. He interpreted Tessa's death as a sacrifice to the shark. He said Tessa was a *Bodhisattva* (person who has attained enlightenment).

He also believed that his one-year-old daughter, who was born in Santa Fe in 2007, might be a reincarnation of Tessa. Eido's daughter had very dark eyes and dark hair, and her eyes locked onto Indigo when in the same room with him. Staying with Eido and his family was a high privilege because they were Buddhists. We meditated with them in the early morning, and evenings we attended to projects at his hostel and the Saving Women Foundation.

I am continually amazed by the inner workings of life, especially when visiting third-world countries. One hour in a Nepali, East Indian, or Tongan village is like being thrown back in time. A week passed in moments, intrigue mounted quickly as we accomplished Tessa's goals helping marginalized people, a privilege to unite and balance efforts between our ways and their traditions.

At the end of our Nepali journey, Indigo and I stayed in a hotel so we could have hot showers, sleep on thick mattresses with regular pillows, and use electricity. Although we couldn't wait to get to the hotel, we both felt awkward knowing that outside the hotel's walls, people were starving, and some rarely had clean water, let alone hot water. We were constantly reminded of environmental racism in this country, which invokes feelings in us to share everything we can.

That night, I dream of being with Eido, his wife, and children: *We are eating delicious food his wife has cooked and drinking rice wine. Eido's father is serving us. The wine has sparkling colors, and we are at the cherry oval table. They are saying goodbye to us on the veranda in my parallel reality. I feel guilty that we didn't spend our last night with Eido and his family.*

Return to Tonga

*Arrival in a kingdom
without a king.
A talking chief,
his family of women,
entering slowly
the history we have
of mourning, mourning again:
Our first encampment, "Utuʻone"—
the sandy land by the sea—
a tour with Sione
to the edge of that sea.
Turtle rocks kissing
Tessa calling
her mother.
The food changes.
We change. Slower
tropical time prepares us.
We cannot refuse
the calling to return.
Where this circle leads
to memory and renewal,
there is no stopping,
only willing new friends.
We fly again
an airplane like a sausage
propellers spin
islands in turquoise water, Vavaʻu.*

Chapter Twenty-Seven
TESSA TRAIL BACK TO TONGA

Tessa's trails of the past led our organization to carry on planting and carving out intentions. The Saving Women Foundation in Nepal became a beneficiary for some of the donations the Tessa Foundation was receiving. Two years after rescuing the three girls in Kathmandu, we circled back to the Kingdom of Tonga, where the goal was to complete more of the work Tessa had begun. From one end of the world to the other, Tessa had left her legacy, a path now for us to follow.

After a twelve-hour flight, I arrived in Tonga at 8:15 in the morning. Air New Zealand only had two flights a week, with an hour-long stop en route in Samoa. I couldn't sleep, anticipating the bittersweetness of returning to the kingdom. I had no idea what to expect; I knew only that someone from Komoto's family would be waiting for me. Komoto held the position of talking chief for the new king, as he had under the previous king.

Because there were so many people at the airport, it took an hour to get through customs. Then I found Komoto and his daughter Ema waiting for me. Ema, who was close with Tessa, now had an eight-month-old daughter named Marcella. They took me to their house so I could change into a formal outfit.

Komoto, Ema, and I went to see Crown Prince Topouto'a and

Princess Nanassi. They had been present at Tessa's Tongan memorial, and in fact they had helped to organize the event. Komoto and Ema had to sit on the floor away from us while we ate and enjoyed tea. This was so weird, such a stupid custom here. I snuck some beautifully rolled-up sandwich-like snacks in my purse to give to Ema later.

The crown prince had his son with him, twenty-two-year-old Prince Ulukalala, who now owned the village of Tu'anuku. It appeared he made his decisions with the advice of his parents who I suspected were trying to encourage his involvement. He was very shy and seemed preoccupied with matters more important to him, such as smoking, girls, and his social life.

I talked to him about sustainability and making Tu'anuku an example through utilizing water catchment, a community garden, and wind power. The crown prince was very enthused about all the ideas, which could be a feather in Prince Ulukalala's cap if the organization of possibilities went as planned. I also needed to get permission from the royals for a CBS crew to film Tatafu in Tu'anuku. I mentioned the possibility of Tatafu traveling to the United States to learn some garden and water catchment techniques, but the prince said he preferred that we come back to the village and teach Tatafu and the locals here.

Tatafu didn't have a birth certificate, and I asked if they would help make that happen so he might one day be able to travel. Though the royals can make things happen, they don't like to be bogged down with minutia. They referred me to the legislative assembly.

I next met with Lord Filalakepa, the chairman of the parliament when King Topouto'a was alive and now a member of the parliament. He was able to make things easier for me and scheduled appointments with all the necessary people, including Houali, who was the communications director and Filalakepa's niece. They arranged a meeting with Saiu Vaipulu, chairman of the whole house.

After my meeting with the prince and princess, Komoto came back for me with his other daughter, Voni, who was twenty-nine and beautiful and drove me around whenever Komoto was not available.

They drove me to meet with the chairman of the whole house, Saiu Vaipulu, who was from Vavaʻu. He wanted to use Tuʻanuku as a pilot project for wind and water catchment.

I next met with the town officer, whom we met on our previous visit. He said he would consider allowing a plot in the village for the community garden.

We also needed responsible people to watch after the library. The Peace Corps didn't seem to want to place another volunteer in Tessa's village, nor were they very cooperative or sensitive to the situation there. I would have to either look for help from an outside organization or ask the town officer for a village volunteer. I thought the governor of Vavaʻu might make it a priority at that point. When Komoto shuttled me over to the Minister of Education, I met with his assistant, Winnie, who was working to find funds to make environmental options available in the country.

Everyone in Tonga who knew Tessa asked about her siblings and friends and expressed their hope for movement in our cycle of grief. While American culture tries to ignore, move on, and even forget after a death, Tongan culture is very attentive to carrying on the wisdom and strength of a beloved person who dies. The person's family is responsible for carrying on their loved one's legacy. I fit right in; the legend of Tessa lived on.

After my meetings, Komoto and I returned to his house. Komoto's family was curious about my family, and of course, the girls had endless questions about Jazie. They wanted all the details about the kids and their lives. We shared sweet stories of family. I had my laptop with me, and I showed them a slideshow, which elevated their spirits.

We planned to view the Tessa memorial film at Filalakepa's house the next night and talk about the new film project, a segment for Shark Week on Tessa's attack.

The film crew was scheduled to arrive the next night, and Komoto had been instructed by the princess to alert customs so they would have no difficulty. This was very thoughtful of Her Royal Highness.

The next morning, the roosters hollered at 5:30 as usual, sounding like messages, exuberant warnings, or territorial recitals. I flew to Vava'u. Both my feelings and traveling companions were different from my previous journey to Tonga.

That evening, the CBS cameramen arrived. The crew were on a job for pay and rather detached from the extreme sensitivity, sentiment, and tenderness that permeated the village. I had no idea what was going to transpire in the following days. The crushing of memories and the unraveling of what really transpired is the focal point this time.

Our family had given Tatafu the glory for trying to save Tessa. CBS was filming a segment about Tessa's death as seen through the eyes of Tatafu, his friends, and the other villagers. When Apolosi and Atiata recounted the story of Tessa's attack from their vantage point, raw emotions surfaced in me. I felt my composure slip. I was right there in the village, on the edge of the water where Tessa had died, listening, trying to take in the details. My Tongan friend Vaasi interpreted because the story came forth in mixed English and Tongan. In those moments, I would get vivid images of Tessa as a newborn child in a manger, being submerged in water, minus her leg and bleeding.

The accumulating grief in my gut gave me a feeling of drowning from water-boarding. Tears choked my ability to breathe, my knees buckled and took me down on the ground. I was convinced I was suffocating as panic crept up on the surface of my skin the way goat-head stickers attach all over you when you get caught in a patch of them. My reaction to the absence of my child scared me into taking slow deep breaths. No one noticed I had lost my balance.

I knew the villagers of Tu'anuku would never forget Tessa nor deny her existence. The people who had tried to save her life truly cared for her. They realized that she had transformed them significantly in a short time. Her generosity and humility opened a window of ideas that would eventually enhance the village culture.

As difficult as it was to go through that process, by the end of those days together, we had become accustomed to speaking of her death as a new part of her life. The internal tide line that had built up inside of me was pulling back into calm. I was grateful for the new closeness and relaxation that had loosened the astonishing rigidity of loss.

As the filming progressed, I was offended at how the cameramen and crew would shove release forms in front of the village people as we were talking intimately. I remembered I had signed a release form and couldn't recall what I had agreed to with CBS. To my disbelief and regret, I was to find out later.

Culminated Mementos

My body is my closet filled with treasure, special dresses, and scarves.
My heart has drawers opening with past souvenirs:
recollections, paintings, jewelry stuffed away in miniature.
I have memorized the shoes I've worn during particular sections of my life.
I feel the structure, which tries to fit space.
Last night, I lay holding your hand in my mind.
The sense of you was clearly vivid,
Floating in my heart, preparing my lungs for breath,
Complete with rhythm painted in between my eyes.
Tracing an emblem with your fingers threading back through my heart
Drifting closer through a dream of real wrapped in coral cotton lavender.
You became my daughter, my teacher.

Chapter Twenty-Eight
CULMINATED MEMENTOS

Tessa's colleagues of Ski Santa Fe ski patrol began the Tessa Ascension Race in 2006, and they have continued the event for more than twelve years. Each year, there was a different kind of celebration with sensitivity and sentimentality. We will be walking through the labyrinth of her visions with attention on other young people who care about their sacred vessel, planet earth.

Our entire family has been moved by the industrious efforts of Tessa's colleagues, who keep the memory of her generosity and commitment to serve alive. The tendency to honor people like her makes everyone feel like they are an active part of remembering Tessa, rather than being sucked into sadness. These events allow our family, friends, and community time to revisit, connect, feast, laugh, dance, and recall.

In 2011, we held a *Dia de los Muertos* event to recognize eleven families of Santa Fe and Aspen whose children had also died. The local celebration honored the souls of those special children whose deaths came in close proximity to one another and who were connected to through athleticism, academics, spirituality, siblings, or parents. Seven of the families joined us in an altar ceremony and the third screening of *Peace by Piece*.

The gathering encouraged bereaved parents to share their losses and to find hope in new possibilities. Tessa had a passion for organic gardening that inspired us after her death. I encouraged the other parents to think of their own children's interests and consider what they might be able to do in honor of them to keep the spirits alive.

In Tessa's name, we began a community garden. We have sponsored raised garden beds in Tonga, Nepal, Mexico, Colorado, and New Mexico. These sustainable initiatives allow people to pass knowledge and food security to future generations. It's never too late to light the spark that ignites the change.

When I get that ripping feeling in my gut about the loss of my child, I remind myself that many other parents have had the same experience. Death has a high frequency, and I've learned that when the conditions aren't right, some people don't stay in physical. As Thich Naht Hanh said, "The conditions have to be right for a baby to birth into this world, and the conditions have to be right when they die."

Later that year, I put my house on the market and began to dismantle the contents, hiring a company specializing in estate sales. This seemed to be the most practical way to end my clutching and grasping of material possessions. My children chose to take whatever they wanted, and I distributed the rest of Tessa's belongings to friends and extended family. I tried to detach from things and memories; the task was a practice of excruciating emptiness.

I planned to sell most of my things. I kept telling myself that if everything sold, we would have many thousands of dollars to finance the Tessa Foundation and support the efforts Tessa had envisioned.

When Tessa left for Tonga, she took only essentials with her. While I longed to become minimalist like her, I feared that without possessions, there would not be anything solid on which I could stand.

I dreamed I was sailing away on an island of plastic, cardboard, broken furniture, and paintings made into sculptures, going into the vastness of a sea as if I had never been Viva, Tessa's mother. The process of letting go was emotional. Walking away from the house and allowing businesspeople to make the decisions about selling possessions that took me fifty years to acquire was disheartening.

I had to take myself as far as possible from the sale so I wasn't tempted to go to the house to watch or change my mind. This was a devotional act for my daughter and me.

Doratea, Declan, and I drove to Aspen for a reunion with many acquaintances and friends from the 1970s. A guy named Lalo, a Zen Buddhist who both Doratea and I had dated at different times took a particular interest in visiting with us as Declan wandered around looking for folks he had known. We shared the intimate details of Tessa's passing with Lalo and our interest in Buddhist studies. He was interested, pensive, and compassionate. He spoke of his path of Zen Buddhism and the changes he had made in his life.

The gathering and visiting with people distanced me from the clenching and challenges of letting go of so many personal possessions. Lalo had never been married or had children, and he still lived in the valley with travels to Mexico during off season.

We reconnected with people we had known from the 1970s. I realized we had only known each other superficially. Back then, every single one of us wanted to make our own rules and our personal direction was oriented toward freedom. None of us were conventional, ordinary, or conformists. That was our common denominator.

I had attended four different high schools and several colleges, and this was the closest I would get to a reuniting with people from my past.

I've come to understand my flaws in regard to expectations of people. I also tire of things easily and look forward to change and this might be why I have indulged in many careers. I have been a dancer, model, painter, shop owner, therapist, interior decorator, poet, and most importantly a mother. I've had many short-term careers and done them well enough, not an expert at any—until I had my children. I immersed myself in them. They were my queendom, my heart, my creative purpose. I believed I was in charge of them. I wanted to keep their lives merged with mine.

After our reunion, while we drove over the mountainous Independence Pass from Aspen to Santa Fe, I clung to the memory of my possessions—especially my mother's blue China, one of my concho belts, some of the jewelry, and certain paintings. I grasped onto these things in my psyche, reconnecting with material things and imagining filling my closet and my future house with stuff again. That sensation overwhelmed me with sadness after the initial thought I had associated things with memories. My memories were a scribe of the soul, and I had to relinquish the accessories.

I pulled over to the side of the road and threw up, something I was usually unable to do without my mother. Doratea and Declan were alarmed, and Declan took the wheel while Doratea sat in the backseat with me, holding my hand. Marme was long gone from physical and could not hold my head and abdomen anymore, like she did only a few years before. Doratea wisely talked about the delight in loving and caring, rather than the possessive action involved with materialism.

Declan dropped Doratea off at her house and took me to my friend Hazel's house. I couldn't bear to return to the house alone. I shared our experiences of the happenings in Aspen. She said that she'd been thinking about my process of letting go and suggested that she buy some things from me to keep them in my view—like my mother's blue China, my concho belt, and some specific art pieces. She said they would at least still be in the family. I could still see them and even wear the concho belt on occasion.

When we opened my front door, walked through the vestibule into the great room, we saw a five-by-five-foot pile of household remains. Everything else in the house had vanished. The blue China was gone, the concho belt was nowhere to be seen, and not one painting hung on the walls.

Hazel and I were frozen in shock. I started to laugh, then Hazel started laughing. She grabbed hold of me, hugged me, and said, "Hey, it's a new beginning, a fresh start."

Three weeks later, I packed my few bags in my car, said goodbye to my dearest and closest friends, bowed to the house, and drove myself to Aspen to isolate and figure out how to move forward.

After arriving in Aspen, suddenly I felt as if I were inside a psychological thriller, trying to pace my entry into each corridor of my life, as if stepping fearlessly off a cliff. My children were settling into their own lives of college and careers. Francis lived in Aspen, so the children could visit him and also see me.

I thought perhaps taking myself back to Colorado might help mend the shattered vessel. I needed to build myself into a woman who could run a foundation, break a cycle of grief, and become a strategic thinker. Time is our true currency, and arousing exemplary behavior was a way of preservation and purpose, to carry on the legacy with Tessa's visions as an activist and advocate for change. The question was: Did I know how to awaken and keep my hearth productive, solid, and useful? Could I be a humanitarian?

My Buddhist friend Lalo had invited me to live in Aspen with him. Lalo was patient, accommodating. His Zen practice gave him discipline, focus, and structure that I didn't have. Moving in with him, I was going on a long retreat completely different than the way I had lived all my life. He tore up the carpet in his two-story cabin built amongst the trees, replaced it with wood flooring, and allowed me to take over his place—except for his office where he wrote and meditated. With Lalo's permission, I spent a couple of months redecorating and transforming his place into a colorful yet calm environment. I felt I was inside a warm vessel.

Eventually, Lalo insisted I get a job because I had become so isolated. He got me a job as a baker in a restaurant on Aspen Mountain. I had to ski to work—there was no other way to get to the restaurant. The fresh air, responsibility, and exercise were healing and rejuvenating. Lalo looked after me and inspired me to disconnect from grief.

A longtime acquaintance from my younger days in Aspen offered her property down-valley from Aspen for a Tessa Garden. The soil was rocky and desolate, but the quarter-acre had great possibility. I met with Indigo's high school girlfriend, a delightful young adult who helped me design the layout of the garden. She had known Tessa. I persuaded her college counselor to consider giving her credit for the garden project because her major was environmental studies and permaculture. This was a great exchange of support and experience for us.

The property was filled with river rock and difficult to clean and clear; however, our many volunteers were able to enrich the soil, remove the rocks, and add compost. Within five weeks, the garden was designed, cultivated, planted, and ready to be blessed by the sun, moon, and water. By the end of the summer, we had harvested many times and given food to the house-bound, underserved, and kitchens around the valley that prepared food for those unable to shop, drive, or integrate into the outside world.

We also sold vegetables at the farmers' market to repay the several thousand dollars we had spent on augmenting the soil and garden-building. We broke even on our expenses while sharing and giving to marginalized people.

Tessa's Gardens became important initiatives and continued in various parts of the world where Tessa had been inspired to include gardens in her continual action for enhancing change.

After working in the garden, I often went home and spent an hour reading through Tessa's journals. This was my ritual during the week, especially when Lalo was at work. He was a summer ranger on the same mountain where he was a ski patroller during the winter.

After reading one of Tessa's journals about Mexico and Guatemala, I came up with the great idea of footprinting those places she had traveled. I wanted to see for myself the people and places she wrote about in her travels. Lalo spoke Spanish. He had gone to Mexico a number of times before he assimilated me into his life. I spoke with him about designing an expedition with me.

Tessa enjoyed traveling to Mexico and Guatemala, I wanted to find projects there for the Tessa Foundation. Lalo was keen on the idea, and we decided to travel with our mutual friend Lupe, who owned a shop called Gypsy in Sayulita, Mexico.

Traditions

A bowl sits atop silver mines, tunneling,
circling the underbelly of Guanajuato
smothered in colored smells and sounds of life.
A mortar and pestle mix mediums
music, basilicas, food, art and history.
Haunted Victorian Spanish decor
slices mystery to pieces as the past looks
to be deteriorating, quietly and gallantly.
Women continue making food for their public.
An accordion player begs to be appreciated.
Mariachis sing, bag pipes play, a guitarist around
the corner sings Jim Morrison's
"The End."
The medieval festival participant's parade,
and days later Mexican worker's line behind
the local marching band with their dump trucks
and flat beds.
The contrast speaks volumes
for the importance and pride of one's own life—
celebratory time for the collective,
all of us the same in those moments of thumping,
heightened exchange;
the resonance rocks our souls
in precious reverence.
A balcony in the sky is a terrace I've danced before,
shaping the images of saints.
I dream of small horses talking in frequency,
no words,
simply essence of experience.

Chapter Twenty-Nine
SANTA SEMANA

Following Tessa's path took Lalo and me to Guanajuato, Mexico. The city, which means "hills of frogs," was built in the shape of a bowl and sits on top of old silver and gold mines. Coincidentally, Tessa had a small collection of stuffed and porcelain frogs.

Lalo and I made our way into Guanajuato by bus through old mining tunnels, which had been turned into roads circling the city. In Mexico, first-class buses are more comfortable than any domestic airlines in the United States, with lots of leg room and spacious seats that recline all the way back.

In the city, we hired a taxi that drove us through underground dark eerie tunnels, swallowing us into the darkness. Then suddenly, there was light for a minute, then immediately another dark scary tunnel. Cars were parked in some of the tunnels; one could leave a car there and walk out as if from a labyrinth. Fortunately, the roads in the tunnels were all one way, which made the driving less chaotic. I was glad we didn't have to drive ourselves in the city.

Our first meal of the trip was on the evening of Good Friday, consisting of Lenten pudding made of bread, onions, tomatoes, and cheese, held together with corn tortillas, then brewed overnight. The flavor was surprisingly sweet rather than savory—not my favorite Mexican cuisine.

Later that night, in our bed and breakfast, I was dozing off, hoping to sleep, and swiftly Tessa and I were talking at the oval cherry table. Her friends from her travels whom I had been introduced to in her journals were talking with her about experiences. I woke up, hoping for a breakfast without Lenten pudding so I could think straight and trying to recall what Tessa and her friends were discussing in my dream.

Guanajuato is a multicultural experience, vast and rich. I was unprepared for the Easter celebration, *Semana de Santos*, the celebration of the saints, which began before our arrival. The city was already filled with visitors from all over Mexico—and other places.

The population of the city at the time of our visit was approximately 140,000, similar to Santa Fe, and about 2,000 of them were Americans. We met a few of those expatriates. Because we were obviously Westerners, they would see us on the street and ask, "Are you European or American?"

Mariachi bands were everywhere, performing with the greatest of ease and fully decked in their traditional bling attire. They were drenched in passion from their vocal cords to their fingertips, faces and necks corded with thick veins from the thrill of performing. I was captivated.

The *teatro* on the central plaza had many steps filled with people. The last two weekends we were there, a musician clown performed with his own kind of exuberance right below the *teatro*. We also saw an outdoor ballet performance by high school girls below a huge Don Quixote sculpture.

The miniature plazas all over the city each had something unique. The churches were exquisite, with domes on top of most of them. I was fascinated with the inner design in each church, trying to see them all before we had to leave. The city architecture was a mix of Italian, Victorian, Art Deco, Spanish, and of course, Mexican. Many of the buildings were deteriorating, but to me that made them more desirable and mysterious.

We stayed in a place above the city and had to ride the funicular, a rectangular boxlike tram the size of a middle-class family tomb or a hearse tipped on the hood. The incline was steep, but it moved quickly, taking only two to three minutes to get up and down.

Our room was appropriately named *Balcon del Cielo*, and it had an amazing view of the city. There was also a magnificently large clay sculpture of *El Pípila* near us on the hill. He was obviously important to the Mexicans, and I vowed to study him before our visit ended.

There was a Medieval Renaissance fair at the old bull ring, now a baseball field, with knights dueling, beautiful damsels dressed to luxurious heights, eagles, hawks, owls, and precious children. I remember thinking, *Gracious sakes, I'm living in a parallel universe yet again.*

One morning, a marching band prancing down below in El Centro woke me up. I watched them from our balcony. After the band passed, a parade of dump trucks and flat beds followed. I laughed and even teared up with amazement and awe. These frequent festive ceremonies were thrilling.

VW Bugs were the favored car there. I saw lots of red ones and other cool colors. I learned that this used to be the home of a VW manufacturing plant.

During these days of celebration, the town breathes from the huge thumping heart with caged energy, the nightclubs vibrate with electronic rock and roll, mariachi trumpets, and bagpipes. Each night, the rising reverberations from below seeped into my body as I prepare to have soulful dreams. I paid attention to the uniqueness of each genre as I dozed off.

Triumphal enjoyment saturated the air the following morning. The open balcony gave me room to dance willingly, and I became overtaken with exuberance. The colliding sounds penetrated me with deep gratitude for the fullness of living. WOW! The science of people is fascinating, spell-binding, and frequently confusing.

There was a profound aliveness present in my creative sphere, soaking everything up like a sponge. The thrumming of delight amplified and enlarged the thought of Everybody Is Somebody!

In the evening, firework explosions colored the walls of the sky with aliveness. At all hours of the night, the dogs and coyotes howled. There were gunshots and celebratory shouts, in honor of the many saints, sounds of lifestyle festivities, more vibrant due to the bowl-like valley in Guanajuato.

On our last day, enjoying a quiet breakfast listening to classical music, we heard "Ode to Joy" in the central *zócalo*. No one had been in the restaurants except the waiters because the locals were accustomed to a slow, late start for breakfast, usually around 9 a.m. We were fortunate to find a lovely place before departing to visit several other places where Tessa had spent time in Mexico and Central America, including Chiapas and Guatemala. The first order of business on the Guatemalan border was money, converting pesos to Guatemalan quetzals. Eleven pesos to the dollar and thirteen quetzals to the dollar, more or less. *Too many different money systems*, I remember thinking. *Why can't I just use beads for fair trade?*

Vibrations, movement, and sights on the streets in the morning were the same and constantly changing. There was a foggy mist hanging low when I woke in the village of Panajachel, beside Lake Atitlan in Guatemala. I could see the volcanoes around the lake, even if only slightly outlined. Every morning at 6:30, I watched from my second-floor terrace as a man arrived to assemble his booth for market on the street below, usually the first to arrive and diligent in his preparation. An hour later, his wife would arrive with coffee and breakfast, and they would set up their street booth with a beautiful array of textiles.

One Sunday morning, some young boys had a firecracker standoff to see who could be the loudest at sunrise. The culture seemed unrepressive. Adults didn't protest, and no one seemed worried about the children's safety.

Outside the apartment, a group of kids depended on me for change and a treat as soon as I stepped out the door in the morning. My departure time varied daily. Although they tried hard to talk me into buying stuff, I preferred instead to give them money and food. After all, I worked so hard to get rid of all my possessions that the last thing I wanted to do was accumulate. I eventually ran low on money, probably a good thing that I had no idea how to use the local ATM.

The favored transportation in Guatemala was the tuk-tuk, a three-wheeled cab that is nothing more than a decorated golf cart. They reminded me of bumper cars. We rode in one for the experience, but I preferred walking or traveling by boat. The restaurants on the street where we lived were Europeanized, offering plenty of interesting food. We found a place with brown rice and vegetables—Café Jasmine, which reminded me of Jazie.

The water was scary, and we had to be careful not to get it in our mouths when showering. Brushing your teeth with the stuff was out of the question—same as in Mexico. I got a bit queasy now and then from an accidental dribble while showering or washing my face. But we had hot water regularly—a great luxury, and not the case while we were in Mexico.

I was fortunate to hook up with an organization in Guatemala called Mayan Families. Our last weeks I volunteered in the village of San Jorge de la Laguna and helped with the organization's food program for the elderly and orphans. I met a young single mother of six children, named Teresa, in this soup kitchen. What an experience. I started laying plans to partner with Mayan Families to build Teresa a house. We negotiated with her father on a small piece of land he owned inside that village. If he signed over the property to her, Tessa Foundation would finance building her a dwelling. The casita was erected and finished within six months—small but better than where she and her children had lived previously. Mission accomplished.

In early 2012, Jazie got pregnant with her first child. She finished college at UNM, then her first child was born. I left Lalo's house to return to Santa Fe to give her support and attention.

My daughter and Gabe included me and Gabe's mother, Valerie, in their birthing of her baby boy, Makai Tatafu Martinez on February 9, 2012. Makai means toward the sea, and his middle name honors Tatafu's trying to save her sister's life.

Later that year, Xavier got very sick in California with a decubitus ulcer, which manifested into osteomyelitis. He had seventeen surgeries, and the infection got so bad they told me his health was precarious.

We tried everything possible from the surgeries, hyperbaric chambers every weekday for several months, then stem cells. I rented a house near the hospital so I could be available for Jazie and Xavier.

We were at another pivotal challenging time for the family.

Makai's birth gave the family happiness and hope. We were all scared Xavier might die. I made him healthy food every day, and Jazie, Gabe, and Makai visited him regularly. We moved him to a hospital in Denver because a doctor there specializes in his condition and felt he could heal Xavier. Declan and I took Xavier to Denver in a rented van rather than by ambulance, and I stayed with him there for a couple months. By 2015, Xavier was much improved. We lived in a rented house by the hospital.

Xavier became an advocate for a young boy named Valentino Tzigiwhaeno Rivera of Pojoaque Pueblo, who had been well known for his hoop dancing by age six. Valentino also had been injured in a car accident, leaving him with a serious spinal cord injury. His father had been governor of the Pueblo.

> Witnessing Valentino Rivera's mesmerizing hoop dance at the museum was a moment that marked the beginning of a deep, unexpected connection for me. At six years old, Valentino—or "Tino" as I came to know him—was already a renowned Native American hoop dancer from the Pojoaque Pueblo, just north of Santa Fe.
>
> The Riveras, including Tino; his father, George (the governor of Pojoaque Pueblo at the time); and his mother, Felicia, were promoters of native children's dancing. George's reputation as a Native American sculptor caught my interest, and I became eager to look more into Native American culture in New Mexico. So I visited Museum Hill here in Santa Fe to check out some history. At the time, I was recovering from an infection I'd caught while surfing in LA. (We wheelchair restrained suffer infections often.) I was seeking diversion and new knowledge, which has been a family tradition passed down from my grandparents to my mother, Viva.
>
> Anyway, tragedy struck the Riveras after a devastating car accident, leaving Tino with a severe spinal injury and his sister Paloma in critical condition. Our hearts ached for the family. A year later, Tino and I became fast friends and mentors for each other, as fellow voyagers in wheelchairs. I tried to help him adjust to his injury, which had also left him unable to walk. From there on, our

two families' lives became intertwined in many ways. Fortunately, his sister Paloma recovered quickly and went on to become a hoop dancer herself.

Inspired by my new kinship with Tino, I worked hard to strengthen my muscles, dreaming of standing upright for the first time in public, with Tino as my witness. This I couldn't have done without the determination and support of my mother.

When the day arrived, in the presence of Tino's family, I took my first vertical steps publicly in an exoskeleton. Hoping to inspire Tino, I dedicated that brief, but giant walk to him. The bond he and I shared from that moment profoundly impacted the Santa Fe community, who followed our teamwork closely. So many were rooting for us then.

But tragedy struck again when Tino asked his parents to let him go. I'm not sure of the circumstances exactly, or how that went down, but he passed away at the age of eight in 2016, leaving me in serious despair and confusion.

Tino's untimely death ignited a search for answers and led me down a path of distractions, unable to comprehend why such a young, extraordinary talent was taken while I remained alive. I got more involved with my personal physical and emotional pain. I began using more pain medicine than I should have. Let's just say, I needed to medicate my "self."

What an honor it was to meet Tino and be around his big spirit at such a young age. I only wish I could have had more time with him. I know he is one of my spirit guides out there somewhere, and I can't wait to dance with him again someday.

Thank you, Felicia and George Rivera, for sharing his bright smile and life with me and my family.

—Xavier Horan, *Facebook post 2016*

Jazie had another child, Cash, whom I call Butter Buddha because he is so round and awakened. Eido came from Nepal to visit his daughter Pema in Albuquerque, who graduated from nursing school. Eido's presence in the house was uplifting, and I felt great that I could take care of him and do things for him the way he and his family had been so hospitable in Nepal to Indigo and me.

Eido is so lovable. My children and grandchildren feel comfortable with him. Everything was flowing nicely.

Then we got news of a devastating earthquake that happened in Kathmandu. Eido was frightened for the safety of his family. In a few days, we learned that his family had survived, and no one had been hurt, but at least 6,000 people had died. He went to Albuquerque in a few days to be close by Pema and the airport in hopes to get back to his wife and family.

Shatterings

*Accomplishments
no power tools.
Leaders emerge from
circumstances.
How far will any of us go
to make life "better" for another?
What do people want?
Who's asking?
Questions of authority
order of politeness
wrapped around
curious quests.
Hearth of suffering sways
while leaning into others.
Adapting and striving…
the framework of respect.*

*Receding to
instrumental movement
stimulates obvious resources,
reclaiming personal wealth.*

Chapter Thirty
SHATTERINGS

On the border between India and Nepal, one of the most widespread tragedies is human trafficking. Despite its proliferation in many parts of the world, this underground crime flourishes largely with impunity.

Sajita had seen Rama on the street a couple of weeks after the awful earthquake. He wanted to sell her fifteen girls. Rama requested some electronics and money. His family business could not afford to keep them, and some of their housing had been compromised. Sajita phoned me with her ideas.

Our strategy was to move the young women from the critical dangers of Nepal—the mudslides, monsoons, earthquakes, and abuse—to a safe place in India, a country I knew very little about and where I had no experience and few contacts. Sajita wanted me to help move the girls from Nepal to India via the Chitwan jungle over a porous border into India. I didn't think twice and said absolutely I will help financially and will show up physically.

I wondered why she would want me to come and help when there are people more skilled in her community. Perhaps she wanted me to experience how grim life can be in a natural disaster. And truly I've not been in the midst of earthquake devastation. There are many ways to be taken down, ravaged, or broken in our world.

Sajita kept ten of the girls in Nepal. She is a warrior woman, a diva for the marginalized women and children in her country. Her shelter's strong brick building that houses many stayed standing erect, and the residents worked together to clear the mud and destruction around the buildings.

Sajita moved the girls over the border without me, and I met her in Calcutta. My Indian friend's mother lives in Calcutta and had found housing and promised to train the five girls to cut hair and give facials. I spent a few days in Calcutta getting them settled, then went to New Delhi to meet friends of Sajita. After a few days in the horrible smog of New Delhi, I went to Mumbai to meet up with my good friend Willat. He and I investigated the city and worked in slums while doing research on human trafficking.

On top of the horrific enslavement of women and children for sex, human trafficking also takes the form of labor exploitation, domestic servitude, and agricultural work. In all its manifestations, this business has become one of the largest criminal industries in the world, ranking just behind weapons and drugs. The despicable ease with which traffickers are able to manipulate government systems, boundaries, and country regulations is astounding and heartbreaking. The environmental racism is a result of an agenda of the wealthiest and most privileged class of people. The world has enough technology and resources to solve poverty, hunger, and climate change. The new generation must create a better system for the future.

We can gradually unshackle people from this slavery if a spotlight is shone on the corruption that causes this worldwide predicament. To work for human freedom against this modern slavery has to be part of an improving world.

Once again, Tessa Foundation left Santa Fe for a service journey to the Kingdom of Tonga. While we were en route, death called again, this time for the king of Tonga, His Royal Highness Tupou the fifth. His father was king when Tessa died, and now his brother —who was formerly the prime minister and then the crown prince —would be king.

The royal family was very respectful and involved in facilitating our family's needs when Tessa died. When we visited in the past, the former crown prince (the new king) and his wife took time to invite us to their private residence. We continued to receive the respect of the royal family. Lavaki Gary, the talking chief for Prince Ulukalala, was the embodiment of this respect. He had become attentive to the Tessa Foundation. He appeared in the Air Pacific Office attached to Utu'one, our bed and breakfast in Nuku'alofa.

Following the king's death in Hong Kong, preparations for his return were under way throughout Tonga and especially in the capital Nuku'alofa. The buildings were draped in purple and black —black to signify mourning, purple to signify royalty. The funeral rites were to be held that Tuesday, and the ceremonies promised to be respectful, complicated, and elaborate.

I noticed a ranking in Tonga that flows like water. Everyone knows their place and what is expected of them. The society is patriarchal, yet the women hold the highest position of respect. This would become evident in the details of the ceremonies for the funeral. Perhaps this was also evident in the respect shown to Tessa and to me.

Lavaki Gary took time from his responsibilities as talking chief to assist in Tessa Foundation efforts. One of our main goals was to find Tatafu. I had wanted to see him again and visit with him, to tell him that Jazie, Tessa's youngest sibling, had named her son after him.

A main concern and goal was to finally get Tatafu a birth certificate and passport. (With the support of Prince Ulukalala and Lavaki Gary, this mission has since been accomplished, and Tatafu has possession of his papers.)

After a few days, we located Tatafu. He and I spent time talking, with Lavaki Gary interpreting for us. Tatafu understood English fairly well, but he was still uncomfortable speaking it. He is the youngest of fifteen children, and he turned thirty-two on July 17 while we were there. He told us he was the only unmarried child in his family, partly because he was obliged to take care of his mother financially.

I was again in Tonga, reviving the compassion Tessa shared with the Tongan people. Tatafu and I were abruptly caught up in grief. We saturated ourselves with quiet for a few moments, then we began planning the projects she had imagined for the village of Tuʻanuku and other villages where she had lived for homestays.

I feel something magical about continuing Tessa's visions on both pragmatic and intimate levels. And though difficulties arose meeting even the simplest of daily needs in Tonga, both my own and those of the local residents, there was no doubt this was the support the people of this developing world imagined.

Traditions are intriguing, and they can often lead the way to more understanding of countries like the Kingdom of Tonga. After the king's death, on the main island of Tongatapu, people prepared the road on which the body of the king would be transported. All the fences, walls, and houses were covered with purple-and-black fabric. Grass was cut and burned, trash cleaned away, and a fresh and honorable path made. The side of the road would seat the common folk with their heads bowed as the cavalcade passed. It was all part of the deep connection between commoners and the royal family. The people were diligently involved in preserving their cultural identity. During the forty-eight hours before the burial of the king, citizens from all the islands of Tonga brought offerings of food to a site near the palace for a feast for all the people to share.

The burial of the king took place nine days after his death. Prayer continued throughout the day and night before the ceremony and through the next afternoon when the services were complete. At the burial, 1,000 ex-students witnessed the procession from the palace to the tomb and took turns carrying on their shoulders the wooden "house" covered in black fabric that was built to carry the king. One of the bearers in the front was the king's nephew. The new king and family walked with the body. After a service and a few hymns by the Methodist minister, the new king, Tupou the Sixth, departed first along with overseas dignitaries. The rest of us followed.

The next day, we flew to the island of Vavaʻu. The Tessa Foundation group volunteers and I set up a base at the Hilltop Hotel in Naiafu as we had done on previous visits. The following day, we hired Mafu to take us to Tuʻanuku. We were greeted in typical Tongan fashion by Heamasi (the town magistrate) along with his family and other village residents. Seeing the familiar faces was emotional. After many tears and embracing from Heamasi's wife and other women from the village, they took us to a plot of land so we could help them plant a community garden. We brought seeds from New Mexico and introduced some new vegetables for their consideration.

We helped Lina (Tessa's friend), Vaasi Kupu (my friend and our hostess at the Hilltop Inn), and two of Komoto's daughters complete applications for the 2013 International Folk Art Market in Santa Fe. They would represent Tongan culture with their craftwork. The worldwide application and acceptance process was quite complicated, and only 200 out of 500 applicants were accepted. This was an amazing opportunity for the women and their villages.

The logistics were quite involved, so I wrote a letter to the Tongan ambassador seeking assistance with visas, funding, and organization. There were rigorous rules, regulations, and preparations to get these women and their craftwork to the United States.

The Tessa Foundation sponsored the young Tongan women who had become friends with Tessa during her time in Tonga. They represented themselves and also the community of artists within their country. Their work included a wide range of basketry, goods woven from local grasses, as well as tapa cloth made from the bark of the mulberry tree and painted with natural dyes in geometric designs.

Tessa's legacy rests in part with these women, who strive to better their lives. One of Tessa's dreams was to empower her friends in the village to connect them to the world at large through their remarkable craftwork.

Those of us who went to Tonga that year had a long list of projects to complete. My good friend Austin headed up an art program for the fifth and sixth grade students. The women continued to tend to the garden, which was only a five-minute walk from the village.

When I first went down the hill to see the site, I was appalled by the amount of trash leading down to the location. I lost my composure and mild-mannered Tongan attitude. I spent the walk back up the hill to the village expressing my strident opinions to my friend and guide that day, Kato. I urged her to go to the weaving house and tell everyone how I felt. My impression was that she heard (and felt) the strength of what I was saying. I wanted them to have pride for their village, their heritage, their families, Mother Earth, themselves, and their country. My hope was that the village would become a model for the rest of the country.

There are no water wells in Tuʻanuku—all water in the village comes from rainfall—so it was a great relief for the villagers when we repaired the gutters at the school, which hadn't been maintained. They had lost much water, but now it would again fill the *simavies* (concrete water tanks) with improved water catchment.

We hired a local craftsman to carve a wooden sign for the school, which was installed by our team and the sixth-grade boys. The children of the village were an enthusiastic and energetic bunch, jumping wholeheartedly into every project, unlike the more laidback adults.

Austin and a few of the boys worked on installing the new library sign, while Brandon and Kelly of the Peace Corps, along with others, helped me plant about thirty tomato plants down below the school. The children climbed a nearby coconut tree to procure us hydration, and they brought us other fresh fruit.

Another project that we took upon ourselves in the memory of Tessa's wishes was to make recycling bins and transport them to the village. We purchased enough material in Neiafu to make three bins and got approval for some Peace Corps volunteers to weld them together. The actions of Tessa's vision after her short time in the village was brought to fruition.

Smoke Ghosts

Born from whose womb?
Heartbeats sing a whale's song.
We, unborn, see through other faces,
other eyes, and unknown places.
Intoxication of intimacy
brings us into being.
We are twins,
invisible to one another for too long.

Chapter Thirty-One
BROKEN MYTH

In late fall 2017, I went to Aspen to attend a remembering at the Jerome Hotel. J. Silverman had passed away. Whenever a longtime friend dies in Aspen, there is an assembly of comrades who were once a close-knit group and had gone separate ways.

Later, in the Jerome Bar, I visited with my friend Reen. A handsome stranger approached, introduced himself, and politely asked if he could have a word with me.

His presence was intense; he seemed to be gazing right through me. His confidence gave me a feeling of knowing him from before. His liquid voice was calming, and at the same time I felt a sense of urgency. He immediately gained my full attention.

I was curious as he leaned into me and said, "I've been asked to relay a message to you, a story of which you are an integral part."

His voice and words made my heart race and my head spin. He handed me a card, which had only a phone number and said, "My name is Ramon. I look forward to seeing you in the morning." Then he turned and walked away.

"That was weird," Reen said. "I think I should go with you."

"Yes, of course you will," I agreed.

I needed a witness to decipher information. We were both intrigued, jumpy, and skeptical.

The following morning over coffee, Ramon spoke to us in a cryptic manner and mentioned a family reunion.

"What do you mean, 'reunion'?" I asked.

"I'm sure you will be grateful," he said, then handed me flight information and ticket to Ottawa, Canada. "You'll fly out of Albuquerque to Chicago and on to Ottawa."

I was stunned and looked at Reen, who smiled.

"Relatives I know nothing about? Ottawa? Delicate information?" I asked.

"Yes," Ramon replied. "And by the way, I am well acquainted with a longtime friend of yours: Jon Hollinger. As you know, he is Canadian and lives in a village not far from Ottawa. He will be happy to accompany you on the flight. Do you have any questions?"

Yes. I have a thousand questions, I thought.

But then, Ramon stood to leave. I stood. We embraced, then he was gone in a flash.

Reen's eyes widened. She laughed, shrugged, and said, "Another Viva adventure."

Two days later after Christmas, I met Hollinger in Chicago. We flew to Ottawa together. Upon our arrival, after the meager customs and the usual airport nonsense, Hollinger introduced me to two people, Avna and Baru. We all shook hands.

Then Jon hugged me and said to call if I felt I needed him. I clung onto Hollinger's hand as if I were a child and he was my father. My palms were sweaty, and I felt nauseous and faint. I started to cry and closed in on Jon's chest for safety.

Avna held me from behind while a rapturous thumping took over my body as my brain clawed at my skull. My mouth was gulping for air, and I wanted to scream and be curled up in a fetal position on a cozy bed with covers. I opened my eyes, and everything looked sterile and modern. I was pushed into reality as Jon was coaxing me to breathe and let go of him. I was charged with confusion, feeling that at any moment the combustible information would vanish in a dream.

That was how I met my twin brother, Baru, and our birth mother, Avna.

I turned to face them as Hollinger slipped away. It started to sink in that I had a twin brother and another mother.

"Come here, sweetheart," Avna said. "I know this is too much and not enough all at once. Let's go to our billet so we can get settled and move through the details."

Avna was light-haired and looked similar to my mother Ruth—except for her dark brown, deep-set eyes and dark eyebrows, like mine.

The particulars are complicated, especially the feelings. Being with them was enigmatic. Avna explained that my cell phone must be dismantled temporarily and turned off. This made me feel uneasy.

"Hollinger knows where we are and you are safe, but technology is not our friend," Avna said and explained they did not have phones on them.

I learned that my biological father is named Alfonzo, known as Zo. Zo, Ruth, and KW have all died. Avna is my sole surviving parent, and now I know I have a new, original brother.

We spent five days together. We went to museums and enjoyed meals. Avna shared her history with both me and Baru. He, of course, knew more about our parents than I did. She told us how she and Ruth met in France so many years ago. I felt love from Avna and Baru, and I know they fell in love with me, although we were vacillating between joy and awkwardness. I was accustomed to feeling amateurish.

They called me Salodius at first and then Savna as a nickname. I was in a trance watching their gestures and studying their features, faces, and movements. We were strangers, and at the same time completely illuminated, occupied, and knowing one another.

One afternoon, we went in the Ottawa museum, and I learned that my biological parents were art forgers. Baru showed me a classic painting that our father had forged, which hung as an original in the museum. I was astounded. There was too much to unpack.

Avna told us about our birth and how we got our birth names. My name Salodius was Ruth's grandfather's name and Byrd was Zo's grandfather. My twin was named Byrd Ruth Salodius, and I

Salodius Avna Byrd, which translate in short to Baru and Savna as our monikers. My name means "she who creates herself." I was in the midst of multiplicity, duality, and nowhere close to simplicity. I had another mother and brother and now an actual parallel life assigned.

Baru had known of my existence. He had spent time with our parents throughout his life, although he too had been raised by another family, in Switzerland. The circumstances didn't make me feel reluctant the more time we were together.

I was stunned and not surprised at the same time to hear that Zo, my biological father and Avna's protector, had seen me on several occasions during my life in Aspen, New York, and Europe. Zo had an easier time moving around the world in those days. Avna had seen me twice in Madrid, Spain, when we came on a family vacation. Zo had expected for us all to reunite. I could see in Avna's eyes how she deserved the loyalty of Zo.

Their lives were complex and dangerous, lurking in safehouses, crossing borders at night, committed to resistance against the fascist regime in Spain. Zo was assassinated, a result of a vendetta held against Avna and their families. Detestable strained cryptic details arose and unraveled little by slowly. I tried to soak up these vast, intimate, descriptive pieces of a story that seemed mythical.

Being with Avna and Baru, even for a short time, was bewildering, uplifting, and rewarding. I didn't want to leave them, my original family. We would be together again soon. Baru returned my phone and reinstalled the SIM card. I called Hollinger so he could collect me and take me on an adventure before my departure the following day.

After our meeting, I recalled Tessa's journal and things I had read that seemed private, cryptic, and secretive between her and Marme. I will reread those journals again when I return and interpret if Tessa knew about Avna and Zo. I have a suspicion that she knew things that might help me understand some of her travels through Marme's life.

I arrived home after the new year 2018 and made plans to go to Mexico to do service in Oaxaca. Avna and Baru met me there, and we worked with an immigration hostel and the gypsy kids in the street. I had not been to Oaxaca. Later that year, I went to Spain to be with them. I studied about the Basque country and Franco's regime before going to rendezvous with them.

In 2020, Sajita called from Nepal asking me to help with an Afghan family who had been evacuated from Kabul. They were two brothers and a sister deposited at a military basecamp in southern New Mexico. Their mother was an activist in Afghanistan and a friend to Sajita. I know nothing of Afghanistan except that a journalist friend of mine had been kidnapped by the Taliban in 2008. Thankfully, he was released after two months.

I constantly think of the word *vision* and wonder about the science of people: their psychology as the science of the soul with compassion having its own laws. We were able to have the family moved from the makeshift camp at the base to a nonprofit focusing on Afghan relocation. After a thorough review of this family, who were all in their late teens and early twenties, we became part of their action team. They stayed with a sponsor family while the Tessa Foundation quickly set up a household for the family. This was rewarding and another learning curve that we integrated into our world of eternities between cultures.

The Covid-19 pandemic came at the world like a monster, and life as we knew it previously shut down. We started the Tessa Garden early that year so we could feed people, if necessary.

That year, Tessa's longtime friend Matt Maienza died under circumstances around the Covid term "sheltering in place." He was tasered by the police in North Carolina on his own property, and his heart gave way. He was naked in the driveway and someone in the area called the police. He and Tessa had traveled, and they had a history of rafting, skiing, and biking together. I was available as a death doula for his parents and tried to soften the blow of their loss.

Stringing words together into a palatable language for parents who have lost a child is the most difficult way to commune. I try to curate an approach that makes an imprint on the strengths of turning tragedy into a goal of triumph. We dedicated the garden to Matt and his family, and the harvest fed many people.

Matt's parents, Joe and Janice, made a trip from Boston to Santa Fe to help us work and finance the garden on their son's behalf.

They got to visit with friends of Matt and Tessa's because he had lived here in Santa Fe for many years.

Let me tell you about my other children. These days, Jazie is becoming the matriarch of the family, determined to eviscerate herself from my patterns and be a better mother than her female predecessors. She is influenced by observing and wanting to make her life more functional and protected. If she only knew all the historical upheavals.

When I watched her give birth to her first child, I acquired new information about her strength and independence. She rules now, in charge of how we spend holidays or gatherings together. Her focus is on her husband, her children, their household, and her career as a nurse. She doesn't consume any substance except caffeine in the morning. She is in charge now and has plenty to say about me, her fathers, and relations. Less is more for her.

This is why I am attentive with learning the ways of both my daughters, Tessa and Jazie, as they reeducate me. I work on changing and following. I am no longer in charge. Jazie doesn't hold back with reminding me of my flaws. She and her father, Francis, are quick, sarcastic, and hurtful in their tongue lashings. She practices harsh love on me to prepare for what lies ahead with her boys growing up. I feel vulnerable in those moments and want her to accept my strengths and put my flaws and mistakes behind us.

I also believe she notices my resilience and ability to take care of myself. She has a keen bullshit detector. She impresses me with her ability to read the inner workings of people and stays clear of uncomfortable situations. I can stand my ground with her when absolutely necessary, but I choose my battles carefully. She is pitiless with me and loves me all the same as she utilizes me to mend her own wounds.

Perhaps she is releasing her anger around the issue of how I have used men to my advantage, moving from one man to another when their usefulness wanes.

The other day, I asked her why she was so protective of Declan and Francis, and she responded, "Moma, you are like a weed. You always survive, and I don't like that you say they are emotionally deformed. That's just wrong."

I've made it clear to Jazie how grateful I am for Declan and Francis because they love their children and grandchildren completely. She is protective of her fathers and not comfortable with new people anyway. I keep my lovers at a distance. They are like salt: A little makes my life better; too much ruins the dish. I have learned from my own mistakes.

Indigo is his own story. He has always been different. Noticeable indicators began when his brother was injured and seven years later when his sister died. Since the severity of these life changes, he has tried to dial back what and how he communicates. When he gets triggered with his rendition of memory from the past, he blames one of us in the family. He can tear into the person who he holds responsible for stimulating the manic episode, then later he will apologize for his behavior. He has signs of a brilliant mind, and he can be dear and contemplative, yet always unpredictable.

My children have always held a mirror up to my soul, reflecting who I was when they were younger. I saw myself as a force of nature, the Earth Mother whose only real purpose in life was to direct these children who had come from my vessel, my womb. I believed they would succeed in whatever they decided to pursue. I suppose I assumed that we parents would inspire their success.

The hardest thing for a mother—at least for *this* mother—is to dissolve the strings of expectation and let her children choose their paths and develop their own personas. I am especially accepting that Indigo has his own way of perceiving the world. Francis watches over him and provides him with a work ethic and a roof over his head. He has learned to be flexible with Indigo's fluctuating personality. This is challenging for Francis. We are all concerned about how Indigo will fare when we die.

Xavier, on the other hand, wants to be seen as mysterious. He has moved to Albuquerque and is living with a girlfriend. I am thankful he has someone who cares about him and helps him when things go south with his body.

When Xavier got better and back into a life of his own, his defense became secrecy. I've learned not to press him for information. This is one of the hardest things for me because I believe it is one of my strengths to suss the order behind appearances. When I call out Xavier on some doubtful behavior of his, it only sets up stronger resistance. I guess this is called "letting go." Not easy. What I keep telling myself (especially with my boys) is I have to have unconditional tolerance.

Xavier is seeking answers. He doesn't want to be sculpted by others. The years since he was injured have obliterated his psyche as his continued challenges seemed to become an ambition. There was always something he had to learn to overcome. He constantly seeks possibility and change, not necessarily physically but emotionally, financially, and mentally.

A friend suggested Xavier consider going on a wellness retreat and take an Ayahuasca journey in the jungles of Costa Rica. In the midst of finding himself cocooned in the hot, humid jungle with eight other people—also seekers—he saw he had a choice to remain in his paralyzed body or to go through a portal into nonphysical. Xavier chose the latter, and during the ceremony, he passed into the other dimension.

Xavier wrote the last pages in his journal before leaving for Costa Rica to join eight others in a shaman-guided spiritual retreat.

I've been a paraplegic for twenty-five years. Now I'm seeking change for my future, and there are serious problems in my path. I often hear the voice of my sister Tessa when she made her swearing-in speech for the Peace Corps. She says she's seeking change for her family, the world.

Now I want to change my addictive habits so I can understand the mystery of my existence. The secrets I have are what keep my private reality in the shadows. Yes, I feel empty, and burdened, because of my broken promises. My bold little sister, Jazie, has drawn distinct boundaries around me to protect her boys—my nephews—from my habitual ways. She refuses to let me be with them until I clean up my lifestyle. And she disapproves of my risky relationships.

She said something interesting to me the other day, "I think, X, you've mistaken the secrets you keep with some people for love."

I feel how my little nephews show me the way to happiness with their innocence, optimism, and unconditional love. To this day, they have kept me inspired to live. When we're together, I feel unburdened. How has my life come to this? So much pain has taken me to a tougher existence that I must tolerate. Now I'm detoxing, trying to eat well like I did when growing up and staying away from caffeine, alcohol, and cigarettes.

I'm committed to going to Costa Rica for this Ayahuasca retreat. Preparing to go is tough. To be honest, I'm nervous and scared while packing for this trip: white clothes, shoes, toiletries, bug spray, swimwear, three pants, sweatshirt, jacket, this journal. I feel I must choose an offering, a sacrifice. I'm defenseless and on the edge. I swear I'm going to let go of my pain pills forever. The sum of my sacrifices will be a decision I'll face in Costa Rica.

I wear Tessa's ashes around my neck in an ampule. I need her with me to help reconstruct my life. I carry them for our honor, lives, kinship, joy, and the suffering we shared. After this journey, I will return to California to reinvent my life and career, hopefully as a changed man.

Xavier asked for his cup of Ayahuasca. Soon, he could feel himself slipping through veils to some true core, and he heard his mother's voice begging him to stay.

Tidal Waves

Crumbling,
the replicating feeling sneaking up on me again,
I perish under heavy womb water, recalling birth.
Immensity of regret and delusion weigh my flesh,
plunging my lungs.
Swallowing and breathing are impossible.
The obese grief wants to be painful and long.
Ah, the faces of his siblings, my grandchildren, his friends, and their children
pull me from the trenches and insist I endure the loss.
They convince me to awaken from the nightmare of the illogical truth
and stand in my flesh like a warrior.

The Bread Truck

I notice the bread truck is parked illegally in front of the house. I am worried because I have so many parking tickets. I start toward the truck when I see Doratea stick her head out of the driver's window with an erect index finger held up before her lips, shushing me. I stop in my tracks.

Something funny is going on. I hear faint music coming from inside the truck. Doratea beckons with the same finger for me to come toward her. She gets out of the driver's seat and opens the big sliding door on the side of the truck. There's a lot going on inside. My first impression is the vastness inside of the space. I can't see all the way to the back. I can't even see to the other side.

My brothers are somewhere inside. I hear Xavier's voice, singing over the drums and piano playing. They're still making music. I think that might be Leonard Cohen singing "Everybody Knows." I'm sure Xavier convinced Cohen to join their band because he is so convincing when he wants to be.

I see the beautiful oval cherry table on the veranda in front of me that is always in my parallel reality. Xavier is at the head of the table. All the women are seated casually around the table, leaning this way and that. None of them have noticed me yet. They are all busy chatting, laughing, smoking cigarettes and pot, and sipping tequila with him.

I stare at them, dumbfounded. Avna is doing something with Marme's hair. Oh, she's putting extensions in the back. Doratea grabs me by the hand and *swirls me around in dance steps. Xavier joins us. He is such a good dancer. She whispers in my ear not to worry about the parking tickets; she's got that covered. Doratea tells me Jack Silverman stopped by today and was fit as a fiddle. She said he became bemused when he saw all the girls, asking again how so many beautiful women could have such a myriad of hardships and still keep a sense of confidence. I listen as I watch Flicka calm her son, who has had another seizure. Xavier is down on the floor beside him, helping.*

Then Tessa comes sliding up to the table on her skis with six-year-old Jazie on her back and says, "Hi, Mom. I'm giving Jazie a lesson on how to pretend. She says she is a pro at pretending, but I know better. She pretends she knows stuff all the time. Really, though, for so long I pretended not to notice how you miss me. I've been with you all along. You are pretending to be shocked that we are all here, so it's you who's bluffing. You're the real pro at dissembling. Remember when Indigo was little, he would take his stuffed animals out under the tree, cover himself up with them, and pretend he was dead? Even though he was so fearful about our grandparents dying, his way of keeping fear contained was pretending. We learned that from you.

"Well, let me tell you, death is all white light and celestial sounds—not music really, just those vibrations you have when you're asleep and feeling very good that you don't have to get up and do the laundry in the morning. Stuff like that. Isn't that right, Xavier?

"I can tell Jazie is getting impatient since she doesn't believe any of this is happening. She enjoys me being the teacher and she the student, even though we're pretending."

Then Tessa schusses off with Jazie still on her back. Xavier, now on skis, chases after them. Jazie looks back at me and rolls her eyes. She's so good at that. Marme puts her arms around me. I know they're Marme's arms by the smell—a combination of silver and gold.

"Who told you we'd be here, honey?" *Marme asks.*

"Marme, this is crazy. I have no idea. I was worried about another parking ticket."

"This is not a dream, dear. You know I can read your mind, and don't be cross with me. You think you are imagining. KW went out for a pizza—whether you like it or not. The kids all wanted pizza and Cokes, and he can't say no to them. Now, why don't you sit down here with me and tell me what's troubling about this scenario," *Marme says, then gently takes my elbow in her hand and* leads me to the table. Even though the table seems to be a few feet away, minutes pass as we walk there. On the way Avna gently takes my other elbow in her hand. Both of my mothers begin to whisper into my ears—one in my left ear and the other in my right ear, and I have the clear sensation that I have a third ear somewhere near the top of my head that is translating what they are saying, a word from Marme and then a word from Avna. The translation is not in words but images. Xavier is in between them.

Suddenly, the veranda and table are surrounded by a lush jungle. The topography has changed. Avna holds Xavier's hand, and Marme kisses me. Marme pours cold clear water into my mouth, and Avna wipes away what has spilled on my chin. Xavier laughs with Avna, and Marme cries. Marme takes a magnificent shawl from around her shoulders and throws it in the air. The shawl encircles all four of us, four-fold images, such as the four stages of the moon, adorn it.

"Let's pretend we're dead," Avna says and laughs so hard tears brim.

Marme and Xavier are infected with this laughter, like people always are. We start screaming like banshees, and the whole bread truck begins to rock and roll, especially because the boys are in the back and have turned up the amps full blast. Xavier goes to them.

"Pizza! Who wants pizza?!" I hear and see KW's back as he is going toward the rear of the truck.

Zo is with him, and I try to make my way to him. I want to have time with him. The girls and Xavier are all in chairs around the table, and they beckon me to sit with them. There is a slice of pizza on a plate and one of those old-fashioned glass bottles of Coke in front of each of us: me, Ruth, Avna, Zo, Tessa, Doratea, Xavier, KW, Flynn, and Jack—who have all passed away. The table is longer than usual, but everyone is close.

They all laugh. Suddenly, there is music playing in the back of the truck. Avna stands and softly taps her Coke bottle with a spoon or maybe it's a fork. "Brethren," she says.

Suddenly, the little boys flash by, each with a slice of pizza in one hand and a bottle of Coke in the other, screaming at the top of their lungs. Xavier is given a piece of pizza and joins them. They are moving toward all the men in my life who are lining up on the veranda. They have provided, propelled, and protected us in their own way. I can't flirt with any doubts now. I wonder if I'm about to die too.

Tessa, sitting next to me, leans over and says quietly, "You can never get it done. You can never do it wrong. Keep trying to complete the circle."

I see Tessa has a microphone in her hand, and I realize everything she has said has been broadcast to the tribe of people. There is a round of applause.

Tessa hands the microphone to me and says, "Go ahead, Mom."

Acknowledgments

There are so many people to thank.

The Tessa Foundation continues to advocate for young activists and visionaries who strive to make the world a better place for future generations. Their initiatives include environmental justice and generational empowerment for food security, climate change, and educational opportunities.

We acknowledge the Lightning Boy Foundation, who are also focused on young people, especially young Native American hoop dancers.

Young people are the most valuable resource we have. They are the heart and soul of the future.

Salutations to our manager and editor, Maureen Geittmann, who weaves us through a myriad of options in the publishing world.

We recognize our copyeditors, Tim Cooney and Emerson, for their continued eyes on this project, voice talents Daniela Chacon and Michael Meade, and publisher Jennifer Bright and her team.

Many thanks to our logistics manager, Daniela Chacon, who contributed many young vital ideas for Tessa's voice and made a supreme contribution to editing.

Our deep gratitude to all those who have worked as a team to keep this project moving forward: Jim and Lyn Avery, Rob and Paula Peck, Boyd Willat, Eb Lottimer, and Anna Darrah.

And to the family and friends of Tessa, Xavier, Flynn, and Craven, who inspired this novel.

"When you cease searching, then you will find."—Zen proverb

About the Authors

Kristena Prater resides in Santa Fe, New Mexico, and began writing poetry at the age of eleven. She invented a personalized form of yoga called Chayo and practices a spiritual and moral discipline inspired by Buddhism. Prater has been an art therapist, mask maker, freelance writer, and death doula and is the mother of four children and grandmother to six boys. She and Salodius have collaborated on this novel, which was created from the sequential organization of actuality that culminated in a fictitious narrative.

Salodius Byrd lives in the Basque Country of Spain and spends several months a year in the United States and Canada. She prefers anonymity and has spent most of her adult life out of the limelight.

She is a ghost writer. Through novellas, prose, poems, books, and articles that are a compendium of her layered experiences, she enjoys writing vicariously. Byrd avoids being photographed because her privacy is of utmost importance.

She spent the past few years traveling and interviewing the siblings, extended family, and friends of Tessa, the remarkable young woman who spread inclusiveness and compassion like seeds wherever she went. Along the way, Byrd met many who were inspired by Tessa without having known her, but what makes *Tessa* so trenchant is how well Byrd knows Tessa's family and friends. To them all, she dedicates this story in their honor.

Milton Keynes UK
Ingram Content Group UK Ltd.
UKHW021305301024
2472UKWH00029B/128/J